UNHEARD MUSIC

Also by Ursula Perrin

Ghosts
Heart Failures

Ursula Perrin

UNHEARD
MUSIC

 The Dial Press   New York

for Randy Stiles

Published by
The Dial Press
1 Dag Hammarskjold Plaza
New York, New York 10017

Copyright © 1981 by Ursula Perrin

Manufactured in the United States of America
First printing

Library of Congress Cataloging in Publication Data

Perrin, Ursula, 1935–
    Unheard music.

I. Title.
PS3566.E6944U5   813'.54   81-9678
ISBN 0-385-27201-4   AACR2

Prologue

Mail.

A glossy brochure from Wayside Gardens, an invitation to join (oh, irony) the Metropolitan Opera Guild, and a catalogue of dirty diversions from Eros, Inc., based in the place that invented eros: California. Also two envelopes (one mauve), stuck face to face as if mating. She opened the white one. Official business.

"Why, you bastard," Tonia said out loud, reading the letter again. The check, pale leaf green in color, indicated, in lawyer Amy Kornblau's petite and rigid hand, half the usual amount. "Regret inconvenience," "client at earliest possible opportunity," "whereabouts presently unknown," etc., etc. She would have cried, but she hadn't cried for years. Why now, for God's sake? These were his kids too. Calm down, Tonia. Still. It wasn't just the money (was it?) but the fact that he could so easily, so smoothly, without a break in his stride through life, disengage himself. Disappear. Well, shit.

And then hot on the heels of red-eyed anger came pale-winged worry. He was down and out, drinking again, sick in some ratty hole. Oh, come on, let's be rational, Tonia. You don't know. There may be an explanation. Don't tell the kids.

She ordered her hand to stop trembling and poured herself another cup of coffee, drank it slowly, staring at the other, mauve envelope, which she had propped against the sugar bowl. The sugar bowl, a birthday gift from her son Joey (he, at least, was still hopeful of her), was in the shape of a white china grand piano sprinkled with pink painted roses. It was a kid's five-and-dime-store gift and its top had never properly fit, consequently had been broken twice and mended, first with rubber cement and currently, temporarily, with Scotch tape. Like me, thought Tonia, chin in hand, brooding upon the mauve letter, which had a British stamp and was postmarked London. Her life, too, seemed always in need of Scotch tape. The letter of course was from Charity and she didn't particularly want to open it. Years ago, when the heiress had taken her up, she—Tonia—had had the promise of a glorious career. What had she now? Nothing much, an ordinary life, not even a promise to balance the glamour of Charity's name and money. Why, then, she wondered, did Charity go on pursuing this so-called friendship? What interest could she possibly have in her? Was it sentiment? Noblesse oblige? She tore open the letter, read it, began to smile. Feeling more cheerful, she read the letter again and buttered her toast at the same time, carefully licking each finger so as not to besmirch the thick mauve-bordered, cream-colored stationery. When the kids came downstairs, she apprised them of Charity's news.

"Yuck," said Elizabeth. "To that faggot?" which Tonia thought very perceptive for thirteen, or maybe just a shot in the dark.

"Gee, that's nice, Ma," said Joey, brown eyes lit up. He wanted Tonia to get married again, to his very own father, of course, so that they could all sit around over buckets of fried chicken, smiling, as families do in TV commercials. Well, she thought, Charity has made a career out of marrying, she's good at that. Soon, Chare, you will have all your dough and you will be Living at last, sitting in European cafés behind black sunglasses. As for me, what is it I have? You, Tonia (she told herself). Don't get depressed. Look, it's nice out. Hear the cardinal? Hear the cardinal? Hear? The telephone rang. She covered her ears with her hands.

I

Allegro con Brio

Olympia:
"Oh, this is my s-o-ong
of love!
Yes, this is my s-o-ong
of love."

"The Doll's Song" *The Tales of Hoffmann* Act I

1

"Foster, McKenna, Slupe—this is the new girl, Tony Hassleteen. Did I get that right, Hassleteen?"

"It's—uh—Antonia, Miss Berry, and Haseltine. As in Hazelnut? And *tine* rhymes with *fine*. Or *kine*." Her timid joke. At the desk near the window, a brown-faced girl nervously laughed. The other two girls merely stared. The office was a long fluorescently lit room with a large window at one end. The window was half obscured by a briskly humming air conditioner. New York City was having a heat wave.

(You see, at that time in her life, when she was twenty-one and had not yet met Charity Mullet—yes, *that* Mullet, of the rich-and-notorious Mullets—she thought of herself in her neat dark blue drip-dry shirtwaist dress as a singer disguised as a typist. Innocent Tonia—there were two things you wanted, only two things you cared about: love and music, music and love. She wanted to sing. She wanted someone to love. She hated typing. Still, one must eat.)

"What are you laughing at, Foster?" said Miss Berry. "Don't you have any work to do? Did you finish that letter yet? Well, let me see it. Come, come, hurry up. Goodness, girl! How slow we mortals be. Here. What's this? And you went to Katharine Gibbs? I've never thought much of Katy Gibbs and I see I'm entirely correct in my opinion." With a crisp self-satisfied motion, Miss Berry tore the defenseless letter in halves, eighths, sixteenths, and dribbled the flecks into her wastepaper basket. "Try again, Foster! Work on that spacing. Use your eyes, Foster. You don't need glasses, do you? That's your desk, Hassleteen, right here in front of me. Girls? Girls! Hassleteen has just graduated from Brynlee. That's right, Hassleteen, isn't it? It was Brynlee, wasn't it? Who turned on the air conditioner? Foster, *never* turn on that thing without permission."

"I didn't, Miss Berry," said poor Foster, whose brown complexion was now more of a beefsteak color, cooked medium rare.

"I don't care who it was, Foster, don't touch it. McKenna, if you don't have any work to do at least remove your hand from your chin and place it upon the typewriter keys. Try to look busy. That's what we pay you college girls for, looking busy. Where's Smith?"

"Out at the desk," said McKenna. She had a peculiar way of speaking. She simply lifted her small upper lip and allowed the words to make an escape attempt through clenched white teeth.

"What?" said Berry.

"At the reception desk," said McKenna again, louder, more hissingly, and slid a sheet of paper into her typewriter's roller.

The long room had six desks. Miss Berry's large glossy-topped desk was directly in front of the window, poor Foster's desk was just to the right of Berry's, then came McKenna, and then nearest the door came Slupe, a round-shouldered girl with incredibly lank dark hair and thick glasses. Slupe typed with two fingers in a slow tempo reminiscent of a funeral march and her bent head continually swiveled from copy to machine, as if she were watching a tennis match played by gnats. Her WPM must have been all of ten.

"I don't know," said Miss Berry mournfully, sitting down and addressing the air conditioner, which was now turned to Off. "We hire these girls and give them a chance to work in a wonderful place at a perfectly marvelous salary where they have the opportunity of seeing with their very own eyes the most famous artists and writers of the day—do you hear me, Foster? Does it mean nothing to you that you work among greatness?"

Poor Foster—whose little brown fingers were furiously flying—stopped and looked up, dazed. There was something in her of the trapped squirrel: her brown hair looked matted, her eyes were bright and scared.

Miss Berry leaned forward and coquettishly placed her wrist under her chin.

"Foster, my dear," she said, "let me give you some advice. If you want to be a success here at the *Beau Monde* you must learn to listen. Consider working here, Foster, as a privilege; a girl with your limited background, Foster, ought to appreciate that. Finished yet?"

Foster's typewriter carriage rolled—a sound not unlike a tumbrel rumbling toward La Guillotine. Foster stood up and walked (no, tottered) the three steps toward Berry's desk and delivered the letter into Miss Berry's red-nailed, blue-veined, only faintly age-spotted hand.

Silence. Slupe's pitiful tap . . . tap . . . ceased, McKenna's steady drumming died away. Miss Berry, who did not wear glasses, held the sheet of paper first out at arm's length, then brought it in to the waist of her pale blue linen skirt, then held it out again. Her small dark blue eyes, which were (to begin with) much too close together, now seemed about to enjoy meiosis at the bridge of her tiny nose.

"Incredible," she sighed, and delicately this time, tore the paper in two. "Try again, Foster," said Miss Berry. "That's the route to success. Try, try again." She waved Foster away and turned in her swivel chair. Slupe's tap . . . tap . . . resumed and so did McKenna's stoical clacking, and after a brief snuffle into a wad of Kleenex, Foster sighed and began typing again, first slowly then faster and faster and yet still faster, in the frantic but futile rhythm of a treadmill worked by a little caged pet.

A girl (tall, big-boned, freckle-faced) came clicking into the room. She had thick straight auburn hair, wore high-heeled patent-leather shoes and an orange dress. She threw herself into her chair and jerked the cover from her machine and tossed it over her shoulder. She yanked open a drawer of the desk and fumbled noisily among the paper clips, making them sound like ball bearings. Miss Berry looked up.

"Where have you been, Smith?"

"Out at the reception desk," said Smith, sullenly.

"Now, Smith," said Miss Berry. "Artists and writers, creative men, they're different, my dear. That's the way young girls get into trouble, you know . . . loitering."

"I wasn't loitering," Smith said irritably. In her high heels, Tonia thought, she must have been six-two and certainly looked as if she could fend for herself.

"Then what were you doing out there?"

"You *told* me to go out there," said Smith. She popped an orange Life Saver between her lips and rolled her eyes across the aisle at McKenna, who did not respond.

"Oh," said Miss Berry. She shrugged and turned a page of the *Times*. "Has Miss Mullet come in?"

"Yeah."

"What?"

"She's *here,*" said Smith in a loud voice, and added in an undertone, "only an hour and forty-five minutes late."

"Oh," said Miss Berry.

The work of the office proceeded. Tonia had uncovered her typewriter and sharpened her pencils, checked the drawer for supplies, and still no one had given her anything to do.

"Miss Berry?" she said. No reply. She cleared her throat, stood up, and walked—on tiptoe, she had no idea why —to the front of Berry's desk.

"Miss Berry?" Miss Berry's small blue eyes leaped, not quite in concert, up. "What? Oh. Hassle . . . er. What is it?"

"Is there something you want me to do?"

Berry leaned back in her chair and stared. Tonia blushed. "That is an excellent question, Hassle . . . er. Why do you think I hired you, my dear?"

"I know . . . but no one's given me . . . I don't have any . . ."

"Sit down, Hassle . . . whatever your name is. Sit down. Something will turn up. Arrange your supplies. Make sure your typewriter works. By the way, Hassle, have I mentioned to you that you are never, never, to touch the air conditioner? The air conditioner is solely under my direction. Now sit down, Hassle, and get to work."

Tonia sat down. It was beginning to get very warm in the office. Slupe looked sweaty and Foster looked sweaty. McKenna did not look sweaty. Occasionally, McKenna would raise her eyes and then look down again. She had a long square white immobile face upon which jesting nature had placed a teeny mouth and two small furry-lashed blue eyes. Black, already gray-streaked hair sprung up above her square forehead. Foster was still typing furiously (she must have been on letter number seven), and Slupe pecked dismally away between upward shoves at her eyeglasses and frowns at her copy. Tonia saw that Slupe's lips moved as she read. She looked a little retarded. Smith, having noisily hurled about the contents of her desk, slouched down in her swivel chair, folded her arms, and rolled her eyes at Tonia. Suddenly she sat up straight and began to do arm exercises, counting under her breath as she flung her arms out to the sides and folded them up again. Then she sighed, stood up, and announced loudly that she was off to lunch. Miss Berry did not look up. Smith click-clacked out the door. After a moment, Miss Berry folded up the newspaper and began inserting herself into the pale blue linen suit jacket that was draped across the back of her chair. Daintily, she picked up her pocketbook, a wicker bag as big as a picnic hamper, and walked jauntily doorward, tilting her head to one side and patting the back of her hair. She was almost five feet tall and had to be, Tonia figured, at least seventy. At the door, she turned, a sweet-faced, white-haired, grandmotherly type, and said, "Now, I want no one—no one, Foster—to touch the air conditioner. I am going to lunch. If an emergency arises, I want"—her blueberry eyes bounced from desk to desk—"you, Slupe, to be in charge." Slupe looked up. Her chin dropped. Her glasses slipped. A crystal tear of perspiration fell from the tip of her nose.

Gone. Relief. Someone sighed. Down the hall the elevator doors clanged, opening, closing.

"That *bitch,*" said Foster. Her voice was unsteady, her eyes red-rimmed. McKenna stood up and marched to the air conditioner. Click! Delicious cool air streamed into the room.

"Well, Hassle," McKenna said, stopping in front of

Tonia's desk, "do you want to go to lunch with me now or go out later with Slupe?"

"Now," said Tonia, rising. Slupe didn't look like much fun.

"You see, Hassle—"

"Call me Tonia," she suggested. They were passing the reception desk and she glanced at it curiously, but the receptionist's chair was empty. A thick paperback, Dickens's *Bleak House,* lay face down on the desk and a cigarette lay in the ashtray, slowly dying.

"You see, Tonia, if you take the early lunch you get two hours, but if you take the late lunch you only get half an hour."

"Really? Why's that?"

"Because," said McKenna, glancing at her sideways, the words sliding out of the corner of her little mouth, "Berry always takes two hours and fifteen minutes. Get it?"

"Yeah."

"And, Hassle . . . ?"

"Do you think you could remember Tonia? I mean, it's really not very hard. T-o-n-i-a. Short for Antonia."

"Okay, T-o-n-i-a; if you have any letters to write, T-o-n-i-a, bring them in."

"Letters? You mean my own personal letters?"

"Uh-huh. Also, as soon as you can, get Slupe to change desks with you. Slupe is hopeless anyway, she's been here two weeks and still hasn't caught on to the lunch routine. It's much better to have a desk by the door. Get it?"

Tonia got it. "Maybe," she said, "Slupe won't want to change."

"Tell Slupe," said McKenna, "that you have bad colitis."

An empty elevator arrived. They stepped in and turned

around. "Well, fuck," said a low voice somewhere in the hall. The elevator doors closed on the nineteenth floor, whose walls, ceiling, and rubber tile floor were all decorated a deep oily gray. With a name like *Beau Monde,* Tonia had hoped that the office might be, well, glamorous, but in fact the office resembled a long subterranean tunnel and the writers who worked there scurried furtively along its walls, like sailors clinging to the tipped sides of a torpedoed sub. It occurred to Tonia that "Well, fuck," were the first clear words she'd heard spoken in the hall.

"Was that Mullet?" she asked McKenna as they slowly descended. McKenna's little mouth moved sideways into what Tonia saw was meant to be a smile. "Uh-huh," said McKenna. "Our very own heiress. If you're real lucky and move fast, you might get to see her this afternoon."

They chose to dine not in the Chock full o' Nuts but more elegantly, in a sandwich shop up the street where they could sit in a booth. McKenna ordered a hamburger. Tonia had a bowl of tomato soup and crackers.

"Dieting?" asked McKenna.

"Sort of," Tonia said, although in fact she was broke.

McKenna sat back in the booth. Her fur-fringed eyes were small and blue. "What do you do?" she asked.

"Do?" said Tonia.

"Do you write or draw or edit or what?"

"No."

"Then why do you want to work at the *Beau?*"

"I needed a job. I saw an ad in the paper and answered it."

McKenna's little mouth pursed. "So. Old Berry's reduced to ads in the *Times,* eh? Who would have thought it? Usually in June there's a whole slew of college girls all dying to work here. That's how we got Slupe. Slupe went to Radcliffe. She's a poet. And Smith? Why, she's going to be a great novelist."

Tonia said, "Did she go to Radcliffe?"

"Uh-uh," said McKenna. "Mount Holyoke. Do you type?"

"Of course I type."

"That's too bad," said McKenna.

"Why?" Tonia said.

"Because," said McKenna, "you'll get stuck with all the work. Slupe can't type and Smith can't type. If I were you, I'd fake it. Just pretend you can't type either."

Their orders arrived. The tomato soup had a shimmer of oil on the top and a mass at the bottom that resembled maggots but must have been noodles. McKenna looked at the soup and sighed. "Don't ever let her know you need your salary."

"Why not?"

"Well, the way I figure it out is, it's sort of low-class to be a girl and need money. If Berry thinks you really need the money she won't give you a raise. She likes to think that everyone—every girl, that is—who works at the *Beau* is a nice class of girl. She picks on Foster because Foster needs her salary. Foster's divorced and supports a kid."

"She does? But she's only—"

"Twenty-two. And Foster didn't go to college. Berry's given Slupe a raise—"

"In two weeks?"

"And Smith's had a raise, but Karen—that's Foster—hasn't had a raise in six months."

"How about you?" Tonia said. "Have you had a raise?"

"I've had two, but I've been at the *Beau* a long time and I started at a hundred and ten."

"*What?*"

"See," said McKenna, "when I interviewed for the job she asked me what college I'd gone to. Well, I went to this little college nobody's ever heard of and I knew she didn't like that. Then she asked me what my father did. I didn't want to tell her that he works in a sauerkraut factory, so I said that he was chief counsel for the Niagara Mohawk Power and Light Company."

"You did?"

"Uh-huh. She's been pretty nice to me. You know Mullet? The receptionist? Miss Mullet?"

"Not yet," said Tonia.

"Mullet's rich—I mean, her family is—and she's had five raises. Berry's nice to her because she knows she can't get to her. That's the way to get on with Begonia—don't let her know she gets to you."

"Begonia? Is that her name?"

"Uh-huh. Begonia Berry. Sometimes," McKenna said, lowering her fur-fringed eyes and smiling slyly sideways, "we call her Beri-Beri."

Back two hours later, they passed the reception desk again, where the paperback lay face down and a cigarette was burning and the telephone was ringing. McKenna reached across the desk and picked up the phone.

"Good afternoon, *Beau Monde,*" she said, waving cigarette smoke out of her eyes. "Who is calling? Huh? Who? Oh. She's not here right now. What? Okay. Uh-huh. Wait a sec." Tucking the phone under her chin, McKenna took a stubby pencil from the desk and for want of anything better, turned over the novel and wrote on its inside cover: "Call Ben. BU8-8200 ext. 35." Behind them, the elevator doors opened. McKenna put down the phone and straightened up.

"Why are you out here, McKenna? And you, Hassle. You're not just coming back from lunch, I hope."

"No, Miss Berry," said McKenna. "We were on our way to the ladies' room and we heard the telephone ringing."

"Just let Miss Mullet take care of the telephone, please. And there's no necessity for pairing off to go to the ladies'. This isn't grammar school, you know."

But indeed, in the next six months Tonia descended the whole upward arc of her educational experience and became —between the hours of ten and six—her second-grade self. Later she wondered why she'd lasted that long. Though at first she was bored, pretty soon she had plenty to do. Smith's lunch hour had lengthened considerably—she was having an affair with a man more than twice her age who wrote occasional book reviews; consequently, was invisible from eleven to three and *très fatiguée* afterward. Slupe was suddenly plucked from their little midst—she'd been promoted to "reader"—and one day McKenna simply did not appear. She was instantly replaced by a girl named Willie, who was rosy and blond and had gone to Wellesley and wanted to write like Chekhov but could not type and Foster slowly but steadily deteriorated. At first she had crying spells in the john and only shook while seated at her desk, but later she cried all the time. One week she did not come in. She'd been taken to Bellevue, where they spent three days flushing Valium out of her system. Mullet spent the week taking up a collection for Foster's kid, who, because there was no place else for it, was in the Bellevue children's ward.

And one day a year or so later, when Mullet—Charity, that is—and Tom and Ben and Tonia had been to the theater, they passed Foster on West Forty-third Street. She was holding up a lamppost in the traditional pose (one knee cocked) and had on (it was summer) red satin short-shorts, white boots laced up to the thigh, and a low-cut black vest covered with sequins and fastened with just one snap.

"Why, Karen," said Charity in her low voice, going right up to her and offering her a hand, "how are you? How've you been? Why don't you ever come see us?"

Tonia hung back, smiling at Karen, nodding vigorously and waving from a distance of ten paces. She was afraid to shake hands, afraid she might get VD, which would put an end to a possibly glorious career. She was very careful of her health and the only whores she wanted anything to do with were Violetta, Manon, and Giulietta. But here was Charity, looking at Karen in her odd way and smiling. Sometimes it seemed to Tonia that Charity's whole life was other people's lives. She took people up the way other people take up scuba diving or contract bridge. Charity seemed to have more friends and acquaintances than anyone Tonia had ever met, so that Tonia pictured Charity in a four-star uniform and boots, standing in front of a large map of the world sticking little pins here and there for her various footloose acquaintances. She talked with ease about people Tonia had only seen pictures of or read about: Dorinda Snyder of the billion-dollar Snyders, and Mort Smythe of the aluminum Smythes, and Peggy Potter (fourth grade, Chapin School), who married the king of a small rocky Himalayan kingdom, and Laura Allwood, of the bark and pulp Allwoods, who was engaged to a would-be shrink. Poor Laura, said Charity. He wanted to marry her for (1) looks, (2) dough, (3) connections, but not really for herself, said Charity, because Laura had no self, that is to say, she had even less self than she, Charity. At which Tonia would say, on cue, "Come *on,* Charity," and she would roll her eyes and say in a meek little voice, "Poor me. I have no thelf."

"Oh, Tonia," Charity would say in her low—well—
*dull*ish voice. "You just don't understand. You don't understand what it is to have . . ."

Tonia knew that except for the nauseated look on her
face, Charity would have said, "nothing." Tonia thought it
funny, this poor-little-rich-girl act, and when Charity took
her up she was pleased and flattered and hoped, of course,
that Charity would introduce her to a man—not just any man,
of course, but one who was pretty rich and/or loved skiing
and music.

2

Many years later it would seem to Tonia that all her life her
ancestors' qualities had met in her and canceled each other
out. The hard-working but small-minded Van Klocks
(mother's side) negated by the artistic but moody Mercers
(also mother's), and both of them put to rout by the Haseltine lust for pleasure, experience, high life, and crescendos
of love, for the Haseltines, although not exactly slaves to
feeling, were of sanguine temperament and (as her father
used to say) liked to live close to the line. Later, much later,
she would think: What has remained? The simple dogged-
ness of the Stuckeys (father's side), those generations of
obscure farmers and mill workers who hardly exist anymore
except in my imagination and upstate New York?

In high school, she had asked to take singing lessons, but
her mother (who herself had a fine voice) neither encouraged nor discouraged her: there simply wasn't enough
money. "We'll see," her mother said, meaning, "Not right

now." Still, Tonia knew she had the gift—her voice, that beautiful instrument handed down to her through generations of musical Mercers. All the Mercers loved music, just as the Haseltines loved sports and liquor and the Van Klocks loved land and cows. There had been a singer or two in every generation of the Mercer family as far back as anyone could remember. Her mother said that what had attracted her father to her was that she could sing. William Haseltine could not, but was able to recognize a fine voice when he heard one, and so they were married and went to live in New York City. Tonia's earliest memory of the three of them together was of her mother playing the piano and her mother and she were singing and her father was a long bulky brown smile under a pair of twinkling glasses. He was charmed with his wife and his daughter, and sometimes, in a pathetic toneless dum-de-dum, a drab monotone so different from his rich speaking voice, he tried to sing with them. It made her cross, his never being able to hit the notes squarely—he was always just a little above or below—and at age two and a half, so went the family tale, she went to him and pounded his knee with her fist and cried out, "No, no, not right, Daddy, sing this way." He was delighted and roared with laughter, for already he saw what she would become—not a mere artiste, or a singer, but a lady of style and accomplishment.

Tonia's mother said that if you went to her Grandfather Mercer's for Sunday dinner, there would be the usual small-town talk of church politics and Republican gossip, but that a kind of unease, an irritable restlessness seemed to accompany the passing of mashed potatoes, of applesauce and sliced roast pork, and it was not until after the chocolate pudding had disappeared and the tablecloth had been brushed with a little silver brush kept on the dining room mantel for that purpose, and not until the last dish had been dried in the humid kitchen, and the men had run through their entire repertoire of jokes in the cigar-smoke-filled parlor, that a kind of family feeling took hold. Aunt Mildred would sit down to play the piano and Uncle John would sing baritone and everyone had a different part and was expected to stick to it and if you couldn't read music or sing in key you were excused.

At Uncle Bob Haseltine's, on the other hand, on summer Sundays you were supposed to come in your old clothes and play softball all afternoon long in their field until the sky was pink and you were starved standing way out there in the outfield waiting for the littlest Haseltine to have his turn at bat. After which (on a long wood picnic table spread with a red-check paper cloth under willow trees) there was beer and baked beans and cold ham and potato salad and the entire meal was spent in dissecting little Junior's stance at bat and wasn't it too bad that bucktoothed freckle-faced Ernestine was of all the young Haseltines the best ballplayer and a girl, too. While at the Van Klocks', who looked the poorest but were the richest of all these relations, there was hardly any talk at all; the noise was the clink of dishes circling around and despite the huge amounts of steaming food, everyone ate as fast as possible: one ate in that household to restore and maintain the body, for bodies were not instruments of delight and pleasure (the Van Klocks, after two hundred years in the Valley, were still Dutch Reformed) but of work and were attended to with the same religious composure and attention to mechanical detail as the tractor, the reaper, and the milking machine. The only subject (said Tonia's mother) that she ever heard discussed at table, and then briefly, was the price of milk and what it would be next week, and oh, yes, that parcel of land on Route 32A so long disputed between Great-Uncle Henry Van Klock and Sam Haseltine, Tonia's (drunken) grandfather.

Once when Tonia was nine her mother sent her to spend

an educational week on Great-Uncle Henry's farm outside Veddersburg. It was August and it seemed to Tonia the smell of manure was everywhere—in the barnyard, in the fields, in the house, in her very clothes—and this dung smell was accompanied by the continual buzzing of huge blue-black flies. The only place to escape was, as it turned out, the barn, where a golden haze of hay dust hung in the air and so infected her sinuses that she spent her chore time in there with streaming eyes and nasal passages blissfully swollen shut. This week was educational indeed, for she never again had any sentimental notions about farm life. All the Van Klocks went to bed at nine and got up at five and even her two rides on a broad-backed dappled mare named Maggie were accompanied by the smell of ordure, the itchy tickle of hay, and a viciously pronged fly that kept circling patient Maggie's doleful head. She went home to the reassuring feel of city concrete under her sandals and the exciting smell of city soot; the very doggy litter in the New York gutters seemed preferable to all that "fresh" farm air and peace and crude farm quiet.

Her parents had both grown up in Veddersburg, New York, an old red-brick textile mill town on the Mohawk River which people pass through nowadays to get up to Lake Placid or over to Saratoga Springs. Her father's parents separated before he was a year old: Alva Stuckey couldn't stand the farm and/or Sam's drinking and she moved into Veddersburg and got a job teaching sixth grade. Sometimes, surveying her genealogy, Tonia saw that her father's ambition was an awful mystery. Most people like to stay comfortably right where they are, but every once in a while, every generation or so, there's a restless soul who longs to see the world. Thus Tonia's father. He must have been ambitious, he got into Harvard, and one rainy spring Sunday before he

graduated he consented to go to church with his mother—
she wanted to show him off and he wanted to show himself
off—and there, after the offering, was Mary Mercer in her
white collar and black choir robe about to sing "I Know That
My Redeemer Liveth." It was Easter. Suddenly the clouds
parted and a pale green shaft of sunlight fell through the
plain glass at the top of the tall nave window and this finger
of light pointed straight at Mary as she lifted her head to sing
and lit up her pale hair, encircling it with a soft suffused
brightness, and her clear voice, ringing out in those first
notes, in the white and gold church coolly scented with lilies,
became (whenever later he thought of it) charged with
beaming splendor so that her hair, Handel's music, her
voice, all flowed, melted together for him into one shimmering instant of dissolved gold radiance: love. He knew it at
once, and standing to sing a hymn, felt, when he drew in his
breath, a sharp visceral pain, as if he had run many miles
without stopping.

The Mercers were better off than the Haseltines. Gerritt
Mercer was first vice-president of the Veddersburg Savings
and Loan and had a carpeted office within the gloomy mar-
ble-pillared tomb of the bank on Main Street. Mary seemed
cool to William (she was, of course, shy) and inaccessible and
intelligent and she was going to Skidmore in the fall. The
grandson of the town's richest man was in love with her. And
besides this obstacle, William's father, old Sam Haseltine,
was a drunk, as everyone knew, and furthermore had for
years been carrying on a feud with the Van Klocks over a
strip of land on Route 32A. Everyone was against the marriage, but after four silently stubborn years on Mary's part,
they were married and moved to New York City, where
William was finishing medical school. They hardly ever went
home again. When Tonia's father died—of a massive heart

attack—it turned out (oddly, since he hadn't been prudent in any other regard) that he had left instructions for his burial: it was not to be in Veddersburg.

3

"You—uh—what's your name? Tonia. Where is it you go at night?" the receptionist (Charity) asked her, a couple of days after she'd been hired.

"Oh," Tonia said vaguely, putting her off, "just out." She never told people that she was a singer, for she wasn't yet; it was only her innermost life.

"You fly out of here," Charity said. "You can't wait to get out. You meeting somebody after work?"

"Not a man in sight."

Charity narrowed her eyes. She was small and anxious-looking and pretty, with a headful of red-gold ringlets, a small pointed face (lightly freckled), and pale lips (somewhat chapped), and her eyes were small, pale-lashed, and in color a greenish blue. She had a habit of speaking with her head down or obscured by long gray plumes of cigarette smoke. She smoked constantly and wore awful clothes. Each of her dresses was the size of a small tent and so full you had no idea whether Mullet was fat or thin or bony or slight or maybe a teensy bit pregnant. The dress she wore most often was purple, with gold and green and red flecks that looked like large commas, and reminded Tonia of the curtains hung by transients in a storefront window to screen off their palm-reading quarters. She did not, Tonia thought, disappointed, look one bit like an heiress.

"I just can't figure out why you work here. You obviously hate it."

"Don't you?" said Tonia.

"No. I like it. It makes such good stories to tell at cocktail parties. And besides, there's nothing else I currently want to do."

"Why not?"

"Why not?" Charity frowned. "Well, because. I can't think of anything. If I had any talent, I'd like best to write stories, or maybe write old-fashioned novels. So far, though, nothing much has happened to me, so there's nothing much to write about. I am kind of waiting for it to happen. Meanwhile, I might as well work here. How about you? I'll bet you're going to law school at night."

"God, no!"

"You're getting a Ph.D. at Columbia."

"No."

"Then what?"

"You'll never guess. Tell me where you buy your clothes and I'll tell you where I go at night."

"Well," said Charity, "I don't know. I'm particular about my clothes and don't want anyone copying my style."

Tonia smiled.

Charity said, "You don't like my clothes, do you?"

"Oh, no! Sure I do!"

"Take this dress," she said, and stood up, and like a little kid held the dress out with both hands. The dress she wore on this particular day was not the purple one with commas, but a dress that was striped orange and black like a café's awning and seemed to be made of similar stiff material. "It's an Alfonso."

"Who?"

"You've never heard of Alfonso?" Charity said.

"No."

"He's a famous designer. You see, I've always liked good clothes."

"Oh."

"Now tell me about you."

"I get my clothes at sales."

"No, no—where is it you *go?* I won't tell anyone. Honestly." She looked solemn and held up one hand, the nails of which, Tonia noticed, were both bitten and painted, a combination she hadn't seen since sixth grade.

"Nowhere. Just home to Queens. It's a long subway ride."

"Why don't you get a place in town?"

"Too expensive."

"Couldn't you get just a cheap place? Say!" She snapped her fingers. "I've just had a great idea. We could room together. We could get an apartment together."

"What? Oh, no—I don't think so, Charity. I could never afford it."

"Yes you can, yes you will. Oh, this is the best idea I've ever had. Listen, I'm going to a party Friday night. Want to come?"

"Friday . . . Friday . . . Friday. No, I don't think so, Chare. Thanks."

"Why not?"

"Well, for one thing, I don't have a date to bring."

"I'll take care of that. Just leave it to me. Friday night right after work." She picked up her telephone and dialed with a small stubby red-nailed forefinger whose cuticles were ragged and sore. "Mr. Vaughn, please. . . . Teddy? Hi! Charity here. I've got a girl I want to bring Friday. What? Tonia. Antonia. Mmm. She's really . . . What? Oh"—her eyes moving over Tonia as if she were beef on the hoof somewhere west of Chicago—"five-five, darkish blond . . . She is *not* fat; just because last time . . . What? Mmm. Six. Ciao. . . . Well," said Charity, folding her little hands on the desk and looking up at Tonia.

"Well," Tonia said. "About this Teddy."

"Oh," Charity said, waving a hand, "he's not your date; he's an old old old old friend. The party's at his place. He has them all the time. His parents are in Europe. I have someone else in mind for you. Soon now," she said, "we'll have you all taken care of. And tomorrow we'll have lunch together and talk and get acquainted." And then, dismissingly, she opened her paperback book.

Tonia smiled and shrugged, thinking: She's funny and nuts. It was sometimes an enjoyable combination, and she was awed and impressed that she'd been asked to lunch by an heiress and so she said, cheerfully, "All right" (Charity did not look up), and ambled back into the office to type an endless fact piece on the mating habits of mayflies, told in true *Beau Monde* stiff-upper-lip style, with no laughs and a lot of irresistible information which would be ingested by hungry readers all over the world, then promptly forgotten. Ephemera.

Well, thought Tonia, why not? Aren't we all?

4

Tonia's father, William E. Haseltine, lived in her memory as a tall, large-framed man with small brown eyes twinkling behind his rimless glasses, a big smile, vast energy and charm. He loved New York City. He liked to call himself a "hick" and a "country boy," and although he was neither, perhaps he really believed it, for he spent a lot of his life trying to counter that impression by collecting some very sophisticated information. He liked to learn and he loved to teach and Tonia thought that what she represented to him when small was a rich but untilled little piece of earth. Her mother sang with her, her father took her to museums on rainy Sundays. In fact, she remembered the Metropolitan Museum when it was not an ongoing circus but was dim and richly gloomy and she and her father and three other people were the only ones there.

On fine Sundays they went for long walks: those golden October New York Sundays when the blue transparent light dies in a haze of smoky violet and the streetlights and headlights suddenly bloom in the billowing dusk. They went to secondhand bookstores and antique stores and had greasy meals together in terrible restaurants. He took Tonia to his office and sometimes to the hospital—he was a cardiologist —and told her about his patients. They walked everywhere in the city—on the Lower East Side, through the Village (where they lived), along the decaying docks sinking by inches into the Hudson River. William had wanted an apartment on the Upper East Side but Tonia's mother insisted on having a garden, so they bought a house on Charles Street and her father commenced giving large parties. He was, Tonia thought later, just a typical small-town boy wanting to make good in the city and so he worked too hard and lived too hard and spent too much money. Some years after her father died, Tonia found an old notebook of his with a list of names—it must have been a guest list. There were names that later she heard Charity Mullet mention and names even she knew: painters, writers, politicians (and in that list even a Mullet, but with dots after it and a question mark as if—

flying too high, perhaps?—he had reconsidered and finally crossed it off), and Tonia wondered if any of these celebrities ever thought of her father after he died. He was forty-two. The house on Charles Street was heavily mortgaged and his life insurance had been heavily borrowed upon and so, in June of the year he died, Tonia and her mother moved to Queens.

Driving across the Queensboro Bridge, her mother talked to Tonia about the value of peace, quiet, and fresh air. Tonia was suspicious, of course (she remembered the farm), and when her mother pulled off a broad busy street onto a smaller one, dotted with look-alike houses and struggling trees, Tonia was incredulous. She had, even at ten, a delicately tuned social sense. Their new home had a gable, a front porch, a backyard, and was painted a rusty brown. Narrow driveways on either side separated it from houses that were, in everything but color, identical. The house to the left was done in the kind of asphalt siding that emulates brick and the house to the right was done in the same kind of stuff but mimicked fieldstone. In front of each house on the street was a small frail Norway maple and, gasp, across the street was a scene peaceful indeed. There were no houses at all; instead, a high retaining wall made of cobblestones held back a grassy bulge of earth upon which, at a level just over one's head, were gravestones, thousands of them. The little house had been a real bargain because of its location, said her mother. Some silly people, said her mother, minded living near a cemetery, but, said her mother, when you thought about it, wasn't it nicer to look at willow trees and cedars and grass plantings (and gravestones, thought Tonia) than a lot of houses?

"It's not a bad neighborhood," her mother said, "once

you get used to it." She had gotten a job as a typist with a nearby law firm, Weingarten and O'Connell, and could walk to work but as soon as Mrs. Haseltine became "breadwinner," something peculiar happened to her—her facial expression changed from delicate Mercer to dogged Van Klock. Her jaw squared, her eyes narrowed. Once she had been graceful and charming and shy and now she became: stolid. Her mother sold the grand piano—there was no room for it in the Queens house (it turned out they were to live only on the first floor; the second floor was rented to a hard-working childless German couple named Schmidt, who never drank until Friday night) and besides, after Tonia's father died her mother never sang again.

Her mother seemed at ease in the new neighborhood. As for Tonia, she was wretched. She hated the school, she hated the narrow dark house, she hated the kids who said "erl" for oil and "berl" for boil and the "goils" and the "fellas" who wore funny clothes in tasteless colors. She made no friends in her new school and didn't deserve any and when she was loneliest she would go across the street and climb up the cobblestone wall and walk through the cemetery, and under three large pines that formed a sweet-scented grove she would, when there were no gravediggers present, sing. She imagined that she was on a large stage and that her stony white audience was applauding. Her father's daughter, she didn't want to live in Queens, she wanted to live in New York City; she wanted to be accomplished; she wanted to be cultivated; she wanted to have lovely clothes and a lovely apartment and never again live in a dark little house, and when she was fourteen she read that in 1870, Adelina Patti, the legendary soprano, got ten thousand dollars for a single performance. Ten thousand dollars! And besides this, she wanted (how very *much* she wanted) to fall in love and she knew that if she was to get out of purgatory—Queens—it would be by singing, and more than anything else in the world, she loved to sing.

5

Charity Mullet did not show up for work the next day so Tonia assumed that their luncheon date was off, but at ten twenty-two the telephone on Miss Berry's desk rang.

"Who?" Berry shrilled into the phone, plugging up her other ear with a forefinger. All typing ceased. The girls waited, fingers poised, to see who the call would be for. "There's no one here with a name like that! You have the wrong number." Berry slammed the receiver down, the girls silently looked at each other, the telephone rang again.

"Idiot!" Berry said, picking it up. "Some people can't . . . Who? Oh, good morning, Miss Mullet, I didn't recognize your voice. How are you feeling, dear? Coming in today? That's too bad; I'm sorry to hear it. What? There is no one here by . . . Just one moment." Berry blinked and looked around the room in a slow clockwise circle that began with poor Foster, moved to McKenna, fixed on Slupe next to the door, took in Smith, and finally swiveled back to six o'clock and Tonia. "You! Will you take this call, please? And from now on kindly remember that we do not make personal calls from this office."

On the telephone, Tonia had heard Charity's low voice say, "Lou's Tavern on East Forty-third Street, at twelve-thirty," but by one o'clock she decided it had been a mistake to stand in front of the restaurant. She should have guessed that Charity would be late, and it was beastly hot, and three men, all of them practically senile, thirty at least, had offered to buy her lunch before she saw someone she thought might be Charity wafting unconcernedly down the street. The creature was wearing black sunglasses, a white nylon dress that looked like a domestic's uniform, white socks, and white tie shoes. She was carrying a tennis racquet, but held it so that the racquet head swept the walk in front of her in a light one-two rhythm. With her blinkered face lifted up to the sun, she gave a pretty fair imitation of a blind person, except that every now and then she whacked a crumpled paper or a cigarette wrapper into the gutter. She would have walked right by if Tonia hadn't called out. Charity turned around, surprised. "Oh, hi," she said. "Are we eating here?"

"Yes," Tonia said.

"But why here?" Charity said.

"Because you picked this place out. You said over the phone, Lou's Tavern. This is Lou's Tavern and I only have thirty-five minutes of my lunch hour left."

Boldly, Charity strode in ahead of Tonia with her tennis racquet tucked under her arm, catching ("Ughnnn!" "Oh, pardon me, sir!") an elderly diner in the abdomen just as he was coming out. It was hard to see. The place was as black as Hades and twice as smoky, one of those taverns that specialize in German food and the businessman's lunch. The air smelled of beer, garlic, and tobacco. There was a continual rumble of deep male voices, punctuated now and then by the tinny clatter of trays and occasional shouts from the kitchen as the swinging doors burst open, like seed pods expelling white-aproned waiters. No one seemed to notice the girls. If there was a maître d', he was myopic, or maybe that wasn't the custom in this strange place, maybe, thought Tonia, you assembled at twelve and there was a starting gun and you got into your crouch and raced for a table: men were so competitive. At last, after Charity tugged at his sleeve, a tall waiter looked down upon them with a grunt of surprise. He snickered, led them to a table, and made a great gentlemanly show of pulling out their chairs for them, to the enjoyment of all the surrounding tables. They were the only women in the place. Tonia felt mortified.

"Why here?" she whispered across the table to Charity. "There's a cafeteria down the street. There's a Schrafft's near Forty-fifth."

Charity sighed, removed her sunglasses, blinked, looked up, down, and around, then focused on Tonia. Beneath the tender palely freckled skin, faint lines fanned out between her small aqua eyes. "Now," said Charity, "let's finish our conversation. Where is it you go at night?"

"Oh, for heaven's sake," Tonia said. "That again. Why do you care?"

"If I tell you about me, will you tell me where you go?"

"Why are you so curious?"

Charity thought for a moment. "I don't really know. I've always been curious about other people's lives. Maybe it's because I . . ." She stopped and looked around distractedly. "But also because there is this man I told you about who I think might be perfect for you."

"Why?"

"Why what?"

"Why do you think he'd be perfect for me? You don't even know me."

"I am trying to know you."

"And what's wrong with him—can't he get his own girls? Is he blind, or crippled, or what?"

"He's busy."

"He's too busy to look for himself?"

Charity nodded.

"Well, in that case," Tonia said, "I certainly don't want him. He obviously has no initiative. What do you do, get a commission?"

"Of course not! He doesn't know I'm doing this. He wouldn't approve."

"Then why do it?"

"I want to see if my hunch is going to work out. When I saw you there in Berry's office, something inside me said: Yes. She is the one. But I need to know where you go at night. You sure there's no other man?"

An oval basket of poppy-seed rolls and rye bread slices skidded across the table and rocked to a stop in front of Charity.

"I was engaged for a while," Tonia said, "but it didn't work out."

"Why not?" Charity said. She took a roll, broke it in half, and stuffed a piece into her mouth.

Tonia was scornful. "He thought he had an ear for music. He kept telling me I sang sharp."

"Is singing your hobby?"

"No. Listen, Charity, I like men and I would enjoy meeting someone that I could, you know, care for, but I don't want to get tied down. I want to stay kind of footloose, you see. Ready to travel, that kind of thing. Eventually," said Tonia, and a dreamy, satisfied look came over her face, "I'll have to be on the road for months at a time. Waco, Texas; Dubuque, Iowa—all over the United States."

Charity's pale eyebrows rose. "You're a singer! What kind of singer are you?"

Tonia lifted her head. "I am going to be an opera singer."

"Oh, that's terrific! I'd love to be a singer."

"I thought you were going to be a writer."

"I'd much rather be a singer. You see," Charity said, explaining this carefully to Tonia, "singing is so definite. It gives your life such an exact shape. You either—one—succeed, or—two—fail." Charity beamed, Tonia shivered. "Whereas in my—uh—life . . ." Charity stopped and turned her head to the side. She seemed to have lost the thread of her thought.

"Yes?"

"Well, you see," Charity said, focusing on Tonia again, "I don't have a life right now."

"You keep saying that," Tonia said, rudely. "What do you call this?"

"This?"

"This right now. This . . . us . . . *here.*"

"Oh, this. This is—uh—this is . . . I'm waiting, you see."

"But what is it you're waiting for?"

"My period."

"What?"

"Do you happen to have a Tampax? I think I've just got it."

"What?"

"Just now. And I don't want to mess up this dress; it's not mine, it's Irene's. Irene is our cook. She's taken care of me most of my life. She's been like a mother to me. My mother is dead, you know. My parents both died when I was a child. We were in Maine and it was the last day of the summer and they wanted to take one final sail together? They never came back. No, they never did. They were found months later, off Deer Isle on Christmas Eve, frozen stiff, still in each other's arms. Forever inseparable, kind of. Except they had to hack them apart, of course, for the funeral. What roles do you like to sing best?"

"Shouldn't we go to the ladies' room?"

"Oh! Yes! I forgot. You see, if I had a talent like yours —if I had something definite I could do . . . The difficulty with writing is you have to have a form and a style, and to have a form and a style you have to have an ego, and to have an ego you have to have ego boundaries. Now, I have no ego boundaries. At least, this is what Dr. Krull says. Writing all comes from the inside and I don't have any."

"Any . . . ?"

"Any real inner life. I've had a lot of problems, you see."

"Uh-huh. Shouldn't we . . ."

"Wait." Charity's red-gold head suddenly disappeared. She had bent or fallen over and when her head came back into view she had something in her hand—a thin sheaf of typewritten papers, folded once down the middle.

"What's that?" Tonia asked.

"My autobiography," Charity said. "I started it for therapy. Dr. Krull makes me write it. He's my psychiatrist."

"How long is it you've been going to a psychiatrist?"

"Oh . . ." Charity turned her head and squinted off into smoky space. "Off and on for—uh"—she looked at Tonia— "eleven years."

"Eleven years! God, aren't you cured yet?" Tonia couldn't suppress this outburst: she couldn't help but reflect on how many singing lessons eleven years' worth of analysis would have bought.

"No, but I'm better. I'm much better. Don't you want to read this?"

"I think first we'd better go to the ladies' room."

"Right!" said Charity, and stood up so abruptly that despite the billowing volume of noise in the place, heads turned for ten yards in every direction. Tonia stood up too,

smiling calmly, perspiring only a little, and planting herself
(in their long circuitous march around tables and chairs and
long outstretched legs) squarely behind Charity's white-
nyloned fanny, just in case.

"You see," Charity said, as they walked thus closely in
tandem toward the door just off the kitchen (Oh, God,
thought Tonia, in what turned out to be an inaccurate predic-
tion, she is going to spend forever explaining herself to me),
"I think we ought to get to know each other because—"

"Wait!" said Tonia. "Here we are, right here." She
grabbed Charity's arm and guided her through the door that
said Ladies and while Charity went into the booth to check,
Tonia stood wondering hopelessly how she had gotten into
this. It wasn't the first time this sort of thing had happened
to her. In fact, crazies picked her out. On any New York
public conveyance—subway or bus—a mumbling wild-eyed
stranger in torn overcoat would zero in on her, always on
her, to tell her his confabulations. Bag ladies clawed at her
in the street; elderly demented messenger boys followed her
for blocks, raving; and in Queens their little Chinese laundry-
man, half berserk with loneliness (his sweetheart was still in
mainland China), wrote her love notes in Chinese; it had
gotten to the point where her mother had to pick up the
sheets. Couldn't life let her alone just for a while? All she
wanted, really, was to sing.

"Fine!" Charity said, emerging with one hand still
tucked up under the white dress. *Snap* went the elastic of
Charity's underpants, and she briskly tugged the dress down
around her hips as the green-painted door of the booth
swung shut behind her.

"You don't need a Tampax?"

"No! I do! At least, I think I do. I hope I do. Do you
have one?"

Tonia groped in her black patent-leather purse and wondered what to make of "think" and "hope."

"I admire resourceful people like you," Charity said, and went back into the can. Her voice floated over the door of the booth, which, Tonia saw, was engraved with scratched penciled offerings: "Call Myrt, RH8-3211." "I'll bet you are extremely organized. I'll bet you would make a great roommate."

Tonia sighed. Back to that again, were they? There was no way she would ever room with this nut. Charity came out at last, peered into the dim mirror, put all ten stubby red-painted fingers into her hair, and fluffed upward. They went back through what seemed by now a cheering audience to their table. Two plates of knackwurst and red cabbage sat steaming upon paper mats. Sitting down, Tonia looked at the greasy plate and a knot in her stomach tightened. She wasn't one bit hungry. Across the table, zestful Charity was cutting into her knackwurst; Tonia averted her eyes. The dull knife blade cutting into the plump sausage made a dreadful popping sound.

"And don't forget," said Charity, looking up, chewing. (What ghastly table manners she had, Tonia thought. She ate just like the Hallorans, their low-class neighbors in Queens.) "I want you to read this." Charity tapped the folded papers with the butt of her knife.

"I'd like to read it, Charity, but isn't it getting late? Do you see a clock?"

Charity squinted and swiveled her head. "One-fifty," she said, peering over Tonia's shoulder.

"One-fifty!" Tonia said. "Quick, let's get the check. I'll be fired!"

"Wait a minute," Charity said. "You haven't told me your last name. We can't room together if I don't know your last name."

"It's Haseltine," Tonia said, rising.

"What?" Charity said.

"Haseltine. As in *fine!* And *kine!*"

But the heiress had fallen over in a dead faint. In the ensuing confusion, Charity's sheaf of papers drifted off the table onto the floor and someone walked off with her tennis racquet.

6

In my globe, Krull [Charity had written, meaning, in her head—see "My Life: Version 1"], I see my grandparents eating. My grandfather, von Hoffmann "Jack" Bayard, sits on a straight chair munching meticulously, his thin lips compressed into a scythe-like grimace under his hook nose, his mulberry-stained cheeks slowly rotating, his blue eyes vacant, his fists—knife in left, fork in right: he ate in the British manner—resting on the damascened table edge, while across the crystal and flowers and silver, my grandmother, Sophronia Dagonet Bayard, sat supported on all sides by a silk-cushioned armchair. She was exceedingly fat and white and I saw her when very small as an undulating landscape: the rounded peach-satin-covered knees, each one with a curved glimmer of highlight, on up to opulent thighs, traversing the upward flow of large abdomen, upon which giant convexity rested two large soft quivering lace-covered mountains, climbing again—excelsior!—to come upon a gentle white incline, then three puffy hillets attached to a hillock of chin, a plane of a cheek, a small monadnock nose, two round perfectly blank blue-eyed lakes, and a brow so serene, so unconstricted by the knot of thought, it was a pleasure to clamp on your crampons and head up to the pinnacle, a crest of tightly curled white ringlets which lay as close as possible to that skull and kept warm whatever dim synapses twinkled therein. In this, a "still" out of my very own home movie, I see my grandmother always in that second before the feat is accomplished: she is leaning forward; the silver spoon (it is full of something . . . what? blackberries in syrup!) held by a small, dimpled, garnet-beringed white hand is halfway to her cupid-bow mouth, which, lips parted, reveals tiny black-berry-stained teeth. Her large round blue eyes are fixed on her reading material, for she always read at table and had, for that purpose, a brass music stand in the pretty shape of a lyre on the cloth in front of the centerpiece and to the right of her goblet. She read all the time. I have never known anyone who read more with less perceptible effect. If you asked her on Tuesday P.M. what she'd read on Monday, she couldn't tell you. My grandfather, on the other hand, seldom read but could give you, when prodded, a pithy description—two or three words—about anything. I think of the word "utter" when, in my globe, I hear him speak: a word part prophecy, part stutter, uh-uh-utter, that so perfectly describes the sounds he made when he deigned to converse, as if twenty years of cerebral constipation had brought out these words —distinct, oblong, hard—from the coiled depths of his otherwise hollow mind. My grandmother smiled but never spoke at all. She never—that I recall—said one word to me.

Her reading habit, however, descended unto the next generation. My mother, too, read constantly, but with this purpose: she sought to discover some role for herself. One day she was Daisy, a madcap debutante, the next Catherine, who married money, not Heathcliff, and shy solemn Jane Eyre and Ms. Evans's Dorothea longing for vocation, and sunny little Esther Summerson, the happy chatelaine. This made my mother hard to get to know; moreover, she formed complementary roles for my dad. One day he was to be surly Heathcliff, a role that suited him only when drunk; he had not the mettle for arrogant Mr. Rochester; did somewhat better as that dear old infant Herbert Skimpole; was best in the role of Gatsby, because Dad's heritage was dubious, at least I never so much as laid eyes on my Mullet grandparents, who lived somewhere in that hill-and-dale never-never land west of Yonkers, although one day my father told me (drunk, maudlin, crying) that his grandmother's name was Esther and his grandfather's Israel and (herein lies eighty years of compressed American sociohistory) they had started out of steerage talking only Russian on some filthy, littered, pushcart-lined street on the Lower East Side. I pressed him for real details but he sobered up and assured me, the next day, with his usual waxen morning-after smile—he was in slippers and a paisley dressing gown, reading Malraux—that he had made the whole thing up, that he had for one bloody moment there fallen into my mother's fantasies and come out a hybrid: Scott Fitzgerald X Henry Roth. I loved my father. He was small and, except when drunk, cheerful. He had black hair, always beautifully combed, and pink cheeks, and very blue eyes, and had met my mother on a train—he was going back to Princeton, she was coming home from a college-girl visit to Saint Louis. He was asked to be a fourth in her roomette bridge game and my mother said she fell in love with him instantly when in a masterful fashion, on his partner's weak bid of three hearts, he made slam and then fanned out the cards with a brisk *thirp* of his gambler's thumb. He was addicted to cards, horses, drink, my mother. (If you saw him at breakfast in the morning, he would say, "Four to one it rains before one twenty-eight." Or: "Ten to one you can't keep your A in social studies.") Still, the odds were against him.

He finished Princeton ingloriously, Lucille found him a benefice somewhere in the less obvious echelons of the Company (then merely Dagonet and Bayard, now, through my Aunt Lucille's maneuvers and business acumen, the world's largest conglomerate). There he had his own three-window office, several plants, a large desk, a secretary (Miss Cropper), and almost nothing to do. I have no idea what his goals and aspirations might have been, but when I knew him last he didn't have any. He came to be that wholly unfabulous creature the falling-down drunk. My mother took on various roles—sainted wife and martyr, degenerating into ironic matron and adulteress. None of these seemed to help. She went on reading, only occasionally lifting her head to inquire, "Is that you, Charity? Why is it you're always lurking? I've never seen such a child for lurking about!"

Now, when in my imagination I wander again through the silent rooms of my childhood (a sigh, a cough, a rustle, the turn of a page), I see myself, a pale-freckled quirky ghost of a child, not so much unwanted as merely superfluous. I was more of an eye than an I and became what every child sometimes is—a spy in Their World—and discovered, therefore, various hiding places at our various homes: behind the heavy draperies in our New York apartment (when stirred they exuded a ticklish odor of dust), under a chintz-covered settee in *ma mère's* dressing room, behind the leather sofa in the library. At my grandparents' house in then rural Peapack, New Jersey, there were outdoor places as well: next to the swimming pool, behind a boxwood hedge, I dug myself a tiny foxhole and used to sit there hours at a time, spreading a tiny feast of berries in acorn cups for all those little guests who would never come and one day when thus employed heard a loud click-clacking and looking up saw through the fancifully pierced boxwood screen my grandmother. She was advancing in my direction down the flagstoned left bank of the swimming pool dressed in nothing save her mountain of opaline skin—a child's dream of a vast confection, like the whipped-cream swirls and gobs (which my father always called a "charlatan's ruse") they used to sell in paper cups on the streets of New York. She bobbled, rippled, dimpled as she teetered by, a very white fat woman with, just above midline, two surprised-looking pink nipples and, at center, a dark patch of nether hair. Her bulk amazingly tapered to two slender ankles and tiny feet in pink high-heeled satin mules and on her face was an expression both bashful and bliss-struck: she was heading downpool toward someone who seemed to be waiting (I am slightly myopic), a man who resembled my grandfather but was gnarled and brown instead of pink and white and usually wore the grayish habiliment of Figaro Pool Service ("Jack" was the name machine-sewn on his workshirt pocket). Had the long, powerful, priapic equipment of his profession incited her lust? I know not, but it seems to me now that it was not very much later when one day, at play behind a stack of trunks in the Peapack attic (old, romantic steamer trunks with the pasted-on labels —Southampton, Cherbourg—of other ports, other times), I heard rustles, giggles, and the creak of floorboards. Peeping from behind my donjon, I saw Lena, our very fat laundress, lying supine on the kind of fringed Victorian chaise ladies of a stiffer era took to in the afternoons (or at least so I imagine it) with novels and bonbons. Lena, half-shuttered eyes agleam, lay there naked, her shining body the glazed brown sugar color of cinnamon buns, her hands playfully locked behind her head, black hair bushes in her armpits, and knees indolently outturned to reveal a pod-shaped orchidaceous slit that reminded me of the world-weary mono-eye of some undersea creature. Hearing a chortle or cackle, I saw a naked pink-pronged arc fly through the air and attach himself to luscious Lena's very center: my grandfather.

And who—who—had become the unwitting instrument of all this dalliance? I had been made to take to my grandfather a note from my grandmother asking him (on pool service day) to perform an urgent errand in town, and had taken a note from *grandpère* to *grandmère* on the day Lena came, saying that he could not, unfortunately, accompany her to cocktails at the Abingdons', he had a headache. Duplicity, treachery, betrayal.

And in town, my mother. Her visits, those endless visits, to the doctor: she seemed in such good health, but leaving our apartment house how cross she was, tugging and pulling at me as if I were a cinder block, block of wood, blockhead, and in the cab she unsnapped her purse, unsnapped her compact, frowned at the oval mirror, snapped it shut, straightened her little veiled hat, tugged at her gloves, up-smoothed her silky hose, and ran the pointed pink tip of her tongue over the cherry red of her little mouth. In his waiting room I slumped into a chair and read a Nancy Drew–covered copy of *The Amboy Dukes*—I was nine and precocious—and waited for her to emerge, which in time she did, with a sigh and a dewy-pink full-faced look and a final adjusting wiggle with accompanying downtug of foundation garment, which muffled snap from beneath layers of silk and tweed gave me great pleasure, for I saw in my mind's eye the cruel garter satisfyingly bite into her rosy flesh. Afterward there was always My Treat: an ice cream soda at Schrafft's.

So that what I learned—not with my mind but with my very pores—was this: duplicity, treachery, betrayal. And who in this farcical world, this life like an *opera buffa,* had any real feelings? My father. He loved my mother (God knows why) to distraction, past distraction into addiction, and past that into pain, and sometimes at night I would get out of bed and wander down the hall to the doorway where just one lamp burned and see him there in the library, in his paisley dressing gown, sitting, looking at . . . what? the smoke of his cigarette curling, rising, and I wanted to—oh, I don't know —pat his shoulder. Misery so absorbed his life that there wasn't much left for me.

There was, of course, a message in this for little Chare: that real life is only a long fiction in which you pretend to suspend disbelief, in which you pretend there is Something Else, in which you pretend that your feelings are real, but *en garde!* always *en garde!* for the punishment for feeling is pain and sure enough misery and even death. (Books are better! Literature is safer!) Then why is it, Krull, when I've guarded myself for so long, that I feel so—uh—dead? Save me, Krull, for I am getting cold; it is lonely here in my globe and I want to get out. Save me, Krull—I am tired of other people's lives; I want some real life of my own. Once, light-years ago, when I was small, I dreamed that New York would be my island and I would be Prospera, but instead I have ended up as . . . what? a spider, a spinner of webs and intrigue, or more simply put, that drollest of creatures, a rich eccentric and cunningly evil matchmaker.

7

"Ooo-hooo, Tonia, did you forget? It's Friday! We're going to a party!"

All week long Charity had been out sick (office rumor had it that she was not sick at all but at her Aunt Lucille's place in Maine), but on the following Friday, as Tonia stepped out of the building and into the six o'clock mob, she saw the heiress in a candy-pink dress leaning against the headlamp of an MG that was silver-colored and double parked.

"Hi!" said Charity. "Hop in. I'll get in back, I'm smaller. Prepare yourself—with the top up, this car is hotter than hell. Ted, this is Tonia—Tonia, Ted. Teddy, take us downtown first, will you? I want her to see our apartment."

"Charity?" said Tonia.

"Get in, Tonia, quick. Here comes a cop."

Teddy was not tall and thus fitted with miniature perfection behind the MG's wheel. If small he was nonetheless handsome, with a hooked nose and lovely skin, and he flipped his long gold hair back in the British manner as he gunned the car forward. Puzzlingly, Tonia did not find him attractive.

"Downtown?" Teddy said. "That's not like you, love. I don't think you can be happy downtown. How far down are we going?"

"All the way," said Charity. She had squeezed herself into the little shelf at the rear of the car, knees tucked up almost to chin. "Tonia, you are just going to love our new place."

"Charity?" said Tonia. "The thing is, I can't really afford an apartment. You see, I've got to pay for my lessons. And I certainly couldn't live downtown. My singing teacher lives *up* town."

"Oh, *damn*," said Teddy. They had gone only two blocks and jammed at the corner of Fortieth and Fifth, the city's descending aorta already clotted with mad Friday night escapees. Teddy twitched and lit a Kool.

Charity said, "Teddy? Don't you think Ben and Tonia would be divine together?"

"Marvelous," said Teddy indifferently. "Of course I'm not one bit fooled, love. I know why you want to move downtown—you just want to get away from bad old Aunt Lucille."

"Charity, I think I'd better get out right here. You see . . ." and the traffic came unstuck and they moved jerkily forward, all New York fleeing beside them toward New Jersey and fresh air. As they moved down and south, the air in the little car, which had been merely unbreathable, became an aggressive presence, sucking at their vacuoles.

Oh, damn, thought Tonia, how do I find these people? Stuck right in the middle of the old fruit and nut bowl. As for Charity, Tonia was onto her. She had roomed with a rich girl freshman year at college. Sheila had come complete with the interesting credentials of having been bounced out of every girls' boarding school in the East. Who in Administration, Tonia wondered, had sicked Sheila on her? At first Sheila borrowed only perfume and sweaters; later whole outfits began to go. Six months after Sheila moved in, Tonia was down to two bras and a pair of jeans not her size, and an English term paper had come back marked "E—SEE ME" in stiff block print across the top. Sheila, too, it appeared, had chosen to write on *Crime and Punishment,* had coincidentally used Tonia's very theme, and had somehow come up with the exact wording of Tonia's culminating masterstroke and conclusion. Sheila had gotten her paper in first and would never know the palpitations of a scholarship girl whose toehold on the Dean's List had been anyway threatened by exotic needs like men and skiing. What to do? Rat? Tonia took her E like a lady, got C for the course and as a reward for her gallant behavior had the pleasure of listening to Sheila quote her at the dorm dinner table for the rest of the year. Meanwhile, the city—Tonia's city—flowed by in the late gold glow of a six o'clock June Friday. At Twenty-third

Street a plain appeared, intersected by the Flatiron Building, very *fioritura,* with trills and arpeggios of architecture. Its windows were all abeam from the sun but it looked sad, soulless, as if it knew its case was terminal. They turned down Twenty-third, where a millennium ago the old *old* OLD Madison Square Garden had stood and where P. T. Barnum had imported Jenny Lind to sing. Here cloud-capped skyscrapers vanished, rows of smaller buildings jogged by, and as they turned onto Second Avenue, not even the vigorous peristalsis of the little car bouncing over cobblestones could shake the gloom from Tonia's soul. How had she hooked up with this rich nut who no doubt thought that living downtown would provide her with at least a month's worth of conversation? Charity would take off for Maine the minute Tonia got her throat cut, leaving her voiceless and stuck with two months rent, plus deposit.

"Oh, look!" said Charity, hunching forward and jutting her small profile into Tonia's airspace. "Doesn't all this life sort of give you the goose bumps?"

Indeed! thought Tonia. They were on Sixth Street now and Dostoevsky's Raskolnikov would have felt immensely at home. The chorus line of buildings had further degenerated into a police lineup of old drunks blearily leaning against each other. Fire escapes were the main form of decoration and this hot evening people leaned on them, sat on them, played cards on them. The streets, too, swarmed with bodies, abandoned furniture, torn sacks of garbage. Through the windows of the car the orange sunset glow seemed full of ripe odors, not just gasoline but rot and a stifling greasy smell Tonia could not identify. There was a stir, a restlessness, a hopeless seething in the air as before jailbreak night on Devil's Island.

"There!" Charity said. "See that building, Tonia? Isn't that sweet? They've painted the lintel bright blue."

Teddy sighed. "Lovey, I do think I'd better stay with the car. In fact, I'll just keep driving around the block. Will you be all right?"

"Course," she said, and prodded Tonia's shoulder. "Out."

They hopped over a gutter full of dog shit and mashed garbage and passed easily enough under the bright blue lintel—there was no front door to impede them—then on into a hall Tonia had seen only in imagination when reading Fyodor: a floor of dirty cracked tiles, greasy brown walls, a crooked staircase, and overhead, a dangling empty light socket. She didn't want to touch the banister. The stairs were narrow and steep. There were four closed doors on each floor and each one constrained a bulging world of sound—la TV, the ball game, a rickettsial baby crying, a couple arguing in something Slavic. The tenement trembled with noise and only the thick, mainly garlic-scented air seemed, by exerting a constant outward pressure, to keep it afloat.

"How much farther?" Tonia asked on the fourth floor. Charity pointed up. The last flight of stairs was well lit by a cracked skylight. Giddily arriving at the top of the tenement, Tonia felt as breathless and oxygen-deprived as if she'd just climbed Mount Marcy.

"Here it is," Charity said. "What do you think?"

They stood facing an open door. A painter, largely inept, had been lately at work. The walls of the room, once a vile green the color of pond scum, had been halfheartedly smeared over with whorls of white paint. The room was very small.

"This is," Tonia said, "it?"

A stride away, at the back of the room, two crooked windows looked out at the blistered brick of other tenements, a crisscross of clotheslines, debris-filled yards.

"What do you think?" Charity asked. Tonia stifled a

laugh or a sob. Down below, noisy Raskolnikov was coming up the stairs. He clattered up the first flight in broken rhythm, two at a time, took the second flight *a poco,* and more slowly still *(lento, lento)* the third. The girls moved closer together. Someone dark in a red-and-white striped shirt appeared, carrying a bag of groceries. He looked, Tonia thought, more Iroquois Indian than Puerto Rican.

"Hi," he said, in English, stopping at the top of the stairs to breathe. "Going to take that apartment?"

He was thin-faced and of medium height and suddenly smiled.

Oh! thought Tonia. Oh, no! And the tip of something metallic pierced her thorax and sent a delicious *chaud-froid* shiver through her system. Love! She knew it at once. Wordless music sang in her ears, her vision blurred, and an ache made her want to cry. Dim-wittedly she smiled, and he, too, smiled—not at Tonia (she who since adolescence had coolly brushed away droves of boring boys and sophomore year in college wrote concurrently to men at five Ivy League schools), but with great charm and incipient passion at Charity.

"Why don't you," Charity murmured, lifting her little head, "go on in, Tonia, and look around."

Tonia stood fast. "What's there to see?"

"The plumbing," Charity said with unexpected firmness.

Tonia stumbled over the threshold. The room was (she saw from her vantage point, close to where they were still deep in smiles) much too small. There was a kitchen area—stove, refrigerator—and past this a bathroom with a new tub not connected to anything, lying unconscious on the floor. Tonia could hear Charity's voice, and then his voice, and then she stepped back out. Downstairs, from miles below them on the sweltering street, came the MG's toot.

"Tom, here," Charity said—Tom! Tom!—"thinks he could help us move in."

"Tom *who*?" Tonia asked.

"Tom Ferrier," he said, still smiling, whitely, widely, and his long brown bony hands shifted the groceries, idly squeezed something round—a grapefruit?

"This is out of the question," Tonia said. "Charity, for heaven's sake, there's no kitchen sink."

"One uses the bathroom," Tom Ferrier said.

"It's cheap," Charity murmured, looking down at the floor.

Teddy honked.

"We've got to go," Tonia said, and took Charity's elbow. The old dog-in-the-manger dodge: if she couldn't have him, neither would Charity. "Nice meeting you, Tom," she said.

"Why don't you," said Charity, fluttering stubby lashes up at him, "come to a party we're going to?"

"Charity!" Tonia said. "We've got to go!"

"We'd just love to have you," Charity murmured. My very thought, thought Tonia, but another tug at Charity's elbow failed to dislodge her and she started down the stairs alone. Tonia could hear him say something, and then she said something, and then he, then she, and then a door opened and closed and Tonia went on down the stairs. The MG was double-parked and Teddy was furiously smoking. She got into the car. Teddy turned to face her, green-eyed, white-skinned, amused twitch of handsome hooked nose.

"You do realize," he said, "that Charity Mullet is quite quite mad."

Tonia said, "Do you have a cigarette?"

They smoked.

The orange sunset had dwindled to a yellow haze that

gave the crumbling street the oily look of an old, badly preserved Venetian painting. From an open window nearby she could hear a couple arguing in Spanish, and above this window a baby whined, and above this yet another layer of human sound, and then, from far above this, a singing voice, recorded but unmistakable, unfurled out of the top-story window. The voice hovered over the turbulent messy sounds of poor street life, so rich it seemed to Tonia a ribbon of rainbow slowly unwinding, and unwound, it fluttered, floated, then soared in ascending loops and whirls, a comet that came so close it singed her heart and then suddenly swerved, retreated through eons of cold space, and in delicate deliquescence, against the apple green of a far-off sky, melted away. Gone. *Fini.* She loved singing. It seemed to her infinitely glorious to spend one's life in time at something so fleeting.

"What the deuce was that?" said Ted.

"Liebestod," Tonia muttered. "Flagstad."

After many minutes, Charity appeared. She came hurrying out of the building with eyes modestly downcast, smiling, thighs under the candy-pink dress crossing at the crotch as neatly as a figure skater's.

Tonia longed for an ax, but instead they went on uptown for the evening.

8

"Good morning."

"Nnnn."

"How was the party?"

Yawn. And a stretch. "Okay."

"Who brought you home?"

"Hmmm? Oh. It was nobody special."

"Whoever *it* was, *it* was nice to drive you out here from Manhattan."

"Mmmm."

"You didn't like him?"

"I can't remember. I fell asleep before we got to the Fifty-ninth Street Bridge."

"There now," her mother said, "I told you to hang on to Andy. A bird in hand. I don't know why that ended the way it did." She was teasing. She'd hated Andy.

"You know why. He was bossy."

"Get used to it. That's the way men are."

Pianissimo: "Shit!"

"What?"

"Skip it." Even now, when she was past voting age, her mother's cool Mercer demeanor threatened to bring out the mad Haseltine urchin in her. When she was little and angry, she used to go up to her mother's closet, close the door, stick her head in an empty hatbox, and let it out: "SHIT! FUCK! SHIT! FUCK! SHITSHITSHIT!"

Her mother smiled, took up the coffeepot, and poured coffee for her. Her mother had on a new housecoat, a blue-flowered cotton robe, and wore with it a white chiffon scarf. Pretty fancy for around the house, unless someone had bitten her on the throat. Lately, thought Tonia, she's been buying clothes. Lately she had her hair done a lot. It was cut short and sprang up curly and white around her face. She never wore make-up. She had beautiful skin.

"So you didn't really have a good time?"

"It was all right. I just didn't know many people."

"Was it a pretty house?"

"Oh, yeah, fantastic. The Vaughns are filthy rich. The

living room was two stories tall, with long glass windows, pointed like Gothic arches. And there was a deck over the garden, and inside, a spiral staircase that went up to the balcony where the bedrooms were. You won't believe this."

"What?"

"There was a Goya—not a copy—in the living room. And Matisse prints—signed—in the bathroom. And . . ."

"What?"

"You won't believe this, either."

"Yes?"

"Someone stole my purse."

Sa mère l'a regardée, eyes glinting with humor. "Which means?"

"Could you loan me some money? I hate to ask, but I have a lesson on Monday."

"Tonia. Baby. Do you really think you're going to be a singer?"

The old seesaw. Protective maternal ambivalence. When Tonia was little her mother would buy her tickets for the opera but forget to come when she had a soprano solo at church. "Just do your best," was ever her mother's motto, carved into the splintered wood of the teeter, but on the totter side, "Don't try too hard, you'll get hurt."

"Am I going to be a singer? Let me think this over." Tonia looked meditative, and then, with a display of confidence (more, actually, than she felt), pounded her fist on the table and said through gritted teeth like McKenna, "Yes." Her mother jumped, the coffee cup leaped up aghast, and the red and white check of the coffee-splotched place mat assaulted Tonia's eyes, just as, all of the evening before, Tom Ferrier's red and white striped shirt had teased her peripheral vision. She saw it first moving up the stairs to the balcony and edged her way toward it, but it vanished, only to reappear twenty minutes later at the glass door to the deck. She had stepped around people and over glasses and ashtrays heaped with butts, but there was no one on the deck at all except Charity in her candy-pink dress, who had taken her by the elbow and said, "Come, there is someone I want you to meet." Leaving the party, Tonia had seen from the vestibule of the Vaughns' house Charity and Teddy Vaughn, standing with their arms around each other, a petite little pair like a wedding cake couple.

"Jesus! Ya can't berl me a yegg?"

"Ach Gott, lass mich nur ein Moment im Ruh'."

Now, in the house across from their Queens driveway, the Heideggers had started their weekend: first the preliminary fireworks, then a rapid fusillade; later big guns would move in, mortars, then tanks, and it would end in the usual verbal carnage:

"Bitch!"

"Bastard!"

"Slut!"

"Pig!"

Her mother stood up to shut the window.

Tonia said, "They're getting worse."

"She's lonely. She doesn't know a soul and she's stuck in the house all day with those babies."

"She" was the booty Joe Heidegger had brought back from his tour of duty with Uncle in Germany.

"Tough luck," said Tonia. "She traded in her inheritance for a mess of Coca-Cola."

"Oh, don't be so smart. Why are you so hard on everyone? You're too young to know anything. Women have lots of reasons for getting married."

"There's only one good one. When I get married—if I get married—I am going to be just crazy in love. And. I'm going to earn money. I'm going to sing my way into big bucks. I will not be a dependent."

"Stuff," said her mother. "We're all dependents. Besides, yesterday you said you were going to marry rich. What happened? Bad luck at the party?"

"I was joking, of course," said Tonia, and in order to cut off the conversation, opened the *Times* to a music review. ". . . young soprano . . . affected presentation of . . . blurry top notes . . ." leaving Tonia with, on the one hand, a feeling of gleeful satisfaction ("My top notes are great") and on the other, depression ("Am I affected?").

Upstairs, the Schmidts' door slammed and the ceiling vibrated as they boomed down the stairs. They were in their fifties, weighed two hundred pounds apiece, and both of them worked—he in a copper-smelting plant in Brooklyn, she in a knitting mill. Saturday morning they cozily grocery-shopped together, loading up their little black Ford with enough brown bags to feed a battalion. Saturday afternoon, dressed in their gaudiest rayons, they bar-hopped. Saturday night they stumbled back up the stairs and about 11 P.M. commenced beating each other, which ended, somewhere past midnight, in an incredible quickening rhythm of ceiling shakes. Like two beached whales they flailed in a vibrato that rose from march time *(un poco crescendo)* to hemidemisemi-quavers of passion. Sunday morning they limped down the stairs—she in a black dress, hat, and gloves, with a patch of adhesive under her eye, he in a shiny black suit, his face as pale and spongy and gray as a newspaper left in the rain. Just outside the front door he would offer her his arm and they would walk down the street to eleven o'clock mass at St. Stephen of Hungary's.

"I'm going to drive into the city later," her mother said. "Theo and I are going to a movie. Want to ride in with me?"

"Mmm. I might go over to Juilliard and check out their fall workshops."

"It's too much for you."

"What?"

"Working and taking lessons. And coming back here every night."

Tonia shrugged. Her mother broke off a corner of dry toast, then began torturing it into crumbs. She said, "You ought to have a place of your own."

"I plan to, eventually. Not right now, though—Blakova costs too much. It's funny you should say that, because Charity Mullet—the girl I told you about?—she wants me to share an apartment with her. Lord. She is one screwball. She went right ahead and found us a place, you won't believe where."

"Where?"

"The Lower East Side."

Her mother looked thoughtful. "I imagine it's cheap."

"Mother. For God's sake, it's a ca-rummy tenement."

"We all have to start someplace."

"Oh, please. Let's not do the *La Bohème* thing. I don't care where I live as long as it's cheap and close to Blakova. This place is as far away as you can get. Besides, Charity's nuts. I don't think I could live with her."

"It might be fun. Perhaps you ought to try it."

"Try it!"

Her mother sighed. Started to put a piece of toast in her mouth, put it down. Lately she'd been dieting. "I'm thinking of selling this house." She lifted her eyes—they were Mercer eyes, a beautiful shade of blue.

"But why? Where will you go? Back to Veddersburg?"

"Veddersburg! Heavens, no. Why would I do that?"

"Well, where then?"

"I'm not sure yet. We're still looking."

"You mean you and Theo?"

Her mother shook her head. "Oh, no, I could never live with Theo. No. You see"—playful exasperating smile—"I'm thinking of getting married."

For eleven years, ever since they had moved to Queens, her mother's life had seemed to flow on with the monotonous smoothness of a complacently gleaming object gliding serenely down time's conveyor belt. Weekdays from nine to five she worked at the law firm, typing. On weekends she went to the city, saw an old college classmate, came home again. Every summer for two weeks she went back to Veddersburg to see her parents. Was it some man she'd met up there? She had never, as far as Tonia knew, gone out with a man, had never mentioned a particular man.

"Really," said Tonia. "To whom?"

"Mr. Weingarten."

"Mr. Weingarten?"

"Yes."

"But . . ."

"What?"

"He's shorter than you are."

Her mother looked up at the ceiling. "True. But not much shorter."

"But . . . have you been seeing him?"

"I see him every day, Tonia. I have for eleven years now."

"I mean, have you been going out?"

"Well. Yes, we have."

"But . . . what about his wife?"

"He's getting divorced."

"But . . . when did this happen?"

"Why, he decided to get a divorce in . . . let me see . . . March."

"But . . . does she want it? The divorce?"

"Mrs. Weingarten? No, I don't think so. No. I'm sure she doesn't."

"Mother!"

Her mother got up from the table.

"Mother!"

"Let's talk about it later."

"I can't believe you'd do this."

At the door to her bedroom, her mother paused and smiled. "You see," she said, "I'm tired of typing." Then she opened the door and closed it behind her.

Driving into the city, Tonia felt queasy; her mother, in a new dress the subtle blue of a submerged iceberg, remained calm, and possibly to divert Tonia's mind, started in on her grandparents, how didn't Tonia think that just once, this summer, now that she was engaged (that was how she described herself: engaged), Tonia might . . . Oh, no, said Tonia. Firmly. No, no. Again, no. She really couldn't take time off from her exciting new job.

Her grandparents had been divorced for six years. For reasons of economy, they'd decided to stay in the same house but with a plastered-up wall down the middle, like a cleaver stuck into a wedding cake. The north side of the house was his, the south half, hers. This living arrangement had necessitated an intricate game of avoidance. Mondays, Wednesdays, and Fridays, *he* went down first to get the mail, and Tuesdays, Thursdays, and Saturdays, *she* did. On even Sundays *she* got to stand on the front porch waiting for a ride to church, but on odd Sundays it was *his* turn and *she* had to cut through two backyards and wait for her ride at the corner of Market and Blair. For thirty years of marriage they had coldly avoided each other, but divorced, they'd become as dependent upon each other as opponents in any boxing match. No one in the family much liked Tonia's grandmother Tilly, and with some good reason. Tilly was small, wiry, and brown; a hard pure light poured out of her eyeholes as if someone had aimed at her face and fired a double-barreled shotgun. She was always ready to tell you what you already knew or half guessed about yourself and hoped no one else would notice. The summer that Tonia was twelve she was morose: she had no breasts, not even a menstrual cycle, but instead a pimple had appeared in the exact center of her forehead as if all her coursing adolescent anger had been drawn to that spot, which was not even a pimple, more like a small and outrageously active volcano. It would not go away. Her mother said calmly, "Just leave it alone." (Huh! thought Tonia. Your answer to everything!) Nighttimes, secretly at work in the bathroom, she would squeeze the loathsome thing, which seemed obediently to diminish, only next morning to reappear flaming and fiery, with a magma-filled center and a crust oozing a sickly, sticky exudate. She hated it and herself. They went upstate for The Visit. When her grandmother saw her, she said (instead of hello), "You have a pimple." As if her house were not full of wincing mirrors. When Tonia's grandfather was thirty or so, Tilly told him what he already knew: "You're washed up." He worked in a bank and after that the cogs stuck, his few investments failed, he did a real estate deal that is a still-told joke in the lower Mohawk Valley (bought land at optimum price from a vacating cowlord and sold it for less—much less —to the state nature conservancy). He withdrew, thereupon, to his radio and his phonograph records. He hated most kinds of popular music, and Tilly, who was tone deaf, regularly got his goat by turning on full blast Johnny Polarski, the Valley DJ, and his ongoing waves of pop, rock, and Polish polkas. When they got divorced, relief went through the family like a blue breeze in sultry August. Except now the news from upstate was that Tilly was getting married again. Why her? thought Tonia, moodily. She's seventy-two. I am twenty-one and I can't seem to fall in love, at least not with someone who loves me back.

"I feel so sorry for Dad," her mother said. "God knows what he'll do without her."

Tonia inquired as to the lucky bridegroom. Mr. Eliot, her mother replied, was selling his hardware store. They were moving to Florida. Tilly wanted to change her life.

They were halfway toward the city now, speeding along the Long Island Expressway, which Tonia thought resembled a road out of an old movie, circa 1943, starring Paul Muni and a skyful of strafing Stukas. Tires, hub caps, chrome trim strips lay on the road like the abandoned belongings of refugees in flight; the potholes were as big as bomb craters and the cars that bumped along next to them as intent on the drive as if fleeing before an advancing army. At last Tonia said rudely, bringing the conversation full circle, "Do you love him?" She half expected her mother would ask: "Who?"

Her mother blinked. She had on pearl earrings and bright pink lipstick. "No," she said, "not yet. I do like him. I expect I shall love him."

"Maybe," Tonia said cruelly, "his wife loves him."

"Maybe," her mother said. Lightly.

"I don't understand you at all."

"You haven't spent eleven years typing."

"You keep saying that."

"It's true, my dear, I'm tired. I'm tired of typing. I want to do something different."

"How can you?"

"Tonia. I am forty-eight. Have you ever wondered what would happen if I got sick? Would you be willing to come and take care of me?"

"I just don't see how you can be so *crass*. Breaking up a marriage."

"I didn't seduce him, Tonia." The word "seduce" sounded as shocking as if she'd said "fuck."

"Besides," her mother went on, "look at it this way: Now you won't have to worry about my old age."

"What about her?"

"Mrs. Weingarten?"

"Yeah. What's going to happen to her?"

"I don't really know. Maybe she'd like to type for a while."

"God. I can't believe this is really you."

"It is. It's me."

"You sure had me fooled."

"You fooled yourself."

"I always thought you were . . ."

"Dead?"

Tonia rolled the car window all the way down and put out her arm and leaned her heavy head upon it. The Queens air smelled of burned rubber. "I never thought you were . . . dead. Only different from me. Content. Not wanting so much."

"And we turn out to be not so different after all. Wanting something."

"I thought you'd already had what you wanted. Married to . . . my father."

Her mother said nothing, but in profile her face took on a cunning Phoenician look: her eye seemed to elongate and her mouth became a sly upturned slit. "It's funny about life," her mother said. "One does keep on wanting. Besides, your father never really asked me what I wanted." Tonia grimaced. Aha. She'd been reading again: the ladies' mags, Ann Landers, pop psychology on creative emoting.

"Oh," she said, "did you want something different then, too?"

"At first," her mother said, "only him. And I didn't have that."

Tonia turned her head. "How can you say that when he loved you so much?"

Her mother pursed her lips. "Sometimes," she said, "I think you are just unbearably naive. He loved me in his own way. In the same way that he loved many things. Get out some change, will you? For the toll."

Tonia was dropped off at Fifty-seventh Street. "So," her mother said, stopping the little blue Plymouth. "Perhaps you'd better think it over."

"About what?" Tonia asked, getting out.

"About your friend's apartment."

Tonia slammed the car door and her mother took off in a blast of gray exhaust.

She didn't go to Juilliard that afternoon; instead, she stood dumbly looking after the car and then walked east on Fifty-seventh Street and south on Lexington. Her sandals were a little too loose and kept slipping, her canvas shoulder bag kept slipping too. It was hot, but a city breeze full of grit and lethal monoxides and cigarette wrappers kept things briskly moving. At Thirty-third and Lex, a short, potbellied, blue-bearded man who reminded her of Mr. Weingarten tried to pick her up. Glancing at him, she did the whole thing in her head—went upstairs in the hotel elevator, took off her sandals, unwrapped her skirt, lay down naked on the dirty chenille bed cover—then she shook her head at him and laughed. At Gramercy Park she slowed her pace, walked with the wistful pleasure of a have-not beside the soothing intricate furbelows of the wrought-iron gate. What a safe pleasant scene the fenced-in park made, the green shrubs glossy in the June sun, inside children peacefully playing, an elderly couple sunning themselves and reading newspapers. But when she got close to these little vignettes, she saw that the kids were having a fierce tug-of-war over a battered green dump truck, and two nursemaids, each jiggling an English carriage, were having a loud Celtic argument, and the elderly man reading the newspaper was being bitterly harangued by the elderly woman. Clearly today the city was giving her a gift: this metaphor of her mother's life. All these years, then, she had assumed that her mother was not unpleasantly skimming along on the surface of things, when, underneath, she had been as full of contentious life as the locked-up park. Tonia wondered why she had gone on placidly for so long. She had never complained. Tonia had simply assumed that: (1) she had already lived; (2) her life was over; (3) the memory of her father, sacredly enshrined in her mother's head, was enough to keep her busy until death. It seemed bumptious, rascally even, to overturn that urn and demand . . . what? Joy, sorrow, pain, feeling . . . life? She had always thought her mother intolerably passive, at least set beside her father's turbulent whirlwind motion. Had she gotten that way in self-defense? Still, Tonia knew that passivity was its own strength, a discreet but stubborn strength, and that her mother could be, when pushed, like a city under siege—implacable, with long reserves of fortitude and patience, until by her sheer ability to wait she would win. She was indeed "long-suffering," stoical, enduring, but with all the ability of stoics to make those around them bear the usual burden of guilt. Apparently, for eleven long years she had suffered in silence for—oh, damn—Tonia.

At a coffee shop on the corner of Third Avenue and Nineteenth Street she bought a Coke and a forbidden pack of cigarettes—let Blakova fulminate—and then walked on. In the heat, people had taken to the streets and fire escapes and they sat in the stifling air listlessly fanning themselves or playing portable radios, or sat in doorways on camp chairs and played cards on orange crates, and ate and even diapered babies on the stoops of buildings. On Sixth Street she passed a boarded-up abandoned building with a dead white-bellied rat lying in front of it, and then saw the blue lintel of the tenement they'd been to the day before. After the dirty, threatening street it seemed like a haven. She climbed the crooked staircase again and passed the same number of open and closed doors and arrived again, breathless, on the top floor. No work had gone on in "their" apartment; the ladder, the dropcloth, the white whorls on the scum-green walls were all the same. She stood looking at the little room, hating it. She wondered why she'd come down all this way: to look at this ugly room? And time telescoped forward and she saw herself in miniature at the other end of her mind's magnification, an older, grimmer, maybe even fatter Tonia, in this very room, a flop as a singer, still typing, singing in some Greenwich Village café, having (if she were lucky) occasional lovers. And nothing else. She felt terrified. Help! Someone help! She peered at the scrawled name card tacked to the next door—no, not this— and the next—not this, either—and, at the closed door at the front of the building, knocked. Knocked again. Inside she heard a rustle, then a thud—feet planted on a bare floor. The bolt was pulled back, the lock sprung, and the door opened a crack. It wasn't Tom Ferrier. They stared at each other. She had on a blue terry cotton bathrobe, much too large for her. She opened the door wider.

"Why, Tonia," Charity said, "how nice." She was as formal as if this were Park Avenue and she were wearing a hostess gown. "Do come in."

Tonia noticed that under the bathrobe she had nothing on.

"Do you have a Band-Aid?" Tonia asked weakly, and pointed to her foot, where a leper's sore had appeared at that point on the toe where thong met skin. Except for the rumpled bed and a green leather chair draped with flimsy underthings, the room had only a desk, a chair, and a bookcase full of books—all medical texts. A greasy little breeze slid in under the window and from its spot on the floor a small fan droned and preened.

"Is that what you wanted?" Charity asked. "A Band-Aid?" (With, Tonia noticed, only a minor note of hostility.) Charity sat down on the bed, then drew herself up into the corner, against the wall. They looked at each other. "I guess you think it's strange," they said, more or less simultaneously, and then looked away and smiled.

"Sit down," said Charity.

"I'm sorry," said Tonia. "I didn't realize you two were —uh—"

"It's all right."

"Look, I guess I should take that apartment. If you still want to. I mean, it's up to you."

"Really? Oh, that's terrific. Why'd you change your mind?"

"My mother. She's getting married."

"She is?"

"Yeah. And she's selling the house."

"Why, aren't you lucky! Now you won't have to worry about her."

"I don't know. It does seem to be a marriage of convenience. He's already married."

"They often are."

"He's getting a divorce."

"Love will find a way," said Charity. "Think of it like this: she's handing you your freedom."

"Uh-huh."

"God. I wish I had that."

"What?"

"Freedom," said Charity. "Listen, do you think you could do me a favor?"

"What?"

"Come back with me and tell my Aunt Lucille I spent the night with you?"

"Oh, no," said Tonia. "I couldn't. It's not that I mind lying, it's just that I'm not a good liar. Besides, why lie? You're twenty-one. It's none of her business what you do."

"I wish that were true, but it's not. You see, she's kind of in charge of my life and there's not much I can do about it. At least not until I'm forty."

"Forty! God. You could be dead by then. I don't understand."

Charity looked tired. "It's a long story. Well, never mind. I guess I'd better get dressed. Would you believe it? Someone stole my shoes last night." She stood up and slipped into a pair of white tennis sneakers that flopped comically on her feet. "These are Teddy's. I had to stuff the toes with Kleenex."

"You're lucky," said Tonia. "Someone stole my purse. Ben had to drive me home."

"Ben did?" said Charity, looking up and smiling. "Now isn't that nice. I'll tell you what: tomorrow let's all go on a picnic together, you and Ben, Tom and I. Bring sandwiches

for two—Ben likes ham and cheese. Want to share a cab
uptown?"

"I had planned on taking the bus."

"In that case," said Charity, "let me drop you. I've got
some money."

You sure have, thought Tonia. If I had your money! If
I had your money I'd never darken the door of the *Beau;* I'd
move uptown near Blakova and concentrate on my singing
and polish my languages and try out for a competition in a
year and wow them in Milan in two. Freedom. Me? You
must be kidding. I'm a slave to my paycheck and furthermore
I don't want to live down here and play at being poor. I've
been poor and it isn't play and I can't quit when I get tired.
Don't you see? Tonia wanted to tell her, *It's not a game.*

9

Sea, sun, sand, that magical old combination. The sea at
Sunken Meadow State Park was glassily pale blue with a hint
of stippled haze at the horizon. In the tattered gray sky the
sun looked runny, as if someone had squashed it, and the
sand was littered with orange peels and Dixie cups. A family
beach—lots of wailing infants and skinny adolescents. Ter-
ritories had already been established, each family enclave
separated from another by skimpy boundaries of sand. A
large preserve some yards away was dominated by a fat red-
haired woman in a black bathing suit, sitting like an Oriental
dowager under a yellow umbrella. Around her in a circle
were spread six smaller beach towels, each one inhabited by
a red-haired kid. The kids also ran to plumpness. Off to the

side of this ménage sat a pale long-nosed gentleman in baggy
blue swim trunks. The father. He had thin red hair under his
green tennis visor and sat grimly reading the Sunday papers.

Still, the air smelled cleanly of salt and pine and a wild
rose hedge ran amok at the edge of the dunes and looking
out toward all that blue expanse—in all of Queens, Suffolk,
and Nassau counties the only real space left—Tonia remembered that she loved the sea. She was not a believer in old
racial myths and was even skeptical about national character-
istics (God, what a hodgepodge we all are), but somewhere
on some chromosome she owned there was a saltwater tingle, a bit of DNA that remembered Haseltines who, two
hundred years ago, before coming to this brave new world,
had lived simply and sailed off the shores of the cold North
Sea. So she loved the sea and he, Tom, loved Charity and
they had spent Friday night together, *con amore.* Or maybe
it was only sex. She'd heard of that—just doing it for sex—
but had never herself tried it, and furthermore, couldn't help
wondering why things were so scrambled. Why couldn't Ben
and Charity love each other so she could have Tom? It
seemed like a simple solution. Besides, she was almost sure
that the creased snapshot in Charity's desk at the *Beau* was
of Ben, and there was (she thought) a certain sly lovelorn
way Charity looked at Ben when she thought no one was
watching. There they were down on the beach gathering
shells, Charity in an outsize orange bathing suit that hung to
her knees from bazooms so padded each one resembled half
a deflated football. Ben, the sunburned scientist, had treated
Tonia coolly, as if she were a not very interesting bit of cell
life on a slide, or maybe he was just retaliating, for driving
out on the cluttered parkway, Tonia could not take her eyes
off the wheel of Charity's convertible, which Tom's bony
brown hands twiddled in and out of lanes with the ease of

a TV criminal. Tom's dark dark hair whipped up in the wind, filaments of sun-red-gold, and his profiled smile was wide and white as he turned to say something to Chare, who, for the drive out, had swathed herself in clothes from head to toe, like a bad-burn victim encased in bandages. Or a mummy. Sometimes Charity did seem a thousand years old and otherwise petrified. How was it they'd spent the night together? Still. All was not lost. What was one night when what she wanted was a thousand thousands of Tom's night-time attentions and daytime attentions and how about right now?

He, Tom, lay a length away reading and she lay under sunglasses, sizzling in suntan lotion and with a mighty effort at detachment concentrated her thought on her old high school boyfriends, starting with Big John Oker, the baseball player—tenth grade, chewed gum, never said a word, had lovely deltoids, and trapezius muscles so developed he was more or less neckless—with whom, feeling horribly ashamed of herself (he was mentally so much beneath her), she learned how to French-kiss in the back of Bull Martin's beat-up Chevy. High school summer Saturdays! They used to go to Rockaway Beach and bake and swim and bake and tease each other and then on, at night, to the Shamrock Bar and Grill for illegal beer and pizza and cigarettes and making out all the way home, till sleepy and sunburned and gritty she got dropped off where her mother waited on the back porch, arms folded, eyes cool.

"Hello."

"Hi!"

"Have a good time?" Swift sidelong look at Tonia's clothing. What was she checking for? Handprints? Blood spots? Sperm?

"Sure!" Slam and into the bathroom, still weak from

repressed sex because certainly she didn't love Big John, it was only . . . only . . . and a quick wriggle out of puzzlingly damp underpants.

Then skinny Arthur Akers of Stuyvesant High, the walking mental gym. He knew her head, took her to concerts, and later they used to hold hands over Cokes and discuss music and lit-a-cher. She never let him kiss her. Freshman year at Harvard (scholarship boy, his father a Queens bartender), for reasons unknown, he hanged himself.

And Danny Reilly, whom she might truly have loved; many sparks there, humor and craziness. God, he was daring! One New Year's Eve, thoroughly drunk, they drove the wrong way toward oncoming traffic down Cross Bay Boulevard. He loved speed, booze, country music, and, oddly, books. The army got him and sent him home an accountant. A would-be CPA with a dead-white face, wanting her to drop out of college, turn Catholic, and live—oh, my God—in Queens.

She considered this, then, how in her love life there had always been this primary oscillation, a pendulum swing between body and mind, soul pretty much getting left out of it. Wasn't there someone, somewhere, whom every bit of her could care for and love? And who, in turn, would love the Princess, the Urchin, and (she knew she was moody) the Witch, as well as the Singer? This Farrier or Ferrier, now. Intelligent warm lit-up eyes and the dim ocher freckles that lived under his tan. When shedding their topmost layer of clothes down to bathing attire, she saw, as he politely turned to unzip his fly (with a sound like a paper heart tearing), a stipple of dark brown moles between prominent shoulder blades. Why not him? Why was it, then, when she looked at him, his eyes clouded over, he became very polite, some sort of invisible barrier of awfully good manners descended like a curtain, and kindness, like a lead shield, warded off her eye rays. She didn't know. Was it Charity? That . . . rich robot? Something hurt. An ache under her ribs made her sit up. He politely smiled and shut his book. Propped on his elbows, he squinted at the sky.

"Looks like it just might rain."

"Yes!"

"On the other hand, it just might hold."

"Might!"

Oh, witty Tonia, always so glib except when the chips are down. Finally, unstalled, they talked, exchanging little histories. Of course: she'd known all along: upstate New York. Five generations of Ferriers, or was it six, from Johnsford, just up the river from Veddersburg; father a doctor, granddaddy too. She often fell in love with the same sort of guy, someone bedrock calm and kind, with the roots of a three-hundred-year-old oak, roots deep enough to exert a downward gravitational pull on her lateral restlessness. Next question (this is getting serious): does he ski? and she gave him the flash of a smile she hadn't turned on any man for far too long. Come on now, you've got to ski, why, everyone in Johnsford skis.

"Oh, sure," he said, and smiled (that wide white smile). Why, everyone in Johnsford skis. Isn't she a singer?

Yes, she's a singer, or will be someday, not yet. . . . What was that he'd just said?

". . . the piano."

He plays the piano!

". . . used to hate it. I'd have my lesson on Mondays after school and to get to Miss Mulcahy's house I'd have to walk past the back of the chewing gum factory where the other kids hung out. I got so I'd rip the damn music right out of the book and fold it up to about, oh, the size of a postage stamp and stick it in my pocket. Miss Mulcahy never said a word, she'd just take it out to her kitchen and iron it flat. Poor woman. Couldn't play herself, she had such bad arthritis. Her right hand was all cramped up, like that." He showed her with his hand: a hook.

"Do you still play?"

"Play?"

She blushed. "The piano!"

"Oh, no. Not anymore. I like music, though."

Likes skiing, likes music! We've got everything in common—I'll take him! But what was that he'd just said and why was it he was looking not at her but steadily seaward? With the extreme gentleness he would someday use to tell some non-benign-tumored patient the good news, he was letting her know tactfully, gradually, but nonetheless firmly that through Ben, whom he'd known for years (years?), he'd met Charity last spring (last spring?) and that, well, they were Very Close, and, well, There It Was.

Followed thereupon a dreadful moment. Inside Tonia's head the sun went under a cloud and she felt a prickly chill on her skin: Am I dead? Is it winter so soon? I could go away and die. I could crawl under this very beach towel. I could get up, taking my flash of a smile, and walk into the water and never come back. She reached for the beach towel and draped it over herself, making of it a dark reclusive cave.

Hidden in her towel, she stood up, thinking dully: All right, all right. I do understand. She needs you. You need her to need you. Sighed. Shrugged. Looked down the beach, where a kind of running blob, eight-legged, like some larger-than-life arachnid, inserted itself into her focus: four lifeguards running seaward carrying a bobbing lifeboat. A needle-fine spray of sand made her turn. She gave the fat man running past a menacing look and he said, yelling over his shoulder in apology, "A kid's missing!" Already the beach at water's edge was dense with people. She saw Charity's orange bathing suit and standing next to Charity, Ben, and then Tom appeared next to Charity. She saw mothers carrying infants and fathers holding toddlers and kids darting here and there and from all up and down the sand, bathers were running calamityward. The lifeboat was out on the water now and two of the lifeguards had jumped in. Why, that's crazy, she thought, no one could drown out there. There's no undertow, there aren't any waves, it's just a few feet deep. The fat man turned and yelled at her (the space between falling-down swim trunks and shrunk-up T-shirt a sunburned red eye), "They say it's a little kid. He had a raft. They say his mother can't swim. She leaves him out there on a raft— can you beat that?" He shook his head. Where one of the lifeguards had gone under, a white geyser of water appeared, and he came up holding on to something large and bright and blue—a child's raft—and the crowd at the water's edge was profoundly silent.

"Make way now, clear a space here!" someone on the beach shouted. Silently, the crowd parted. The two lifeguards swam, then waded ashore, the lifeboat arrived and the crowd drew back. She couldn't see clearly what was going on, everything was very still, then came a terrible groaning cry and like the slowly unfolding petals of a flower the crowd began to move out from its center, men with their arms around their wives and women clutching at children. She saw the large red-haired white-skinned woman supported on either side by a lifeguard but sagging between them like a sack of wet meal. The woman lifted her head and again came that terrible cry, which went up, then down the scale. The fat man came back, and trudging past Tonia, remarked, "Dead." In his sunburned face, his small blue eyes were circled by white rings.

Then she saw in the center of the slowly dispersing crowd the body—so small!—wrapped in a blanket, the fat woman, whose head had slumped to one side, and all the red-haired kids, the two plump little girls holding each other, an older boy with his arm around a younger one, and the father in his tennis visor and baggy trunks, looking stupefied, holding the baby.

Tom and Charity arrived together. Charity looked pale. Her lips were blue. Tom bent, picked up her white terry cloth dress, then reached for her hand and drew it into a sleeve. He pulled the dress up on her shoulder, then placed Charity's left hand in her left sleeve. From far off they heard the spiraling wail of an ambulance siren—it was, of course, too late—and in a low voice Ben said, "Let's go home."

10

The house was dark when she got home, and stuffy. All the warmth of the day had collected in the little locked-up rooms and she sat for a long time in her nightgown on the back porch, waiting for a breeze. None came. The black air was thick and smelled charred as if, down the block, the crematorium were cooking. At least it was quiet; instead of last summer's hot night screams and whines from the Schmidts and Heideggers and Hallorans, this year they got the steady synchronized hum of bedroom air conditioners. Technology will save us all. Will they cremate the kid? What's one more kid, there are so many already. Three years old, bug-eyed in water and gasping for air. Kids? Hostages. In her head, Kanfer, her twelfth-grade English teacher, points at: "Wanda?" from whose red-smeared lips a pink blob of gum grows into a bubble, oddly divided and seamed like a scrotum. Snap. The bubble collapses. "To fortune." "Huh?" Repeat: "Hostages to fortune." Wanda doesn't know. Arnie Flegel also is stumped. Kanfer looks at Tonia over his glasses, but lost in a lazy Monday morning haze of post-weekend erotics, she doesn't want to answer; the whole weekend comes and goes in black and white like clips from a scratched film and Kanfer shakes his head at her, smiling, and she loves him, this teacher who, as if they were real people, calls them by their first names, who, in a school like a barbed-wire zoo, wants them not just to pass the Regents but out of his dignified humanness, shares with them his sad love for words. "My dears . . . so young . . . your children . . ." (Twitches, rustles, Arnie Flegel farts.) "Vulnerable through one's deepest attachments: Get it? *Verstehen?*" She got it, she got it; she would never have children. She would maybe love, but would never marry; she would live like Blakova in a cluttered empty room; she would dedicate herself to her music. She went inside and put a record on.

Another mistake. Flagstad: the *Wesendonck Lieder.* All weekend long she had thought about love, not music, and the voice, sinuous and powerful, came up like a city weed through the slab of her chest, opening up a familiar abyss: *Tonia. Baby.* She would never sing like that. No, never. No power, no range, no talent, no drive, no heart, no will, no voice. Who can save her soul from the fiend? This terror waiting in the dark who crawls out of a corner and grins and with one swipe of a paw wipes out her whole inner world. What did she have but her singing, her singing, her singing? Opera! Grand opera! Her performing art. Sometimes it did seem ridiculous.

Headlights flicked across the wall, picking out blue sprigs of wallpaper. Wayward mother was home from her date. The front door rattled. A light went on in the kitchen. She heard the refrigerator door open and close. She heard ice clink in a glass and then, in a voice faint with disuse, heard her mother singing: *"Misterioso! Misterioso!"*

Oh, Lord. Her mother was falling in love.

"Tonia?"

And there was that. Someone to hold your head in the dark.

"Tonia! Phone!"

Maybe just that.

"Tonia. Phone! If you don't want to talk to this Ben, tell him so yourself."

His voice heard over the crackle of Ma Bell's wire was deep, ringing, clear. Why hadn't she noticed before? Maybe he sings. And he said before hanging up, "Sleep well."

And she needed to laugh.

Or to cry.

11

The next night, a Monday, Tonia took her lesson—promptly at seven—with Madame Blakova, who had a studio apartment in a building on West End Avenue. It was a lovely old building, very European in character, with both a wide marble staircase and an airy gilded antique elevator that looked like a giant birdcage and creaked and swayed dangerously when you set foot inside. Tonia always took the stairs. Madame was on the third floor, and climbing those wide marble stairs, Tonia could hear from behind closed doors various

instruments—it was a house inhabited by teachers of music
—a piano, a flute, the human voice, all in harmonious dis-
cord. Often, if she was early, she would sit on the step outside
and listen to the lesson before hers—Madame did not allow
interruptions, not even the trill of a doorbell. The girl was
a mezzo-soprano with a bit of a strain in her upper register
but—as much as Tonia could hear through the heavy oak
door—a mellow woodiness of sound in her middle register,
a grained richness, like the pink and gold of unvarnished
mahogany. The first time she heard the voice she imagined,
sitting there on the cool marble step with her music on her
knees, that the girl would be medium-sized and heavy in the
hips like a small bass or a cello, but when the door opened
and she came out, Tonia saw a small, frail young woman who
was slightly round-shouldered, had Mediterranean coloring,
several unattractive black moles on her cheek, and a large
hooked nose. She gave Tonia a dark-eyed contemptuous
look over her shoulder before clicking off to the elevator.

"Come in, please," Madame said briskly. Tonia went in
to her living room-studio, where, through most of her hour,
she would sing and, seated at the piano, Madame would
occasionally accompany her, but most of the time, eat. It was
her dinner hour. She had agreed to take Tonia evenings only
as an exception. Tonia rather resented the fact that she ate
on her time and besides this, watching her take deep bites of
a corned beef on rye, slathered with brownish mustard, accompanied by a cool succulent slice of green pickle, she had
trouble concentrating, her *s*'s slithered in her mouth like
hungry serpents, and her stomach, unattended since noon-
time, rumbled and groaned.

Blakova had narrow, heavily mascaraed eyes, a long but
delicate nose, and a steep shining pile of braided dark-brown
hair, around which she liked to tie ribbons or velvet bands.

She wore, always, winter and summer—wool or chiffon—a scarf around her long throat and had a whole repertoire of stoles and shawls, and even on the hottest nights of the summer drank glasses of warm tea from her samovar. She encouraged Tonia to drink tea too. Not too hot, of course. She was to remember not ever to ingest anything too hot or too cold. Ice cream was strictly *nyet.* Never put ice in cukacula; hot let your coffee seet unteel ees culd. Good health was everything! The voice reflected the mind and the body. Do not push the voice during the menses. Avoid drafts. Avoid seek pipple. Avoid peels. Who knows what craziness in them? On winter nights before retiring Tonia was to lubricate her throat with petroleum jelly and pin around it a piece of flannel; this was not only to keep the cords warm but to preserve the line of "your beautiful throat," for who wanted to look at a singer with a wrinkled neck?

As she got to know Blakova better, her teacher began to give her bits and pieces of her personal life, unfortunately also on Tonia's time. Madame claimed to have been the mistress of two famous conductors and her studio-living room, hung with dingy red damask drapes and cluttered with cheap porcelain, was made tawdrily rich by the signed photographs everywhere—on the walls, on the dusty mantel, on tables, and upon the bureau, from which, often, the tip of a scarf or the toe of a stocking crept out of the topmost drawer. Tonia would have preferred to listen after her hour was over, and besides, these anecdotes and these reminiscences of Blakova's life inspired Tonia with an awed sadness. After a lifetime spent in music, was this all? Photographs? Anecdotes? Still, Blakova knew, had known, so many singers and musicians it was like listening to a catalogue of twentieth-century greats: Flagstad had been a glorious ox, Galli-Curci the most human, Lotte Lehmann the best, perhaps, technically, of all of them. As for these new singers—poof. A dismissing wave of the hand. Thees new Jezebel, for example, all emoting, no voice. A screech at the top of her range. Ees no nice.

That night, Tonia told Blakova that she would have to reduce her lessons to one a week. Madame was eating a plateful of stuffed cabbage sent up from a deli down the street and she stopped, fork in midair, and asked, "Why?"

Tonia told her.

"Ah," Blakova said sadly, "money." She thought for a long moment. "You must get some work seenging. Now ees diffeecult. Summer? Naw-teenk."

Tonia stood silently by while she finished her cabbage and scooped up the sauce with a piece of rye bread. She sighed and put down the plate, frowned, took a black notebook from the piano top, rapidly turned the pages with her skinny dark-red-tipped fingers, then thoughtfully tapped a page with a curved nail. "Maybe een fall."

There was a silence between them. Madame sat with one black-clad arm—she always wore long sleeves—on the keyboard and looked down at her skinny hands, flexed them and sighed. Here it comes, thought Tonia, the old locker room lecture. To leeve ees to seeng. To seeng ees to sockreefice. Weeth you, who can tell? Nice clarity, beeg range. Voice not yet of course mature. Gets better? Gets worse?

"I myself," said Blakova, "prefer more slower to mature the voice, otherwise flash een pan; thirty years old, all burned out. Steel. Ees not everything here"—again the dab at the throat—"but here." A tap at the forehead, the sign Americans use when they mean "nuts." "Also," Blakova went on, with a sharp stab at her chest, "here! Courage! It must be deesire, stronger than anyteeng else. Now," she said, looking up, and spreading her hands on the keyboard at last, "Seeng for me now what from *Hoffmann* you did last time not so good and remember please that you are not hoor like Giulietta and not wood like doll Olympia. You are young girl in love, but sad, sad. Your father forbids you to sing, and do not please sing from back of throat on way down scale—out, *out* with the notes."

Blakova turned, put her hands on the keyboard, and began to play, and Tonia was there—in the opera set's old-fashioned music room with a harp and a piano, its French doors open to the sunset. She knew in that moment exactly how to sing Antonia. She would create a long sustained pure line, not colored too richly with the resonances of age and experience but sung in pretty simplicity, with an occasional fine flash like a startled head turning, or like the swift brittle glance of a mirror hung in a fruit tree to frighten the birds; and only here and there perhaps a special softer glimmer, a note that in the mind's blackness would recede like the golden glow of an old-fashioned oil lamp, which first burns brightly and then, as the wick is reduced, merely gleams and at last falters, a radiant squiggle, and fades into the encompassing dark.

Blakova, taking the part of Dr. Miracle, sang: "All this will you sacrifice, for gray daily life, for the cries of small children which your beauty will destroy," and then Tonia sang, letting the song lead her up into an almost shrill terror, keeping it very white:

> *"No, tempt me no more,*
> *For he has sworn to be true*
> *And love me forever.*
> *Oh, who will save my soul from the fiend,*
> *From my own self?"*

Blakova was silent when she'd finished and sat for a moment quietly.

"Ah," she said.

The tall clock chimed the hour. Her lesson was finished.

"What a shame," Blakova said. "You must study now fool time. It must become your life or else . . ." She hunched her shoulders and turned her long palms outward. "You must seeng, seeng always, seeng constantly, sometimes only een head, but you are always seenging. Ah," she said coyly, "ees exhausting, yes? For young girl like you there are good times, parties, young men?"

Not so much that, said Tonia. It was more like no money.

"Then, my dear," said Madame, "let me give you some advice. Find nice young man—one who earns a little money, yes? Sometimes the right marriage ees good for an artist. You should of course peek the correct person." She sighed and twitched her silk shawl down around her shoulders. "For me was mistake. Two artists together—disaster! Find nice young man, lawyer, busyness man, doctor. You will make him proud and he will earn money for you. But"—she warningly raised one skinny forefinger—"no children. Thees keels the voice." She quickly shuffled together the rest of Tonia's music and handed it to her. Waiting outside Madame's door was a tall, dark-eyed, already balding young man who was rapidly pacing the hall. She greeted him with a cry.

"Gino, my pearl. Queekly, queekly; thees one has stayed too long."

Who was he? Tonia wondered. She knew Blakova had no more lessons at this hour. Could it be that she had a lover? It was cheering to Tonia to think that Blakova had someone —anyone—in her life and not just a dismal room cluttered with memorabilia, and she walked down the marble stairs feeling as tired and exhilarated as if she'd just done a thirteen-mile ski run. Tonight her voice had had a surprising agility, a coiled springlike power, and at the end, singing pianissimo, she had felt her voice as an eerily effortless weight, had let it fall softly—a feather, a snowflake—let it float downward, and even on the dangerous icy brilliance of a chromatic run had sustained it from turn to turn, note to note, in perfect form. Leaving the cool marble lobby of the building, she felt as she opened the door—despite the upward rush of moist dank air from the heat-swollen street—cool and contained and complete and enormously happy.

12

Tonia was so full of her music that she had actually gotten on the Eighth Avenue subway to Queens before she remembered Ben: she had promised to meet him in midtown for dinner after the lesson. She was late, he was cranky—something he expressed by looking coldly at a spot over her head and saying not one word to her until after they'd ordered.

"Wine, sir?" the waiter asked, holding out the long tasseled wine card.

Ben looked up. "What do you recommend?" The waiter murmured. "All right," said Ben, and the waiter left. "Frankly," he said, looking at her at last, "I know nothing about wine. We were strictly a Scotch and bourbon family."

"For breakfast, lunch, or dinner?" Tonia asked.

"Never before five," Ben said, "except of course on weekends. When are you going to move?"

"Saturday."

"You don't look happy about it."

"I hate, loathe, despise that room."

"Then why take it?" he asked, cocking his head. His eyes were bright blue. The day at the beach had turned his brown hair reddish; his forehead was spotted with tan; his blunt ridged nose was peeling; his neck was a painful scarlet.

"I don't know," Tonia said. "Charity seemed so determined and I needed a place to live. It was the course of least resistance. There's a part of me that cares about where I live and a part of me that doesn't."

"Can't you get another place?"

"I've already paid for this one. I've signed the lease. Look. I've got to live on my salary. My mother's supported me all these years. Now she's getting married to a man who has two kids in college and one in law school. And a wife who needs alimony."

"Money," he said. He picked up his fork and dropped it. The salad course arrived. The waiter was tall, thin, balding, with a long Gallic nose. He grated pepper on Tonia's lettuce, then dished out upon it grated Parmesan. His cuffs were immaculate. He had a class ring on his right hand. Tonia's high school. She sighed. The waiter left.

"Are you always more than an hour late for dinner dates," Ben asked suddenly, looking up, "or is it you're just letting me know that you're not too interested?"

She looked down. He would never believe the dopiness of what she'd done.

He shook his head and muttered, looking off to the side, "Yesterday at the beach I got the impression that you didn't like me much. You seemed so hostile."

"Then why did you call me later?"

"I'm stubborn."

She laughed at him. "It wasn't hostility, it was passive resistance. Charity seemed so intent on my liking you."

"And instead you liked Tom."

"My. You are direct."

"It's a time-saving device. Everyone likes Tom. It's his air of being at least seventy-five and knowing exactly the right thing to say and do at all times."

"That doesn't sound as if you like Tom."

"Sorry. Just envious, I guess. Since he seems to have your complete attention."

"Are we going to spend the evening discussing Tom?"

"No. I was just going to point out . . ."

"What?"

"About Charity and Tom . . ."

"Well, I know all about that now, though nobody thought to tell me before. And I do like Tom. He seems to be such a . . . giving person."

"He is indeed. And Charity needs a lot of that."

"I sense I'm a taker, so watch out."

"I don't know what I am, except maybe a backer-offer. Here. Stop that. You cannot have my roll."

He caught her wrist between his thumb and middle finger and shook her hand like Fido wrestling a bone. The roll dropped on the floor and bounced over the shoe of the waiter, who was silently removing their salad bowls. She saw that she was beginning to like this Ben. He was smart, he was honest and funny and tough, and tonight as they'd walked through the restaurant heads had turned, starting at the north end of the bar on southward to the kitchen, as if with their health, blazing sunburns, and good looks they'd brought to life all the jaded flowers in the place. As they had passed the end of the bar, a blonde—faded, bleached, freckled, ten pounds of mascara on each lid—had turned and, half slipping off her stool, given Ben a wink that left a row of black surgical stitches on her upper cheek. She had walked into dinner supported on the arm of a tanned gentleman in a blazer and polka-dotted silk throat scarf (his hair that special color of dye-bottle blue) but nonetheless with the uncertain gait of a late stroke victim, and just at their table had attempted a change of direction. The tack failed, she stalled, wobbled, and fell in a soft heap upon Ben's shoulder. He immediately rose to steady her and said, "I'm terribly sorry; my feet must have been in the way." Now, thought Tonia, that really is awfully kind. The blue-haired gentleman nodded coldly, the couple moved off. Tonia could hear in her mind just what Danny Reilly would have said: "Jesus, lady, what the fuck's *wrong* with you?" She had gone to high school with a bunch of hoods and was thus moved nearly to tears by the New England prep school good manners of Benjamin Durham. Looking across the table at him, she said, with a little smile, "I'll bet you ski."

He lived in three basement rooms of a brownstone, with an old sea chest for a coffee table, a sofa covered in oatmeal tweed, and a wall full of books—medical texts, sailing, history, no fiction or poetry, and (that's odd, thought Tonia) no records or stereo that she could see. On the wall a watercolor in rosy pinks and blues of a sloop sailing at twilight (or was it dawn), with a single star scratched into its sky, signed B. Durham. The second room was a small windowless sleeping alcove with the feel of a ship's cabin; the bed—it seemed awfully wide for a bachelor—hung between built-in bookcases. The third room was a dining room and kitchen, and the fourth room—they stepped right out—was his garden, which he had made out of what had been a yard full of trash and boards. A tall paling fence enclosed it. He had put in a brick path. There were shrubs and a small struggling paper birch and in the middle of the little yard a flower garden, tiered like a wedding cake. "Why, it's beautiful," said Tonia.

"If you didn't look up you'd never know all those buildings were there."

He went inside to get two beers, she sat down on a canvas chair. The garden had a funny cloistered feeling with its paths and careful arrangement of shrubs and plants. Looking up, she saw a woman in the window of the brownstone that leaned over the yard; she was smoking and naked and stood with one arm up against the side of the window. Then the woman pulled down the shade.

"Your neighbor likes this garden too," Tonia said when Ben came back.

"Who's that?" he asked, handing her a cool dew-covered bottle.

"The lady over there, up on the fourth floor. She didn't have much on."

"Sometimes," he said, "she has nothing on."

"Oh, really? And do you know her well?"

"Only by sight. Actually, she's sort of sad. She's not a bad-looking woman. I've seen her at D'Agostino's sometimes. I think she's a little bit crazy."

"Does she live alone?"

"I've never seen her with anyone."

"Does she often stand at the window with nothing on?"

"Yes," he said.

Tonia's head felt hot. She put the cold bottle to her cheek. "Don't you have a stereo?"

"No. I've got a radio."

"Why don't you have a stereo?"

"Don't need one."

"Why not? Don't you like music?"

"Not much."

"Are you kidding me?"

"Nope. Got turned off on music at an early age. My

mother used to play the piano, but only when she was really mad. She'd sit down and play something loud with crashing chords. I guess it's a good thing I'm tone deaf."

Tonia warily laughed. "You're not *really* tone deaf."

"I don't mind music, I just have no ear for it. I think it's genetic. My father's the same way—can't tell major from minor."

"I don't believe you. Anyone can tell major from minor."

"Not me."

"Maybe you've just never listened."

"No. I am honestly tone deaf."

"But that's terrible."

"Why?"

"Because music is . . . because it makes me so happy."

"Well, lots of things make me happy. Music just isn't one of them."

"What a shame!"

"Why?"

"I was just beginning to like you."

"Can't you like me anyway?"

"I really don't know."

"Ah, well," he said, "then it's mutual. I could never cope with a singer."

"What do you want, a nice indentured servant?"

"I haven't narrowed it down to a category. What do *you* want?"

"I don't have a category either. I expect I'll know when I find it."

"Someone rich, I guess."

"Rich? Yes! That would be nice."

"I'm not rich."

"How about well-off?"

" 'Fraid not. My father gave up working when I was thirteen."

"He did? Why?"

"He wanted to drink instead."

"Then how are you getting through medical school?"

"Poorly. I'm kind of really in debt. I thought Charity might have mentioned it."

"Don't be silly, she wouldn't know the difference. It's all flow to her—comes in, goes out. That sort of thing."

"I thought maybe that was why, when I called, you were so unenthusiastic."

"Nope. Just being cool."

"You weren't trying hard to get in touch."

"Hey."

"What?"

"Stop it."

"Okay. I do have one other question."

"What?"

"It's a very direct question."

"What?"

"Do you want to go to bed?"

Why was it, why was it, she tried to remember later, that she hadn't headed straight for home? For what is life after all without its games, tourneys, and jousts, and who in the skirmish of the sexes is so totally without imagination as not to enjoy the battle almost as much as the score? Perhaps because it occurred to her, sitting there in the flat black and white of a badly illuminated garden, that she was getting on in years, her grandmother had first married at seventeen, her mother was no doubt regularly finding some sort of satisfaction with her new beau, and she was hoarding up in a little drawstring purse pennies of virtue which, in the long run, might get her only a single room in some downtrodden midtown hotel.

And she sort of liked him and she knew she didn't love him, which could, in the end, prove damaging and he had taken off his coat and tie and she remembered suddenly with a pang of modest lust that he was tall.

She said, "My, you're suave."

"Because if you don't, this sure is a waste of time."

"Now, that hurts. You don't like my company."

He put out a hand and it seesawed: so-so.

"You mean," she said, "if we don't jump in the sack tonight it's all over?"

"Not exactly, but along those lines."

"So what you're saying is," she went on, stalling, stalling, stalling, "if I don't go to bed with you right now, it's goodbye?"

"I'm not saying that; I'm only saying if you're not interested in that sense, let's skip the whole thing. I mean, if you're going to moon over Tom. Or if you just want to sit around and talk. Sex is one of the things that make me really happy."

"Don't you think we should wait a little while?"

"Why?"

"So we could, you know, kind of get to know each other."

"I know you."

"You do?"

"Sure. Look. It's all a risk. You could know me for twenty years and there'd still be a risk. But hey. It's up to you."

"It's just that . . . I can't."

"Why not?"

"Well, as long as we're being so honest, I might as well tell you."

"If it's the usual female reason, I won't mind."

"*What?*"

"It's not that?"

"No."

"You've got a disease?"

"No!"

"For Christ's sake, what then?"

"There is just one little flaw in your personality, you know that? You don't catch on really fast. I am," she said, mustering a large amount of dignity, "inexperienced."

Silence. "Oh, no. Oh, me." A hollow dejected laugh.

"Besides, I'm not on any sort of birth control."

"Oh, no; naturally not." He sighed. And stood up. "Okay. Let's go inside."

In the kitchen, he snapped out the lights. Passing into the little alcove bedroom, he put out that light too and then stood there glumly for a moment before he went into his living room and put out all the lights but one. Then, with the dogged expression of a French resistance fighter awaiting a full night of Gestapo torture, he began accumulating at bedside a number of things—towel, Kleenex, condoms, ointments, jellies. Why not, thought Tonia, pliers and a scalpel?

"What's all this *stuff* for?"

He muttered something.

"What?"

"I said, I sure can pick 'em."

"I can always go home."

"Hell, no. Let's just get this over with."

"You're making me feel really good."

"That's often the point. This unpleasantness—how'd you happen to avoid it for so long?"

"Just lucky, I guess. Or virtuous."

He laughed and began unbuttoning his shirt. "Why

give up your virtue now? You could bank it with someone and draw the interest."

She gritted her teeth—oh, you funny guy—and decided not to answer, and as his shirt fell open, remembered with a sense of tightening under the ribs that despite his scalded skin he'd been beautifully made by an expert craftsman. He carefully lifted the shirt off his shoulders and winced; transparent pieces of flesh adhered to the collar and drifted slowly to the rug. He tossed the shirt into a corner. In the slant of light he stood in, his sunburn glowed a bright neon violet.

She said, "Aren't you going to kiss me first?"

He knelt to untie his shoe. "Nope."

"Not just a little?"

"Certainly not."

One shoe, two. Socks. Long sunburned feet.

"Couldn't we just *hold* each other?"

He drew up his chest and unbuckled his belt. She politely looked away. Then heard a sound that struck her as most peculiar or at least inappropriate. Was he crying? No, in the high-pitched hee-hee-hee of someone who on five drinks is watching a late night TV rerun of something zany, he was laughing, laughing unrestrainedly, with his head on his forearm, and his arm on the wall for support, laughing so hard he was crying. Well, damn your hide, thought Tonia. I'm about to bed down with a crocodile in tears.

"Ben?"

Gasp.

"Ben!"

A partial lift of the head and then another collapse into laughter. In jig time, more or less furiously, Tonia had snaked out of her dress and stepped over to him in her underwear. He was leaning feebly against the wall, cheeks wet, eyes crinkled up. She prodded him with a forefinger.

"Ben."

He hiccuped, then groaned.

She slapped his sunburn, hard. One fierce eye shot open. She said, "Why are you laughing?"

He smiled down at her, swaying, then turned and put his hands on her shoulders.

"Tonia?"

"Yes?"

"God, you feel so *cool.*"

"Yes."

"Listen, Tonia, try not to—ah—touch me too much, okay? And don't touch my back, all right? It really hurts."

And so to bed, as if they were both eighty-four, and a long struggle to sort out, among parts tangled, locked up, or sunburned, the two that will best fit in a position that will afford the least amount of pain to the participants, and ouches and groans from him, and from Tonia, tight-lipped stoicism: holy smoke, this *hurts.* But later, in the sleepy middle of the night, the heat his skin gives off ignites hers and she puts a cool hand upon his back and he swiftly turns. She murmurs something. "What?" he asks, and she says, "Let's try that again," and this time the pain is sweet and they frame between them a musical symmetry, a rising arc of rhythm which, pure delight, ends in a cymbal clash of ringing—oh!—colors.

Then a peaceful coda, thud of heartstring bass and adagio tears, and against the sonorous notes of a dying cello, a sad sweet Mozartian clarinet.

"What?" he asked, when she came back to bed.

"I had to call my mother," she said, climbing over his legs and under the sheet.

"This late?"

"It's only one."

"What did you tell her?"

"I said I was staying with Charity."

"Oh. Well, as long as she doesn't call Charity."

"Charity is quick. Charity will tell her I'm right there."

"No she won't."

"She won't? Why won't she?"

He stretched out under the sheet and put his hand on her hip. "Because Charity isn't home."

"How do you know? Is she in Maine?"

"No." His hand stroked her hip.

"Then where is she? Is she all right?"

"I suppose so. She's in Maryland."

"In Maryland? What's she doing there? Ben, stop that."

He lay still for a moment, then yawned. "She's getting married."

"She is?"

"Yeah."

"You mean she and Tom?"

"Yeah. I thought she'd told you. You said at dinner you knew."

Tonia looked up at the ceiling. "When did you find that out?"

"Tom called me last night."

"Oh *Lord.*" She sat up. "Oh, damn it, damn it, I knew she'd do it. She's stuck me, don't you see? With that hideous little room. Oh, damn her anyway. Now what am I going to do?"

He got up and went into the kitchen. In a moment he was back, wearing a cotton robe and carrying a glass. "Here," he said.

"What is it?" she asked.

"Gin," he said.

"I don't want any gin," she said. "I just want to beat her head in. Why, oh, why did she get me into this deal? I don't understand it."

"I don't think," he said, "that they'd planned to get married. At least not right away. It was a last-minute decision."

"I was supposed to chaperone her, was that it? To make her moving down there all right with her Aunt Lucille?"

He sat down on the edge of the bed. "I really don't know. I haven't yet figured Charity out. Still, it can't be all that bad. You don't have to live there permanently. You could live there for a while, and then look for someplace else. Or just skip living there. You could live here for a couple of days."

"Here?" Tonia said sullenly. "No, thanks."

"Why not?"

"Because," she said, "I'm a singer. I've got to practice and you don't like music."

"True," he said, a little too quickly, she thought. "There is another solution."

"What?"

"Get another job. One that pays more money. Why don't you try teaching? That way you'd have vacations off to study your singing."

"Your singing." He made it sound like a crack-brained hobby. But he was right, of course; he was certainly very practical. She lay back on the bed. He took the glass out to the kitchen and came back with no robe and a hopeful look, but she turned her back on him. She was still angry—at Charity, who she knew had somehow conned her, and at Tom, her accomplice, and at Ben, who with Charity's connivance had maneuvered her into bed. She was determined, in revenge, not to love him.

This wasn't hard, for in the morning he was gone. A note explained that he'd be in his lab for the day. She dressed and left for work. Passionate romance did not ensue. He had neglected to tell her—among other things—that in a week he was moving to Baltimore, where he was going to intern. Cool guy. More fool she. Seduced and abandoned. In spite of herself, Tonia cried (she didn't know why; she thought she didn't love him), and that next weekend moved into her tenement room, alone.

13

It was Tom Ferrier who finally told Tonia Charity's bizarre story, but what struck Tonia as chillingly odd was that Charity's parents had died just two days before her own father's heart attack. Charity had lied to Tonia about her parents—they hadn't died "forever inseparable." Instead, one cold March day (when both girls were ten years old), Charity's father shot her mother in the Schrafft's restaurant on East Fifty-seventh Street.

Charity had gone to the ladies' room and when she came back, carrying her patent-leather purse by its little gold chain, the restaurant was in chaos, people were running everywhere, women were screaming, and a trayful of dirty dishes had fallen and lay on the carpeted aisle. No one seemed to notice the little girl. She got to the table and saw her mother sitting slumped back on the banquette smiling (or was it a smile?), and her ringed hand was pressed to her pink-chiffon-covered breast, and from between her fingers, blood slowly oozed out. Then she gave a doll-like blink of her eyes and fell sideways. On the floor, next to the table, lay her father.

After shooting his wife, he had put the gun to his ear, which was no longer there but instead, at the side of his head was a curious fringe-petaled, red-lipped hole that looked like a tropical flower. Charity didn't know what to do. A waiter kindly said, "Get outta here, kid," and she turned and walked out of the restaurant.

It was very cold. She had on her new spring coat, navy blue with a white lace-trimmed collar, and her new straw hat with red streamers down the back and an elastic under the chin. It was too cold for the thin coat but she'd wanted to wear it anyway. They had been having a special treat, she and her mother, lunch out, then a matinee; her father had not been invited. Where had he come from? She walked up the street. In her purse she had a dime in a small leather change purse that was made to unfold like the petals of a flower and that would later always remind her of that day. She knew her parents were dead and that her father had killed her mother and now she realized that she had been waiting for it to happen. They had fought a very great deal. Her father drank too much. He had a bad temper. Sometimes he would cry. "Going to pieces" was a phrase she remembered someone saying. She didn't know when the trouble had started. Lately, there was always shouting and slammed doors and her mother had a funny way of looking at her father—as if he were a bug or a snail. "Irritating," her mother would say. "Don't be irritating, Ralph." And would, as if he didn't exist, as if he were invisible, go on buffing her nails.

She walked down Fifth Avenue. She looked in the window of F. A. O. Schwarz and then decided to cross the street and walk toward Central Park. She knew that if she hadn't gone to the ladies' room he would have killed her too. It wasn't that he didn't love her, but she knew he would have killed her. It was only a mistake that she was still alive. A couple was crossing Fifth Avenue—a tall man and a woman in a black veiled hat, with silver fox furs wrapped around her neck. She walked along at the woman's side. "Hello there," the woman said, looking down at her and smiling. "You're not lost, are you?"

Charity shook her head. She wasn't lost. She knew exactly where she was. She kept on walking until she got to the entrance of the park—the one near the zoo—and then she went in, past the balloon seller, whose breath came in long white streams, who stamped his feet in their thick boots and rubbed his chafed purple hands and who had one white forlorn, wandering eye, and she passed the blue and yellow umbrella of the Sabrett's hot dog man and went on to the monkey house and went to see the polar bears and whenever she saw a couple she stood close to them, as if she were their child. She wondered what would happen now. Would she be sent away to school like Jane Eyre and wear brown uniforms and eat gruel? What was gruel? She would like to go away. She had often been lonely. While her parents fought, she sat in her room and silently played with her dollhouse or silently read.

In fact, her life changed hardly at all. Lucille, who had just been divorced, came and lived in the apartment. Irene and Maria stayed on. After school she sometimes played with Sally Summers. On Mondays she took piano lessons, on Thursdays she went to dancing school, and on Fridays they drove to the country. She read a lot and played the piano and painted. She wrote poetry:

> *Oh where has summer fled?*
> *The pansy's color is bled . . .*

"Bled?" Lucille said. "Well, not quite." She was amused by Charity. She told all her friends what an amusing child Charity was. She believed, however, in absolute honesty and felt duty-bound therefore to convey to Charity that she had no talent. *"Bled?"* Charity did, however, have one very important thing.

What is that? said Charity.

Oh, said Lucille, smiling, her pen held in midair—she was always writing something: checks, memos, orders. It was something special and there was quite a lot of it.

What? said Charity.

Money.

Said Lucille in her melodious voice.

Charity was disappointed. Is that all? she wanted to know.

Lucille said, It is quite a lot of money, my dear, and money is a grave responsibility.

Charity thought and said, "I'd rather have a talent. I'd rather paint or write."

Well, said Lucille, we have to make the most of what we have.

She smiled at Charity and went on writing. It was true that Lucille loved money: not in itself—she wasn't a miser—but she loved the game of making money. Nothing excited her so much as that delicious moment when, sitting downwind of a company long desired, she would delicately sniff the air and note decay or maybe just a tremor in the stock price and then, with a galvanized twitch of vulpine muscle, pounce: tender offer! Dagonet and Bayard coming in with a rush so sudden that before you knew it the shareholders had sold out lickety-split and for mere peanuts D & B had gobbled up yet another company to add to their already engorged roster: diversification! She cared nothing, of course, for the firms themselves (some of which had been patiently built up for generations); the firms were managed by blank-faced managers in New York and Houston who balanced businesses as if they were stacks of poker chips: Succeed—terrific. Fail—tax write-off. It was all dollars and cents, pluses and minuses, a game on paper, and Charity, when Lucille talked to her about business (which she didn't do very often), saw Lucille as a very large spider spinning a very large web all across the United States: oil in Texas, petroleum products in New Jersey, sheep in Idaho, publishing in New York—why, there was not one facet of life that Lucille's web did not touch and ensnare.

But, said Charity, I'd rather be a play writer or maybe write stories.

Someday, said Lucille, looking up, the lamp casting a slant of gold light across her face, you are going to be a very rich woman.

Aren't I now? asked Charity.

No, said Lucille, you are not. You will always have enough money to live on, but when you are forty years old you will be very rich.

But who has the money now? Charity asked.

It is there, Lucille said, in what is called a trust fund. That is a nice safe place where the money your mother left you is earning still more money.

Did my father leave me money too? Charity asked. Not really caring, just curious.

No, said Lucille coldly. She had never liked Charity's father.

But suppose, Charity asked, that I wanted the money earlier?

Then you couldn't have it, Lucille said. You see, your mother wisely decided that when you were older you'd be better able to handle your money.

Why do I have to wait that long? said Charity. Forty is really old.

Not at all, said Lucille, who was thirty-nine. You see, often when a girl has money—oh, how am I going to tell you this?—well, sometimes men want to marry her not for herself alone, but for her money.

Is that what happened to you? Charity asked boldly. She knew perfectly well that this was an impertinent question, but had learned when very young how to ask a difficult question and look extremely innocent.

No, Lucille said. Then after a pause asked, Who told you that?

Nobody, Charity lied. It was the cook, Irene, who had told her.

Well, said Lucille, not amused, to protect you from that kind of situation, your mother and I set up a trust. When you are forty you'll have a very nice amount of money and no doubt a very nice husband too. Do you see? Someone who will marry you for yourself alone. Do you see?

Charity nodded. She saw. She was one of those children who are not quick, not bright, but instead deeply, quietly intelligent. "Little Still Water," her father used to call her. In fact, although she hardly ever spoke, she had always seen too much. One thing she did not see was "herself alone." Who was that?

And because your mother knew that I loved you and that I understood about money, she made me the administrator of your trust.

Administrator? Charity asked.

I take care of your money, Lucille said.

Until I'm forty? Charity asked.

Yes, Lucille said. Do you understand now?

Charity understood. It wasn't very hard to understand. She understood that her gift, her talent, would not be for art, or music, or writing, it would be for money, and that until she was forty, Lucille would be in charge of this gift. But how very far away forty seemed. And what was it she should do meanwhile?

14

By the time Ben called Tonia again it was months later (Huh! she thought, what manners! He didn't even thank me for the nice time) and she had a new job and a new apartment, a two-room flat on West Ninetieth Street that she shared with a college classmate named Trixie—a name that suited her roommate in every respect, except that fortunately for Tonia, Trixie preferred going home with her various (and they were many) amants, leaving to Tonia the tall-ceilinged dingy flat where the view was of an air shaft but no one minded occasional bursts of song.

In September, when Ben called, Tonia was teaching music to seventh- and eighth-grade girls (wriggle, wriggle— giggle, giggle) in a private school part-time and he was in Baltimore, Maryland, where he had gone to do his internship. Would she care to join him? She scoffed: Are you serious? The vanity of man, his incredible belief that you will readily give up all you have—your body, your heart, your very soul—to join him in what he thinks should be the most important enterprise of your life: his career. Certainly she would not, Tonia replied. Why not? Ben asked politely, as though simply curious. Because, Tonia explained, her life was singing and one sang in New York City. He took this news quietly; in fact, he was very annoyed. In the next three years, while he finished his residency at Hopkins, Tonia thought about Ben a lot, heard about him from Charity and Tom, but saw him only occasionally. Sometimes (each time looking taller and thinner and paler) he came up to New York and they all had dinner together. When she did see him, in these widely spaced intervals, he seemed to Tonia to have developed all the identifying marks of his abstruse profession: he was brusque, he was cold, he was arrogant. He seemed only indifferently interested in Tonia and of course not at all in her alter ego, the Singer. (It was the Singer, after all, who Ben felt was his rival, and who had rejected him.)

"Still singing?" he would ask with wonderful irony, as if singing were a somehow inconvenient disease that might, if left untreated, go away. She only smiled quietly at him, but the truth was, although no one had ever attracted or interested her as much as Ben, she felt angry with him, too. Singing came out of her deepest self, and it was this self he so courteously ignored. He was, she knew, seeing a couple of ladies in Baltimore, and for her part, she went out with a number of men, some musicians, some not, some rich, some not, some of them interested in marriage—she was, currently, not. Her career was going well. She had acquired an agent who got her part-time jobs singing: as a waitress in an Italian restaurant in the Village called La Bohème; in the chorus of the Jones Beach summer theater; and she was the voice of Madame Nightingale, a very fat opera singer, in a Saturday morning TV cartoon for children. Sundays were busy. She sang nine o'clock mass at a Catholic church uptown, then took a cab (when she could afford it) to get downtown so that she could sing the eleven o'clock service at a Presbyterian church in the Village.

Now and then she saw Charity, who still puzzled and amused her. Charity had continued on at the *Beau,* perhaps because, thought Tonia, she liked the contact with people that it gave her and besides, Tom, who was a resident in medicine at Bellevue, was gone long hours. Often, with one of her various young men (she slept with two of them, or was it three?), Tonia had dinner at the Ferriers' and of these evenings she remembered only Tom sitting in his green leather chair in his white resident's uniform, his head leaning wearily on his hand, his feet stuck out, his black socks crumpled about his ankles, one funny thick pink rubber-soled shoe turned sideways, as if his ankle were broken. She felt that between his chair and the edge of the sofa where she sat ran a current of understanding, which he always buffered with his habitual kindness. And if Charity left the room for any reason he would instantly get up and wander about, looking at everything with curiosity, as if for the first time.

There was a lot to look at, too, because Charity was no housekeeper; the two rooms of their apartment were stacked with magazines, newspapers, dirty clothes, overflowing ashtrays. In the middle of a conversation a foot stuck under a chair would dislodge a plate full of crumbs, a cheese rind, a smeared knife, an apple core. It seemed to Tonia that marriage to Tom had not solved any of Charity's problems. She was as lost and puzzled as ever and now often seemed listless, like a person waiting . . . for what? A baby? Whereas old-time fairy tales always ended with the prince and princess happily hitched and left forever after up to them, the male novelists of the early sixties all recommended babies, as if a great plague of infertility were abroad in the land, or as if they couldn't quite figure out what their women wanted and a baby would give even the most undirected heroine's life a happy ending. Bull! Tonia thought, slamming a book shut. Baloney! She knew from her years in Queens, the only child of staid Protestants

squeezed between the Catholic Heideggers on the one side
(three years, three children) and the Catholic Hallorans on
the other (four years, five children), that babies cried all
night, that they were smelly and exhausting, and after they
weren't babies anymore, once they could toddle and walk,
they needed watching every second.

"Poor Margaret Halloran!" her mother used to say.
"Look at her! She's not even twenty-six and her hair is as
white as mine and she's had all her teeth out. I'd like to slip
her a little classified information." And poor Joe Halloran
too. B.A.C.—before air conditioning—Tonia had overheard
some of their choicest hot summer night arguments: "Christ,
Maggie, I'm workin' my goddam *butt* off—Saturdays, Sundays, overtime every night. I can't make any more goddam
money."

"Oh, please, Tonia," said her mother when she was
dating Danny Reilly (it was the only time her mother would
say anything about one of her boyfriends), "please be intelligent about this. I don't care who you marry, he can be purple
or Moslem for all I care, as long as he isn't a very strict
Catholic." Tonia was relieved that she wasn't a Catholic. She
was relieved that she was not only intelligent but a well-
informed graduate of an excellent women's college and that
—thank God!—she didn't need babies. Her life was all in
focus: she had her singing.

The spring when she was twenty-four and living in New
York was a beautiful spring, as tender and tense as loving
someone who is far away, someone you cannot go to bed
with. Outside the windows of the school's second-story music
room, leaf buds appeared, each one furled as tight as a baby's
fist, and a warm fresh breeze from the river kept wandering
in through the windows. She was singing well and felt that
her singing was growing with a richness that wasn't merely

technical—perhaps after all there was something to growing up and older. Why was it, then, that her career seemed at a standstill? There were auditions and more auditions. And no one called back. Is it me? she asked Blakova. Why? Am I not good enough? Blakova shrugged and shook her head and said: Wait.

One night in April, Charity called. They were leaving the city, going to some godforsaken place in West Virginia. Other friends of Tonia's married, got pregnant, left the city. Tonia began to smoke again. Blakova said, "My child, what is wrong?" She couldn't answer. What was wrong? Blakova left in June to go to Paris and died there in August. Tonia saw it in the *New York Times.* Her mother and Alfred Weingarten had gone to Europe. Trixie was in Easthampton. One morning she woke up and couldn't get out of bed. She couldn't eat. She was tired and agitated and depressed: what was the point? There seemed to be no point, as if all those airy connections that tie you to the world, of love and friendship and work, had been cut at one swift stroke. For a week she didn't leave the apartment, she didn't pull up the shades, she didn't answer the telephone. Mail piled up, unopened. Roaches scattered like buckshot when she turned on the kitchenette light. At night she heard something gnawing in the walls and began to imagine her heart's walls were full of rats. She lay on her bed and drank straight Scotch and slept—it was pointless to be awake—and then one night there was a pounding on her door. It wouldn't go away. She covered her ears with her hands but it wouldn't go away. In her filthy bathrobe she went to the door and asked, "Who is it?" Her voice came out a croak. She hadn't talked in a week.

"Tonia, open the door," said Ben.

She whispered, "Go away."

"Open this door, Tonia," Ben said, "or I'll get the super."

Slowly, with fingers that wouldn't bend, she undid the three bolts and opened the door.

"Tonia," Ben said, "what . . ." His blue eyes were bright. He was wearing something khaki-colored with shiny gold buttons. "Oh, Tonia," he said, "oh, baby, what's the matter? What's wrong? You haven't answered my letters. I've called and called." He lifted her up and carried her to a chair and sat holding and rocking her.

She said, "I'm a nothing. I'm just a nothing. I don't have anything."

He put his face against hers and when she dumbly looked at him she saw that his cheeks were wet with tears.

They were, those first months they were married, enormously happy. Tonia's Great-Aunt Millicent Mercer (married three months, widowed forty-two years: "men have no staying power") had, when Tonia was still very young, given her this advice: "Better-class people, decent married people, use twin beds. All Presbyterians use twin beds. If you can't find a Presbyterian to marry, look for an Episcopalian. They are often well-off enough to afford separate bedrooms." Ben, an Episcopalian, didn't even own a pair of pajamas. All night, every night, he slept curled up tightly against her, with his knees locked into the back of her knees, and one day he took all her long nightgowns out of the drawer and tossed them, one by one, out the window of their German apartment, right past the astonished blue gaze of Frau Drobach, their German landlady. They had gone to Europe with the U.S. Army and six months after they'd settled in, a much-forwarded letter arrived asking Tonia to join the Gandolph Opera Company in their next season. The company would be on tour for six months. The season was, of course, half over. She smiled and laid the letter aside.

She didn't really care. They were, those first months they were married, enormously happy.

15

Once upon a time, Krull, when I was ten [Charity wrote in "My Life: Version 2"], I stopped talking for three whole months. I thought my head had become a crystal globe and in it was a radiance that made me squint blind at the rest of the world, and a high-pitched ringing that necessarily took my attention. I had to walk very carefully, of course, on tiptoe so the globe wouldn't crack. I avoided men with tools —hammers, axes—anything that would threaten my globe, and at night when I went to bed I had to place my head just so on the pillow and sleep on my back without moving, like a little corpse in its little coffin. It was a terrible burden to carry the globe and yet I knew that was all there was left of me. After week one, Lucille sent me to see our minister, Reverend Redneck. He was tall, fat, jolly, with red cheeks and a large laugh. He bundled me upon his black-clothed knees and talked in a faraway voice—I caught only a word or two—about God, and Jesus, and Love, and Obedience, and Stubbornness; and as he talked, his knee kindly jiggled and his hand—as big as the bladder of an ox—kindly strolled up my shin and under the hem of my dress, while his stertorous voice rumbled on and his breath first walked, then trotted, then galloped, until at last I felt the poke of a forefinger under the lace-trimmed rim of my underpants. His face was

wide and purple and his breathing—I think here I squirmed
—turned into a gasp. He shuddered and gagged. *Uuuuhh.*
Shoved me, at last, off his lap. Took out a pocket handkerchief as big as a parachute and wiped his brow. Told me,
suddenly cold: Stay here. I heard him on the phone with
Aunt Lucille: I was naughty, corrupt, and not to be re-
deemed. So much for religion. The next step, I knew, was
medical science. All the while, of course, the globe kept
growing, the ringing had blocked my hearing, and the light
in my head made it hard to see what was going on.

I wish his name had been Dr. Schlagwahn or something
lip-smackingly Viennese, but it was, instead, J. Alan Mater-
bury. He was, with his tweeds, and pipe, and good British
manners, the most credulous fool I had ever encountered.
Right from the start I had his number—he would believe
anything. He was perplexed by my muteness and it was
decided that during our fifty-minute hours I would write it
all down—the truth, of course, the whole truth (but my truth
varied from mood to mood and day to day). My mother? I
invented for J. Alan Mat. an obliging classic, a mother so
grim and aloof that half an hour with her would have
wrecked the psyche of Pollyanna. I described her bedroom,
with its mirrors and silk scarfs and dead corsages and chiffon
robes and odor of spilled Vol de Nuit, and the little knife she
kept on her dressing table, and the way her pink face contorted when she said, lifting her eyes from her novel,
"Mummy loves you. Straighten those filthy socks." For him
—how I wanted to please—I presented this lady tied up with
enough pink ribbon to double-bind a Chinese gymnast, and
all the while J. Alan stoically puffed and occasionally *hmmm-*
ed or wrote something down in his red leather book—he had
two: red for girls, black for boys. Then on, of course, to my
father, a shattered hero (I said) who came home from World

War II with a sleeve pinned to his chest and death in his eyes and his head (a leftover field mine) exploded into psychosis, and the rest J. Alan knew from the pictures and text in the *Daily News* (also front page, but lower-left-hand corner, the *Times*). I described for him my chilly childhood alone in my room and my mother's hard white hairbrush and the country house in Peapack where she once locked me up in the stable and lessons and school and nothing I did was right and nobody loved me and so on and so forth, when in another truth, my mother remained in her sacredness at the base of my globe, a radiating presence who, deep summer nights in the country, fiddling insect music all around us, used to sit with me on the glider and tell me stories. And my father, poor man, loved us both to addiction and I don't know why, don't know why, don't know why.

One day, three weeks and two months after my speech had ceased and I knew Lucille was losing patience fast (next step, a nice quiet nuthouse with cozy jackets to wear and a little bit of shock—so what if you kind of lost your memory marbles), I had Marvin drive me to J. Alan's office, but after Marvin was gone I stepped out from behind the potted evergreen at the door and fled crosstownward. I took a Fifth Avenue bus and rode to the Village. From there I moved eastward and slightly south and appeared—it was Thursday, cook's day off—on Irene's Lower East Side tenement stoop.

"Lord love us!" she cried, leaning out of the second-story window for a look-see, her fat arms cradling her breasts. She came right down and led me up the dim stairs. How strange the place smelled—of onions and cabbage and mildew and sweat. She made me some lemonade—it was June—and turned on the electric fan and we sat together in an upholstered rocking chair whose stuffing leaked out at the very frayed corners, and despite the globe I took in everything: the dull linoleum shine of the pitted floor, the an-timacassars on the bowlegged sofa, the stockings drying on a line over the stove. She sat with me and we rocked and she said, "It won't ever be all this bad, love, not for long. It will go away someday and you can bear it." She held me and I remembered that for three whole months, since my parents had died, no one had touched me, no one at all—even a slap or a tug is better than nothing—and she said, "Ain't I yer friend, love, you can trust yer Irene. Why, you poor little thing, you're like a great doll, all china and wood and trained so purty, fancy manners and dancin' school and pi-ana. Poor little doll, when all you want is to be a little live girl." I wanted to ask her, and I did. It was hard to talk. I said (I thought she would know), "Tell me why I am alive." The globe trembled, the radiance flashed, and the ringing screamed. She said, taking my globe, my head, and pressing it to her breast—she was sweaty and smelled of onion—"Ah, someday, love, you'll know. You'll love someone and you'll know."

She held me a long time and then showed me her special things: a music box from Italy that played the "Barcarolle," and a little china ballet dancer in a gauze skirt. I went to sleep in the old stuffed rocker. When I woke up, the globe was much reduced, there was only a remnant left, a little residual footlight glow and the usual stage peopled with tiny actors and a faraway ringing like applause and my body, my feet, legs, arms, hips, and where he had put his finger were all my own again. Marvin came in the car to get me. I suppose this is why, Krull, whenever I feel a pressure in my head, I look for a warm male body. But not love, Krull. Never for love. I have to protect my core. My radiant core! For anything you love—lover, husband, children (no children, no children, no children, no children)—will be loved against you.

II

Andante

Giulietta:

"What I ask of you
is your reflection:
your dear face,
and your glance,
your whole being,
Give me your reflection!
And I'll lock it forever
in my heart."

The Tales of Hoffmann Act II

1

"Jesus Christ!"

"Huh?"

"Look at this. My God, don't you have any considera-
tion? Why is it you have to spend Sundays changing your
clothes and dropping them everywhere? I tell you what—
next weekend *you* can take Jamie and the baby and the dirty
laundry and go down to the basement and use the washer and
dryer, and then you can go to the dry cleaners and don't
forget to pick up your shirts at the Chinese laundry."

"What the hell are you so upset about?"

"Just see how you like mushing through the slush dragging a two-year-old by the hand and pushing a baby carriage
with the other and don't forget to pick up some wine on the
way to D'Agostino's."

"Okay, okay, I won't change my clothes ever again.
Listen. What is wrong with you?"

"Wrong with me? Why, nothing at all. It's just become
exactly what I expected. You go off to your lab every day,
including Saturday—weekends around here are fabulous fun

—and come back at ten at night. Your food's on the table, your clean clothes are in the drawer. My, what a perfect life. You really were smart, you know that? You got yourself some cheap domestic help."

He didn't say anything. He was tying his tie and his face was perfectly composed.

"Jesus, just *look* at this place. I hate this awful apartment. It's like being in prison, it *is* a prison, I've only been out of here five times in two weeks."

"Why don't you get a sitter?"

"Get a sitter! What's that, some kind of joke? They do like to be paid, remember? On what you give me, I can barely buy food. Besides, with Jamie sick so much of the time, nobody wants to sit for us. And what kind of doctor are you, you're so worried about all these diseases nobody's ever heard of. Look *around.* Your son's had an earache for two months."

"It's February, Tonia. Things are always rotten in February."

"Things are rotten period. How did it all get so out of whack? I used to be a nice person, now I'm a bitch. This awful life is turning me into a bitch, Ben. All you do . . ."

How trite this is, life's oldest story, the glorious first months of marriage turned into crumbs and egg stains and the smell of sour milk and unclean diapers. Tonia was not surprised—she was horrified. She had been put off her guard by extreme happiness. She hadn't expected marital happiness, she'd expected to fight a lot about things like toothpaste caps and where to go on Saturday night, but instead they had had a nice time talking to each other and making love, and furthermore, it had developed that she liked him. He wasn't so brusque after all, nor was he arrogant, and sometimes, on a Sunday morning, watching him move about in his rented

German garden among his plants, with that tender respect every good gardener has for living things, she'd felt a painful and warm feeling rise beneath her sternum, as if she had a suppressed cough—herself felt a tender respect for the living thing he was. He had told her, after they'd been married a month, that he'd read up on music while he lived in Baltimore. He now knew Bach, J. S. (1685–1750) from Beethoven, van (1770–1827), and Mahler (1860–1911) from Alban Berg (1885–1935). Or so he said. She did not notice any improvement in his aural perception but thought it touching that he'd tried. And it turned out, after all, that she was attracted to him and when she got pregnant, was she wildly unhappy, as any great diva should be? No: she was overjoyed, full of wonder and pride that they had done this miraculous thing together. Which turned out to be fantastically easy to do. No sooner was Jamie a sturdy one-year-old when it seemed somehow, and despite mechanical appurtenances of all kinds (she superstitiously refused to take the pill), that she was pregnant again. Ben was honorably discharged from the army, they came back to the States and rented a New York apartment in a very high rise. It also had very high rent, and because it faced a small courtyard, a dingy gray light fell through the windows, even on blue sunny days. She hated it, no doubt he did too, but he was in it a lot less (she thought) and she wished that instead of an idealistic young doctor on a skimpy fellowship, he were one of those doctors she was forever reading about in the newspapers—uncaring, callous, and rich.

The birth of Elizabeth brought out the maniac in her— she screamed all the time. The more she screamed, the more he withdrew, and she felt all that winter like a madwoman rattling the bars of her cage or like someone in a Kafka story who has been accused, tried, condemned (by whom? for what?), and imprisoned in a forgotten tower. She cried, she complained, she hated herself—this termagant she had become. Sometimes she felt (he was, of course, the only adult in her life) that he was her accuser, her condemner, and her rescuer at the same time, and when he came home at night with a little bunch of wilted carnations bought at the subway stop, she didn't want to cry, but who else did she have to complain to? She didn't have his resources. She didn't have a lab to go to. In fact, she had nowhere, mental or physical, to go.

"I hate it here, I hate it. Is this why you married me? I'm a prisoner—that's just what I am. Look! My fingernails are bloody from scratching at the walls."

He didn't smile. He had finished tying his tie, had given his shoes a swipe with a rag, had put on his vest, his suit coat, his overcoat, and now stood at the door, immaculately groomed and smelling of Alfred Dunhill cologne. He turned, looked at her in her spotty bathrobe, and then opened the door and stepped out. Without a word.

"You bastard! You miserable cold son-of-a-bitch!"

The door closed. She picked up the cereal bowl full of baby oatmeal and applesauce (mixed) and threw it, full force, at the quietly vibrating door. It shattered on the door and fell. Brown rivulets oozed down the wood she had painted herself just two months ago. Brown lumps and crockery (mixed) lay on the floor.

Jamie stood in the bedroom doorway looking at his mother with round blue eyes. His mother turned and looked coldly at him. He ran back into his room. If he had whined just once she would have hit him. Suddenly she could understand the deranged woman who beats her child. In his room she heard a *ping* of bedsprings, then all was still. She sat down panting and had a cigarette—she was now smoking a pack a day—and looked, depressed, at the door. Leave it. No. Clean it up. What the hell. Jesus. Soon she would be twenty-eight.

At twenty-eight, already a world-famous mezzo-soprano, Maria Malibran had fallen from a horse and died. At twenty-six, Nellie Melba had walked out on her husband and small children and gone to Paris to sing. This, then, was the fatal flaw in her artistic temperament—she could never leave her children. What sweet children they were, too, a lovely little girl and Jamie—who wouldn't love Jamie? Already he could sing—perfectly, without a quaver and exactly on key—all the songs from the Mother Goose record she had bought him. Something soft touched her knee. She looked down. Jamie was holding his blanket, a little pink flannel patch with the edging her mother had embroidered in blue blanket stitch, and while he held one comforting corner to his cheek, he silently offered her another. Her stone heart melted. Once as a joke, she had taken his blanket and put it to her face and imitating him had happily sucked her third and fourth fingers. She lifted him up—he was a warm heavy weight, a big sturdy blond boy—and cuddled him into her lap. He leaned his head against her breast and drew a shuddering breath and sighed, a satisfyingly deep sigh.

"Mummy's darling," she said, nuzzling him. Then hoping insidiously to poison his mind against his jailer father, whispered, "Bad old Daddy's gone."

He said reprovingly, lifting his head (he was always irritatingly fair), "*Mummy* frew dish." The telephone rang. "I get it! I get it!" he cried. She let him pick up the phone. She was too drained to care.

"Ha-woooah? . . . Jamie! . . . Yeth! . . . Noooo! . . . Bye!" *Clunk.* Mummy's lovely little boy had hung up. Her last avenue of escape cut off. Trapped. She began to feel resigned and the next step, she knew, was lethargy, then death. She saw herself on TV's six o'clock news, a blanketed lump on a stretcher, with two little stretchers beside her. Mother kills self and children. Horrible. Hideous. She understood it. The buzzer rang. Well. Let him get that too. She didn't care.

"Ha-woooah?" Jamie said, delighted, into the speaker. And then cheerfully, "Ho-kay!" and pressed the door release.

"Who is it?" she asked him dully, no longer even curious.

He looked at her brightly. "No no," he said, meaning, "I don't know."

Who could it be? She thought of burglars or bill collectors or maybe a ski-masked rapist. Well, she said to herself, anything would be better than this. Come on up! And awaited the arrival of their unexpected guest.

2

"You see, I don't think I ever loved Tom, I just liked him. And then this awful thing happened. I still haven't figured it out. I still like him in a way but I don't want to sleep with him, I don't know why. God, this place is a mess. You were always rather neat. And—well—you're a mess too."

"Thanks," said Tonia, and thought: Go on. Don't stop. Tell me what happened. What was the awful thing?

Charity had gained weight from the neck down and looked triangular. She had changed not so much in herself as in what she was doing with herself: the pale waif had turned into something more knowing. Her face was coated with orange make-up, her cheeks were daubed with a bronze-tone stain, her eyes completely encircled with black pencil, the lids dusted with green. She looked like a painting by a German expressionist, a demimonde effect that was more or less ineffectively contradicted by her clothing. She wore a gray wool dress with long full sleeves cut like a monk's robe, with a ropelike sash tied around what once was her waistline. Tonia said, "You're not pregnant, are you?"

Charity started, then sighed. "No. Can I have another cigarette? Funny. Did you always smoke this much? I don't seem to remember you smoking."

"There's not much else to do. Besides, I feel dead already, so I might as well smoke."

"And you have Ben," Charity said with a mocking grimace. She had on black stockings and little fur-lined boots.

"You had Tom," Tonia said.

They looked at each other and made similar faces.

"How is Ben?" Charity asked, head down, mouth turned up.

"I hardly know. He's so busy with his T-cells that he rarely has time for those of us here at home. He never says much unless he runs out of clean socks."

"Sounds divine," Charity said.

"Yeah," said Tonia.

Charity lit her cigarette and slowly waved out the match. She looked around. "You ought to move," she said.

"Thanks," Tonia said.

"No, I mean it. It's ghastly to live like this."

"I agree."

"Why don't you get out of the city? I've got a friend— a Chapin classmate of mine—who lives in New Jersey. I could call Laura and we could go out to Summerville and look around."

"Laura? You mean Laura Allwood? Isn't she the one you always said was strange?"

"Did I say that?"

"Yes."

"Oh."

"Besides, I don't want to leave New York. I just want the babies to be a little older. I want spring to come. I want to walk around outside. On those rare days when I'm allowed outside the apartment, I feel terrific, and I plan to start singing again."

"You're not singing now?"

"No, I'm screaming. Once Elizabeth is on a good schedule—this spring sometime—I'll start again."

"Wouldn't it be easier for you out of the city?"

"Oh, please don't say that. The city's my only hope. Besides, look at you—you grew up in the city."

"We always went to the country on weekends. Lucille and I."

"How is Lucille?"

"Fine. How's your mother?"

"Fine. Ben and I are like people who've been married too long. Mother and Alfred are like newlyweds. You really are getting divorced?"

"Mmm. You see, at first I just came up to visit, and then I found I didn't want to go back. I figured if I didn't want to go back enough to see Tom, there wasn't much there."

"What did you do down there, anyway?"

"Nothing. Smoked a lot. Drank some. Read a lot. Waited for Tom to come home. Now I am waiting to get divorced." She lifted her eyes to Tonia, looking puzzled. "I am like the traveler who never gets on the boat—I just stand there on the dock and one ship after another passes me by."

"But you're the one who's always moving around,"

Tonia said, frowning. "I'm the one on the damn crazy boat that moves all the time and doesn't go anywhere." She felt irritated: the selfishness of this girl. Charity had everything —money, time, freedom. She could go where she wanted, do what she wanted to do, whereas she, Tonia, was like the mythological god what's-his-name. Every morning she got up feeling reasonably healthy and sane, then within five minutes came the day's first whine or cry and she knew she was chained to the rock. All day long the children would nibble and peck at her. Life, hope, energy would be consumed long before nightfall, given back to her in sleep only to be consumed again, peck by peck, the next day. She glanced bitterly at Charity, whose face—orange-coated, circled eyes glassily green—was lifted in fear. Ah, God, Tonia thought wearily, she is crazier than ever. Why does she come to see me? What does she want? Doesn't she see I'm in a mess? I haven't the strength for one thing more. Then, without knowing why, she tentatively laid her hand—she had slim strong hands— over Charity's stubby nail-bitten hand, which still had the starfish shape of childhood. Charity started.

"Tell me what you've read," Tonia said. "I have one friend who reads, but she only reads things in Russian."

Charity blinked and said, turning her head away to the side, "Oh, I read everything. What am I reading?" she asked herself, and then said, in the same peculiar questioning way, "Virginia Woolf? *To the Lighthouse?*"

Tonia removed her hand and said sullenly, "I hate that book."

"But why?"

She shrugged. "Because. I'm afraid it will be me."

Charity looked down at the floor and Tonia knew she understood her. Now and then, when she could get out of herself long enough, Charity had strange flashes of insight.

If only, Tonia thought, she could stop thinking of herself every minute.

"Last night I couldn't sleep? And I read one of her essays. There was something, though, I didn't understand. Do you understand what this means? 'We are the words, we are the music, we are the thing itself.' "

In the right hemisphere of Tonia's brain a little light no bigger than the waggling blue-green tail of a summer-night firefly blinked and blinked again. "Oh," she said, "say it again. 'We are the words, we are—' "

Crash.

"Dammit," Tonia cried, and got up to see what Jamie was doing.

"Can't even have a fucking conversation," Charity said pleasantly in her low voice.

"Right!" Tonia yelled from the doorway of the babies' room. "I *can't*. I can't talk, I can't think, I can't hold on to an idea for more than three seconds. Jamie, what are you doing? Oh, look! Look what you've done."

"That's the way I felt in West Virginia, as if I'd been lobotomized. People down there are right friendly, and right stupid."

"Not stupid," said Tonia the egalitarian, "just uneducated. Look who's telling me to move." She came back and sat down on the floor too fast and as she did so she felt her full breasts rub sorely against the cotton cloth of the nursing bra and painfully tingle. Christ, she thought, I am just one huge brainless cow. "Moo," she said to Charity.

"What?" said Charity.

"Nothing," Tonia said. "Now tell me about Tom."

"Who? Oh, Tom. Tom is just very very busy. He loves his work, he loves helping people. The Albert Schweitzer of West Virginia. Pardon me if I sound cross. I *am* sorry. Maybe if we'd had children . . ." She shrugged.

"Not necessarily a help."

"No," said Charity, looking around. "What's that stuff on the door?"

"Oh, just—uh—stuff. Wouldn't he come back to New York if he knew you missed it so much?"

"I wouldn't ask him."

"But why not?"

"Because," Charity said, and carefully tipped her ashes into her cupped palm.

They were both sitting cross-legged on the floor. Tonia pushed yesterday's coffee cup toward her with a bare toe. "Use that. Because why?"

"Because I don't want to be married to him anymore. I have . . . no desire for him. I don't want to be married to someone I can't go to bed with."

Something inside Tonia delicately twanged. How acutely she remembered wanting to go to bed with Tom. Did she now? No, mostly she felt she didn't want to go to bed with anyone, ever again. She felt ugly and messy and old and as susceptible to sperm as other people are to pneumococcus or cold virus. Some awful vindictive thing inside her, some thing that hated the Singer and all the other better, finer Tonias, just reached down and snatched those poor wandering sperm right up.

Tonia said, "I wonder what kills it. Desire, I mean."

Charity lifted her green-lidded eyes. "I don't know. Maybe . . . I just don't know. It was probably all my fault. I can't get pregnant. I mean, what happened was, I did get pregnant, and then it turned out it was ectopic—you know? Stuck in the plumbing? And I got sick. Well. He was so busy"—sarcasm—"that he didn't seem to notice how sick I was and by the time I decided I was really sick and had gotten to a halfway decent hospital, I was pretty washed out. They took out everything. So. I ain't evah gonna be a mothah, brothah.

I'm sorry, I sound like I'm blaming Tom. I'm not. It's just that, really, I had nothing else to give him. Except money. And I didn't want him to get stuck with me out of pity. You know: 'Here's this poor woman I've stuck it to'—pardon the pun. I knew he felt like that. I could sense it. He felt he'd done something terrible to me. Poor Tom. He always has to assume he's responsible for everything. He was so sweet afterward, but not very interesting.''

She ducked her head and her mouth went sideways into a little hook of a smile. "But," she said, dropping her cigarette into the coffee cup, "now I feel marvelous. I've met the most wonderful man. He's so beautiful that the first time I saw him I wanted to say, 'Take off your clothes! This minute!' Pietro— You've got to meet him, his name is Peter Pontini, I call him Pietro—he's absolutely divine. He's a sculptor. We've got a place down off Hudson Street. I bought a huge Victorian bed and put it right in the middle of everything. It sits there all alone, kind of totally out of place and yet just right. Sometimes," she said dreamily, "we go to bed at two in the afternoon. One of the benefits, my dear, of not having all one's equipment is the marvelous sex life you can have. No pills, no foam, no diaphragm, no nothin'. Terrific. Just unbridled lust."

From the children's bedroom came now the soft sound of cooing and then a thud and then the sound of something rattling and the baby began to cry.

"Jamie!" said Tonia. "Jamie, come here, will you? What are you doing?"

The rattling went on. She stood up. "He thinks he's rocking her."

"I'll bet," said Charity.

Jamie appeared in the doorway. "Mummy?" he said. "Mummy? Baby cwying!"

She changed the baby and let Charity hold her while she sponged oatmeal off the door. She thought of Charity living in the Village and remembered suddenly their house on Charles Street, the house they had had when she was small. She had wanted, when they first came back to New York, to live downtown, but this building was closer to the medical center. Maybe they should move. Yes, maybe they should move downtown. She saw, glancing out of one of the gray windows, that it was snowing and thought of the Village and its little houses and saw snow falling on little stoops and ivied gardens and thought: Yes, that's what we'll do. We will move downtown. The thought was immensely cheering, so cheering she made bold to ask Charity if she could possibly stay with the kids for half an hour while she ran out for a quart of milk, and although Charity looked wary and resentful she agreed, and Tonia, out on the street for the first time in days, felt happy and healthy and young and full of hope. Yes. In the spring they would move.

3

In early May, with the leaves just unfurling on the city trees, the sanitation men went out on strike. The garbage piled up and all over New York, people who ordinarily went silently on with their flaccid daily routines talked to strangers in elevators and parks, talked to strangers while walking dogs and carting groceries and hauling laundry ("Isn't this *awful?*"), so that daily the atmosphere grew more lively and intense and ironical and cheerful.

Nothing, Tonia decided, was so good for the human

psyche as an occasional crisis. How boring good health was until you were sick and how boring routine was until you didn't have it, and how boring, she thought, as their little Saab dove into the Lincoln Tunnel, it would be to live in New Jersey. On the New Jersey Turnpike, she looked back and saw the city, already unreal as a stage set behind its filmy curtain of yellow smog. Ahead of them, on the blindingly white highway, there was nothing but blue sky, and to either side, against a backdrop of yellow chemical haze, were coughing chimneys, bubbling vats, and humming electrical power lines.

After the turnpike, three towns blended into each other with topographical economy, as look-alike as three molecules in a benzene ring. There was another highway, an Indigestion Alley that featured very fast foods (doughnuts, fried fish, eight kinds of name-brand hamburgers), and then they drove up a steep hill and under a railroad trestle and then made a left-hand turn. Quiet. Tall trees. Sun-sprinkled streets. A sense of idle floating, as in a gondola on the Grand Canal.

Summerville sat on the crest of its terminal moraine, blissfully soaking in sun and ignoring equally: the three major highways that girdled it round, making of it an island of green; the smoggy glitter of the Newark Basin (N.E.) and (S.E.) the already very distant, paper-thin cutout skyline of New York City. At a real estate establishment, housed in a "quaint" nineteenth-century farmhouse, they picked up Betty the Realtor, who on their tour of the town talked only to Ben, not to Tonia. Perhaps because Tonia looked angry. She smelled money and boredom. Inside the well-kept-up Tudors and colonials, she saw uniformed black girls dusting, and outside, under maples frilly with buds, on grass as smooth and richly green as a lawn in an English country house scene from Henry James, she saw black men in T-shirts, raking. It could have been La Grange, Georgia, in 1850. The real estate prices were astronomical. For a home no bigger than an upstate New York henhouse, one was asked to give up an arm and both legs. The shaded streets were awesomely quiet. Where were the children, the dogs, the household mistresses? On the town's highest hill, they passed a tall stone wall over which massed rhododendrons leaned, and behind the shrubs yet another screen of tall oak trees, and past this threefold screen caught a glimpse of a stone pile of a building, built in the gloomy late-nineteenth-century beer baron style, and on the steps of this building, in little groups, chatting, chatting, stood women—all blond —in sunglasses and short white dresses, carrying tennis racquets. Tonia shuddered. Ben looked pleased. It occurred to her suddenly that their dreams—his and hers—had revealed themselves and clashed. Did he see them actually living in this boring town where women shopped and played tennis and husbands dutifully brought home staggering sums of money? Her father's daughter, she saw them in the city, the only City, living in a spacious apartment so high up it seemed to stand in a wreath of clouds and where, looking down from their terrace at night, they would see the lights of New York sprinkled like icy tinkling stars at their feet.

"Now, this house," said Betty, slowly halting her im-maculate brand-new squeaky vinyl clean Chevrolet, "is what we call a low-maintenance property. It's compact, of course, but isn't it *darling?*" And four other houses, not one of which was much bigger than their two-bedroom New York apart-ment, then on to "I do have one more"—said thoughtfully, with a frown and tight lips. "It's been on the market a year and the old lady who had it"—harsh laugh—"never did a thing to it, so, as you can see"—nod in direction of turrets and towers and porches behind tangled mass of vines—"it's slightly in need of repair. But"—brightening smile—"it does have, well, a certain amount of charm."

They had a celebratory dinner on Route 22, in a place with red damask walls and fake plastic beams glued onto the ceiling. Ben smiled and twisted the stem of his martini glass. Tonia cried.

"Tonia, listen," said Ben, reaching for her hand, which she drew away and wrapped, as if it were wounded, in her coarse red dinner napkin. "If you don't like it, we'll cancel the deal."

She inelegantly wiped her nose on the back of her hand.

"It just doesn't make any sense, Tonia, living the way we have been. Look. This will be so much easier for you. Much easier. You won't have to drag the kids to the park, they'll play right outside. You'll be able to get sitters and there are lots of nursery schools and the public schools are good."

"How do you know?" she asked. "That's only what *she* said. And by the way, does she lower her commission if you sleep with her?"

He said with a martyred look, "I didn't ask."

"Well, you should have."

"She said it was a good neighborhood."

"I heard her say that. And I heard her say that the Merkles live right behind us, 'another *darling* young couple.' You know who they are? They're friends of Charity's. She's an utter stick and he married her for her money. Can't you see us hanging around the old neighborhood together? We can have great conversations about the Junior League or how to improve our needlepoint. We can all lean over the back fence and discuss stock prices or power mowers."

"You don't have to see the Merkles," Ben said. "You

can see anyone you want, though Charity did say she thought maybe we'd like them. She also said—"

"Who—Betty?"

"No, Charity."

"When did you do all this talking to Charity?"

"We—uh—had lunch together, last winter."

"Really. You never mentioned that to me. She never did, either."

"She came into the hospital one day for a checkup. While she was there she called me and we went out for a sandwich together. All right?"

"You never mentioned lunch. I hope you let her pay for it. It can come out of all that dough she's going to get when she's forty. Is she the one that put you up to this? God, I wish Charity would stop diddling with my life and do something with her own."

"She has; she's married Pietro. Tonia, Charity didn't have that much to do with our coming out here. We've been thinking of this for a long time."

"You have. I haven't."

"What is it exactly you have against moving out? I honestly want to know your practical reasons."

"One: I hate the atmosphere in the town. It's rich and clubby. Two: I like New York. It's full of people. Three: I am still, believe it or not, a singer and there are people in New York I can sing for. Did you notice how when Betty drove us downtown everyone looked alike?"

"I didn't notice that at all. I saw two Indian women in saris, a Chinese couple, and several blacks."

"Maids, gardeners, the owners of the local Chinese restaurant, and I don't have an idea who the Indians were; maybe they were just visiting. What am I going to do about my singing?"

"Can't you sing out here?"

"I hate you. I *hate* you. I don't even want to be married to you. Just when I'm ready to start auditioning again, and I've got a great voice coach, you pull this. Why, Ben, why? Sometimes I think it's sabotage."

"That is truly paranoid."

"I don't want to leave New York."

"Why didn't you say so before? Before we signed the contract and handed over the check?"

"I did say it; you didn't listen. You never listen."

"I've been listening to you complain about the city. You can't get out, you can't get sitters. I don't know, Tonia—why don't you figure out what you want? You keep putting me in this awful bind: I'm damned if I do something, damned if I don't. The truth is, I don't care where we live, so long as you're happy—happier than you've been."

"Maybe," she said, "I just needed to scream for a while. I resented the unfairness of it. We had those babies together —they're *ours.* Why do I keep having this feeling it's just me, all alone?"

"It's not you, all alone, but somebody's got to earn the dough, babe. Look. It is really your decision. Just ask yourself this, though. Were you happy in New York?"

"No," she said firmly.

"Then what's the problem?"

"I don't want to be happy, at least not in that way. All that playing tennis and stuff—that's happy, all right. And moronic. It would be terrible for my singing."

He wearily leaned his head on his hand. "What's good for your singing—unhappiness?"

"No. Something in between."

"How about safety?"

"What?"

"Remember the day that junkie followed you home from the park? And the time Tanya almost got raped in her hallway?"

Tonia sighed. The waitress—in a short black skirt that barely came to the top of her thighs—arrived with two wilted salads in two lopsided wooden bowls. Saucily, she nudged Ben's arm with her hip. He blinked, but did not alter his expression, which was alertly expectant. Clearly, obviously, he had won, but in fact he had won many hours before—this was just her final rally—when Tonia, looking out through the cracked panes of the dining room window (a window that hadn't been opened in fifty years, in a room that hadn't been painted in fifty years), saw Ben standing below in the over-grown garden. He was looking serenely about him at the honeysuckle vines that hung everywhere and he lifted his head and looked up at the apple trees, which were covered with a velvety black fuzz, and he smiled. Her gaze followed his and she saw him look toward the back of the garden, where in a magical swarm of color, an old barn stood completely draped in drooping lavender wisteria, and around it were blossoming peach trees, and quince, and crab apple and pear, and a large cherry tree that had lately shaken off the lacy shawl that lay in delicate shreds on the tall grass around it, and this flagrant parade, this seductively costumed chorus line, continued right on up the rise—drifts of pink and white dogwood, mounds of pearly spirea, azalea garishly colored coral, salmon, raspberry red. He wistfully smiled. And shook his head. She saw then (her heart turning for him) that they would move to Summerville, and she thought, standing at the window, Make Me Strong, for she saw Summerville as a kind of Venice, set on swimming pools instead of lagoons, where life had an Oriental air of jeweled insouciance, of gilded ease and of luxury, where no one was ever too young or too old; where want—of the body or mind—seemed not to exist; where all day long birds sang and goldfish swam and where beautiful women decorated their husbands' palazzos and where (except on her property—Tonia, the property owner!) nature was so cosseted, so pruned, so exquisitely ordered and arranged that the lawns and gardens of the town seemed to her less Nature than Art, almost Byzantine in their jeweled precision, like a series of painstakingly executed Fabergé pieces, and even the birds warbled so decorously she imagined them in their leafy bowers as a twittering mechanical aviary, made each one of beaten gold, with rubies for eyes. In the sweet air of the town, which smelled of lilac and lavender, *she* smelled myrrh, incense, corruption, and she felt—my singing! my singing!—she was moving to a seraglio. And a seraglio, as all sultans and sultanas know, can be very Expensive and Difficult to Maintain.

The Durhams (funny how in New York they were Ben and Tonia but in Summerville at once became a blandly faceless amalgam) bought a barbecue grill and a sandbox and a swing set and traded in the dented little Saab for a large sleek station wagon and set up a plastic wading pool under the dying apple trees. The Welcome Wagon lady came with gifts and discount coupons. Ben hacked at the vines. They rented a piano. Tonia sang and painted furniture. Tonia's mother and Alfred came to visit and brought two large house plants, a Schefflera and a Ficus Benjamina. Ben's mother came to visit, and while Tonia was out at the A & P, rearranged the living room furniture. Jamie found a friend named Jimmy, who lived down the street and spent most of his time at Jamie's house. Tonia did not meet his mother, Mrs. Kerston, for two whole months. She appeared one morning at seven thirty-five in a tennis dress and asked if

Tonia would please not give Jimmy tuna fish for lunch, he was allergic to it, and also should an emergency arise, she would unfortunately not be available as she was playing in a tennis tournament, could Tonia handle that? And, inquired Mrs. Kerston, did Tonia play? "No." She didn't? "No." Did her husband play? Tonia didn't know. "You don't know?" It had never come up. There was a pause and a strange light-eyed look came over Mrs. Kerston's face, as if she had eaten a bad clam. "What," she asked, "do you two talk about?"

Ben liked their new life. On Sundays he gardened and puttered and pruned. The yard was marvelous for the children (and Jimmy). Sometimes Tonia took her children for walks down the shady streets of the town. She never saw anyone. Where were the people? She missed New York. She was lonely. In New York at least there were stores to look at and policemen and dogs and delivery boys and drunks and junkies and old ladies. It occurred to her that she had merely exchanged one prison for another: she had been transferred from a high-risk facility to the state prison farm, where they send criminals who are not dangerous, only asocial or slightly retarded. One day, desperate for company, she walked around the block and knocked on Laura Merkle's front door. The door was opened by a black girl in a pink uniform.

"She nah home," said the girl, who had a cigarette in one hand and a can of Diet Pepsi in the other.

And there were days when everything seemed perfect, days when the children delighted her and the house behaved and in the tall cool spaces of the large, largely unfurnished living room, she would sit down at the piano and find herself, after an hour or so, singing. On rainy days when Jamie clumped wildly through the uncarpeted house, and the baby cried, and the piano seemed as out of tune as her voice, she could not sing. Ben would come home (he loved his work: he was an immunologist working on T-cell research), she would sit silently at their very late dinner table, and he would look at her carefully, then clear his throat and take his coffee cup and go into his study and she would listlessly put the plates in the dishwasher and go upstairs, to the sleeping, softly breathing children's bedroom. She would go to bed herself and fall fast asleep, but wake up completely at three or four. In an old-fashioned white nightgown, with a baby blanket draped like a shawl around her shoulders, she would move from room to room of the dark damp house. It seemed to her that something had gone slightly awry. What was it? She walked through all the rooms and then sat in her favorite room, a tiny under-the-eaves space at the back of the house, which they were using for storage. She would look out across the yards, through black-leafed trees, at the massed presence of the Merkle house. Once, sitting there, with her head against the window, she suddenly saw a light come on, just one small light at the back of the house, and this startled her, as if across the variegated blackness of two nighttime suburban gardens, or like an answering bleep from another galaxy, there was life she hadn't imagined in a place she hadn't counted on.

"Tonia?"

"What?"

"What's the matter?"

"Nothing."

Ben traced with his finger the reticulated curve of the fully nightgowned back she had turned to him. She moved her shoulders rapidly, as if shrugging off a fly.

"Stop it, Ben. I'm tired."

"You're always tired."

"I am tired."

"Maybe we should get you some help."

"Help? What kind of help? Psychiatric help?"

"Household help. It's a big house."

"Help. What's that, a joke? On what? We're back to Jell-O and macaroni as it is. Okay, let's get some help, but right now will you please leave me alone? I've got to go in and see Ecklund tomorrow and audition for that thing in the afternoon, and I'm beat."

"What thing?"

"The Diaper Soft commercial." Ironically: "I should be perfect."

"What about that church—uh—group, whatever it was."

"I told you about that; I got it but I'm not going to sing there until the fall." Ironically: "Unless I get pregnant again, of course."

"Are you still upset about that tour with—uh—"

"The Gandolph Opera. Yes, I'm upset. No, I'm not upset. I knew I couldn't do it. It's months on the road and the kids are too small to leave that long. I just auditioned for practice. Please move your hand, okay? I'm not in that kind of mood."

He sighed.

God.

Something had gone awry.

4

Ben's father, Dr. Latimer Durham, had been a well-known neurosurgeon. One day in the middle of a cervical disc operation—an operation that he had done a thousand times and could have done in the dark or in his sleep—he suddenly said to his assistant, "Take over, Harry. I've got to get out of here." He left the operating room, stripped off his gloves and mask and cap and gown, and left. He went down to the hot, dirty uptown New York street, found a cool dark bar, and got good and drunk. He never operated again. He liked drinking. In the short white horrifying spaces of time in which he was unhappily sober, he picked up odd medical jobs: doing insurance exams, beef inspector at a fat farm, medical director of a second-rate summer camp. He had spent, after college, eleven years preparing himself to become an excellent neurosurgeon, and after fifteen years of practicing excellent neurosurgery he was incalculably bored. He had put some money into stocks, the mortgage on the house was paid up. His wife, a small vivacious redhead who liked to shop, tried to get him to "get some help." He good-naturedly went through all the appropriate programs, but in truth he didn't particularly want to be cured of his addiction: What, then, would he do with his life?

And so the Durhams went on—with fewer amenities, it is true: they sold the house in Cushing, Maine, and the new thirty-foot sloop; and Mrs. Durham, Ben's mother, who had always had such good taste, opened up a pretty little store in the village and went to work as a decorator. They managed to eke out a fairly good show of a middle-class life. On a remnant trust fund the kids all went to boarding schools and college— except for Belinda, who wanted to be an actress—and their northern Westchester life went on, straitened but not impossible. No one would have guessed, looking at their large colonial-style house (clapboard with dark green shutters) surrounded by a charming dry stone wall and spattered with the shade of an old, gnarled apple orchard (each small May breeze bringing down a snowstorm of pink-veined petals), that inside the house everything had gone to hell. John, Ben's older brother, went off to boarding school and never came home again; he found himself roommates to visit and jobs in out-of-state places. Belinda, Ben's younger sister, locked herself into an ongoing daydream of Hollywood fame; and Muffy, two years younger than Ben, was a good girl who did everything she was told to do—that old familial have-a-heart trap of perfect adjustment that doesn't exactly kill, only sucks the guts, liver, lights, and heart out of an adolescent. And Ben. Who knew best how to shelter himself. Who would, while apparently physically remaining within the confines of the Durham family prison, effectively retreat to an interior island of stubborn resistance. On his island he had built himself a thatched shack and had stocked it with science books and some watercolor paints and a girl and a modest supply of Scotch, and riding at anchor out past the reef, a little sloop. In the outside world, he invented for himself a couple of interesting dangers: he was a good though slightly reckless skier, and when friends asked him for seashore weekends, a very competitive sailor. He found a pure, pristine line of work. He discovered while doing his internship that he had little interest in sewing up minor wounds or comforting women in labor. When confronted with very sick patients, what he felt was a keen rage. The wittiness of a mother nature who gives a three-year-old a brain tumor as big as an orange; the irony of a young athlete's dying in pieces from bone cancer; the injustice of an adolescent girl's deterioration from a rare disease that was now oddly everywhere on the increase—systemic lupus erythematosus. Most of all, he felt helplessness—not so much in dealing with the diseases as in dealing with the emotions of the patient: what to say, when he wanted to put his fist through a wall.

Sometime in the middle of his first year of residency at Hopkins he had the awful feeling that he'd made a bad mistake. He couldn't cope with the mother of the mangled six-year-old hit by a drunken driver and he could not handle the young black father in utter despair because his child needed a rare drug that cost twenty-three dollars a day, when his daily salary was twenty-five. He lost weight, could not sleep, started taking amphetamines. Off duty, he drank a lot. He lived for a while with a girl he didn't love (the girl he loved—Tonia—didn't seem interested). Then, luckily, he became fascinated by the problems of what was then a relatively new field of medicine—immunology. The fact that the body can, without known cause, produce cells that attack and destroy its own tissue, that whole groups of diseases—the autoimmune diseases—fall into this category, the fact that very little was known about the etiology or mechanism of these diseases, and the fact that he had very much liked his young patient who had had lupus, steered him in this direction. He acquired a reputation as a hard, solid, gifted researcher. He could have made quite a bit more money in another field of medicine. Years of medical training had left him much in debt and the thatched shack he had bought on Summerville Island turned out to be a large house colossally expensive to run. But he went on quietly working in his lab and working in his garden and paying the bills, and if Tonia, as always, seemed a little moody, he was sure she'd get over it. He loved the house and adored his children. Then why did he have this persistent feeling that something had gone awry? On Sunday nights when they sat together Tonia no longer looked at him and she was smoking more than ever and seemed always lost in an anger he couldn't explain. And at night when he reached for her she pulled away so that, when finally engaged in an act that should have brought them mutual tenderness and delight, he had the awkward feeling he was sleeping with a sullen whore.

In fact, the more Tonia withdrew from him, the more he felt compelled to love her, and he couldn't understand that, either. At any rate, she had stopped screaming, which was something he had never been able to deal with, maybe because it reminded him too much of his parents' home, where his mother—tired of working, tired of worrying—had screamed a lot and where survival in adolescence had been dependent on a certain degree of acutely gauged deafness. He did, however, have an increasing sense of frustration—he thought morosely that it was sexual—and he wasn't totally unaware that a young lab assistant they had just hired lowered her eyes carefully when he looked in her direction. She was young and pretty and he avoided her. He was working very hard. He wrote a paper on the recurrence of diseases in several generations of the same family, all of whom had a faulty beta cell mechanism—a genetic dent, so to speak, in the armor of their immunity. He was more and more often asked to speak at meetings and conferences; he was asked, eventually, to become chairman of his department, an honor, of course, but a job that involved a great deal of dreary administrative detail, which was nicely compensated for by a significant increase in salary. And that was certainly welcome.

Life in suburban Summerville had turned out to be confusingly expensive. After their first few months in Summerville, people began to ask them out, people who apparently had to be "asked back." At the drop of a postcard, a crowd of fifty would appear at his door—strangers whose names he could never quite remember—and these tanned ravaging Tartars, this Golden Horde, would consume whole hams, turkeys, filets of beef, to say nothing of several hundred dollars' worth of wine, beer, and Scotch. In order to appropriately serve all this provender, they bought a dining room table—not just any old table, but one that his mother (who now seemed in collusion with his wife) said was a "steal." ("A what?" he had said, incredulous, writing out the check.) Yes, a steal, an early-nineteenth-century English mahogany three-piece banquet table, which, it turned out, then had to be completely covered with a very long laboriously hand-made lace cloth. To "finish off" the dining room, Tonia ordered drapes. They bought a second car so that Ben could drive in to the city on Saturdays when he worked. Tonia bought a new sofa and carpeted the stairs. Their second winter in Summerville they were asked for a ski weekend in Vermont, and although Tonia didn't ski—she was pregnant again—Ben bought new skis for himself and for Jamie too. Tonia bought carpeting for the bedroom. They joined a country club and bought new tennis racquets and tennis clothes and kept the liquor cabinet stocked and suddenly life in the wicked city seemed puritanically pure and spartan and simple, and every month when the bills came in Ben would put on his bathrobe and retire to his den and emerge hours later, surly, red-faced, and slightly drunk. As for his raise, it assumed all three physical states: at first very solid, it gradually thinned to a liquid and then, mysteriously, turned into a vapor and disappeared. Still, he loved his house, his garden, his children, and most of all, his wife, and the first Christmas they lived in Summerville, although they couldn't afford it, he bought Tonia a diamond pin; the second Christmas he bought her a little fox jacket; the third Christmas he bought her a pair of emerald earrings for her newly pierced ears.

When what she wanted most was her own piano.

5

"Oh, it's lovely. Lovely!" her mother said. "Look how much you've done in just four years. When I first came out I thought: Why, those two are crazy, they'll never bring back that decayed old place."

"Actually, it's four years, four months, six days, and nineteen hours," said Tonia, and thought: Shall I tell her now? All afternoon long, since her coaching session with Ecklund, she'd been hoarding a piece of news that alternately warmed and chilled her, a cold little jewel—"Oh, gleam with desire!"—that flickered at her from the velvety dark of her future. No, not yet. She hadn't yet told Ben, who would say . . . what? She had become so successful at all her supplementary roles—decorator, housekeeper, hostess—gave such a good imitation of being the perfect suburban woman (wasn't that what he wanted?), that even her mother-in-law now approved of her. Did he, she wondered, remember at all that she was a singer? She'd figured out some time ago that she hadn't just married a man (her first naive idea), she had made a deal—apparently the usual deal: he did the money, she did the house and kids.

"And are you liking it better?"

"Pardon?"

"I said, are you liking it better? In Summerville?"

"Oh, I suppose. I like having the space. I still miss things about New York. It's hard to get into the city, and exhausting. For my hour with Ecklund I have to leave here at eight and I don't get back until noon. Then of course I have to pay someone to sit with Joey, and that's expensive. You didn't ask me."

"Ask you what?"

"How Trenton went."

Her mother put her hand to her face. "Oh, no. Tonia! How could I forget? I'm so sorry. How did it go?"

"I think beautifully. We were so pleased. We're going to do five other concerts in New Jersey and there's a possibility of two coming up in Pennsylvania. The fantastic thing is to have found Sonia right out here. Her piano may be ten feet away, but I swear that we can sense each other's vibes across that airspace. The problem is, her mother isn't well and so there's that as well as her kids she's got to take care of. And the other thing is, we can't drive too far. If we drive somewhere and come right back we're both shot, but if we stay somewhere overnight it's expensive. And Ben is—well, you know Ben. I can do anything I want as long as I don't ask him to veer one inch from his established course."

"He doesn't have the time," her mother said. She always defended Ben.

"And I don't earn much money," said Tonia, "so it's my hobby. Oh, God, I wish you could have heard the *'Chanson d'Amour.'* It was just . . ." She lifted her hand in the air, and pinched her thumb and forefinger together: perfection.

Her mother smiled. "I've always especially loved that song. Don't worry about the money. You'll earn more as you go on. If you could be a bit more mobile . . ."

"Yes."

"But that will come and at least you're really working again."

"Yes."

"But . . ."

"What?"

"You don't seem happy. You seem so nervous. And how can you smoke? You know it's terrible for you."

Tonia shrugged. Her mother looked away and then said, smiling a little, "But Ben seems happy. You know, I didn't think when you married him . . ."

"What?"

"Oh, I wondered, of course. Isn't that what mothers are for? Wondering? But he's such a nice man, Tonia."

"Mmm."

"He's such a hard worker and he loves you so much."

"Mother. What's this got to do with anything?"

"I just thought I'd say that because . . ." Her mother stopped and then shook her head. "I don't know. Oh, never mind. Funny. When you were in high school I used to think: Well, Tonia's got talent, but . . ." She looked at her daughter tentatively. Tonia, who knew some devastatingly honest piece of information was coming, sat up straighter, her hands gripping the wrought-iron arms of the garden chair like a patient waiting for the dentist's drill. Her mother sat with her hands in her lap. Her hands were swollen and arthritic. "But," her mother said, "you had such a talent for, oh, life, for living. You were always in love with some awful boy, always on the go—picnics, parties, dances. I kept thinking: Well now, let's just see what she chooses to do."

"It never seemed to me that clear a choice."

"I think it is, for some people."

"I suppose I thought I could do it all."

"You never wanted to give anything up."

"That wasn't it. I just didn't think I could get through alone—with just my singing. It always seemed to me part of a whole—my singing, my personal life. Never mind. I can't really explain it."

One of her mother's hands lightly smoothed the other, then she sighed and her hands lay still. "Yes. I know. I *do* know. The truth is, I never could have done it. I knew I couldn't."

"Is that why you gave up singing?"

"No."

"I don't mean when Daddy died; I mean before that. When I was very small I remember you sang at churches and you did operettas and there was that funny little man, your voice coach—what was his name? Swoboda!—and then it all stopped."

It was almost eight and Ben hadn't yet come home. The

children were all tucked in upstairs, Joey in his crib and Elizabeth in her bed, drowsily murmuring to herself, and Jamie in his room, playing before he went to sleep. From time to time, glancing up, Tonia could see his blond head at the window. It would duck down, then reappear, and he would grin at her and dart off. At the side of the yard, above the black branches of the apple trees, the sky had turned pink and fiery-edged clouds drifted by, all very baroque, straddled by fat-limbed putti blowing toy trumpets as they rode off to grace another ceiling. The flower bed Ben had made—marigolds, miniature dahlias, rust-colored chrysanthemums—curved like a flaming band around the grassy terrace. He had a marvelous eye for color and changed the border with every season: spring bulbs turned into delphiniums, poppies, phlox; in mid-July there were firecracker zinnias and early fall brought this red-orange glow, as if a last blaze of color could lend them enough warmth to get through another bleak winter. Even the apple trees had revived under his care and would live to give them shade many summers more. The trees were a blessing in the hot New Jersey summer. Oh, what was that line? Tanya, a Russian friend she had had in New York, used to quote from an old Russian poem as they sat in the park together, under the shade of a much-abused city tree, watching their children. "Blissful shade, shade of Elysium." It was a poem Tonia had particularly liked. She couldn't recall the rhythm of the poem but remembered its light and shade, gloom and brightness, sleep and awakening, life and death. In the poem, the idly plashing fountain, the quiet cypresses, the sleeping deep-shaded Italian villa, are awakened by footsteps on the villa's threshold: the adulterous couple. Restless life? Is that what the poet called it? Life with its evil passion. At the top of the apple tree a bird had begun to sing.

Tonia's mother (she had on white today, a color that did not suit her) had been looking off toward the back of the yard where a tall redwood fence, a hemlock hedge, and a row of shrubs, forsythia fountains, separated the Durhams from their neighbors. She sighed and looked down at her hands and said, "You see, I lost my confidence." Tonia waited for her to go on, then gently prompted, "Just like that? All of a sudden?"

"Oh," her mother said, "it was more gradual than that. Your father . . ." She hesitated and looked down at her lap, then in a fumbling gesture touched her glasses. "I thought he didn't love me. I felt . . . unloved. I felt . . . worthless. I couldn't sing. There didn't seem to be any point."

Tonia was silent. How odd. She couldn't remember a time in her childhood when her parents hadn't seemed in love. At night her father would burst through the door, shouting: "Mary? Mary! Where are you?" Perhaps her mother had imagined it.

Her mother said, "He was having an affair with another woman. When I found out—this seems so silly now; I suppose nowadays they would say I was clinically depressed—I couldn't sing. I didn't *want* to sing. My will to sing simply died. I guess it wasn't strong enough in the first place."

Tonia cleared her throat. "I'm sorry," she said. And didn't think she believed her.

"Oh," her mother said, "it's all so long ago. And now I have Alfred and we've been very happy. Very happy. But I must say"—she raised her eyes and smiled; her tone was brisker, cheerful—"I'm glad he's gone off to see David and Ellen alone, so that I can have some time with my grandchildren. I wonder if they'll like the farm."

"I hated it," said Tonia.

"I remember," her mother said. "You were always such

a city girl. It's sad, don't you think so? No more Van Klocks in Veddersburg. I hope they'll like California, but I tell you, I wouldn't live there for anything. You can't imagine how brown California is. I don't know why they want to sell the farm."

"Because they can't make a living at it."

"Still. Van Klocks have farmed that same piece of land for over two hundred years. At least your children will see it before it's gone. It's odd, but as I get older I find myself dreaming at night about my childhood. Often I have the very same dream: I'm a little girl and I'm standing in the attic window looking down over the town. The hills are so serene and the river goes on and on. The hills seem to represent something very permanent to me—though God knows what's permanent nowadays—and the river is like . . . oh, time, I suppose, just flowing along, always changing, always the same. I so loved that view."

"But you left it."

"Of course. I wanted to leave. I wanted your father and a different sort of life."

Oh, you, Tonia thought. I have known you all my life and here I am still finding out things about you. So you had ambitions too. You always kept them so well hidden, under your coolness. And who was the woman? No, never mind. If you wanted me to know, you would have told me. I'm not at all sure I believe it; on the other hand, why not? Is it possible to love two people at once? Sometimes I want to ask you . . . never mind, never mind. "I do think you should leave Joey here, Mother. He'll be too much for you."

"Nonsense," her mother said quickly, and dropped her eyes. "He'll be perfectly fine. I will guard him with my life. Henry's girls will help. Don't you worry about a thing. You just have a marvelous weekend alone with Ben."

So that's it, Tonia thought. Ha. Collusion. *He* put her up to this. Another one of those wonderful weekends alone and no doubt I will end up pregnant. No, I won't. Not ever again. Not ever.

The year that Tonia was pregnant with Joey, Jamie came home from nursery school his very first week with a virus that attacked the throat, ears, chest, and eyes. Except for Ben, they were all so sick that she simply put blankets down on the living room floor and she, Jamie, and Elizabeth lay on them in a daze of fever, graham cracker crumbs, orange juice, poppit beads, Play-Doh, and TV commercials. When she tried to sing, her voice sounded (in her plugged-up ears) very faint, fuzzy, and far away, as if it were Schumann-Heink singing Fidès on a 1912 Red Label Victrola record. All that year the virus (a cunning little green fellow with pop eyes on striped eye stalks) lived with them, reappearing whenever she gave a local concert or attacking the children whenever she planned a coaching session in town. As she grew larger and more cumbersome, as if in some crazy-house mirror Ben seemed to mock her by growing thinner and more graceful. In the mirror of their marriage she thought she saw herself in her husband's eyes as a piteous object, a large, clumsy, very pregnant dependent, drowning in domesticity. So it was for this—this brainless, songless existence—that she had passed so many appropriate examinations, attached herself to so many scholarships and honor rolls and prizes for music. It amused her now that when a senior in high school, she had gotten a prize for biology. Biology had outwitted her. Ben remained obstinately cheerful. His career was zooming along and he was—all alone, of course—going to Dallas and San Francisco and Chicago and New Orleans and Saint Louis. She knew that Ben was probably—all those times away from her

—resolutely faithful, when what she sometimes hoped was that he would pick up a girl, get a disease, and the whole apparatus would drop right off. And then she remembered how, finally, with a starchy rustle, the nurse had come in, and bending over her with the smile of a moon giving the earth light, placed the baby in her arms. It had been wrapped up and pinned into a blanket and moved only a little. She had dreaded this moment. The pregnancy had been so full of sickness and anger that she feared she would not love it, but when she looked down, the baby was staring up in blue-eyed blindness and already there was on its little face a tiny frown, a look of intelligent anxiety, and already—how absurdly early life stamps its design on us—he had the look of a real person. He had thin reddish-brown hair and (she was certain of this) her father's eyebrows. Although there was only the merest feathery hint of reddish brown, the shape, the width of the brows, seemed as well known to Tonia as her own. Looking down at the baby, who seemed still to be frowning, she smiled and stroked with her fingers those funny little brow feathers and felt such a deep attachment to the little thing—who already seemed to know that life was difficult and sad—that she wanted to comfort him and make him happy. So in a little whisper she sang to him and he lay very still and seemed to look up with strict attention as if (of course, it was impossible) he heard and enjoyed the song. She felt deeply happy. She could not imagine not loving this child and because Ben was not home—he was in Chicago— she dialed Charity's number and asked her (it came to her suddenly, very spontaneously, as she heard Charity's New York telephone ringing) to be the baby's godmother. "Look at it this way, Charity," she said. "Every baby needs a Mother Greenbucks."

Charity was amused and not hurt and told Tonia that she

would accept "with very great pleasure." It was only later
that Tonia thought she might have been tactless.

"Shouldn't we go in?" her mother said. "It's almost
dark. Does Ben always get home this late?"

"Yes," Tonia said, "he does."

"That poor man," her mother said, getting up slowly,
stiffly. "He works so hard."

6

After the Durhams moved to Summerville, Charity and
Tonia talked to each other only occasionally on the telephone, and when they did there was, on both sides, an acer-
bity that they did not care to acknowledge. Especially after
Joey was born—so unplanned, unwanted, and very much
loved—Tonia thought of Charity's life in New York with
envy: to have an income, even a small income of one's own,
and all that unencumbered time and freedom. Her freedom,
how Tonia envied her that. Charity thought of Tonia's life
—a loving husband, a talent, children—with envy too.
"Blessed be the ties that bind/Our hearts in human love."
She, Charity, had no ties. True, she had a husband, but it
turned out that Pietro wasn't exactly loving: he was handier
with a checkbook—her checkbook—than he was with sentiment or tenderness, and Charity found after not so many
months of her new marriage that she was back to her bad old
habits: reading all night, sleeping all morning, walking the
streets of the city in the afternoon, and having more fre-
quently now than ever those attacks of panic in which her

whole world tilted upward and she seemed to be endlessly falling into a white, downspinning vortex. She saw her psychiatrist, who put her on Stelazine and said at the end of her session, "You've got to learn to put yourself first." First before whom, she wondered.

She joined a consciousness-raising group. At the second meeting, one of the members, a tall, thin girl in boots, wool plaid shirt, corduroy pants, and single long brown braid, did an analysis of famous prisoners: Zenda, Monte Cristo, Mary Queen of Scots, and Rapunzel. Wherein it was seen that fairy tales, fiction, and mythology convey to us that men must rescue themselves while women are rescued by men. And, the girl added, tossing her long braid, "having long hair helps, ladies!" General laughter. Charity put her hand up and felt her hair. She had just cut it with a pair of large, clumsy kitchen shears and it stuck up all over her head in red-gold whirls and commas. Sitting there, over wine and cheese and cigarette smoke in the West-Beth apartment as big as an airplane hangar, with its white-painted pipes and Moroccan cushions and brass tables from India, Charity felt a familiar panic. Cold and lonely, walled up within the stone tower of her self with (to make it worse) one narrow but insistently beckoning window, she saw that in the landscape below, all the peasant children, their Brueghel faces cruel and absorbed, had found games to play, had hitched themselves onto something: religion, art, drugs, drink, singing, dance, communism, Birchism, feminism, some ism or other, some structure or antistructure, some way of getting on with it from day to day that she couldn't seem to acquire. Why was it, why was it, that whatever she took up didn't last? She had taken them all up, all the modern cures for lost souls—yoga, meditation, scream therapy—and it was always as if she were a stunned spectator at her own life, thinking ultimately: This is pretty dumb. Or: I can't seem to care.

It was a few days past Christmas, and in one corner of the apartment a tall dead fir tree had indifferently begun to shed needles and silver glass balls. Marge, a girl in a long peasant skirt, had taken off her sneakers, and walked around the apartment barefoot, prowling as restlessly as a caged animal. (Another one, thought Charity; she's crazy like me.)

"Right on! Right on!" Marge would shout every now and then, interrupting the orderly flow of intimate confession, another embarrasment to the group, which had long tried to get rid of her, and now Marge walked right over a broken glass ball, leaving tiny bloblets of blood on the polished wood floor. It seemed to Charity in that moment that her own head was as large and fragile as a glass ornament and she knew that this was a dangerous notion—she had had it before—and in order to test the reality of her physical being, she walked to the tree and gathered up some glass shards and took them into the bathroom. Dear God! She looked at herself in the mirror—tufts of reddish hair, small, pale, anxious face—and taking a glass splinter lightly in hand, drew a thin red line, as thin and red as an accountant's pen, across her forehead and down her cheeks and across her small chin. She was put in the hospital, the bits of glass removed, the cuts weren't deep, plastic surgery not needed, she was put back on Stelazine, just for a while. "Take care of yourself, Charity," her psychiatrist said. "Be good to yourself, Charity."

Thus the first time Tonia saw Phil Merkle was not in Summerville at all but in the doorway of Charity's hospital room, the expensive New York hospital room of the expensive New York hospital in which Charity had been, as she put it, incarcerated. Tonia was just going in the door; he stood half-turned near the doorway, saying something humorous to Charity, a tall lean man in a rumpled dark suit. He abruptly turned his head as she came in and gave her, to her surprise, a look that was, under prominent curly brown brows, keen and direct, so direct that she felt astonishment and guilty pleasure. Then he nodded and smiled and walked past her. She turned her head to look after him and Charity said dryly from the bed, in a voice kept smaller than ever from fear of moving her face and cracking her scabs, "Everyone loves Phil Merkle." Tonia had noticed his eyes—they were brown —and that he was pale and had a longish face and his clothes looked shabby. "Is that who he was?" she said to Charity with a laugh. "Do you know, we still haven't met them?" then took in Charity, a frightful mask, an apparition with a stiff little white face streaked with long, dark, jewel-scabbed scars, sitting up looking grim and exhausted. For a while, before she moved on to someone else (she was always moving on to someone else) Phil was Charity's psychiatrist.

When Charity went home she found that during her absence the girl downstairs had moved in with Pietro. Charity stood in the middle of their one-room apartment and in a taut calm voice told Gloria to kindly leave. Which good-natured Gloria did. When Pietro came in, smiling and shrugging and looking quickly at her from under his black brows (he had passed Gloria on the stairs), she didn't say anything. He made her a cup of herb tea and brought her a shawl and silently showed her a small sculpture he was working on, for her. She nodded. Okay. All right. It's all right. Still. She was angry. After all, she supported him and what she expected was minimal loyalty. It occurred to her that although she'd wanted to sleep with him she had never really loved him and so she didn't care who the hell he screwed. He was only someone to live with. That was, she supposed, had always been, her insulation and her revenge. That she just didn't care. Didn't give a goddam. Had no real feelings about it. What had anybody ever wanted from her anyway but money?

7

"Now tell me," Laura Merkle had said, her green eyes widening, "how is it you know Charity Mullet? This is so embarrassing. Charity did call several times to tell me about you, and here you live right behind us and you've lived in Summerville how long? Gracious! Of course, it's true that we were in England for six months and since we've been back it's been just—well—hectic, and whenever I thought of stopping by, something absolutely earth-shattering would come up. I spend a lot of time, you see, in volunteer work. It's such a busy time of life and this is such a busy town—don't you think?"

Tonia wanly smiled. She had lived in Summerville long enough to know about volunteers: the hospital was jammed with volunteers and the public schools were jammed with volunteers and every community service agency in the town had enough volunteers to staff the hospitals of Newark ten times over—except that the ladies of Summerville never went to Newark, of course; it was fifteen dangerous miles away. She had lived in Summerville long enough to know that Laura Merkle was on at least four "boards," that in the abstract her works of unrelenting charity were many, but after ten minutes with Laura, Tonia knew that if you had the bad taste to fall down sick in the Merkle doorway, Laura

158

would, with a little twitter and a ladylike gasp, step right over your twitching body.

"And of course," Laura said, "I thought I'd probably meet you somewhere. At a League meeting, or somewhere. You don't belong to the Junior League?"

"No."

"But you must join. Let me put you up. It's a wonderful way to meet people. And the League does such good."

Poor Tonia. Torn as always between ordinary civility and the other alternatives—a crushing desire to pinch the bitch or possibly vomit—she said demurely, "I really can't. I have other things I do."

"Oh!" said Laura. "Of course. I'm so sorry. Charity did tell me you were a singer."

"Am," said Tonia, feeling her jaw unattractively harden, "a singer."

And Laura blinked and helplessly kneaded her long beautiful jade-ringed hands and Tonia saw that she was wretched and decided to let her off the hook: she smiled and asked if Laura had children, for she saw that poor Laura, behind her highly veneered facade and her protective snobberies, was uneasy inside and that her facade was perhaps the only thing that kept her structure from totally crumbling.

It was June and the party had begun with drinks on the Andersens' old-fashioned screened porch, which was furnished with creaking wicker and gingham cushions and begonias in hanging baskets. The Durhams did not know the Andersens well. Ben looked tired and even before her second drink Tonia felt bored. At nine o'clock the doorbell had rung, and after a few moments Sunny Andersen came back followed by Laura Merkle, who was two hours late. There was a little pause, as if everyone had momentarily stopped breathing, and then the men stood up, all at once, all together, all of them desperately looking into the corners of the room, which is where well-brought-up American men look when they see a beautiful woman. Laura nodded nervously to everyone and sat down next to Tonia, on the cushioned wicker love seat. Her black hair was pulled back from a perfect *Vogue* face. She was wearing a white jump suit with a halter top. Her tanned shoulders gleamed as if she'd oiled them.

"Laura, you look wonderful," said Stu Andersen, a tall, shambling man, easygoing and kind. "Where's Phil tonight? Working?"

"Oh!" said Laura, her eyes widening. "He's in Buffalo! At a meeting!"

She tended to exclaim rather than speak.

"I guess you know the Durhams."

"Oh!" said Laura, abruptly swiveling. "Yes! How are you!" Her lips trembled ever so slightly. "I do know who you are, you're a friend of Charity Mullet's"—and she pronounced Charity's infamous name in a raised ringing tone so that the rest of the room could hear and be properly awed. "Now tell me," Laura said, "how is it you know Charity?"

And the next week they were asked to dinner at the Merkles'.

"The who?" said Ben.

"Merkle," said Tonia impatiently. "Merkle, Merkle. For heaven's sake, they live right behind us. Laura Merkle. You remember, the stunning brunette."

"Oh! Her!"

"Yeah. Right. Do stop leering."

"I wasn't. As a matter of fact, she doesn't do a thing for me."

"I bet."

"No, truthfully. She's too—uh—perfect-looking."

"There's no disorder in her dress."

"Something like that."

"Funny. I wonder what he's really like."

"Really like? Have you met him?"

"No," said Tonia, and went on scrubbing at a black-crusted stew pot and didn't really know why—laziness? indifference?—she'd elided the scene in Charity's hospital room.

Phil Merkle answered the door on Saturday night and again he gave her a direct look and she looked, confused, at the floor and did not offer her hand. They went into the living room. It seemed to Tonia a cold room, "perfectly" decorated with the usual eighteenth-century English antiques or Williamsburg reproductions that most of Summerville thought was good taste, and it was very clean and very drab with a hint of antiseptic room deodorizer in the air and gray drapes and gray walls and a bunch of pale lifeless silk flowers in a bowl on the mantel and nowhere, that Tonia could see, any color: uniform drab neutrality. He got the drinks and brought out a tray of cheese and crackers and Laura did not appear. The doorbell rang. Another couple arrived. More drinks. Finally, after they had been there a good forty-five minutes, Laura came into the room looking terrified but perfect, in a long pale green dress and long jade earrings.

She said, "Oh! Hello!" as if surprised to see them, then sat down next to Mary Herder and began a very animated conversation as if her tightly wound spring had just been released with the tug of a little cord. Phil Merkle sat down on the puffy gray silk sofa next to Tonia in a sudden slump. He looked straight ahead of him and smiled into the gray space of the room as if waiting for her to begin. She said, keeping her fingers crossed, "What a pretty house."

He looked around. "Is it?" he said. "Oh. Thanks. So you're Laura's new friend?"

This bewildered her and she must have shown it, for he said sarcastically, "She said she met you at the Andersens'."

"Oh, yes. You were . . ."

"In Rochester."

"Oh."

"They're interesting people."

"Who?"

"The Andersens."

"They are?"

"Aren't they?"

"You mean rich?"

He looked startled. "Well, yes, I suppose they are rich, or at least pretty well off."

"They why not say rich instead of interesting?"

He said agreeably, "Yes, why not? Though in a way, money makes people more interesting. Don't you think?"

"No."

"No?"

"Certainly not. Sometimes it makes them dull."

"People who don't have money can be dull too. Why are we talking about money?"

"Why not? Everyone in Summerville spends so much time thinking about it."

He smiled deeply and long lines appeared in his face, making it suddenly charming, so that she saw a whole different facet of him, a facet she did not trust. He said, "I think Summerville is a lovely town."

"It is, it's a lovely town, with lovely trees and lovely houses and lovely gardens and lovely dogs and lovely people. The stores are lovely, the clubs are lovely. Why, I had no idea before coming here that life could be so lovely."

"For a lovely woman you sound awfully spoiled. In a

lovely way, of course. You see, my dear, we haven't all had your advantages. I grew up in South Jersey in a town where they can tomatoes. Tomatoes, cranberries, asparagus. If you were lucky, you got a job in the canning factory.''

"And if you weren't lucky?''

"You got to pick tomatoes, cranberries, asparagus.''

"So you were more than lucky.''

"I worked at my luck. Still do. At night, driving home from New York, I feel as if I'm slipping through a curtain into another world, and frankly, I want to keep it that way: two worlds. Summerville's like an oasis to me. I have to deal with that other world all day long.''

"But you see, I need that other world. I suppose I'm afraid of losing touch with it.''

"Laura says you're a singer.''

"*Was* a singer.''

"You're not singing now?''

"No. But I expect to get back to it soon. I always expect to get back to it soon.''

"I've known some singers. It's a tough life. Physically tough too.''

"I think that's what I like best about singing—it's so totally, oh, mental and physical and emotional all at once. It's like,'' she blurted, "skiing,'' then blushed and looking down at her lap noticed that she'd torn her cocktail napkin into fragments, and he reached over, plucked the cottony wad out of her fingers, and deposited it in a large molten-glass ashtray.

He said, "Let me get you another one; you can tear that up too. You know, once, a hundred years ago, I thought I was going to be a composer. As a matter of fact, I majored in music at college. Why are you smiling? Do you think that's funny?''

"No. What happened? You're a psychiatrist, aren't you?"

"I thought about how starvation was such a slow painful way to die. When I was growing up we always seemed on the edge of some economic disaster. I didn't particularly want to go on that way. Now. It looks as if dinner is, at long last, ready. Be nice to Laura about dinner, won't you? She's a terrible cook."

He was right. The dinner was terrible and there were no flowers on the table and Laura had forgotten to buy candles so that although it was June they sat in a somber gray winter light, in the cool sterile air of the air conditioning. At her end of the table, Laura was chatting with Ben; in her rapid mechanical way she was firing a volley of questions at him. He looked amazed. Phil began spooning his pale green soup not up and down but back and forth as if looking for something in it. After a moment he sighed, a funny sigh, the kind of long sigh a child gives after it has been crying, and he pushed away the soup and left his right arm on the table, just a few inches from the edge of Tonia's dinner plate. He drummed his fingers lightly on the cloth and looked down the table at his wife. He said, "She's beautiful, isn't she? My wife?"

"Very," said Tonia.

He said, "I married the most beautiful girl at Vassar."

He turned and looked at Tonia and smiled. She saw that in his calm, pallid face, his eyes under the curly brown brows were very much alive and light brown and mocking, not so much the eyes of a tired husband but the eyes of someone who pretty much gets what he wants out of women. She did not smile back. She lowered her eyes and reached for the water goblet and in her nervousness, knocked the base of the goblet against the rim of the wineglass. It clanged, a tiny warning bell. He scowled and abruptly stood and began removing soup plates. She felt confused. He jerked her plate away and said brusquely, "You didn't eat your soup."

After dinner, he passed around coffee (he ironically took on all the hostess's roles) and then came and sat down next to her again. He declined to talk. He sat there on the gray silk sofa, heavily, broodingly, as if he'd been mortally wounded, and when she at last said something gentle to him, he raised his eyes and looked at her with the kind of painful trust a child shows when he has been wrongly accused.

So long as she knew him, she never knew which Phil to believe in—the Phil of the lazy bold smile or the tired hard-working intelligent Phil to whom she could talk as simply and honestly as if they were children together. At the other end of the room, Laura was still chatting, chatting, chatting, and when at last it was obvious that her spring had run down, they all stood up to go home.

8

"Sit right down," Tonia said to Ben. "Dinner's ruined, of course. You could have called."

"Sorry," Ben said cheerfully. "Hi, Mary, how are you? Ready for the big farm weekend?" He bent to kiss his mother-in-law and she patted his cheek.

"Poor boy," she said. "You work so hard."

Tonia grimaced. "He loves it. It's a pain to leave the lab and come home, isn't it, Ben? And how are all your little cells today? Still swimming around?"

"You'll soon find out," he told her, grinning, and she

glared at him—Don't!—over her mother's bent white head.

"What's this, dear?" Tonia's mother asked, looking up from her plate with fork poised. The Haseltines and Mercers preferred "plain food," coming as they did from a region so remote from the city that chocolate mousse was still called pudding and oeufs à la neige folksily labeled floating island.

"Eggplant and Italian sausage with cottage cheese and noodles."

"Oh," said her mother.

"Looks great," said Ben, tucking in. He had the primary virtue of being able to eat anything and not get fat. "How'd Jamie do today? Get off to school all right?"

"Certainly. He loves it. He got up all by himself half an hour early so he wouldn't be late. He's in the first reading group and he beat up another kid at recess. Everything in his life is terrific. And Elizabeth loves kindergarten and Joey hit little Jack Kerston on the head with a shovel while they were in the sandbox."

"Good," said Ben. "I hope he really brained him. Maybe little Jack won't be back for a week or so. I thought she was going to stop parking her kids here."

"She was sick today," Tonia said, "with cramps."

"You're too nice to her," Tonia's mother said. "You have to be firm with some people or they take advantage."

"I'm nice to her because Joey likes Jack. At least when he's not hitting him."

"Tonia feels sorry for her," Ben said. "Her husband left her."

"No!" said Tonia's mother.

"He switched from tennis to golf and she couldn't make the transition," said Tonia.

"They had nothing left to talk about," said Ben.

"True of lots of people," said Tonia, and when her

mother glanced at her she said quickly to Ben, "I had a coaching session with Ecklund today."

"Oh, good," said Ben humorously, and winked at his mother-in-law. "Another forty bucks shot, I guess. Listen to that, will you? Jamie's feet get bigger all the time."

"Damn," said Tonia. "He's going to be cranky tomorrow."

"He'll sleep in the car," her mother said. "Don't worry about a thing."

"You said that before," Tonia told her.

"I'll just go up and see what's going on," said Ben, rising.

"Why don't you just finish the damn dinner?" Tonia said.

"Be right back," Ben said.

Tonia's mother looked at her, then put her fork down and gently cleared her throat and said, "You certainly have done a beautiful job on the house, Tonia. It's lovely, it really is. Why, I think even Ben's mother would have to admit that it's lovely. I thought when you bought it—"

Crash from upstairs.

"Oh, shit," said Tonia, throwing her napkin on the table. "He'll never sleep now. This is just what he needs— a wrestling match. Ben can be so . . . stupid."

Tonia took two plates off to the kitchen. Her mother sat staring into the candlelight and then reached up and adjusted her glasses. When Tonia came back into the room, her mother thought her blue eyes looked smeared, but Tonia, with a cigarette stuck into her mouth, cleared the rest of the serving dishes, keeping her eyes cast down and squinting against the rising cigarette smoke.

"Oh, please," her mother said, "*please* stop smoking. I can't stand to see you do that to yourself."

Tonia took the cigarette and thrust it into the middle of

her husband's dinner plate, where, on a slice of grayish egg-plant, it hissed and gave up one last ghostly sigh before it died.

With extreme stealth, Ben had gotten out of bed early and cooked Jamie and Elizabeth a farewell breakfast of pan-cakes. They had gone—Jamie, with a plastic sailboat in his hands (the farm now had a pond), and Elizabeth, dragging a bald doll, and Joey, four firm limbs vigorously waving from out of the complicated straps of a large padded car seat. Tonia, waking up late, had called goodbye from the bed-room window and then in her bathrobe went downstairs. Ben was putting a rose into a bud vase on a breakfast tray. Oh, dammit, she thought, the old breakfast tray seduction routine.

"You," he said, "were supposed to stay in bed."

"Why are you still here? Won't the lab fall apart without you?"

"I'm taking the whole weekend off. What would you like to do?"

"I'd like to have my coffee."

"Have it upstairs."

"I'm *down* stairs now."

He poured coffee into a mug and handed it to her. "What would you like to do this weekend?"

"Do? I don't know. I feel disoriented. There are always so many things I want to do and can't, but now that the kids are gone I can't remember what those things are."

"I know what we could do."

"Don't," she said, moving away and sheltering the full coffee mug with a curved hand.

"Why not?" he said. He took the mug out of her hand and set it down.

"Not now, Ben, for heaven's sake."

"Why not now?" he said. "No one's around. Alone at last."

"You know what I'd like to do? I'd like to put on some pretty clothes and go into New York."

"You know what I'd like to do? Take off some clothes and stay home." He had backed her up against the stove and put his hands on her hips.

"We did that last night," she said, pushing against his chest.

"I did it, you didn't."

"I was tired."

"Now you're rested."

"Let go, Ben."

"Why?"

"Because."

"That's not good enough. Why don't we see if we can do it together?"

"Not now."

"Why not?"

"I just don't feel like it."

"Let's try an experiment," he said, unslipping the knot of her bathrobe, "and see if we can make you feel."

"Ben, I have something to tell you."

His hand froze. He cocked his head at her.

"It's not that," she said.

"If it were, it certainly wouldn't be mine."

"Ecklund thinks I should have a New York recital."

He stood still and looked at her. "A what?"

"A New York recital. Next April."

"What's that mean?"

"I sing in New York. You know—songs? That kind of thing."

He leaned against the wall. "Really."

"Yes."

"Okay. What's it going to cost?"

"I don't know yet."

"Want to try for a round figure?"

"Well, we have to rent the hall . . ."

"Which one—Madison Square Garden?"

"And I have to pay an accompanist."

"Of course."

"And there are the tickets and programs, and I'd like to have a party later."

"Uh-huh. Tonia, why are you telling me this now?"

"I didn't have a chance last night."

"I see."

"You don't sound thrilled."

"I'm simply delighted. Where in hell is the money going to come from?"

"I don't know."

"Can I tell you something?"

"All right."

"We are very much in debt."

"I know."

"Would you care to render an opinion on how we're going to pay for this?"

"Maybe I could stand out on the street in red satin short-shorts."

"Lotsa luck."

"What does *that* mean? You don't think I could attract anybody?"

"Oh, I think you could attract lots of bodies. It's the performance I wonder about."

"That's exactly what it is with you, it's a performance. Maybe if it weren't so much performing and more something else—"

"I'm sorry, I'm sorry, I was just joking. If we had the money—"

"We had the money to go skiing. We spent hundreds of dollars to go skiing."

"You, too, wanted to go skiing, as I recall. Or am I wrong about that?"

"No, you're right."

"Don't you see, there's a limit to—oh, Tonia, I'm sorry, really. Look. We will find the dough. Really we will. We'll just—uh—"

She went upstairs and locked herself in the bathroom. When she came out an hour later, Ben was already dressed.

"See you," he said.

"All right," she said. He went down the stairs. She followed him into the hall and called down the stairs, "Don't forget the Sullivans' party tonight," but he did not answer and did not turn his head.

After she was sure he'd gone—the car spinning out of the driveway—she went downstairs. She had a glass of iced tea in the kitchen and looked out the window, feeling drugged. A day off with nothing to do but listlessly walk through the house. In the dining room she ran her hand over the smooth surface of the sideboard—she had refinished it herself, slowly, painstakingly. Later, when practicing, she had often felt she was working on her voice as a skillful carpenter works on a piece of dull shellacked wood until that wood, cautiously sanded and stroked, reveals under a sticky marred surface its rosy, tender, golden-grained, silky heart.

> *"What I ask is your true image*
> *your dear face*

and your glance . . .
Give me your reflection . . ."

Above her head the dining room mirror reflected nothing
but greenish light. They had hung it too high and instead of
hanging it again had simply lazily adjusted.

"My reflection! What do you mean?"

She could practice, of course. In the living room, she
struck one note on the piano, D, but it sang out timidly,
muffled by the humid thick air of the afternoon. No. She had
no desire to sing. She lit a cigarette—oh, this is stupid: *don't
smoke*—and put it out. From the hall, the steep white walls
looked down at her with the calm, impartial gaze of Miss
Elm, her sixth-grade Sunday school teacher. They had not
gotten along. Miss Elm, whose literal faith in Christ was
unshakable, had not liked noisy, troublesome, smart-alecky,
desperate Tonia, who wanted to know: If God was so good,
how come he had killed her father? If God was so good, how
come we had all these wars? If God was so good . . . if! if!
if! why! why! why! God, said Miss Elm, is good. People are
bad. But God made people! God gave people free will. But
God (that huge eye in the sky which always appeared in
Tonia's mind as blankly blue and a little bloodshot) knows
*every*thing—you said so! you said so! Miss Elm had a very
long outcurved white upper lip, which at a certain point in
their "little discussions" she would press firmly downward.
Her movements and gestures were as measured as her voice
—that voice! Tonia could hear it still, and no doubt somewhere out in space Miss Elm's voice had become immortal,
sound waves even now rolling confidently outward from tiny
Earth, past nebulae, galaxies, quasars, and pulsars to the very
edges of this universe and on into the next, with the calm
Midwestern assurance (she was, Miss Elm, originally a Luth-

eran from Iowa) of a great slowly undulating plain that
knows it is secure under God's merciful eye, on and on and
on and on, on a hot Sunday morning with the whole sunny
rose-scented June world vibrating just past the grimy window
Tonia had been allowed to open only a tempting inch or two;
and downstairs, the tread and thump of the choir arriving to
put on their robes in the choir room and still another long
hour of church to sit through and only—brief respites of bliss
—those moments when they would stand and sing. Then
Tonia would feel her whole body lift from the ribs up:

For the beauty of the earth . . .

and the joy, the glad, upswelling, outspilling joy of her own
voice rising in praise of—not God: she was a ten-year-old
atheist—but sun, sky, roses, June, happiness, life. It had always seemed to her that singing *was* life.

She put a hand to her forehead. It was so hot. Hot
squares of sunlight lay on the polished wood floor of the hall,
and in the living room, tall shadows stood in the corners, not
coolly, but looking somehow muffled and draped like bent
veiled women in a Middle Eastern marketplace. Was this her
house? Really her house? And passing the long mirror over
the pier table, glanced at herself. She had on a green linen
dress and gold hoop earrings and a gold bangle and she
thought that she looked as decorated as a Christmas tree.
Who would know that the cambium layer was dying? How
had it all gotten so out of balance? After years of chaos, she
had gotten the children and house—finally—into some kind
of order. Now these feelings (disorderly feelings, disorderly
house?) intruded. Life with its evil passion. I would and I
would not. *"Vorrei e non vorrei."* Sometimes when Ben was
so relentlessly cheerful he only made her feel crushed. "She
is crushed, she is crushed, Olympia's crushed!" Needing to

stay alive. *"Vorrei e non vorrei."* Needing—oh. Didn't she have everything? What was it then that she needed?

9

"My dear," Phil said on her first night out (she had had another brief pregnancy and a miscarriage), "where have you been? This town's been a desert without you."

("I hate you!" she'd screamed at Ben from the hospital bed. "When does this all turn off?"

"You stupid bitch!" Ben had roared, then collapsed into a chair and mumbled, "Sorry, I'm sorry. Look. Give *in.* Just take the damn pill, will you?"

"They give me headaches!"

"Listen. They will not distort the quality of your voice. I promise."

"I hate you! I hate you! I will not mess myself up just so you can guiltlessly enjoy yourself."

Groan.)

"What's he done to you, my love? You're thin as a wraith. We're going to have to fatten you up. Lots of Peach Melba and Potatoes Schumann-Heink. And what about your singing? You didn't have much time for that, did you? When are you going to quit this baby business? Why don't you send old Ben over to Dick Burns at the hospital? He'll give him a nice little badge to wear, make him a member of the broken arrow club. Feel strong enough to dance?"

She didn't.

"Then I'll sit down. I am very glad to see you. Don't ever leave me again. And for God's sake, don't get pregnant.

What's wrong, do you need some good medical advice? Even Laura, zombie that she is, knows how to take care of herself. Someday, when you're feeling better . . ."

Laura danced by with Stu Andersen and darted green eyes at them over Stu's bulky shoulder.

"Someday," Phil said again, and Ben appeared, looking red-faced and sweaty, and taking a handkerchief out of his tuxedo pocket, sat down, blotting his brow.

"Someday," said Phil, smiling at Tonia, "we'll all have to go into town together for dinner."

The next weekend the Durhams had dinner in town with the Merkles and Phil was perfectly cordial and Laura was wearing the diamond wristwatch he'd just given her for her birthday.

"Where's Ben tonight?"

"Houston."

"A meeting?"

"Yes."

"Am I wrong or are you a little depressed?"

"Only a little."

"Missing Ben?"

She said nothing. He smiled. "Tell me about last weekend. Did it go all right? Did they fall out of their chairs? Someday I'm going to rent a hall and you're going to sing just for me. I'll be down there all alone, listening."

She laughed at him. She thought what an odd character he was and understood that he flattered her, but there was something else, too: when she had first met him she felt very at ease with him, as if he were someone she'd known all her life, but at the same time baffled by him and curious. There was something in his eyes—a private unhappiness. He had with other people a conventional, courteous, almost flat way

of speaking, very agreeable, as if he were too tired or unin-
terested to disagree. Yet when she saw him, at all those brief
moments during parties, he was silent or would burst out
with something shockingly personal, about himself or his
children. A few times when on the telephone with Laura she
could hear music in the background and she knew that he was
home. In the wide-eyed, innocent yet canny way Laura had
of saying bitter things, she said once, "Phil sits alone at night
and listens to music," and another time: "Some people drink
—Phil listens to music." And once when Tonia came by on
a Saturday to return a borrowed platter, she saw him from
the driveway, sitting on the Merkles' glassed-in porch. It was
late summer; the shade of the maples made the light of the
room bluish-green. Faintly through the closed glass doors
she could hear music, a string quartet. He was sitting with his
head in his hands. In the deep, slowly wavering goldfish-
bowl light of the room he looked like a man drowning. She
was too frightened to ring the bell, so she left the dish on the
doorstep and went away.

Spring came and at the Andersens' midnight Easter egg
hunt, conducted in jeans and boots and hats and raincoats,
Phil's white face appeared in the beam of Tonia's flashlight,
next to the Andersens' still silent rose-garden fountain. He
said, "I need to see you," his voice expressionless, his face
bleak. Tonia nervously laughed. "Stop it," he said. "Listen
to me. I need to see you."

"Ouch!" said Laura, who was right behind Phil and had
caught her sweater on thorny "Chicago Peace."

Summer came and went with the swiftness of a whole
flock of small scudding clouds, in V formation and following
a leader, somewhere, someplace, and the Hubers had their
annual Labor Day picnic. Tonia saw Phil from across the
Hubers' field. He had on dark sunglasses and was holding

little Kitty's hand and Kitty was trying to tell her father something but he was looking in Tonia's direction. Finally, he bent his head and nodded gravely and Kitty ran off and Tonia turned and went into the house and locked herself into a bathroom. It was cool and dark in there and someone had left a warning copy of *Couples* on the windowsill.

They went to a benefit ball for the New Jersey Opera Society. Tonia went as Violetta, Ben went as Pagliacci, Laura went as Carmen—a role that did not suit her—and Phil came as himself, two hours late, in his usual blazer and crooked tie. When she went upstairs to the ladies', she saw him sitting outside it, on a small gold chair. Women were coming and going, looking at him curiously. His hands were deep in his pockets, his feet—black shoes, white cotton socks—stuck out. He looked up, then stood and came toward her. He said, "You've been avoiding me."

"Not at all," she said.

"Scared?"

"What of?"

"Of yourself."

"No."

"Well, good. Then let's dance."

"Oh, no, I have to—uh—"

He smiled at her and in a parody of cavalier courtesy, bowed his head and walked off.

At a dinner party in early September she saw him in the dining room, switching the place cards. He looked up at her, smiled, and beckoned.

"You're right here, my dear, next to me." He always ironically called her "my dear."

"That's funny," their hostess said, frowning. "Did I put . . . ?"

"Sit down, Tonia," Phil said. "How are you? How's your singing?"

"Fine," said Tonia.

"Fine, fine, fine," said Phil gloomily.

"Oh, look," said Tonia, "we're having beef Wellington."

"Again?" said Phil. He ate in silence and then turned his head, one curly brown brow lifted. "So you're fine?"

"Mmm."

"Busy with your singing and the children and the house and feeling fine. You don't look fine."

"Don't I?"

"You look tired. He doesn't take care of you. Why don't you get some help with the kids, a maid or an *au pair*."

"I don't want an *au pair*."

"Wouldn't it be a help?"

"Right now it would just be confusing."

"It seems odd to me, my dear, how disrespectful you are of your talent. Sometimes I find with my patients— Is this going to bore you? I don't want to get all clinical and pedantic. . . ."

"Go on, I'll tell you if you bore me."

"Sometimes I find that women can be very self-defeating. They arrive at a certain point and simply quit. Usually it's because they sense that someone, a husband or lover, feels threatened by what they're doing."

"Phil . . ."

"Oh. Am I boring you?"

"No. You're being tacky."

"Sorry." He smiled. "How does Ben feel about it?"

"About *what*?"

"Your singing."

"How should he feel?"

"Don't you know?"

"I suppose after all these years he's used to it."

"Used to it! Doesn't he feel delighted? Proud? Or, possibly, inconvenienced."

"Inconvenienced? By my so-called career? Don't be stupid."

He smiled again.

She said, annoyed that she'd let herself be so trapped into exposure, "Oh, what are you doing?"

"You know what I'm doing."

"Then stop."

"You're scared. What are you scared of?"

"What is it you want me to say?"

"That you care for me." He had not lowered his voice and on his left Mary Herder lifted her small head on its long thick neck, and blinked. He said in a low voice, looking down at his plate: "Tell me what to do. I don't know what to do. What am I going to do with Laura? She doesn't . . . she's so . . . Yesterday she went out for the whole day and left Kitty all alone. No sitter, nothing. Do you think a five-year-old should be left all alone? The sad thing is I don't think she knows the difference. What in hell am I going to do with her?"

Tonia, too, looked down at her plate, and said in a low voice, "Sometimes I just can't believe you. Can't you get her some help? *Not* household help. My Lord, Phil, you're a psychiatrist; don't you see she's . . ."

He lifted his head and in a painful gesture drew his palm across his face and pulled at his mouth. Tonia looked away.

"Sorry," he said abruptly.

And indeed she did feel very sorry for him.

And so, through a couple of years of dinner parties together and cocktail parties together and dances and buffets together, she had arranged in her mind a whole scrapbook of his remarks and pasted them up to make a life and that hot humid Saturday in September drove down the turnpike to the South Jersey town where he had grown up. She recognized it at once—another variation of Veddersburg, only hotter, lazier, almost Southern, with its streets sun-glossed in the center and smelling of melted tar, and shadily cool at the edges, whole rows of crook-limbed maples darkening the sidewalks, and the patchy front yards where birdbaths and silver reflecting balls grew and revolving sprinklers idly turned, throwing up, now here, now there, cool silvery arcs of water that dampened the walks and brought up a deep earth smell. The houses: small, frame, with ferns in pots on wicker stands and barberry bushes and hydrangeas.

She parked the car and walked downtown: a Sears, an immutable five-and-ten, an ancient Egyptian temple for a bank, a movie house (peeling, degraded, boarded up), and a drugstore, now part of a nationwide chain. His father had been a pharmacist and his mother a piano teacher. She went to the town library. There were the usual characters—a prim librarian, not yet wholly resigned to virginity; and the two elderly men full of lively animosity for each other who came in every day at nine to read newspapers and beat each other out for the one easy chair; and the freckle-faced little woman in socks and saddle shoes who for eighteen years had been doing research on her family's genealogy, trying to prove that her great-great-grandfather had been the illegitimate son of Napoleon Bonaparte; and a tall boy with dark gold hair, leaving with three books under each arm and a furtive look around, hoping none of his friends would see him here on a Saturday. Phil's house. Which one? That one, perhaps, set off from its neighbor by a hedge of scraggly lilacs, stained-glass lights on either side of the front door, where a piano tinkled mercilessly all day: "The Indian's Walk," "The

Happy Farmer," until full-bosomed sixteen-year-old Marianne Wallop arrived to play, in clumsy gushes, Chopin, and hope, heart thudding in her warm freckled teen-age bosom (armpits damp with sweat), that maybe Mrs. Merkle's son might clump up the stairs as she sat playing so soulfully for him, for him, for him. "Pay attention, Marianne!" said Mrs. Merkle, who had hard, very hard green eyes and who, the other girls said, watched her son like a loving hawk. A house he had described for her, not elaborately, but in chance remarks here and there, as pious and boring. She could smell without even getting close its hot little rooms and in winter the heat rising through the grillwork register to his bedroom over the kitchen. Pious and boring. Economy. Cabbage. Methodism. Two weeks every summer in Ocean Grove, New Jersey. Sun, sea, sand, no booze, and no—certainly not!—sex.

He used to help his father in the drugstore and his father, tall, white-haired, with a deep-dimpled charming smile, would hold the ladies' hands just a little too long as he handed them their wrapped pharmaceuticals or occasionally, coming out from behind the counter to reach with his kickstool some bottle or jar of suntan oil stored too high up, would, upon descending, brush a breast or a thigh, for which he was always elaborately apologetic, and would, when the lady had left, turn to his son and deliver himself of a long wink. At home he was mild, kind, harmless. Estelle, Phil's older sister, got out of the house as soon as she could and went to New York. Small-time model followed by big-time marriage. His mother—she had been musical and bright and a beauty but burdened with a pious upbringing so that she married early—wanted for her son: everything.

In the little town library, with its slow, whirring electric fans, and smell of old books, and the librarian's hopeful springtime perfume (lily of the valley), she looked up his high school yearbook: young Phil, pale and solemn, stared out at her. But his classmates had decided about him, in italics under his picture:

> *A handsome head,*
> *A roving eye,*
> *This musician makes*
> *The ladies cry:*
> *Philip—from the Greek*
> *meaning Lover.*

She smiled and shrugged and driving home again thought: Ego. It's only my ego. And wanted, suddenly, Ben.

It is sad, or funny, or ridiculous, how many of life's decisive moments are chance matters of mood: why should a simple matter of time, two or three hours on a warm, beautiful September evening, make any difference? If Ben had come home earlier . . . for at six o'clock, sitting on the terrace, the humid September air now lightened by a breeze, Tonia looked around and thought how lovely her life was, thought, with a Pierrot half-moon rising behind her and Venus ascending into the greenish sky, how much Ben had put into this house, this garden, this life, and how much he loved her and the children and (a little breeze picked up and ruffled the leaves of the apple trees) how hard he worked and that although he sometimes infuriated her, no one, no one, had ever made her laugh like Ben. But at seven, sipping her second glass of wine with the night closing in, she felt her mood slip, and at eight, as the sunset began to die, a slender reclining pink streak crushed between the transparent far-off purple hills and a sky that pressed blackly, suffocatingly down upon it, she felt rigidly angry. She glanced at the Merkle house and then, turning her head, saw a figure—Ben's—in the French doors that led from the dining room to the terrace. He seemed not to see her. He was standing in the shadowy half-dark looking out at the garden and for a reason she could not explain, she thought of a painting, a Matisse, of a piano with a scrolled music rack and a silent triangular metronome and thick black lines, and you felt, when you looked at its heavy blues and grays, not music but silence, not joy but oppression, not harmony but something static and forbidding, every part of the canvas shut off into its own little arc of isolated paint, as in a Chekhov play when the players are all on stage together but so separate in their perceptions, so alone, that they come together as if by accident, their encounters as random as the chance collision of molecules. She stood up and walked toward him. He looked so content standing there in the gloaming, with what she saw as a half smile on his face.

"Ready?" he asked, looking across the space of the terrace at her.

"For what?" she asked.

"Aren't we going to the Sullivans'? Or were you counting on going alone? I guess our neighbor could get you home."

She had thought that they might, before they went to the party, discuss the recital, but now went instead to get her purse. In the purple half light of that warm September evening, she walked by him so coldly that she felt her movements as stiff as the string-propelled twitchings of a marionette, and although she passed by him only a few feet away, she did not see, did not see, that his eyes were blurred with tears.

10

"What's going on?"

"What do you mean?"

"You heard me. Just what is going on? Will you put out that goddam cigarette?"

"Ow! What the hell do you think you're doing?"

"Breaking your wrist."

"Then who would do your laundry? And do you have to drink so much? No one ever sees you without a drink in your hand these days. It's marvelous for the kids."

"The kids! What kind of shit is that? You don't give a damn about the kids."

"It's all I do care about."

"I don't believe it. All you care about is yourself, and your singing, of course."

"You've never understood that, have you?"

"Understood what?"

"That it's one thing—me and my singing. We come together."

"You and who else?"

"What?"

"You and who else come together? It sure ain't you with me."

"Stop it."

"Why?"

"Jamie's right there in the sunroom."

"I don't care, for God's sake."

"Oh, I know it. Talk about me—you're the one who doesn't care. You never cared about anything but your damn lab. The rest of us out here—we're just really irrelevant. Well, I can't stand it anymore. God, you make me feel com-

pletely dead, as if I died years ago. I don't have one real
feeling left."

"You! You and your feelings. Jesus, you don't know
how lucky you are. I can't *afford* feelings, I don't have the
time for feelings, I've got to support this family and all of *their*
feelings."

"Oh, what a martyr! Onward, Christian soldier, bravely
marching into work each morning. Bull! Bullshit! You were
the one that wanted this lovely home in this lovely town. You
wanted to live out here, remember?"

"I wouldn't really call it living."

"Neither would I. I'll tell you something: there is no
one else, but if you go on this way—"

"What way? Are you threatening me, *my dear?*"

"Ow! Let go of me. Will you leave me alone? You are
right out of "March of the Wooden Soldiers", you know
that? *Ow.* Don't you ever do that again. Don't you ever touch
me again. You're a cold, drunken— Jesus! You bastard!"

And so on.

And so forth.

11

Often, sitting in one or another of her hotel rooms, Charity
wrote letters. She never put them down on paper but instead
wrote in great length and detail in her mind. Now she was
writing a letter to Tonia and she knew that as soon as she'd
written it she would feel better and she would go down to
the Westbury's coffee shop and have two cups of coffee, a
small glass of orange juice, and a cheese Danish.

Dear Tonia, she wrote, looking out the window. (There was a bookstore across the street that looked as if it might sell real books instead of games, beads, or plastic reproductions of New Guinea artifacts.) I'm at the Westbury now. Last week it was the Waldorf and before that the Sherry-Netherland. Eventually I'll work my way downtown again, but for now it's goodbye to Hudson Street and all that. Well. I can't say I didn't know it wouldn't last. Six years is much longer than I'd thought. Still, it gives me a desolate feeling, as if everything I do in life is doomed to fail, and more and more, lately, I feel friends, acquaintances, peeling off, everyone with a whole little network they've developed—husbands, wives, children, friends—while I am, I am . . . Is this what I've always wanted? a life alone with no one left to hurt me? Strangely enough, it was that scene in your kitchen that gave us—Pietro and me—the *coup de grâce.* God knows, I've put up with a lot from him, but having him tilt back in his chair and so insolently put his hand on your ass. I'm sorry I screamed at you. I know, I *know* it wasn't your fault. He does these things—how can I explain? He feels he can do anything, get away with anything, perhaps because I've let him. In January, I came home and found him in bed, my Victorian bed, with the girl downstairs: she makes batik as well as husbands. I don't know why I was surprised—it had happened before. Did you notice he's getting bald? Ha! The more his little monklike tonsure grows, the randier he gets. I swear it's true. He'd screw anything on two legs, maybe even four; we've never had a pet so I wouldn't know. He's absolutely obsessed with fucking, anyone, anything but me, of course. All right. Let me confess. I've never been terrific in bed. I can't . . . I don't . . . but still.

The first time it happened, a couple of years ago, I put it down to business. Matty was ten years older than me (he is, after all, seven years younger than I am), but she did own that nice little gallery on West Broadway. Yet he didn't even care enough about me to be discreet and didn't I contribute to his cause? So really, he didn't have to. And then, as he came up in the art world, thanks not a little to my friend Stu Weber over at the Whitney—God, I've known Stu for ages; we went to dancing school together—and his work started moving uptown, it was Lizzie Cling Rabin, the wife of the real estate fella (Lizzie went to Chapin with me, however) that bought a Pontini for the lobby of the new Rabin building on East Seventy-third. One of my favorites, it turned out, the one called *Marriage of True Minds,* which is a long polished bronze oval ring (ten feet tall) intersected by a small rounder weightier bronze ring and mounted so delicately, with such precision of balance, that if you push it, it harmoniously sways in a lovely pendulum-like rhythm. I think it's his best, maybe his only good one—in fact, I don't really think he's much of a sculptor—and I'd always thought he had done that one for me. Well. Maybe he had. At the time. I suggested the title. He can't say I've never given him anything, aside from money.

Damn it! When I first saw him he was so lean and lovely, that coal black hair and those black eyes and that young milky skin, dusky red on the cheekbones. He's fatter and paler now. I think we were, at first, happy. He's not very verbal, as you know, but there are lots of other kinds of communication and I wanted so much to help him, to be a part of what he was doing. And now it's all gone to hell and I feel that besides Pietro, I've lost your friendship. You, Ben, and the children, you're practically my family now that Lucille has gone gaga and spends her days plucking at her hair and sticking out her tongue. I'm sorry, really, that I screamed at you. I had had a lot to drink—we had all had a lot to drink

—and all right, I will have to admit that being there with you and Ben and the children I was overcome by an acute attack of envy. You have always seemed to me to have everything. Your singing, Ben (whom years ago I might have loved), and the children—what lovely children!—and that marvelous house. I know. I could buy myself a house. But for what? Or rather, for whom? And then, of course, Phil acting so peculiarly. Just what, Tonia, is going on there? There we were, in your kitchen after the Merkles had left, me in my black late-thirties evening dress which you didn't seem to appreciate (it's a Worth, my dear) and you in that blue thing, doing the dishes, and Ben having yet another drink and then Pietro just reached over and gently cupped your ass and you turned around and let him have it with the wooden cooking spoon right over the fingers and he was so stunned he could only gasp with pain and I stood up and threw my drink at you and then Ben with the most godawful roar took me by the shoulders and shook me until I thought my teeth were going to drop and then he took Pietro—one hand on the collar, the other on the seat of his pants—and hurled him out the kitchen door. Oh, Lord! It was funny, I guess.

I wish I could talk to you. Someday we'll be friends again, won't we? Oh, please don't desert me now. I am often in such pain. I even went to see Tom the other day. My excuse was a checkup, but I really just wanted—oh, I don't know—to see someone who wasn't a busboy, waiter, or maid. He's back in New York, married to a Southerner, Lulu Belle or Daisy Mae or something. I hear she has a drinking problem. Sounds like Tom, doesn't it? He always was a sucker for problems. . . .

Charity had for some time now been standing with her forehead pressed against the glass of the window and she sighed and straightened up. What time was it? Eleven. She was a late riser and a late go-to-sleeper. Pietro always went to sleep promptly at ten and he was up prowling about at six. She stayed up until two or three, reading, watching late late TV shows on the little Sony. It was one of their points of disagreement. He hated tiptoeing around her in the morning and felt her little night light—she was always careful to shade it—kept him half awake. She, on the other hand, hated days, those long white tunnels of unending time that had to be filled with something—what?—as if with a teaspoon. All her life she had read a very great deal, so that gradually the form and shapeliness of literature, its rhythms, characters, and conversations, had come to replace in her life the drab grayness of real life, real time, until sometimes she felt she had no life of her own left at all. Except—God, yes. She'd almost forgotten. Lunch with Ann McKenna. How are you, Ann? What's going on in your life? Pietro and I have split, you know. Me? Oh, I'm just floating around town. Decided not to get another apartment right away. I never was much for possessions and this simplifies life a lot. I just move around the city from time to time. Remember Karen? I've been meaning to try and find her. We saw her once, you know, years ago. I wonder how her kid is. Someday, when I get my inheritance, I'm going to found an old-age home for prostitutes. What do you think of that? I know lots of women who would qualify, some of them even married. Especially some of the married kind. The one thing I can say about myself is, I've never gone to bed with a man for his money. But then I've never had to. Thank God. If only for that.

12

"Get the hell out! Get the hell out of my house!" Ben had roared. There was the sound of scuffling down the back steps and then Charity, in her black thrift shop dress, went flying past Tonia and out the back door. The Pontinis' car started and shot out of the drive. Ben came in, slamming the back door so hard that the window gave one tinkling shiver, fell out of the doorframe, and slithered to the floor, where it broke into a thousand glittering pieces. He stood there, red-faced and panting. Tonia said coldly, "Oh, look what you've done."

"What I've done? What I've done?" he said, not in a shout but menacingly. He started toward her, his arms cocked, his fists curled, then scooped up the sugar bowl from the kitchen table and threw it full force at the wall. The glass salt and pepper shakers followed, wineglasses she had just polished, glass jars from the spice rack—cloves, mustard seeds, bay leaves—all went spinning through the air and into the flowered wallpaper. Black peppers flew in all directions, followed by cinnamon sticks. Bits of glass stuck into the wall everywhere, along with dribbles of curry powder and ground allspice. When the spices were gone, he jerked open the refrigerator door. After the mayonnaise jar went—*splat!*—she turned and left the kitchen.

She went upstairs, got her nightgown out of their bedroom, went into the guest room, and locked the door. She got undressed and into bed. She could clearly hear the crashes from downstairs. They went on for some time. She lay in the dark wide awake until she heard him come up the stairs, heavy-footed. Their bedroom door slammed. At last. Silence. You beast, she thought. You utter pig. Swine. Jerk.

Dope. Deaf and dumb, deaf and dumb. She would have to get up early and clean up the mess before the kids, barefoot and heedless, came downstairs. She knew what, in his own way, he was telling her. "Here," is what she thought he was saying: "I'm going to make this mess—you clean it up." In the mirror of their marriage she saw herself—reflected in his eyes—as the cleaning help.

That winter had seemed the coldest of Tonia's life. March came and she did not notice. The weather changed or did not change, the forsythia bloomed, snowdrops and crocuses appeared, but inside the Durhams' house the air was cold, as white as January. Her recital was a month away: Ben had not mentioned it. The long windows of the house, its airy arches and curved bays, had seemed, when they moved in, to enclose a safe rounded space, a bit of Victoriana which, when painted white, would soften the sharper angles of their life together. Instead, the space of the old house (frame and stone, circa 1860) seemed now to contain a cold mad fog like a sigh or an exhalation that reminded her, not of happy Victorian families full of children tumbling down the stairs, but of unhappy women, spinsters looking out from behind heavy draperies, sobs stifled into fresh-pressed cambric, madwomen locked into third-story bedrooms, headaches, corsets, birch rods, the smell of patchouli. She wandered from room to room of the large house, wrapped up in a heavy sweater. The furnace expired, a pipe broke on the third floor, the roof leaked right down into the guest room, which they themselves had just painted and papered. She spent hours each week now waiting at the door not to greet guests but instead graciously receiving a whole cavalcade of smirking plumbers, sly-eyed electricians, and haughty roofers, who arrived not in trucks but in long white Cadillacs, smoking

Havanas, and dressed, not in overalls, but in white suits and Cardin shirts.

All winter long Ben had been reserved and she knew she was being punished—for a sin she had not yet committed but that daily seemed more attractive. Not this week, though, she prayed, looking at herself in the mirror. A bad cold had left her with chapped lips and a cold sore at the corner of her mouth, and remembering Blakova, she superstitiously coated her neck with petroleum jelly and swathed it in flannel rags. Every morning, the Singer got up with a headache and a pain in her throat while Cinderella sat and patiently sewed and waited, with eyes cast down and her lips pressed together in a secret smile, for her lover to call. Why, then, when he called, this Comedy of Terrors:

"Tonia!"

"Hello? Oh!" Help! "Phil!"

"How are you? Fine?"

"Oh." Little laugh. "I guess."

"I wondered if—uh—we could reschedule"—he was calling from his office—"your appointment for sometime—uh—on Wednesday afternoon."

"Wednesday!" Help! "Wednesday . . . Wednesday . . . Wednesday. I—uh—can't on Wednesday, Phil. You see, I have to take the kids to the dentist. I've waited four months for this appointment, and—uh—"

This leftover blob of a conscience! When all around her, bodies were happily going to hell, gamboling as gleefully as the little naked sinners on the tympanum of a Romanesque church. Why, just last month, Lydia Carver, mother of four, Girl Scout leader, Presbyterian Sunday school teacher, member of the ladies' A tennis team at the club, while cavorting on some motel bed with her lover, a well-known local orthodontist, had taken a misstep backward and fallen from mattress to floor. What to do? Poor Fred had had to call first the lady's husband, then the volunteer rescue squad (three of them A team players): in the long fall backward, Lydia had broken her neck.

It wasn't her neck Tonia was worried about, it was her life. Unfair, unfair! She was not a nineteenth-century woman, had no patience with the awful current nostalgia, this last hope of infirm minds, this ache for a nineteenth-century past that was, anyway, part myth, part marzipan—the current craze for buying cracked hundred-dollar pots and leaky glazed jars and broken baskets; for wearing lace and ruches and carrying fans and reticules; this outward sign of an inward history that had probably never existed; the current attachment to fake nineteenth-century heroes: Jesse James and Custer come gun-blazing out of a made-up past proving their manhood or the Code Duello, when she saw them as a bunch of syphilitic brain-rotted renegades, half gone into general paresis, and her idea of a hero was—odd, because she had never been religious—Sir Thomas More. Conscience before all and how the hell would she get rid of hers? Her left-over blob of a conscience. Unfair, unfair! She hadn't been to church in years, so why not just be bad and shut up about it? What was she scared of? She didn't want to love Phil.

(1) Practical reasons. Sometimes at night, not able to sleep, she would imagine loving Phil—first a dreary little affair, conducted in secrecy and nervousness at dingy motels on major highways; then the eventual scenes: Ben would throw things, Laura would shake. Then the breakup of their marriages, and here was where she stuck—she couldn't imagine not being married to Ben. What about the kids? Who but Ben would love their dopey kids? And what about Phil's kids? Laura the Robot would get custody—here was a

thought to scare any sane person. Or suppose Phil did get custody, meaning, eventually—God!—Tonia. In charge of six kids! How swiftly, surely, and ironically her imagination leaped forward from the first blissful hours of the affair to the domestic ever-after: six kids to get meals for, six kids to wash clothes for, six kids to prod into doing their homework at night, six clamorous kids, for each one of whom she would attend: school concerts, swim meets, hockey games, tennis matches, soccer games, dance recitals, oboe concerts, art exhibits, piano programs, and all six kids would have to be driven to all of the above—by Tonia. It wasn't really what she had in mind.

Finally, there was (2) Impractical reasons. Or reason. She didn't want to hurt Ben.

And yet. All winter long Tonia had felt Ben withdraw into his world of work, and the more she pondered the ease with which he did this, the angrier she became. How easy, how convenient to have another place to go to when surely most of the heat was right at home in their kitchen. How good it must be to be able to make decisions, clear-cut decisions, when at home decisions were impossible, things simply had to be borne, to be lived with. She felt it as betrayal, abandonment, nothing less and his pretext, as always, was money. As for instance in this conversation, held in rising tones over orange juice at 6 A.M.:

"Hadn't you better come home for dinner tonight? Your kids think you're a myth."

"I'll come home when I'm goddam ready."

"Which, it seems to me, is hardly ever."

"That's right, because this isn't a home, it's just the place I deposit the money you spend."

"*I* spend. You want to eat, don't you?"

"These don't look like food bills to me."

There was a pile of stamped addressed envelopes—bills —on the kitchen table and he had scooped them up in both hands, tossed them into the air and let them fall, the way a kid will toss up dead leaves. They did look dead, these white envelopes scattered on the kitchen table, like a cemetery full of fallen tombstones.

"No, they're not food, they're oil, electricity, gas, water, telephone—"

"What about this?" He craned his neck; a crooked forefinger stabbed an innocent envelope. "Saks Fifth Avenue, Bonwit Teller's, Bloomingdale's!"

"Didn't you just buy a new suit? And five or six or was it a dozen shirts? Why is it every time I buy anything I have to ask your permission?"

"Every time? It's more like all the time."

"I see. I shall wear my jeans to sing in, I guess. In April. That will create a sensation. Are you planning to come, by the way? You haven't said. Oh, you really have a hell of a nerve, you know that? You really think I'm some sort of serf, don't you? You get all my services—"

"Such," he said ironically, "as they are."

"—for nothing, or next to nothing—"

"Oh, no; not for nothing. You've never given anything away."

"I've given years of my life away."

"So have I."

"Only I have nothing to show for it. You're the one who makes all the dough."

"And you're the one who spends it."

Sometimes she felt that she was dead and the Singer, whose union contract clearly specified that she be more or less alive, had taken a liking to Phil because, of course, he seemed to like her. Her singing! Her singing! Little Cinderella had decided to love Phil and the Singer—that maniac who ruled her life with bullwhip and clock—had decided to love him and thus, the morning after the Pontini debacle, a Saturday, Tonia got up, cleaned the mess in her kitchen, then promptly at 9 A.M. called Phil's office. Message: Wednesday is fine. One o'clock (burst of inspiration), the steps, main entrance of the New York Public Library. She would, she added, for the benefit of his icy-voiced secretary (who, Tonia thought, was probably in love with Phil), be glad to help him with his research paper. When she put the phone back on the hook, her palms were cold, her brow hot, and Ben was just coming into the kitchen. His face was red, his blue eyes glittery, he had on a white cotton turtleneck and over that a bright blue Norwegian ski sweater which had worked in, across the chest (where his heart should be, she thought grimly), a pattern of ice crystals. He poured himself a cup of coffee and sat down, turning his chair away from her.

13

Not surprisingly, Ann McKenna had changed everything in her life but herself. After ten years as a secretary-typist, she had taken her little fund of hoarded money, quit work, and enrolled in the Columbia School of Social Work. Now instead of neat polyester dresses she wore jeans and sweat shirts. Her hair had turned white but for a central black streak, which she combed back from her high square forehead. She was still angular, still thin, still had her droll, close-mouthed way of speaking. Walking next to Ann, down a crumbling Yorkville Street, Charity thought that social work would drive her crazy—she had never been much of a do-gooder. Ann was the codirector of a halfway house for juvenile offenders: young car thieves, young prostitutes, young kids temporarily out of trouble.

Primly, in front of a flight of chipped brownstone steps, Ann bent, picked up a banana peel, and put it under the lid of a trash can that was chained to the wrought-iron railing in front of the building's tiny yard. (In the yard someone had planted daffodils and tulips.) A head popped out of a window, a young caramel-colored girl whose dark-fringed almond eyes were uptilted, whose hair was braided into tiny braids, each one tied with a yellow ribbon.

Lord, Charity thought.

"Miz Ann!" the girl yelled. "Tina say she ain' gonna do no more vacuumin', even tho' it huh turn an' ah did it all las' week."

Ann looked up at the girl, smiled slightly, but said nothing. They climbed the brownstone steps and went in the unlocked front door. The hall was painted a light yellow and arranged on a table between two doors was a vaseful of daffodils. On the wall above the table was a long gold-framed mirror. Ann said shyly, "I found the mirror and the table in a secondhand store." Through an open doorway, Charity could see a room full of furniture—a green vinyl sofa and chairs on aluminum legs that looked as if they'd been rescued from a second-rate dentist's waiting room; mismatched tables and a card table and bridge lamps that seemed to have come from some turn-of-the-century seaside hotel. On the living room mantel, as in any other good home, were arranged pictures of the . . . what? wondered Charity. Inmates? Inhabitants? J.D.'s? Offenders? Guests? Ann saw her glance and said, with her little close-mouthed smile, "Our kids."

A tall fat man with a rosy round face, tiny glasses, and a scraggly beard stuck his head out of the doorway at the end of the hall.

"McKenna," he said, "where's Carstairs, d'you know?"

Ann thought. "He said he had to go see a man downtown this morning. Jerry? This is my friend Charity Pontini. Charity? This is Jerry Muller."

"Hi, Charity," Jerry boomed. He had a loud rich voice. "When you see him would you tell him there's been a mixup in the milk deliveries? Also, remind him about that dinner he's supposed to go to in New Jersey. Summerville, I think it is. Some folks there interested in us. Money money money!" Grinning, Jerry made the usual sign, rubbing his thumb against his fingers.

The girl with the corn-row hairdo reappeared. "Miz Ann," she began in a complaining voice. "Do ah gotta do this stuff?"

Ann smiled. Charity wondered how she could order around anyone in this place; McKenna's voice was so small not even a roach would have jumped. "Don't worry," Ann said. "Tell Tina to come see me when she gets in."

They went up the carpeted stairs. "Like the carpeting?" Ann asked. "It seems like a luxury but it's really not. Not when you have sixteen people going up and down."

"Just like home?" Charity asked, pointing to the key Ann had used to unlock the door to her room.

"We all have keys," Ann said. "The kids like that. Most of them come from homes where they've no space of their own, so they like having a room with a key. And I guess," she said, her small mouth turning up, "it's just as well."

She opened the door on a bright room of striped pale yellow wallpaper, a bright green sofa, and wicker chairs cushioned in yellow chintz. A large wicker stand full of plants—ferns and African violets—stood next to the yellow drawback drapes and in front of the little fireplace was a large round wicker basket full of rolled-up magazines and needlepoint canvas and knitting wool. A clock ticked peacefully on the mantel. Through the windows, the new leaves of an ailanthus tree quivered, casting speckled shadows on the wall. The room exuded . . . what? peace, hominess, ardent domesticity. It needed a cat curled up in the sun, and a tea tray, Charity thought.

"How many kids do you have?" she asked, sitting down.

"We have fourteen now," Ann said. "We're really full up."

"Is Jerry the codirector?"

"No, he's a volunteer. He's actually a doctor, a radiologist. He takes the kids to the park and they shoot baskets or he works outside with them. We have a little garden out back."

"And you really like this?" Charity said.

"You mean," Ann said, drawing her mouth up, "do I like it better than typing?"

Charity smiled. "Your room is so pretty."

"It's home," Ann said. Below, in the yard, through a window that was raised a few inches, Charity could hear Jerry's loud voice and the sassy, quibbling voices of kids: "Hey, Doc, looka dis!" "Hey, Doc, why we gotta . . ."

"All my life," Charity said, "I've avoided this kind of thing. I hate thinking about poverty, disease, and crime. Some people do all the time. I don't mean you; I was thinking of Tom, my first husband."

"I don't think about poverty," Ann said. "I just think of how we're getting along, all of us, from day to day and week to week. It's like any other family."

"But don't they—the children—have terrible problems?"

"Lots of families have problems. I just look at it that

way. I guess we know we're going to have problems, so maybe we're better prepared to face them. I think to myself, maybe whatever we do is better than doing nothing. We might not really help a kid. But back where he's come from, he's got no hope at all."

"When I was married to Tom," Charity began, and lifted one shoulder, "I never went down to his clinic."

"Why should you? It wasn't your clinic."

"Yes. That's what I thought. Anyway, I was never very good with sick people. I guess I'm not very giving."

"Well," said Ann, her small blue eyes contemplating Charity, "we all have to find our own work. If you like what you're doing, you're really getting."

Down in the yard, they heard Jerry Muller yell, "Arthur, you knucklehead! Don't do it that way; take the hoe. . . ."

"What a kind man he must be," Charity said.

"Yes," said Ann, and her dead-white skin slowly reddened and she lowered her eyes. Oh! thought Charity, oh, no! and imagined Jerry Muller at home that night with his wife and (no doubt) four children, and his wife would say, teasingly, at the dinner table, "And how was Miss McKenna today?" and Jerry would laugh good-naturedly and flick the smallest kid—a redhead—on the hand for reaching instead of asking and the kid would say, looking up, "Who's Miss McKenna?" and Jerry's wife would say, smiling, "Someone who likes your dad a lot." And here was Ann with her face so painfully red, her furry black-lashed eyes looking down at the green-carpeted floor. There was a knock on the door.

"Come in," Ann said. Charity had expected the child with the tiny braids, but instead a man with a calm pale face, gold-framed eyeglasses, and gray-streaked shoulder-length hair stood in the doorway. He, too, wore jeans and a gray sweat shirt.

"Oh, sorry," he said. "Am I interrupting?"

"Come on in, John," Ann said. "This is my friend, Charity Pontini."

"Hi, Charity," John said. "Any relation to a Father Pontini out in Birch Spring, Minnesota?"

"Father?" Charity asked. She had been brought up a Presbyterian. "Oh. You mean as in priest?"

He flashed her a smile. "Right!" he said, and held out his hand. She took it and felt the bony hand enclose hers.

"John was a Jesuit priest," Ann said, "but they asked him to leave."

"You know, Charity, I knew Ann for a month before I figured out what a straight-faced comic she is," John said. "They didn't ask me to leave, Charity, I asked them. I didn't want to end up teaching math to good little Catholic boys. By the by," he said to Ann, "there's a little problem with Tina: she's gone."

"She'll be back," Ann said.

"She's missed her work detail every day this week."

"She'll be back this afternoon. She went uptown to see her mother, but she told me she'd be back in time to cook."

"What makes you think she'll be back?"

"She loves to cook. She told me she had something special in mind."

"She's got to do her other jobs too."

"Maybe she can trade with Lindsey. Lindsey hates to cook."

"Well. You work it out. I'm off now. Got to see what I can do about Keith. Nice to meet you, Charity Pontini. Oh, say. Can I give you a ride somewhere? I'm going downtown, as far as Bellevue."

"Really?" said Charity. "That would be fine. I did think I'd go downtown today and look at some bookstores."

"Come back soon," Ann said.

"I'd like to," Charity said, not knowing if she meant it or not.

When he opened the front door for her, Charity felt Carstairs glance at her and smile. In his car, a wobbly orange VW, he drove with clip-on sunglasses and an elbow out the car window, steering the car with two fingers. The car engine, in need of a new muffler, made it hard to hear. At the first light he shouted, "Where are you from, Charity?"

New York, she shouted back.

At the next light he asked her what she did, a question that always embarrassed her. Well, she shouted, she was separated, and as she said this, perhaps because she had to shout it, it suddenly seemed true and she winced and thought: Yes, that is what I am: separated. Have always been. Separated. With Tom. With Pietro. Separate. Separated.

She shouted above the engine, which rattled and coughed and roared, that she had liked Horizon House very much, that she really would like to come again, that she'd like to—in fact—contribute a little something. She didn't have much money, she lived on an allowance, but now that there was only herself to take care of . . .

"Terrific!" Carstairs yelled, and glanced at her and flashed her a smile. "Only first you ought to know more about us! Come and meet the kids! Come to dinner! Come tomorrow night—we're having spaghetti!"

They were married six weeks later. The *Daily News* said: HEIRESS MARRIES EX-PRIEST. The Sunday *Times* had a small dry paragraph. The Durhams did not go to the wedding. Jamie had been dead only a month and a half.

14

Tonia stood in the driveway blinking in the pale March sun. The whistle, Jamie's special one, came from about halfway up the blue spruce.

"Hey. Up here, Mom."

Red, white, and blue sneakers, dangling in odd perspective.

"Jamie? How'd you get up there?"

"Climbed, a course. Where ya going?"

"Just out to do some shopping. Is it nice up there?"

"Sticky."

"Don't fall, okay?"

"I never fall. What's Dad mad about?"

"Is he mad?"

"Yeah."

"I don't know. Just leave him alone."

"Okay. When you coming back?"

"In a little while. Would you like me to get blueberry muffins or pecan buns?"

"Both." He grinned down at her from his shadowy perch high up in the tree. She waved and got into the car and drove off, thinking she would bring him the album he'd been saving for. Funny kid, so sturdy and indefatigable, and at the same time his ear for music was uncannily, delicately precise. He could sit down and play almost anything he heard on the piano, and his voice was sweet and true. She had begun playing little games with him: "Jamie, listen to that dog bark. What key do you think that's in?" He would cock his head, in the way he had that was exactly like his father's, and say, "D?" He was never wrong. Funny kid, she thought, funny mixture of elements, her child. And drove off to Bloomingdale's.

Later, in the days and weeks that followed, she would go to Bloomingdale's or Saks or Bonwit's every day, a store for each day of the week, wandering up the aisles, then down, never buying anything at all, but on this day, a Saturday, she bought a dress of sheer flowered cotton and the album for Jamie and came home several hours later with the cakes from the bakery and the album and the dress box in her hand. Ben was at the refrigerator getting a beer. He turned and said, looking at the box in her hand, "What the hell is that?"

"It's a dress," she said.

He closed the refrigerator door and peeled open the aluminum top of the beer can, then leaned back against the wall. "Well," he said, "let's see it."

She thought: He's been drinking, but said, "It's just a spring dress."

"Is it?" he said. "What color is it? Blue? Yellow?"

"Why are you so interested?"

He put the beer down and with a movement that seemed big-pawed and clumsy, like the swat of a bear, took the paper box from her hand and tore it apart. He plunged his hand into the box and brought out the tissue-wrapped dress and held the poor thing up to the light, like a man holding up a dead wife. The tissue slipped to the floor and he squinted at the price tag dangling from the sleeve. He took the price tag in both hands and looked at it closely; it was not an expensive dress, but he suddenly yanked the tag out of the sleeve. With a sound like a gasp the sleeve tore. She reached for the dress and they stood there, the dress hanging between them, and did not see Jamie, who had just come in the kitchen door.

"Let go," she said.

He reached across the dress and slapped her, a hard stinging slap on the side of the head. Tears—of anger more than pain—flew into her eyes and, in surprise, she let go of the dress and put her hand to her head. She shook her head and as she opened her eyes saw him, with a sneering look, tug at the dress where it was torn and tear it in two.

"Stop it!" she cried, and jumped at him and hit him on the arm with her fists. He reached out a fist and hit her ear and her ear sang and buzzed and she thought, clutching it: He's going to deafen me.

"Mommy! Daddy!" Jamie cried.

He hit her on the other ear and she cried out and fell back against the counter and he hit her again in the ribs and she doubled over and sank to her knees on the floor. Don't scream, she thought. Jamie's here; don't cry or scream. Looking up from the floor, its vinyl pattern a blur of fake Spanish tiles, she saw his legs in dark corduroy pants and his feet in their hard shiny black shoes and then saw one foot lift, its sole curiously uptilted like the snout of an ugly beast. She thought that if she could stand she could get Jamie out of the room —he was crying somewhere, far away from her—but before she could get up, he kicked her. Then behind her she heard the other two children crying in the kitchen doorway and she felt ashamed that they should see their mother this way, kneeling on the kitchen floor, not even defending herself. She turned her face to them and foolishly smiled—she wanted them to see that she was all right, quite all right, but they were crying in terror, their arms entwined, as if hiding behind each other. He reached down and hauled her up by an arm and propped her against the kitchen counter and said, leering into her face, "Your *friend* called."

She stood with her arms around her ribs, swaying slightly. She felt something wet near her eye and putting her hand up saw, distractedly, that it was blood. What friend did he mean?

"Come on, didn't you hear me? Your *friend* called."

She said, "What?" Her voice came out a whisper.

"What? What? What friend? Your friend *Phil* called. Doesn't he call every day? Didn't you tell him I'd be safely at work?"

She shook her head.

"And your daughter, your little girl, how nicely you've trained her to take his messages. What a good mother you are. You've trained them so well. She wouldn't even tell me —that's how clever she is, how well you've taught her. But I happened to be in the kitchen when he called. Really. How stupid of you. Or has it gone this far? You don't care, you don't care what I think or what I feel, or has it gone farther than that, even—you're letting me know, is that it?"

She said nothing, but although she knew it was dangerous and couldn't help it, smiled. Oh, why am I smiling? she thought. He'll hit me again.

"Why are you smiling?" he asked. He slapped her again, on the side of the jaw. Her teeth rattled, her ear sang, she felt dizzy and slightly nauseous. If I could lie down, she thought. Had he really called? Why? It seemed an odd thing to do, to call on a Saturday. But that's right—she'd forgotten. She had called him. Her ear began to ring. No. It was the telephone. She looked up at Ben. She wanted to laugh.

"Go ahead," Ben said. "Answer it."

She put one hand on the counter and leaning on it moved the few feet toward the ringing telephone. "Pick it up," Ben said.

What would happen if it was Phil? And what was he doing? Didn't he know that Ben was going to kill her? Did he want Ben to kill her? It seemed incredible to her, all of it, and somehow pathetic and laughable. It seemed ridiculous and her voice when she spoke into the telephone did not function. As she opened her mouth to speak she heard, far away down the street, a police siren go spiraling by, and then a high frightened voice said something fantastic:

"Mrs. Durham?"

"Yes."

"This is Elsie Cummings, around the corner on Livingston Drive. Mrs. Durham, you'd better come right away. Your little boy Jamie's been hit by a car, he was riding a bicycle and he went right through the stop sign down here, I don't know why, he's usually such a good child, and the Langton boy? He was driving the car and going much too fast, they say he's on drugs, you know, he's always in trouble. Please come right away. I called the police and they're sending an ambulance."

"Yes," Tonia said. Funny how she said it, calmly, as if agreeing to a car pool change. She hung up the phone. Ben was looking at her with an expression full of menace, his eyes two glittering slits.

"It's Jamie," she said. "I didn't hear him go out. He's been hit by a car."

He had already been put on the stretcher when they arrived. He seemed, after all, not so big nor so robust. His eyes were closed, his round face pale, a blue vein beat in his forehead under a lock of gold hair and in the cup of one perfect pink-lobed ear was a dark red dot of blood which, even as she watched, grew into a little pool and as the white-jump-suited volunteers lifted the stretcher gently, so gently, spilled over and trickled slowly, his life's blood, along the soft line of his jaw.

Every day, in the morning and the evening, they went to the hospital, parked, took the elevator to the pediatric ward, and walked down the corridor—the yellow walls were

decorated with Mickey Mouse and Bugs Bunny and Cinderella and Alice in Wonderland—to Jamie's room. He had a
private room and they had hired a private duty nurse. It was
always the same: the quiet of the room, the IV slowly drip-
ping, the bustle outside in the hall, the young cheerful nurses
who always, as they passed this room, looked away. At first
Jamie did not move. He lay on the bed with just a diaper on,
his arm taped to the IV, his eyes closed. His eyes were
sunken, with deep blue patches beneath them. Once he did
move in a series of spastic jerks and Tonia cried, "Look!
Look, he's moving!" But the doctor who was in the room at
the time said nothing, his expression did not change, and the
nurse said at last, gently, "It's just reflex, Mrs. Durham.
Clonic movement."

They had given her his clothes to take home, his jeans
and striped T-shirt and the socks and the red, white, and blue
sneakers, and she bundled the clothes together and tucked
them under the cushion of a large wing chair in the bedroom.
Upstairs alone, she would lock the bedroom door and sit
with the bundle of clothes in her arms, as if she could, by
giving warmth to the clothes, give life to her son.

Friends called. Friends sent flowers and cards. Sunny
Andersen called. "My dear," she said, "I'm so sorry. How
is he doing?"

Fine, Tonia said, fine. It was a lie. He was still in coma.

"We are praying for you," Sunny said. "And by the
way, don't worry about car pools. I'll pick up Elizabeth. I've
got to do the Merkle kids anyhow—they're in Spain. You
know Laura. Every time Phil gets out of hand, she takes him
to Europe."

She listened and it didn't matter. She didn't care. Later,
months later, she would learn, and feel indifferent, that he
had had many affairs, that while wooing her he had slept with

many women—patients, nurses, secretaries. "Any body," Charity said. "Literally, any body. Didn't you know? God. He's been at so many chests and into so many drawers they call him the Carpenter. It's kind of sick, really. You know. The score card. The catalogue. The old Don Juan thing."

She hadn't known, but maybe—yes—had guessed. Phil. *"Che per mi scorno amai . . ."* "Whom to my shame I loved."

"Of course " Charity went on, looking at Tonia so coolly that Tonia wondered whether he'd been in her drawers too, "he doesn't feel it's wrong. It's just a game to him, really. People like Phil, who are so detached from their feelings, they simply don't see it as right or wrong, maybe because they don't feel it."

Tonia said in protest, "But that's sick! And he's a psychiatrist."

"Why not?" Charity said. "Maybe it takes one to know one."

More to the point, Sunny Andersen would say, "That Phil! What a perfect life. Out here, Laura with all her dough, and in the city his work and his girls. Two perfect worlds!" Of course, Tonia thought. Conned again. She would listen and shrug and feel . . . what? Indifference.

Outside, spring came at last, the weather turned warm and glorious, and it seemed odd to her that Jamie could not open his eyes to see it. She sat by his bed long hours with her hand on his arm, and although she did not speak to him felt, in a primitive way, that her thoughts would penetrate the layers of cloud and fog to the deep dreamscape where he lay sleeping. One morning just as they arrived at his room she saw that the bed was empty and freshly made. He'd been taken into surgery. They waited an hour. The doctor came out looking sweaty and pale—he had a boy Jamie's age—and he shook his head.

209

Ben slumped into a chair. He gave a deep groan like the sound, in spring, of pond ice breaking. He put his head into his hands and cried. She stood looking down at him. The doctor said, "Are you all right, Mrs. Durham?"

"Yes," she said.

Ben wept. She drove them home. She took the children into the sunroom and told them. Her mother, who had just arrived, came to the door, heard, went white, and half fell into a chair. Ben had staggered into his study and closed the door.

They had a small private funeral. That day, a warm spring day, the noise of the birds' song seemed deafening. She thought how everything had changed and nothing would ever be the same again.

15

What are the wages of sin? The wages of sin are death.

What was the crime? Wanting too much.

Outline the contours of hell:

A tall-ceilinged sunny house on a fine spring day, and a dark tavern—Ada's—with a Schlitz beer sign in the window, pizza on weekend nights only, Italian travel posters— Roma, Venezia—on the walls.

People said: My! Isn't she brave? Or perhaps they said: I always did think she was cold. Or perhaps they said: It didn't matter. Tonia accepted twenty-two casseroles, eight homemade loaves of bread, twelve layer cakes, seven plants, and many arrangements of flowers. Thank you, she said. How kind of you.

Letters and notes arrived. Ben opened them all. He seemed touched by them. Tonia shrugged. She didn't care. What difference did it make? Listen to this, he said, it's from the Grahams . . . the Ormsbys . . . the Kleins. When they returned from Spain, the Merkles sent a huge bouquet of flowers and a note in Laura's handwriting. She didn't care.

Ben had stopped drinking. He stayed home for a week, took the children on small excursions, and then went back to work. Tonia got up every morning and made breakfast. She did the laundry, dusted, and ran the vacuum. The house was much cleaner than ever before. At three she picked up Joey and Elizabeth and they all went marketing together. She drove to the next town to shop so that she wouldn't meet anyone she knew. From four o'clock on she spent her time in the kitchen. She made cupcakes or cookies for the children. She cooked complicated meals straight from the cookbook without tasting anything. She watched herself carefully. She didn't have a drink until five, when she had a small glass of sherry. At six she had Scotch and water, and another at eight or eight-thirty when Ben came home—he drank ginger ale— and she served wine with dinner; he had none. Just before bedtime she had a little glass of brandy. The awful time, the time she could not bear, was the early afternoon when the children were both away and the house was empty. There was a punishing silence in the house. Alone that first day she felt, ascending the stairs, a sense of dizziness and danger; the blood pounded in her ears and something—a giant hand—squeezed the blood out of her heart. In the second-floor hall she stopped, her hand on the banister. Jamie's room was on the third floor and as she stood there at the foot of the stairs looking up, a dust-rimmed shaft of sunlight fell down the staircase from the window of the third-floor hall. It seemed to her impossible that he was gone, vanished, except for the image of him left lying in her brain. And what image was that? A little blond boy lying perfectly still on a stretcher with a dark-red dot of blood in his ear. She said to herself, coldly: Well, he would have died anyway, we all die anyway, he would have grown up away from me and died. But someone else in her head answered: By then you would have been dead. She thought how nice it must be to be dead, how good it would be to be dead and not have to feel . . . anything.

She went up the stairs and stood in the doorway of Jamie's room, looking at his bed, covered with the puffy blue quilt, and his white desk, and the half-finished skyscraper of red and white Lego blocks, and a pile of books next to his bed, and on a small table, his phonograph, with a record, now filmed with dust, upon the turntable. The silence of the room. It was deafening. It seemed to her a dead white weight that pressed against her ears until her head felt squeezed in a vise, as if the silence were smashing her skull. She put her hands over her ears and thought that she screamed. She thought that she screamed until her voice stopped and she couldn't scream anymore.

Evenings, she and Ben sat together in silence. He brought home paperwork and sat at the desk in the study, sipping coffee. When he was through he would come out to the living room and throw himself into a chair and sit watching her. She had, some time before, taken up needlepoint and now sat every evening, filling in colored areas of canvas with bits of colored wool. She didn't read, she didn't listen to music. In those evenings together, they rarely talked, not even about money. The hospital and doctor bills and funeral expenses: enormous. They didn't speak of it. Ben sat slumped in a chair and stared at her as she did her needle-work. He asked her, occasionally, what she had done that day. "Did you do anything interesting today?"

To which Tonia replied, wanly, "I went to a bar, Ada's, and I sat there for a long time."

He gave her his ironic smile and shrugged.

They still slept in the same bed but far apart from each other and if they made love—no, she thought, that was not the right phrase—if they had sex, it was only an abrupt kind of need. It would happen quickly, in the middle of the night, before she was fully awake, and when he was through he would turn away from her quickly and she would feel a sense of shame come off his skin like sweat, as if he were ashamed that he had touched her. She wanted sometimes to reach out her hand across the miles of cold snowy sheet and touch him, but there was always now a part of her that watched and ironically smiled and that told her without words, with only this smile, that no one wanted to touch her and that if she reached for him he might turn away and confirm this feeling she had, that he was ashamed to touch her. She thought how all her life she had taken the most absurd kind of risks for love but could not now do this simple thing: she could not bring herself to touch her husband.

16

"I'll have, oh, just some more white wine, I guess. Chablis. No ice. Have you quit drinking?" Charity looked at Ben curiously.

"What?" He had been studying the white tablecloth and now his head jerked up, he looked at her and glanced away. Charity had on an awful dress—a fuchsia wool knit that was stretched over her ample bosom and had, embarrassingly, a moth hole just off bull's eye on her left breast. Small, pinkish pimples, like the drupelets of a blasted raspberry, decorated her chin. Did she ever look in the mirror? She had got her ears pierced and wore long dangling earrings—pearl teardrops. She looked like a bargain-rate tart. He was fond of Charity, but as they came in the door of the restaurant Ben had been afflicted with a sense of extreme conspicuousness. From the rear, her dress rode up over her fanny, and the long black shiny boots, skin-tight to the knee, seemed to emphasize her thighs, which had the delicate contour of whole smoked hams.

"I said, have you quit drinking?"

"Yes, I have, but let's not get on to that, all right? It's not as if I drank a lot before."

"I thought you were," Charity said in her soft voice. "I thought you were drinking way too much."

Ben frowned. He hooked a forefinger into his shirt collar, tugged at it, and turned his head irritably. His left eyelid ticked. "Come off it," he said rudely. "That ex-priest you live with has tainted your morals."

"I suppose so," said Charity. "I guess that's it." She opened the maroon menu and peered upward. It was two feet tall and decorated with a gold tassel that swept across the butter on her bread plate. "This looks good—filet of sole Veronique . . . yum. I'll have that." She closed the menu and looked about for a place to put it.

"Here," Ben snapped, and took it out of her hands. The waiter came. Ben ordered Chablis and Perrier. Charity said, "Why are you so angry?"

"Sorry," Ben muttered. He looked at her and shrugged. "I'm sorry, really. You won't believe this, but I was looking forward to this—lunch today."

Charity looked down at her plate. "How's it all going?"

"Going?" He laughed. Not a laugh really, a bray: "Ha!"

"I mean, how's Tonia?" Charity looked up. Ben looked down. When Charity was little she used to seesaw with kids in the park. They would purposely try to bump each other hard, teeth-jarring, head-aching. She and Ben were, on the other hand, teeter-tottering delicately.

"Tonia is . . . well, she's . . ." He shrugged. "I don't know." His eyelid ticked again.

"It's been nearly a year."

"Yes."

"She's not singing?"

"No. I don't know what she does. God. I just don't know. It's as if she's been hit on the head." His face flooded and his eyes glistened. He shifted in his chair. "I mean to say, she's not herself yet."

"And she won't get any help? Surely there must be someone—in the hospital or in New Jersey."

"I've tried to get her to see someone. She won't go. She says she's fine. She goes on. She's so . . ." He looked up.

"Lifeless," Charity said for him.

"Yes."

"And how are the children?"

"Surviving, I guess. My mother-in-law comes out a lot."

"I suppose it will take some time."

"Yes. Let's change the subject. How are you?"

"Me?" Charity smiled, but weakly, he thought. "Oh, I'm fine. I've had the most marvelous idea. When I get my dough—my inheritance?—I'm going to fund and staff Horizon Houses all over the country. Don't you think that's a good idea?"

"I don't know," Ben said, and sat back in his chair as if exhausted. "Last I heard, you were going to endow the arts. Particularly sculpture."

"I'm in a different phase of my life now," Charity said. "What I've learned is that living is loving and loving is giving."

"Why, good for you," Ben said. "You've got it all memorized."

"That and a lot of other shit."

"I think you should do that in needlepoint and hang it over your john."

She laughed.

He said, "So John's into Oriental religions. Does he have a mantra?"

"Of course. So do I, but I can't tell you what it is. Wait a minute—I will tell you. It's Buzz."

"Buzz?"

"Yes. As in Buzz Buzz."

"Fascinating. And is John still thinking about India?"

"Oh, yes. He leaves on the nineteenth. I am giving him a scholarship." She looked down at her plate.

"Unbelievable. Maybe he could take Tonia. Sometimes I think she's already reached Nirvana. Sorry. Didn't mean to get back on that."

The waiter came with their drinks. Charity looked at her wine, then with a forefinger drew a wavy line down through the dewy moisture on the glass. She said, "It's not Nirvana. It's hell."

He looked as if she'd shot him. She saw his jaw move in a grinding motion, then he tossed his napkin on the table and stood up so loudly and abruptly the silver and crystal shook and all up and down the dim-lit room, with its rose-shaded lamps and flowers and mirrors, its leather banquettes and thick carpeting and the clink of dishes and talk wreathed in cigarette smoke, Charity saw astonished cartoon faces—white, O-mouthed balloons—floating upward. Watching Ben go, Charity saw his scalded face mirrored in the opposite wall and his features were transformed by a grimace into something skull-like and frightening, the reflection of a corpse. She drank her wine and had another glass. Oh, Lord, how they all had changed. She remembered him as so . . . good-natured. She remembered—she took a sip of the wine, it was her fourth glass—she remembered (it didn't seem so long ago, really) Teddy Vaughn saying to her in his nasal voice, "Do stop trying to fix me up, Chare. But listen, there's someone I want you to meet. A sweet boy, really. I think you two will fall in love and be divinely happy. He's just your type. He's in medical school but a teensy bit artistic. Not awfully artistic; I mean, not enough to be a pain about it. Paints a little. Watercolors, that sort of thing. Do come round on Friday. Do you think you could bring dessert?"

Ben had come in late, straight from his clinic. She had liked him first of all because he took Teddy seriously, allowed him to be just what he was. He sat cheerfully through cocktails with his long legs stretched out, perfectly relaxed. He didn't say much but laughed a lot. He and Teddy were cousins. Extraordinary! Teddy kept saying. My father's the flop in the family, Ben said to her, and laughed. She liked his laugh, a large hearty ha! ha! She liked the habit he had of tilting his head to listen and she liked the way he seemed thoroughly himself. No shell at all, really. None of those awful New York City affectations. No political or literary or artistic New York name-dropping bullshit. She liked his warm, rather sly sense of humor, his straight-faced ability to deliver a double entendre. She had thought him sweet and stubborn and witty and perfect for her and all that year she had been a senior at Smith had wooed him with Maine and sailing and theater tickets and college girl parties and New York parties and herself, all of which he had gracefully declined. Why? She thought perhaps it was her money. It seemed to scare him. Strangely, the more Ben firmly, courteously declined to love her, the more certain she felt that in her entire life she would deeply love only Ben. This gave her an immensely peaceful, secure feeling (is there anything less threatening than ideal, unreciprocated love?), but when he called her one night during her spring vacation and asked her to go out with a friend of his, she agreed; it was that final step down in a nonworkable relationship called easing out. He had thought (she knew this instinctively): I'll fix her up with someone else.

With Charity it was the opposite: it was a way of not letting go completely, of exerting a certain amount of control over Ben's life, that she set herself the task of finding him a girl. Not that she was a kindly matchmaker. It was always with cold curiosity that she brought people together—she wanted only to see what would happen. For Ben she knew she would need not just any girl but one with enough ambition, will, and direction of her own to make the game of courtship variable and challenging—he certainly required a challenge. She'd fastened on Tonia as soon as she saw her sitting there at her desk in Berry's office. There was something about the secret sarcastic way Tonia looked at her work; and the sullen way she typed; and the way she ran out the door exactly at six (her short rough-cut mop of dark gold hair very much in need of combing) that recommended her as a possible candidate. Charity foresaw that if they married —two ambitious people: delicious!—there would be all sorts of hell to pay. It was only a little plus (later it didn't even make much difference to her, she often simply forgot) that Tonia was probably William Haseltine's daughter.

As for Ben's friend? Tom. Dear Tom. That terrible spring night (winter's last blast: icy rain, streets like mirrors) she'd sat at the bar of the restaurant thinking that no doubt she was going to get stood up. Then someone dark-haired, in a white shirt, tieless, with his sports coat collar turned up, had run in under the restaurant's awning. He stood with his back to the window and his hands in his pockets and looked up and down the street, shifting from foot to foot in the cold. Left profile. Right profile. She sighed. His black hair streamed water and needed cutting. He turned and peered into the bar and looked straight at her. She looked away, then thought: So this is the way it's going to be. He is the one. I am going to marry him. It was as if some sort of resolution had been made in her heart and she'd felt both happy and resigned. Yes. He would be the one. She could be fond of him. They would be happy together.

A moment later, a wedge of icy air had attacked her spine and she heard him say at her elbow as the door wooshed shut, "Pardon me, are you Charity Mullet?" His brown face was wet, his dark hair hung in unattractive driblets, his lips were bluish. She had looked in the other direction and laughed. Later they went to the movies and afterward (he was so pathetically dumb) it was she who said, "I'd ask you back to my place, but you see, it's not really my place. I live with my aunt, so maybe we ought to go to your place." He didn't get it. He said, "My place?" She thought: "This poor *dope* of a man. I am going to have to teach him everything." Luckily, he had caught on fast.

Why, then, had it not worked out? The moment she'd married Tom she'd felt stuck worse than ever—an accessory, a confused listless patron at some dim café where the stage show never quite started. It occurred to her after a while that she wasn't really going to share his life, his life belonged to him. And then the other thing happened. Despite fondness, respect, affection, and sex, or perhaps because of them, she began to feel herself loving him. She was becoming dependent upon his love in a way that long ago she'd decided never to risk: if you loved someone too much they could badly hurt you. When she found out she was pregnant again, down there in West Virginia, she drove to Lansing in a rented car that smelled of popcorn. Afterward, the baby gotten rid of, she went back to New York.

Now it seemed that in her marriages she was doing less and less well; after only a few months of this last one, she had had it. John was not awfully interested in bodies, only souls, specifically his own. Frankly, she just didn't care about her soul. Frankly, she just didn't care about immortality or any of that hollandaise they'd peddled along with the wafers and wine. Her problem was not the blank ever-after but the void here-and-now. Every goddam morning she had to get up and face another abyss. Hadn't she tried almost anything? Pain, Krull had said, is what makes us real. Guilt, Krull had said, is what makes us human. Hundreds of souls out there wanting a flick o' the cat and we give 'em Velveeta. But Krull himself was long dead—a suicide. Could you believe a shrink who had done himself in?

"Madame?" the waiter said. "Shall I take your order now?"

"No," Charity said. "Just bring me the bill, please, will you?"

"Certainly, Madame," said the waiter, who knew her and was a little afraid of her—he thought her eccentric and unpredictable. He brought her the bill to sign and as her pencil point hesitated—she was figuring a percentage for the tip—he said, "It is always a pleasure to see Madame."

She said, "Do you know something, Jacques? My husband is going to India."

"To India?"

"Yes," Charity said. "He's going to learn how to be a monk."

"A monk?"

"Yes. Isn't that interesting? He's going to shave his head and forgo those great sins of civilization, red meat and blue sex. Have you ever noticed, Jacques, that most serious religions eschew meat and sex?"

"Pardon, Madame?" the waiter said nervously.

"Skip it," Charity said, and gathered her things together —her orange cape, her black pocketbook, her green tote bag full of books she had taken to carrying everywhere. Lately she spent her days wandering around the city, reading in parks and restaurants and buses. When humans fail, there are always books. Literary friends. Illusions of connectedness. Only temporary, of course. Anesthetics. Anodynes. Like stuffing a Tampax into a chest crater blasted by a terrorist's hand grenade. Lord, Lord (rhetorical). She was bleeding to death.

17

It was hot—the first hot spring day—when Tonia had a flat tire and pulled off the highway into a parking lot. She got out of the car and looked at the building attached to the lot, an old two-story farmhouse converted into a tavern. She pushed through the door and blinked. It took her a moment to be able to see. The air of the bar was dark, cool, and sour. There were tables and a few booths against the knotty pine wall and a long circular bar in the center with blue, mirrored panels hanging above it.

A woman, the barmaid, was slowly polishing a glass as she came in. Under a bartender's apron the woman wore a white nylon uniform, like a nurse or the matron of a prison. The woman nodded indifferently at Tonia. She was stout, had orange-blond hair, and even in the bar's dim light Tonia saw that her skin color was poor, yellowish. The woman was middle-aged and her face was without expression, as if she had seen and experienced so much there was no room left for feeling of any kind. Three men stood at the bar, drinking. They looked at Tonia, then looked away. They were watching a small TV hung above one end of the bar: the ball game. Tonia went to the bar and asked the woman about service stations: were there any nearby? and the woman, looking at her impassively—she had strange yellow-brown eyes, the whites of her eyes were yellowish too—simply shrugged. "Pay phone's over there," she said. Waiting for the mechanic to arrive, Tonia sat in a booth and drank white wine and looked at the travel posters taped to the wall: Venezia, a gondolier, black water, the Bridge of Sighs.

The second time, she went back to the bar to retrieve the sunglasses she had left there and then, because it was hot, and she had nowhere else to go, she ordered a glass of white wine and sat in a booth. The bar seemed dark and safe to her, safer even than looking out from behind sunglasses. She always wore sunglasses now, large black glasses. She thought how Moslem women hid within the privacy of their veils, only showing their eyes, but Western women wore sunglasses, careless about their bodies, souls shuttered. Once when she was a teen-ager, her mother had reprimanded her for wearing sunglasses to church. She had been taught, when a girl, to shake hands and look directly at someone when introduced, and her mother had told her to be sure always to remove her sunglasses. Now she wore sunglasses all the time. She did not want her eyes to be seen—they were dead.

The third time she went to Ada's, she went because it was very hot and Sunny Andersen, thinking to be kind, had taken Joey and Elizabeth to the beach. Left alone for the entire day in the large silent spaces of the house, she had been terrified. Left alone, there was nothing to distract her from the images that she had not even seen but that her mind, with a torturer's special skill, played and replayed for her. Jamie, blue eyes wide open, flying through the air in the moment after impact. If she could have saved him that moment. She was alone too much and yet, even when she went downtown, always behind her black sunglasses, she felt people she knew—friends, acquaintances—looking away, hurrying past her, as if everywhere she went she was like a figure out of some medieval engraving who wore on its forehead *D* for death, a plague figure sent to remind those in the midst of life—who on no account wanted to know—that life, security, happiness, all hang by a breath or a thread. All alone, behind her sunglasses, she went to Ada's and sat in a dark booth with her shoulder against the cool wall. A man named Mac often came to the booth and sat down and talked. She was glad to listen to him, someone who did not know that her child was dead and who looked at her without pity.

He was tall, with short-cropped blond hair and a high hoarse voice. He wore, always, white sneakers, a T-shirt, and a pair of tan cotton pants. He drank beer, had a large square jaw and small blue eyes. His mother had left him when he was four. He and his father moved around the countryside together and his father picked up odd jobs—carnival roustabout, factory worker, farm laborer, whatever he could get. When he was ten, his father remarried and he was sent to live with his aunt, a sister of his dead mother's, who had four children of her own. She was kind but her husband beat him and once for punishment had held his hand over an open gas flame. "See?" said Mac, and showed her his left hand. It resembled a hook, was stiff as a claw and shiny with scars. When he told her this story, his eyes looked cocky, as if he were bragging, proud that he had survived so much, but she saw that when he looked off into space his eyes were frightened and it was because of this frightened look in his eyes that she went upstairs with him. Going up the stairs, they put their arms around each other, but as he drew her close she saw that this was going to be a mistake: she did not like his smell. It was a sweetish, rotting smell like decaying fruit. When she uneasily pulled away from him, his hand clamped onto her shoulder.

"Who are they?" she asked Mac, at the top of the stairs, pointing. At the end of the hall upstairs was a living room of sorts—a shabby sofa, dirty window curtains, a television set. Two children sat on the sofa watching TV. The boy had an odd, dreamy, withdrawn look and his large thin head seemed too big for his slender neck and frail body. He was neatly dressed and his hair was carefully combed. The little girl had long blond sausage curls, the kind of curls little girls wore years ago. She sat on the sofa watching the television set and eating potato chips out of a bag.

"Ada's daughter's kids," he said. "She's I don't know where. New York, maybe." He unlocked the door to a room. The room was dusty and stifling. A window was open a few inches and the noise of the traffic on the highway—trailer trucks hurtling by—came in on a sulfurous gust. "Shit," he said, and slammed the window shut. "It's damn hot." He looked at her. He took off his shirt, his sneakers, his socks, his pants, and looked at her. "What the hell," he said. "What's with you, anyway? Let's *go*."

They went down the stairs together and when they came

back into the room where the bar was he looked at her, snapped his fingers, and laughed. "Jesus, I nearly forgot." He reached into his hip pocket, took out his wallet, pulled out two bills, crumpled them and pressed them into her hand. She looked at the bills, then dropped them on the floor. The men at the bar laughed.

"You wasn't worth much, Mac," a tall man named Al said. "She wouldn't take your dough."

"Crazy slut," Mac said.

After that she never went back to Ada's, but the odor of his sweat stayed with her a long time, that and a pressure on her throat. When inside her, he had put his thumb on her throat and pressed down.

Not that night but months later, while Ben was away at a meeting, she dreamed that she went to Ada's again. There was a small man with a cough and thin red hair who was playing the piano and in her dream she went to him and said, "I used to be a singer."

"Yeah?" he said. "Why don't you sing something, then?"

He played a few chords of a song; the other men stood around with drinks in their hands. There was Rufe, who was short and potbellied and blue-jawed, and Mac, and Al, who was tall and crippled and had dark angry eyes. She opened her mouth but she couldn't sing. She couldn't sing. The men glanced at each other and knocked each other in the ribs and Mac said something she couldn't hear and the other men laughed. They were standing around her in a circle and she wasn't prepared when Mac, grinning, suddenly reached out a hand and grabbed her by the arm. With her arm twisted up in back of her, he shoved her toward the stairs. Looking over her shoulder she saw Ada watching steadily and polishing a glass. Mac pushed her up the stairs, her arm twisted up

behind her, and pulled her inside the room. She heard footsteps on the stairs, then saw Rufe and Al come to the doorway. They were laughing; Al's dark glowing eyes looked
ecstatic. Mac began slapping her—left, right—with little
rhythmic slaps, and when he pulled out a cigarette lighter she
heard Rufe nervously giggle. Mac flicked the lighter on and
held it in front of her face and said wasn't that nice? wasn't
it pretty? She watched him—he was grinning—and the long
bluish flame of the cigarette lighter came closer and she
thought: They will kill me, and in her dream felt relief—they
were going to kill her. She was going to die and that pain—
the pain that was always with her, that made everything but
sleep and drunkenness unbearable—would be gone at last.
A door slammed. Mac blinked and turned his head. The little
girl was standing in the doorway, eating potato chips out of
a bag. Tonia walked quickly past Mac and past Rufe and Al
and said to the little girl, "What's your name?"

"Anna," the little girl said.

"Give me your hand," Tonia said to the girl, and the
little girl obediently put her hand in Tonia's and together
they went down the stairs. Ada looked at them humorously.
"You git," she said to the little girl. "G'wan now, git upstairs."

"Goodbye, Anna," Tonia said to the girl, and went to
the door.

Ada said, "I hate whores. I just plain can't stand
whores," and Tonia went out blinking, into the sun.

"Mommy!" Elizabeth cried. "Mommy, wake up! I had
a bad dream." She had turned on Tonia's bed lamp and was
crying, clawing, crawling upon the bedclothes. "I dreamed
you were dead and you wouldn't ever talk to me. Mommy,
wake up!"

"Shush," Tonia said, sitting up on one elbow. "You're

all right, pet. Everything's all right. Get in under the blanket with me. Come on. There now. That's better, isn't it? Everything's all right."

Tonia put out the light and put her arms around her daughter's small humid body. She must have been very frightened: her nightgown was damp and her face was wet with tears and her hair was damp at the temples. Tonia wound her arms around her daughter and held her close in the dark. At last Elizabeth sighed and fell asleep, but Tonia lay awake a long time. She thought of Jamie looking down at her from high up in the spruce tree. In her mind she would see him always—his round cheeks, his soft blond hair—but would never again be able to touch him. There was no bringing him back. She would have to go on without him. She knew that the pain would get better, be bearable as time went on, and that she would go on living. She would never leave her children. It was only that she could not sing. She did not want to sing ever again.

18

In the spring, a year after Jamie had died, Ben went to a meeting in San Francisco. He came home from the airport in the evening and they all went out to the porch to meet him. Joey said, raising his feathery brown brows, "Hi, Dad. I'm glad you're back." Ben lifted him up and a little muscle —a tic—gave way in his face and he whispered to Joey, "I'm glad to see you, fella. How's everything?" Like a vine, delicate and tenacious, Elizabeth attached herself to her father and said, "Guess what, Dad, I know how to read. I bet I can read anything. Can we get a dog? I want to have a dog so much. Linda Vazzi's got a dog and Mary Lou Orton's got two dogs. Everybody has a dog but us."

They all had dinner together, Ben put the children to bed, and afterward Ben and Tonia sat in the living room. Tonia studied him carefully. He had on a brown tweed suit that she didn't remember. "Well," he said, "home again." He sat in a chair with his legs stretched out.

"How was the meeting?" she asked.

"All right," he said. "How are you?"

There was something rude in the way he said "you." Something she didn't understand.

"Fine," she said.

"Good," he said, and bent and picked up the newspaper. She stared at the floor. She had, in honor of his homecoming, put on a long skirt of flowered velvet and she wore with it a long-sleeved blouse. He put down the newspaper.

"Joey says he wants to take piano lessons and you've said no."

"Oh!"

"Is that true?"

"I thought . . . I don't think he has any talent. He doesn't seem to carry a tune very well, and besides . . ."

"Yes?"

"Lessons are expensive and I thought we should wait awhile."

"Why? Do you think he's too young?"

"Yes, maybe."

"Mozart started when he was two."

"I don't think Joey's Mozart."

"Why not? He has your genes."

"Don't."

"Did you go to see Dr. Lawrence?"

"Yes."

"What did he say?"

"Say?"

"About your voice."

"It's fine."

"What does that mean? Are you singing?"

"I told you. I can't sing."

"That's nonsense, you know. There is nothing wrong with your voice. Nothing. You are doing this—"

"Why are you angry?"

"I'm not angry. I don't understand your motive, that's all."

"There's no motive. I can't sing. I am not going to sing anymore." She got up, gathering her skirt in her hands, and went out to the kitchen. She opened the dishwasher. Clean, steamy dishes. She began to extract them, stacking the plates.

Ben came out and stood in the doorway. There was something—a sparkle of nervous energy—in the way he stood there, very straight but bent slightly toward her, and then he came into the kitchen and began helping her put away the dishes. When he reached for a glass he swore and the hot glass dropped from his hand and smashed on the kitchen floor. She looked down at it, knelt, and began picking up the pieces. He, too, knelt and gathered up pieces of broken glass and then politely, in Alphonse-Gaston fashion, first she, then he, deposited the glass in the trash container.

"Tonia," he said.

"Yes?"

"Let's go into the living room." He took her arm at the elbow and steered her out of the kitchen.

"What is it?"

"There is something . . ."

"What?"

He took off the glasses he wore now and rubbed the bridge of his nose. "Tonia," he said, "listen. I'm not helping you at all. I feel as if . . . Don't you see? I have got to keep things going. I have got to keep on."

"Yes."

"I have somehow got to get in to the hospital every day and do my work. Do you see that?"

"Yes."

"Well, I'm not. I'm not doing my work very well."

"I'm sorry."

"I am talking now about money. Earning a salary. Not the goddam job. I hate it. Did you know that? You didn't see that, did you? You didn't see how it had all gotten to be . . . Who cares? I just go in there every day and . . . Did you know that?"

"No."

"But I have to get on with it. There's you and the kids. Do you see? I have got to keep on."

"I know."

"The point is, Tonia, I am not doing well. I can't even minimally do my goddam job. I am going to get canned unless I change something fast. Unless I get the hell out of this."

"This."

"This. This silent asylum we live in. This abattoir. Please. Look. I'm sorry. I'm sorry for everything. But I have to go on and live and work, if only for you and the kids. Do you see? I can't afford not to work. One of us has got to get on with it."

She stared at him. He had closed his eyes and stood with his arms folded across his chest. He took a long breath. "Look," he said, opening his eyes. "I feel now somehow you are better. Better able to cope with things. But I am . . . uh

. . . Look. I am going to leave for a while. All right? Maybe just for a while?"

"Leave?"

"Look," he said. "Tonia, look. It's survival. You are drowning me and dragging me under and one of us has got to keep on. Look. Okay. I'm not kidding myself. I've been wrong. I didn't . . . I don't know. There were things I didn't do. But you be honest too. Even before Jamie, these last few years, what was this? A marriage? You obviously . . . What was it you wanted me for? The money? Was that it? Was that the deal? You agreed to sleep with me so that I could support you? What a joke. You weren't even sleeping with me, at least not all of you. There's nothing there. There's nothing between us. I wonder now if there ever was."

"No," she said, confused.

"That's true, isn't it?"

"No," she said.

"Come on," he said. "Come *on*. I just showed up at the right time. If you loved me, if you cared for me at all, you wouldn't punish me this way. You know you're punishing me, don't you? Tonia! Look. Come here. *Look* at us. What do you see? Is that you? Is it? Is that me? Jesus, we're two corpses." He had taken her arm, pulled her to the mirror, then pushed her away. Through the silk of her blouse she felt the imprint of his fingers on her arm, deep oval depressions. He turned and went up the stairs. She heard him in the bedroom, opening and closing drawers, then he came down with the suitcase in his hand, the same one he had brought back from the airport.

"Not you," she said, "myself."

"What?" He didn't understand.

"If I could talk to you."

He gave her a weary look. "There's a check on your bureau."

"I don't want any money."

"Take it," he said. "You're going to need it." She saw that behind his glasses his eyes were puffy and red.

"Please don't go. Please let me talk to you."

"Oh, Tonia," he said, "too late, too late. Let me salvage what I can."

He opened the door and went out. She heard his VW start, heard its rachitic motor grumble and wheeze, heard its arhythmic cough and the sound of tires spinning in gravel in the driveway. She stood for a moment looking at the door. She hadn't had a chance to tell him about the leaky pipe in the basement, or to ask him about the cost of the new storm windows. She hadn't had a chance to tell him that she was sorry, sorry for everything, and that while he was gone, as a surprise for his birthday she had ordered a gift certificate from Wayside Gardens. And in truth, after all, he was wrong. She had loved him. Things had just gone awry. She would have to think about this, how so long ago, but not long ago really, they had begun together, two people who loved each other, and how this had turned into the usual deal and the twice-looped lovers' knot had constricted ever more closely until it became, at last, a double bind—the ultimate double bind. They had both given up so much of themselves to the marriage that the marriage had failed.

When she went upstairs she found a check on her bureau. It was for a great deal of money. She wondered where he had gotten this money. Insurance money, perhaps, for Jamie. Not that the money mattered. Somehow, it didn't matter at all.

Fancy philosophers aside, and ignoring most works of modern fiction that deal with diseases of the twentieth-century soul—emptiness, boredom—there is something to be said for life on its fundamental level, of hotting it paycheck-ward five days a week, of—not for yourself, of course, but for those dependent on your support—working for money. Tonia found a job, Monday through Friday, nine to five, and although it did not pay well, it was enough to pay the rent on a small house, and with Ben's very prompt support checks, enough to put food on the table. She worked as a typist. For a long while, through the divorce and the sale of the house, it was all she could handle. She didn't think much about singing, but when she did, it seemed to her that love and music had canceled each other out. She remembered how, when she was young, she thought that she could not live without music, without love, and it occurred to her one day that she had survived the loss of both and was, after all, still more or less alive.

III

Moderato (amoroso)

Antonia:
"Do I love you
because of music?
Do I love music
because of you?"

The Tales of Hoffmann Act III

1

Charity sat at her desk in the dim little room with her hand on the thin sheaf of papers—fifty or sixty handwritten sheets that comprised the opening chapters of her new autobiography. For many years, she had wanted to put her life into some sort of organized form, and it was only here, in the silence and shadows of an early morning madhouse, that she had finally been able to draw parts of it together. Well. Not madhouse, exactly; psychiatric clinic for the very well off was more like it. And although some of the facts were here and all of the feelings, she had discovered in the writing of it that this was not the truth about her life. What was? A series of images maybe, blood-bright blots, yellowish clots, the whiteness of terror laced here and there with startling intermissions of happiness; rainy days spent reading; sunny days spent reading; panic: don't leave me, don't leave me. I can't . . . I can't . . . The unexpurgated truth would have been not words at all but an infinitely prolonged amusical howl, a shrill spiral interrupted by terrifying silences, after which a pit-pit-patter, a sound like the falling of rain on a roof after insane heat and parched, dry-mouthed days. No. The more she gave written form to her life, the less the thing resembled her life; the more she gave truth to the written form, the less it was her truth, the more it acquired a runaway truth of its own. Comedy the obverse of horror, the satirist's mask is a grimace. Where is the nexus? I can't . . . I can't . . . Lucille had died of a final stroke. Three weeks later, Teddy Vaughn and Dr. Walter had brought her here. Now she was much better, but the thought of leaving this place, where for the first time her life had some order and serenity, frightened her.

In a few moments, the daily routine of the hospital would begin—the clink of medicine trays, the breakfast carts, voices in the hall. Dr. Walter would appear, knock lightly, and with an abashed smile limp into the room. He had been in the German ski troops during World War II and his left foot had been shattered by a sniper's bullets somewhere in the Riesengebirge. But excellent skiing, he had said. Best skiing in the whole world. Where the East German ski team trains. He had come to the U.S. just after the war and was now thoroughly Americanized: he drank Scotch with ice, ate his steak blood-rare, and had lost his only son in Vietnam.

She had at this point in time been the patient of many psychiatrists and knew enough about them so that she could categorize them by technique: there were those like Phil Merkle who used the life raft theory—when you were drowning they threw you a slogan: "You've got to learn to put yourself first"—and let you cling to that for a while before the next wave rolled by. Then there were the technicians, who preferred a lofty silence, who examined you as a mechanic examines a piece of extremely beautiful machinery, and you sensed that they were seeking, continually seeking the right button, the catch in the flywheel, the cog that needed just a little adjusting. There were the remnant theorists, mosaic in temperament, who clung to the tenets of Freud as if they were commandments (she had always felt oddly rebuked by Dr. Mann, who sternly reminded her that she must conform to the "laws" of her gender, when she felt conforming would have made life easier for him, not for her). There was, finally, the very fashionable psychiatrist she had gone to, the one she had dubbed the Necrophiliac, who looked like a cadaver, talked like an automaton, and recommended one day that she have intercourse with him right there in the office so that she would feel "alive." She had declined, first because he had very bad breath, and second because she was paying him such a good fee she thought the therapy should be hers, not his.

Dr. Walter, on the other hand, would come limping in, smile gently, sit down, and ask her how she was feeling. They often discussed literature. She had complained to him of having the feeling that only her head was alive, a head full of other people's lives, people who weren't even real, characters out of books, and he had said, "But it is marvelous! What a gift! Think only of the poor people who have not that." She had come to believe, finally, that a good psychiatrist had almost nothing to learn from rational training, that he, too, had to have a gift—an almost psychic phenomenon based primarily on intuition. There was something about Dr. Walter, the calm warmth of an impartial light that emanated from his soul, which made her believe that together they might be able to find the way out. She felt, when very sick, as if she were endlessly falling, and when she began to feel better as if she were in a white wall-less space, groping about blindfolded; she knew the stairs were there, if only she could find them. Dr. Walter had said, "It is difficult, life without props," and she had puzzled over this. Did he mean props, as in the theater? Properties? This made her think of her childhood dollhouse, and Galsworthian property, and furniture and family life and the theater sets of another era: *Life with Father.* She had been taken to see the play when very small and had hated it and remembered almost as well as the play itself her mother next to her, restlessly shifting and fanning herself with the *Playbill* and the large bunch of fake purple violets pinned to the lapel of her mother's white spring suit, violets she always sprinkled with L'Heure Bleu before going out. Blustering father and dumb coy sneaky Vinnie, the old master-slave relationship coated with sticky nostalgia, when she knew in her bones, no matter what time, what place, this was not the truth about men and women and how they were with each other. Maybe life wasn't better now, without Victorian props, but maybe it was more honest. Other props had eroded too, and the problem as they had identified it was this: how to form a life from the inside out. Give some shape to a life when all the exterior props had disappeared. That was the long-range problem. More immediately, her problem was where to go: she would soon be discharged.

From her window on the tenth floor, she could see that the East River this morning was a Whistler's study in shades of gray: early morning fog, the mists of September that would be burned off by a later sun. Brooklyn would emerge, part smoke, part sparkle, and by then Tonia would be up and Charity would call. Tonia left the house at twenty to nine each morning and drove to her job at the Perpetual Insurance Company of America, where she had been, for several years, the head of the typing pool. It seemed to Charity—yes, it was true—that Lucille had at one time been on the board of directors of the Perp. But of what use was that to Tonia? Tonia did not want to get ahead in business; she wanted only, as she had said once to Charity, to "keep her head above water." The Perp building itself (Charity had driven past it once, with Tonia) seemed to Charity reminiscent of prison architecture of the 1930s—a shimmering set of white stone tiers almost entirely without windows, and this despite its setting on the still somehow grassy banks of the Passaic River. Well, Tonia had said, I don't mind the job. It pays almost enough to live on and there are medical benefits and besides, there's nothing else I really want to do.

A streak of glinting silver appeared on the river, like light glancing off the blade of a knife. At the right side of the window Charity could see something, a scow, emerge from beneath the mist and a horn tooted and with dreamlike slowness the scow floated across the window's stage and exited, stage right. She glanced at her wristwatch. Yes. Now. She lifted the bedside telephone and dialed. Clicks and buzzes in far-off New Jersey. Tonia's telephone rang once, twice, three times, and then a small breathless voice, Joey's, said, "Hello?"

"Joey?" Charity said. "How are you? This is Charity Greenbucks." It was their little joke. She thought, feeling vaguely guilty, that she should have sent him something from London, but her memory of London was blurred; she had been walking somewhere in Richmond and then there had been a very young tall bobby, and then a very white London hospital, and then Teddy's face. He had been in Rome and had taken the first plane out.

"Oh, hi, Charity," Joey said. "I thought you were in England."

"I got back a while ago. Is your mother there? I want to catch her before she goes to work."

"She's here," Joey said. "Anyway, it's Saturday. She doesn't work on Saturdays. Wait just a second. . . . Maaaaaa," he bawled, and from somewhere else in the house Tonia answered, "Hello? Charity? Where are you? I just got your letter. You can't be serious."

"I'm in New York," Charity said. "Oh, that. Well, that's temporarily off."

"Now that's sensible," said Tonia. "What were you thinking of? I know you like Teddy, Chare, but ye gods. It seems built-in trouble to me."

"Something else came up."

"I hope you mean someone."

Charity ignored that and went on. "This does, though, kind of put me in a bind. Teddy and I had planned to live in his place, and now, with Lucille's apartment sold, I don't have anywhere to go. So. I have a deal for you."

"A deal? Well, good. No one's made me an offer in a long time." She laughed, hopelessly.

"You know that little garage of yours?"

"Our garage?"

"Yes. I was thinking I might live there."

"Our garage? But it's not livable, Charity. I mean, habitable. It has no heat or plumbing or anything."

"I was thinking that you could hire a contractor—I'd pay for it, of course—and we could fix it up. Into a little cottage. It would be adequate, I think. And then, when I move out, you could rent it. It would be an investment."

"But why would you want to move to Summerville?"

"I don't want to live in New York just now. Too many interruptions. I'm working on my novel again. It's an autobiographical novel."

"Oh. But it would take forever. The construction, I mean."

"You might offer the contractor a bonus."

"I don't really understand."

"I need to get out of New York just now, Tonia. I need to get my novel written. I'll send you a check today."

"But wouldn't it be simpler for you to come out here and rent a place?"

"I've already looked," Charity lied. "I was out with a realtor last week."

"I don't know why you want to do this. It seems so complicated."

"It isn't really. See if you can get the contractor to finish in a month."

"Ha."

"Remember the bonus. Is it a deal?"

"All right," Tonia said. "A deal. Listen, where are you? Where can I reach you?"

But Charity had hung up.

"Hi, Mrs. Carstairs," the nurse said. She had lank dark hair and glasses that slipped down her shiny nose. The white plastic name tag pinned to her uniform pocket said "Ms. Smith." "It's going to be a beautiful day once the fog lifts." Ms. Smith stuck the thermometer into Charity's mouth and reached for her wrist and now, through the partially opened door, Charity could hear the whole routine of the hospital gaining momentum: the PA system beeped and paged Dr. Clyde, Dr. Clyde, and the rattle of medication carts came toward her from down the hall and just past the door an orderly teased a nurse's aide about her new hair color and two doctors greeted each other and then Tom came in. Ms. Smith released Charity's wrist and extracted the thermometer and said brightly, "Good morning, Dr. Ferrier." Charity had noticed how all the nurses seemed to like Dr. Ferrier. They always said, as they plumped up her pillows, "Dr. Ferrier is a wonderful man."

Tom smiled and nodded good morning, and Ms. Smith adjusted the green and orange woven draperies and then with a shy smile at Tom and a shove at her eyeglasses—did she know that he was a widower?—moved out the door, the rubber soles of her white shoes going *squelch-squelch,* and her old-fashioned starchy white uniform rustling. This was an expensive modern hospital that insisted on old-fashioned standards. Like a first-class hotel, patients got the luxury of starch and courtesy and doctors like Tom Ferrier.

"How did last night go?" Tom said. "Did you sleep?"

"More or less," Charity said. "Oh, Tom, look at you. Why don't you get yourself some new clothes? You're Mr. Threadbare himself."

"You did sleep."

"Yes."

"That's very good, since you were off medication last night. Did you eat breakfast?"

"It was awful."

"Did you eat it?"

"Yes."

"Good. Now. What plans are we going to make for next week?"

"Sit down, Tom. I want to talk to you."

He sat, crossed his checked pant leg, linked his fingers around his knee, and sat back looking at Charity with dark, somewhat wary eyes. His gray shirt cuffs were frayed and the gray plaid jacket in no wise went with the maroon and brown checked pants. Sometimes, looking at him, Charity remembered with a sense of pain the first years they had been married, the little apartment on East Eighteenth Street, and the feeling, blissfully secure, of being attached to someone who was more or less required to like you.

"All right, Charity. What's up?"

Charity studied him carefully. He had changed very little in all these years. His brown skin looked a little creased, his black hair was handsomely flecked with silver. She said, "I've just called Tonia Durham."

A flicker of interest? curiosity? wariness? moved across his face, starting with a blink of his eyes that became a frown between his brows.

"Oh?"

"She's going to renovate their garage and I'm going to live in it."

He studied her silently. "Why?"

"Why? Because. I need a place to go."

"I see. And stay how long?"

"Till I feel strong enough to get out on my own."

"Does she know you've been ill?"

"No."

"You're not going to tell her?"

"Not right away."

"I don't think that's fair."

"Shush," said Charity. "I'll take care of everything."

"I think you should tell her."

"She might turn me down."

"That should be her decision."

"I have no place else to go." Charity looked down at her hands. She had given up smoking but was biting her nails again. The cuticles were ragged and sore. "Besides, financially, it will be to her advantage. She'll be able to rent the place later. She is rather hard up. Would you come out to see me?"

"Why?"

"Just to check. I'll pay you, of course."

He looked at her steadily. "No. I'll do it for nothing."

"I'd like to pay you," she said, and blushed. In her head, Dr. Walter said, "Reciprocity! Reciprocity!"

"I know you would. Let's just say I'll do it for old time's sake—for several very nice months we had together, a long time ago."

Charity looked away. "How's Alice?" she asked.

"Alice is fine," Tom said, lifting his head. "She's up in Jamesford, with Fred. She loves it up there. She drives Mary crazy, of course. Her bug collection gets lost all over the house."

"Spiders aren't bugs," Charity said.

Tom looked at her with raised brows.

"And how's Peter?"

"He's off visiting a friend before school starts."

"They're nice children."

"Yes."

"You've had a difficult time."

"So have you."

"You will do this for me, Tom, won't you?"

"Yes." He stood up, waved, went out the door, and in the hall she heard a high young voice call out, "Good *morning*, Dr. Ferrier!"

2

"Mom?"

"Mmm."

"What are you doing?"

"Just some figuring."

"Who was that on the phone?"

"Charity. She's back from Europe."

"Is she in New York?"

"I guess so. She didn't say. She's had sort of a strange idea. She wants us to do over the garage so she can live in it."

"Live in it!" Elizabeth's black brows drew together. "Why ever would she want to live out here?"

Today, a Saturday, Elizabeth wore white gym shorts and a T-shirt that had, emblazoned in rainbow hues in the dip between her little pointed breasts, a blurred mess that resembled old spaghetti stains but took on, with closer inspection, the approximate features of actual or unreal humans, a "group" called Fleetwood Mac. Red and white tube socks reached almost up to her knees and on her feet were the most important item in her wardrobe, genuine white leather Stan Smith Adidas tennis sneakers, which cost fifteen dollars more than Tonia thought anyone, even Stan Smith, should pay for sneakers: Old Mother Scrooge and her children.

"Because she's working on her book and she says she can't work in New York."

"I bet," Elizabeth said.

"What do you bet?"

"First of all that she can't work in New York and second of all that she'll ever finish her book."

"Maybe it's a long book."

"Oh, Mom. Charity will never finish anything."

"You may have a point. Still, maybe we ought to give her the benefit of the doubt. And besides."

"Is she going to pay us?"

"Yes."

"Well, in that case. And is that Teddy Vaughn going to live here too?"

"I think that's temporarily off."

"Good, because he would certainly be an embarrassment. I mean, I couldn't bring my friends home with that *fag* living here."

"Oh, Lizzie, don't be so hard on everybody. There are lots of things you don't know. You don't know he's a fag, and besides, even if he is, it's his business and Charity's business, not yours."

"It's my business if he lives here."

"No it's not. It's my business. I pay the rent."

"You and my father pay the rent."

"Your father didn't pay it this month, my friend. Seriously, do you have to say fag all the time? When I was a kid we didn't tell ethnic jokes and we didn't call people fags. That's cheap, Elizabeth. That's just a cheap little ego boost."

"Mr. La Crosse tells ethnic jokes."

"Who?"

"Our social studies teacher."

"In the classroom? Say. That's dandy. I suppose he's the stage show that goes along with those comic strip books you get. When I was a kid we had real books with real print. This is what I get for living in a Republican ghetto: social studies books with nasty pictures of the nasty inner city. Why is it I go on living here, I wonder."

"Because you can't afford for all of us to live in New York. Anyway, I'd never live in New York. It's crummy and dirty and the people are weird."

"Are you saying this just to irritate me? Because you are, you are really irritating me. Why don't you just go toddling off, okay?"

"You irritate me, too, so we're even. Why are you always picking on . . . my father?"

"I was not picking, Elizabeth. Okay. You asked for this. I was going to spare you the worry, but let me tell you right now that your father sent us half the usual amount this month. So. You can forget about Bloomingdale's this afternoon or any afternoon. If I have any money left at the end of the month I'll take you to Loehmann's."

Long long bitter look over her thin shoulder as she haughtily left the kitchen, her princess. God, thought Tonia, was I like that? In the living room, the jumble of shrieks, groans, buzzes, and other Saturday morning TV noises suddenly stopped.

"Hey, Mom," said cheerful Joey. He was ten years old, a plump sturdy good little kid still tanned from summer. "You look kinda weird."

"Thanks."

"What's the matter, don't you feel good?" His expression was cheerful, but there was something alertly anxious in his eyes and immediately, his brows slanted upward.

"I feel fine, shmoezo. A little old, but fine."

"What did Charity say? Is she coming out to see us?"

"She wants to move out here."

"With us? Where are we gonna put her?"

"In the garage. How's that? Is that all right with you?"

"Yeah, I guess so. Why does she want to do that?"

"I don't know, Joey, but she's going to pay to have the garage fixed up and she's going to pay us rent, so it's fine with me. Going to your lesson?" He had three tattered music books under his arm.

"Yeah. I think I got the rondo perfect."

"Ly."

"Huh?"

"You can play it perfectly."

"Yeah, that's what I said—I got it perfect."

Oh, Joey, thought Tonia, you are such a good little kid, but when I hear your off-key voice droning along as you play the piano, I am reminded that your father and grandfather were both of them tone-deaf. "Don't forget to lock up your bike, okay?"

"Nobody'd steal that old wreck."

"You'd be surprised. Some kids don't even have a wreck."

"Like who?" he asked, and shouldered his way into the

screen door, which had, at the level of his shoulder, a distinct bulge.

Oh, my kids, Tonia thought. They think they're the poorest kids in town and maybe this is true, but it is their town and they will have to adjust.

In truth, once divorced and declassed, she had discovered a whole different town lived beside the other town she had known, as the ghostly photographic image of a face, superimposed in double exposure, becomes quite another face, reveals another expression. It seemed to her now that the town had endless aspects, endless superimpositions, existed as a sort of horizontal archaeological dig. There were all sorts of people in the town, living all sorts of lives; there were artists and harpists and writers and even Democrats, and sometimes at night when she walked down the streets of the town she found herself doing what she used to do when she was a kid growing up in Queens—she would look into people's windows. She would see a lit window and be curious and touched by the little vignette inside: the elderly couple watching TV together, and the black family playing poker at the kitchen table, and the very fat lady in an upstairs window: her head, neck, arms, and bosom appeared and disappeared and appeared again—she was touching her toes. Tonia had a sense of life going on all around her in the town that was sad and funny and sustaining, and she had friends, most of them newly single: bad-mouthed Louise and funny Harriet and Grace from Warrenton, N.C., who ducked her head and moved her mouth sideways when she talked, as when she said (as she did often), "Ah ha-ad no *ah*-deah of what tuh say, so ah jes sa-yud, 'Sc-rew yew.' " Once at a party she had watched Grace carefully listening to a pompous ass—an ass who had made millions in the bond market, who would soon no doubt buy his way into high political office—and Grace had listened for all she was worth, lifting her little blue-green eyes admiringly to his rich, cunning, stupid face, when, in the middle of one of his declamations, she had reached over, and taking firm hold, unzipped his fly. Funny. How funny life is, Tonia thought. It was only that sometimes at night she dreamed that her children were dead and she woke up terrified. *Whoever you are out there: Don't touch my kids!*

She worried about her kids growing up in this town where there was so much and she was grateful, finally, for her own stern penurious upbringing. How to convey to her kids that their true home was not in this lovely town in a lovely house with pool and gardeners and Betamax, but somewhere inside themselves? So that no matter what—disaster, divorce, impecunity—they could live and look around and be curious and interested in life. She had faith in Joey, she worried about her daughter. Elizabeth had the Mercer variety of good looks, was tall and long-legged and thin, with delicate blond coloring and a pink flush that came and went in her moody face. Her eyes were dark-lashed and blue like her grandmother's. Tonia worried that her head would get turned, that she'd fall in love too young. In those little secret glimpses Tonia caught of her with her friends (as if Tonia were someone else and Elizabeth were someone else), her daughter never stopped laughing. Head thrown back, books clutched to skinny chest, eyes a black-veiled blue glimmer. It was only at home that Elizabeth was angry, an anger punctuated every now and then by the sound of a door—ouch! —slamming.

"Where are you going, my pet?"

"Karen's. I've got to get back the albums she borrowed for her party."

"Did you do the bathroom?"

"Yeees."

"And how about your room, my friend?"

"Yes yes *yes.*"

"And take out the trash, please, will you?"

"Okay, okay! I'm just a serf in this house, that's what I am."

And now leave, please, thought Tonia, because I have some telephone calls to make.

"Hi, Cissy. It's Tonia Durham." She used to play tennis with Cissy Boland light-years ago, more often against each other than with, for she never enjoyed being Cissy's doubles partner. If you dropped a shot Cissy glared, and if you lost she wouldn't speak to you for a week. Tonia twice saw her, when they were all four at net, smash the ball from five feet away into her opponent's sunglasses.

"Yes," Cissy said, her voice flat and indifferent. Tonia smiled to herself; she knew this tone of voice. It meant: You don't count. Poor Tonia Durham whose husband left her, no money, no status, works as a typist, not very interesting, had to drop out of the club.

"Is Bill there?"

"Bill?" Hostile pause. "He's playing tennis this morning. Can I take a message?"

"If you would. I'd like an estimate on doing over a garage. I want to remodel it—put in plumbing and some baseboard heat for a studio apartment. I'll throw in a fifteen percent bonus if he can get the job done before the end of October."

Bizness is bizness. A sparkle of interest—dollar signs went up like rockets, decimal points exploded like catherine wheels in Cissy's dead voice.

"I'll certainly tell him, Tonia. And how are *you*? I haven't seen you for *ages*."

"No. Well."

"I hear Elizabeth's growing up so pretty."

"It runs in the family, Cis."

Silence. Aw come on, laugh, willya? Tonia thought, and then—hostility is catching—hung up without saying good-bye. "Bitch," she said out loud to the telephone, and shrugged.

"Mother?"

"Yes?"

"Hi, it's me, Tonia. How are you feeling?"

"Who?"

"Tonia. Remember?"

"Oh, Tonia, I'm sorry—the TV's on. Just one minute." Her mother, a widow now, kept the TV on all the time, for company and to remind herself that six floors down and out there was a world with people in it. Her eyes were bad, her hearing had started to go, and sickness had left her frail. With her health precarious and her senses deteriorating, she was full of fear—of the boys that played around the apartment house grounds, of people with different-colored skin, of noises in the night, shadows, phantoms, shades, all sorts of things that once, younger, stronger, and healthier, she never would have worried about.

"How are you, Mother? How are you feeling?"

"Not very well. Not well at all." To prove it, she coughed.

"Are you taking your medicine?"

"It makes me sick, Tonia. I can't stand it. After I take it I can't eat anything." There was a whine in her voice. At this stage in their lives they had changed roles. Her mother wanted to be mothered and Tonia did it, but badly, she felt. She was too often impatient. She hadn't yet made an accom-

modation to this role reversal and realized to her shame that
she still often wanted a mother too.

"Have you talked to Dr. Graham?"

"Not lately."

"Aren't you supposed to see him this week?"

"I had to cancel my appointment. I didn't have the
money. My check didn't come." Lord, thought Tonia wearily. She and I, always sitting on the mailbox, waiting for our
checks. Sometimes, most of the time, it was just plain tiresome, not having any money. Tiresome and boring. Other
times it was infuriating.

"Listen, Mother, I'll send you the money."

"Oh, no, Tonia, don't do that. You need it for the
children. Don't you worry about me. I'll be all right." The
minor-key whine had modulated into the flat cheery major
of martyrdom.

"I'd much rather you saw the doctor this week. I'll send
you a check on"—she remembered suddenly that her checking account had in it eleven dollars and forty-one cents—"uh
—Thursday." Hell. What's one more overdraft? And then,
to her utter disgrace—why was she bothering this poor old
lady with her worries?—blurted, "Ben only sent half of the
usual payment this month. You know? The child support."

A silence. "Why did he do that? That's not like Ben.
He's always so dependable."

"I don't know."

Another, longer silence. All right, Tonia thought, I
know that when you get right down to it, you think it was
all my fault. Moody, demanding Tonia drove honest, reliable
Ben right out the door. How could I have asked more of that
wonderful man who for so many years supported me? If I'd
been nicer to him, I'd still be living in style instead of in this
tiny falling-down box with no man to look after me. That's

what you think and sometimes, but not very often, I think that too. And further, if I were living in style you wouldn't have to worry so much about me. This worry just makes you sicker (you said so once), and your grandchildren—why, your grandchildren could have the life I no doubt deprived them of: ten-speed bikes, designer-label jeans, tennis lessons at the C.C., and of course, a father. You never did believe that he left me. It just wasn't like him. "Mother, please make a doctor's appointment, will you?"

"I'll see." Another modulation, this time upward into coyness.

"Please."

"And how are the children?"

"Fine. Charity called this morning. She's back from Europe."

"And wanting something, I suppose. Funny how that girl is so rich but has never given you anything. What's she ever done for you, Tonia? She never even sends Joey a birthday card and she's his godmother. I never met anyone like that girl and I hope I never do again. With all her money she could have done something for Joey. Something."

"Joey's fine, Mother, he's just fine. He's a great kid, he doesn't need Charity. Now you call and make that appointment, all right?"

All these endless games, she thought, hanging up. The time I spend now coaxing her to take care of herself. It must run in the family. As the Mercers got older they developed an infinite capacity for sportsmanship. Her hard-eyed grandmother, for example, had kept on running away from her Florida nursing home. She'd pack up her little bundle of belongings and like an adolescent head out the door. They'd bring her back, she'd run away again. Finally, in a cold spell that killed all the juice oranges, she ran away and made it to an orange grove and was found, hard-eyed and mumbling and still alive, the next morning. Brought back and died peacefully in her sleep two weeks later. Amazing. Tonia's mother had cried. She'd always figured her mother hated the old lady, but she'd cried for days. At the end, hate or love didn't matter; it was part of your life wiped out. Her grandfather, on the other hand, had had cancer for two years and in all that time her mother went up only twice to see him. Couldn't stand his pain. So he died and the property went to pay off the medical bills and now, as far as Tonia could tell, there were no more Van Klocks, or Mercers, or Haseltines in Veddersburg and the town itself had shrunk to a few hillside streets. The tall-chimneyed mills by the river stood silent and empty, and broken windows caught the evening sun. Where her grandparents' house stood (white, Greek revival, 1830) there was now a McDonald's that boasted, in the food-bespattered and -dribbled parking lot, a plaque awarded for artistic landscaping; and across the street, where Mr. Jordan, the town's richest man, used to live (his house a stuffed zoo of antelope-tiger-bear-elk heads, rugs, antlers— walking through it as a kid gave Tonia an uneasy feeling, all those sad brown eyes watching from the walls), there was now a Kentucky Fried Chicken. When the last of her mother's childhood friends died, her mother went up for the funeral and could hardly find the town. They'd gotten urban renewal money. The main street was being bulldozed from one end to the other. She had watched them wreck the old Alhambra movie theater, which had started out in the town's palmier days as an opera house, the wrecker's ball swinging against dadoes, caryatids, columns, entablatures; scrolled brackets flew through the air, bricks, painted plaster. The five solid blocks of fanciful mid-Victorian (1840–1870) buildings—one Romanesque, one ye olde half-timbered medieval, one bastard Gothic, and the Moore Building, which had been, all arches and slender columns and minarets, Moorish —gone. The whole street leveled into rubble, flat as several acres in the South Bronx. A dingy little covered "shopping mall" had been put up so that the few remaining Veddersburghers could feel they were as spiffy and modern and elegant as, say, Livingston, New Jersey. Well, her mother had said practically, you can't save everything. But Tonia had felt . . . she felt . . . what was it she had felt? She had only spent childhood summers there, had no real connection, but she felt that her own past had been rubbed clean as a slate, with only a milky residue of clouded memory left upon it. Every summer these past few years she had meant to take the kids upstate but hadn't done it. Now there was nothing for them to see. How to teach kids to plan and work carefully, to take infinite pains, when looking around all they see is the instantaneous and the disposable? The past destroyed thus destroys the future. Ben had once told her that in the eighteenth century in England, estate gardens were planted to come to maturity in four hundred years. The security of a world based on inheritance and primogeniture. And where the hell are you, Ben? Oh, I wouldn't care, but these are your kids too, and despite everything, they need to love you, and I cannot bear—cannot bear—for them to think you've abandoned them. Again.

In her tattered address book, she found Miss Sarah Tornquist's home telephone number. Good old Miss Tornquist! Their relationship even before the divorce had been unsteady. From her windowless cubicle outside Ben's office in the hospital, Tornquist sat at her desk and ruled a tiny cosmos of telephones, typewriter, envelopes, paper clips. Mrs. Durham was just another interruption—Tonia with her

256

all too frequent messages: Elizabeth's temperature is 103; please be home by seven, we are going out; the car needs an axle, a wheel, a bearing; *I* need a bearing; our lives are falling apart. Tonia became, after the divorce, more than a mere interruption—the Enemy. Poor Dr. Durham! He had finally left that dreadful wife of his. Thank God she no longer demanded to speak to the Great Man; she only left messages with wispy, dry-voiced Miss Tornquist, who was fifty-four and unmarried and lived all alone in a small West Side apartment with a crippled mother.

"Who?" she said.

"Antonia Durham, Miss Tornquist. How are you? It's been a long time since—"

"Yes, it has," she said, cutting Tonia off. Tonia imagined that her voice was triumphant, as if all morning long she'd been sitting there waiting for her to call. Right there next to the phone so that she could say, as now she did, "I'm sorry, Mrs. Durham."

About what? God! Is he dead?

"About what?" Tonia asked.

"About Dr. Durham. I know why you've called. I don't know where he is. No one does. Everyone is looking for him. Miss"—sarcastically—"Sampson doesn't know, either." Poor Miss Sampson. If there was someone Tornquist loathed more than Tonia, it was Ramona Sampson, the doctor's—uh —well, his—uh. He had lived with her for two years. At least, Tonia thought, I get points for having been legal.

"Have you talked to Miss Sampson?"

"Yes, of course. She works here, you know. At the hospital."

"Yes."

"And apparently she has been living at another address." Oh, really? Ha. So she left him, huh? Good.

"I even went over there, Mrs. Durham—to his building?" Tornquist would. Good old faithfully trudging Tornquist, with her galoshes and umbrella and shopping bag, and little eyeglasses and clear plastic raincoat. "He'd moved out too, bag and baggage, without any forwarding address. No one knows where he is. He told no one at the hospital where he was going. I don't want to worry you, Mrs. Durham, but Dr. Durham has been acting peculiarly for quite a while."

"In what way?"

"These last few weeks he's seemed very—oh—depressed. He was scheduled to go to a meeting in Los Angeles and never got on the plane. I made the reservations myself. He just forgot. Now, that's not like him. He was always so reliable. We've notified the police."

"I see."

"If I can help in any way . . ."

"Thank you. . . . Miss Tornquist!"

"Yes?"

"How is your mother?"

"My mother? She died years ago, Mrs. Durham. Didn't Dr. Durham tell you?"

"No."

"Yes; I'm all alone now."

"I'm sorry."

"It's all right, Mrs. Durham, because you see, I have Jesus. I'm very active in my church; they're a wonderful group of people. You know, Mrs. Durham, when you've been consecrated in Christian fellowship you can bear almost anything. If ever you need a friend in Christ, Mrs. Durham, call on me. I'd be glad to take you to one of our meetings. I know you're all alone." Not quite, Miss Tornquist, thought Tonia. I still have my mother, my children, my sanity; but she said politely, "Thank you. That's awfully kind."

"And meanwhile," said Tornquist, "I'll send you some of our literature. I've often thought of you, Mrs. Durham, and how you could benefit from coming to know Jesus."

"In what way?" Tonia asked.

"Pardon?" said Tornquist.

"Skip it," said Tonia rudely, and when she hung up, smiled. She knew exactly what her bad-mouthed friend Louise would have said: "Oh, listen to that, will you? I'll bet a nickel she shits ice cream cones."

Sitting alone at the kitchen table (crumbs, milk splotch, sticky smear of jam where her arm rested, shifting trapezoids of sunlight through panes of window glass), now that the kids were out of the house she lit a cigarette. They accused her of trying to give them cancer if she smoked in their presence, so she was reduced to being twelve again and sneaking puffs when no one was around. Why didn't she stop smoking? She didn't know. Maybe because she'd stopped everything else. It struck her as odd that when she was married she was, in every way but one, unfaithful, and now, five years divorced, she was as faithful to her former husband, as maritally chaste as a noble lady locked into a steel contraption while her husband was off whoring and crusading. In fact, she thought that perhaps she was dead from the waist down, or that that part of her head where sex starts had been damaged.

She had gone one night, dressed in black velvet pants slung low on her hips and a white silk shirt unbuttoned down to *there,* to a singles bar with a friend. It was not a New York City Third Avenue scene full of glossy-faced optimistic youth looking for quick connections, but a very suburban singles bar, called by the locals the Meat Rack and crowded with middle-aged divorced suburbanites, but for a moment, sitting there at a table with Dolores, her divorced friend from work, she had the insane thought that she was in high school again and this was their high school hangout. Those same sidelong glances from the bar (instead of the soda fountain); two men, who should have been in basketball jackets but were wearing turtlenecks and tweed sports coats, eyed first them, then each other, and drinks in hand (were they still teammates? did they bowl together? why for God's sake, in middle age, do they still travel in pairs? Ben at least had the guts to get what he wanted all by himself), came over and introduced themselves, if that is what one could call it. In a sort of historical inversion, no one seemed to use last names anymore. A hundred years ago, it took people months or years to work up the ritual ladder from "How do you do, Miss Archer?" to the final downfalling rustle of petticoats. Now they were all universally reduced to the naked anonymity of first names: which implied nothing more, perhaps, than an easy pickup and a fast lay.

"Evening, ladies. Mind if we join you? My name's Bill and this fella, my handsome little friend over here, is named Luke." Friend Dodo had smiled, Tonia's expression would not yield. Bill's gray hair had been artfully cut in layers and his red fat face—German? Irish? who cared?—was good-natured and coarse. Small blue eyes which by some trick of focus looked simultaneously stupid and acute. Luke was smaller, dark, with quick oily eyes and large black-haired hands, and she had, for a moment, an image of one hand clamped on her own bare breast— five-eighths of a hairy-legged spider.

Her little moue did not go unnoticed. She was at once labeled the Snob and for the next hour or so, jovial Bill sat in the crowded aisle with a maroon-socked ankle planted firmly on his plaid-panted knee and, cigarette burning, referred to her (winks, leers, in fact he loved her snobbiness), while talking all the while to Dodo, as "yer snobby friend." The other fella said nothing at all. In Tonia's head, two millstones began grinding up brain cells; she developed a crushing headache. Felt responsible, however, for Dolores. Dodo was her age but dumb and Tonia had gone with her because she thought Dodo wouldn't know the ropes, was amazed, therefore, at how swift Dodo was on the rigging, much more at ease with those two (shall we say) men than herself. Dodo liked them, she thought they might like her, and Tonia saw on her face relief when, with hand to brow, in the ladies' room (pink poodle on the door, the poodle sitting up begging—for what? one wondered), Tonia pleaded: "Sinuses!" "Aw, gee! Sure, that's okay," said Dodo. "I hope ya feel better." And Tonia saw that she would stay and get crocked and then go to bed with one or both of these dolts and on Monday morning during their coffee break, give her a candy-coated, starry-eyed version of this sordid business.

Home again, the sitter discharged, the TV shut off, Tonia had a small Scotch—two and two—and felt nervous and angry (why? why? what had she expected? she was always so hopeful about people until it came down to particulars) and decided to read. She had brought home from the public library three well-reviewed books and, ecumenical to the core, noted that she'd picked out novels by (1) a Protestant, (2) a Catholic, (3) a Jew. The Protestant's elegantly written book claimed to be a love story, but she knew that the next morning the only thing she would remember about the heroine was the color of her pubic hair. The Jew was very funny and thought he was writing about sex when in fact he was a moral didacticist: he had the ancient Hebraic urge to educate and uplift his women, but unfortunately, his female characters were stupid to begin with and she felt he was in for a lifetime of disappointment—you can't make a silk purse, etc., etc. Still, his women were pleasingly, recognizably human. (Or was she, after all, prejudiced? Her mother had married a Jew and they had been happy together.) The Catholic, like so many Catholic men of a certain generation, had not discovered sex until he was forty and divorced and had thereupon become fascinated by the texture, taste, and smell of several hundred vaginas, which he swore were as different from each other as individual snowflakes. Was he right? She didn't know. She had always had a somewhat utilitarian relationship with her own apparatus: there it was, poor lost lonely thing. For years during her marriage it was so squeezed, fondled, stroked, desired, that once in a fit of true exasperation she had threatened to cut it off and leave it permanently in the *letto maritale.* She had asked him, her ex-husband, why? *why?* WHY? he could never leave it alone and he'd looked—well—puzzled. Now, after many noons of dryness, it—her part—still insisted on recapitulating her girlhood themes: the primacy of selection. It did not, rather to her disappointment, want just any old cock. It wanted the instrument to be attached to somebody, some one, some body-mind-soul male she could not only crave but love honor respect. Tough luck, Tone, she said to herself. You had your chance. She knew, furthermore, that she had that regrettable thing—a feminine sensibility. She thought that women did err on the side of sentiment, smothering over just plain old sex with a nauseatingly thick valentine glob of chocolate sauce schlock, but men, on the other hand, protected themselves from their feelings by surgery—detaching parts. It was easier to deal with a part than a whole, easier to deal with a cunt than a mind or a heart. Whenever Ben had to deal with her, he thought he could do it in bed.

Now that the kids were well out of sight, she got out the catalogue from California, which she had, for the nonce, slipped under the morning newspaper. Thought it might be nice, comforting even, to have some sort of sensation between her legs just to prove they, she and the part, were still alive. Madame Tremblefingers opened the plain-covered wrapper and peeked, heart bumping, at page one. There, printed in inks that did not reproduce well, was a composition as complicated and unhealthily bluish in color as a basket of fish-market squid—here a leg, there an arm, half a breast (this was, she guessed, a threesome), the curve of a profiled buttock, and somewhere in the melee, a simple arrow emerged from a scraggly circlet of hair and wanly aimed toward a pinkish wound, which wound was crowned with a thin wreath of brown curlicues—poor porno starlet! The hours she must spend getting her bikini area plucked, shaved, waxed. Tonia tried to think: What do I feel? Tentatively, she wriggled her bottom on the bottom of the hard kitchen chair and glanced up at the kitchen ceiling (cobwebs, flaky paint) and thought: Let's see. What do I feel? What was it she felt? A buzz? A tingle? She felt . . . sad.

Once with a friend (it was fashionable that year) she had gone to see *Deep Throat,* two divorced, suburban mothers deep in obscuring wool hats, tinted sunglasses, scarves—disappointingly, they hadn't met anyone they knew. Sitting there, tensely waiting to be turned on, in the Forty-second Street theater that smelled like all the movie theaters of her girlhood (popcorn, Hershey bars), and glancing around every now and then to see who in the dark theater was diddling with what, she thought, watching the dopey proceedings, that it was boring. Boring and sad. No one laughed or even smiled much; the poor performers went through their motions with the listlessness of panda bears imported by zookeepers to breed. Morosely, she had thought: Shouldn't this at least be fun? I regret now, I regret—what is it I regret? That night, Ben, when we came home from the dance, it was late May and suddenly warm and the mock orange was in bloom and I had worn a pink-flowered red dress, cut low, with thin straps and a flounce like a Spanish dancer's, and I was pleasantly high (you were laughing; I heard your low laugh and your feet on the driveway's gravel as you came around the side of the car to half lift, half pry me out), and as I stood leaning against you with my head on your chest (you held me up by the buttocks—you always did keep such a firm grip on my ass), I slid my fingers between two buttons of your shirt and entwining your chest hair around my fingers said, leaning against you and smiling, "Oh, let's go right upstairs and do nasty things." If cells have a memory, then Joey's cytoplasm remembers the night he was conceived. Now, alone in her bed, on those rare nights when her part demanded some sort of attention, it amazed her that (with her nightgown hiked up to her waist, and her finger slipped in to her own wet depths to stroke that burning spot which, at last having been made to tauten, quivers, comes) it was Ben's face she imagined in the second before climax, Ben's face, then emptiness. Then to turn over and, dry-eyed, fall into sleep, a heavy sleep, the sleep of one dead. A part—a cunt—can be satisfied with mere vigorous manipulation, but the ache in the bosom (old-fashioned phrase—she was an old-fashioned woman) was not so easily brought off.

3

"My God, Chare, you look . . ."

"Awful?"

"Well, yes, I suppose that's the word."

Charity smiled, a smile as pale as the November sunlight

thinly spilling through the almost leafless boughs of the maple trees. She had gotten out of her car so slowly and with such noticeable trouble that Tonia had taken from her the small overnight bag she carried, and as she did so, Charity staggered. Tonia caught her hand and firmly held it.

"Hey. Are you all right? You're not sick, are you?"

"I'm all right," Charity said, and withdrew her hand. She stood still for a moment, looking around. "Oh, it's pretty out here. Look at that—your roses are still going."

"It's been a mild fall."

Tonia saw that Charity stood still because she could not yet go on and she looked at her closely. She had lost a great deal of weight. Her reddish hair was thin and colorless and large black sunglasses hid her eyes so that her small face, rubbed to the jawline with cosmetic pink, looked even more frail. Charity had been very ill—with something. Another one of her breakdowns, maybe. Two or three times in the eighteen years Tonia had known her, Charity had disappeared into hospitals or institutes for living, to emerge paler, thinner, shaken.

I don't know, Tonia thought; how do I get into these things? Mother sick and Ben missing and now I've got her on my hands too. Sometimes I just feel too tired for any of this. With very small steps, Charity was walking toward the back of the driveway and the converted garage.

"I don't know if you'll like it," Tonia said, walking watchfully beside her. "I hope you will."

"Of course."

"I'm sorry it was so expensive. I had no idea what construction costs would be."

Charity stopped and looked at Tonia coldly. "I can afford it."

Tonia smiled. "Yes. You've got your inheritance. How does it feel?"

Charity looked up at the sky and the sun winked and flashed from her dark lenses. Reflected in her tilted glasses Tonia saw the top of the cedar tree suspended above them, as if about to topple.

"It doesn't make any difference. There's nothing I want to do." She turned and went on, slowly, toward the transformed garage. It was an old building, perhaps a hundred and forty years old; no one seemed to know exactly when it had been built, or what its original purpose had been. Too small for a carriage house, it had been simply another outbuilding on the large estate that had, in 1959, been demolished to make way for a subdivision of small houses, in one of which Tonia now lived. The little building, its facade bowed like a wishbone, in the nineteenth-century Gothic style, and done in board and batten siding, with, just under the apex of the arch, a dovecote, had been made into a garage by the first owner of Tonia's subdivision house. Was it he who had planted the wisteria vine or someone years before him? The large vine grew up and around the little white building and now rattled its long empty pods in the breeze. Even leafless and flowerless, the strong curve of the vine lifted Tonia's heart. She had made Bill Boland take special care of it and she saw now with pleasure that everything she'd had done was right. The two overhead garage doors had been replaced with long shuttered windows on either side of a wide Dutch door. The door had fine strap hinges. Skylights in the roof. In my next life, thought Tonia, I will build houses.

"It's very nice," Charity said dryly, and Tonia was disappointed. She pushed open the door and stepped aside so that Charity could admire the high bright room. A stone fireplace opposite the door, a tiny immaculate kitchen built into one wall, furniture all slipcovered in yellows and greens. Charity sat down without seeming to notice and huddled into her raincoat as if she were cold. "I'm sorry," she said dimly. "I'm so tired. Do you think Joey could bring in the rest of my things?"

"Of course," Tonia said. "Look. Really. Are you all right?"

Charity said, without looking up, "No, but there's nothing to be done about it. I am just . . . sick, that's all."

"Is it what you were sick with before?"

"I've had it for a while."

"But what is it?"

"Lupus."

"Lupus?" Tonia was astounded. And didn't believe her. "Lupus! How long have you had it?"

"Oh"—Charity looked vaguely around—"a couple of years. I wasn't going to tell you. I thought you might not let me come out here. You see, I don't have anywhere else to go. You are my only friend."

Who? thought Tonia. Me? She thought of Charity, when she thought of her at all, as someone who had barely touched her life. She had always been amused by Charity and felt protective toward her, but believed they were merely on parallel tracks through time.

"I'd like to rest now," Charity said. Her head hung down, drooped like that of a wilted flower. "I thought I'd do better than this, but the drive out was exhausting."

"If you need anything," Tonia said, "you can just call me on the telephone. It's there on that desk. I put some things in the kitchen—coffee, tea, sugar. I'll shop for you later if you want. Chare? Charity?"

She had fallen asleep.

Leaving the little cottage, Tonia thought: Lupus! I don't know. It doesn't seem to make sense. And then hurried the fifteen yards or so into her own small house. The wind had picked up. The November sky seemed to be at war with itself, half raging gray, half defiant blue. Sometimes, she thought, I don't think I can handle one thing more.

This month, in the letter from lawyer Amy Kornblau, there were two checks enclosed and no indication etc., etc., of the whereabouts of said client. Still, he was obviously alive somewhere and presumably well enough to get together the dough for the child support. Sometimes she thought it would be a relief not to get these checks, to have no contact whatsoever with this phantom who so dutifully, so punishingly doled out money to her. No sense, though, in cutting off one's nose. Kids have to eat. Look at that sky, will you? I have always loved fall, these moody Eastern autumns with their somberness or silver-bright days. I will bake an apple pie, do it my mother's way with a crumb crust instead of pastry and baked in a brown paper bag in a hot oven. I will . . . She looked around. Elizabeth stood in the doorway. Her daughter had on very high wedge heels, which forced the upper half of her body into a dangerous tilt, while in compensation her still flat derriere stuck out under the curve of her spine. This unattractive effect was enhanced by a very straight narrow skirt slit up to God knows where and a blouse unbuttoned to meet said slit. Cheeks pink with her mother's wild rose blusher and a strong smell of her mother's favorite, very expensive perfume. Her look was at once brooding and saucy. Young lady, I should tan your hide. How to deal with your adolescent's sexuality. Good God, I can't even deal with my own.

"Where on earth are you going?"

"Over to Karen's. She's having a party after the game."

"You're going dressed like that?"

"Why not?"

"Elizabeth, it's a Saturday in November. Halloween's all over."

A blush under the blusher; chilly glimmer in cold blue

eyes. "I know what day it is, Mother. Besides, I'm not *forty,* you know."

Why, you rat. "Elizabeth, do not leave this house in that getup."

Rudely, her daughter laughed.

"I mean it. No go-ee out door, kid, or you'll be much sorry."

"What am I s'pposed to wear? You were too *cheap* to let me get that suede skirt. Or maybe"—she flung back her long blond hair, cocked a knee, and with one hand on hip was ready for fisticuffs—"it's the old mother-daughter thing."

"Huh?"

"Maybe you secretly don't want me to look too good. You know? Because of your *age.*"

So. She'd been reading again. How to get along with your aging mom, who naturally hates you. Tonia crossed her eyes, and arms outstretched, pretended to fall, crucified, upon the kitchen counter.

"Oh, Mom, will you stop it? You think you can get around everything by clowning. Be *serious.*"

"Why? Okay. Seriously, don't you have anything more appropriate for a post-football-game party? We all know you're beautiful, my pet. You can afford to be subtle about it. I mean, give these poor boys some credit. They may not look too smart, but I'll bet one or two of them think you're terrific."

Her daughter glared. Tonia knew well that how-dare-you look of hers: You! her daughter is thinking, you who have done everything wrong with your life. And she's right, of course, Tonia thought. I can't, haven't been able to get my own life in good order, if there is such a thing. My own hypocrisy slays me. Luckily, Tonia knew that after reason and humor both failed, there was always, simply, No. Another old Mercer tradition. Her hard-eyed grandmother once broke her mother's little finger—slammed at her hand with an old-fashioned black iron skillet when her mother was thirteen or so. Her mother! Who had always been so demure and good.

And after all, what advice can she give her child, culled from her own long life? The only thing she has learned is this: the punishment never fits the crime. One lady in upstate New York got thirty-to-life for doing her husband in with a kitchen knife, although at the time he had beaten her blind with a baseball bat, and another lady, same prison, from Brooklyn, got one year on work release for hiring a killer to gun down her mate for insurance money. There are other punishments, most of them internal and equally unjust. Some people, heinous criminals, remain unmoved by the acid of sin etched upon the quartz of their souls; other people wallow in sin and write pious profitable books about it; still other folk, picayune sinners, for crimes imagined or unknown, spend years in a hell of their own devising. What advice, then, can Polonia give to her children? Life is not just; life is unpredictable; there are no rules; some things you can't think out. Find some work you love to do and someone you like to love. Still, life will fool you. Here I stand, living proof. I have made too many mistakes. I have lived too much by my feelings. I have trusted too many times. I have been weak too often when I should have been strong, and hard of heart when I should have felt tenderness. I can't give you advice. It's everyone for his/her self. Laugh once a day. Be generous of time with your friends. Laugh at yourself. Don't live just by your feelings. I made a mess of our lives. I was vain, I was egocentric, I didn't see, I didn't see.

"Do you think," Tonia asked her daughter, "you might stay with Jamie tomorrow?"

Elizabeth stared at her. "Jamie?"

"Joey, I mean," Tonia said quickly. "I want to go in and
see Grandma. I'm worried about her; she sounds pretty
sick."

Defensively, Elizabeth blinked, and her eyes changed
from bleak to sad. "Sure," she said, and went off, gently, to
change from tart to teen. Tonia sighed, thought: *Jamie.* Now
where did *that* come from? and stared for a long moment out
the window. It had started to rain.

4

It seemed to Tonia that the fall passed in streaks of silver and
shadow and she found herself wondering, sometimes, if she
were not, after all, a very old woman lying in bed waiting for
death, and with half-shut eyes saw her life passing before her
from childhood to grave, not in a series of images but in swift
alternations of light and dark. It was a sad fall. Joey, missing
his father, had fallen into silence, and Elizabeth was edgy and
mocking and seemed to challenge Tonia on everything—
schoolwork, clothes, friends—until her nerves felt raw and
her patience, long since used up, resembled an old coat,
frayed and sent to the cleaners and returned one size too
small.

"The bastard!" her friend Louise said. Louise was divorced, wiry, black-haired, tough. She was proud of the fact
that she could sleep with almost any man and enjoy it. Or so
she claimed. Why can't I? Tonia wondered. What's wrong
with me? I've read all this fiction out of the sixties and California and all I remember is . . . what she remembered was

nothing at all but his sickish sweet smell and the pressure of a thumb on her throat. "Shit," Louise said. "*He* disappears and the kids blame *you*, of course. What an old ploy. I'd sic the cops on him."

Harriet Desmond, also divorced, said, "Tonia, come *on*, shape *up*. Look around, will you? There are lots of neat men in town. Don't think about Ben. Does he worry about you?"

Charity lived ten yards away but Tonia seldom saw her. Fridays, Charity drove off in her white Porsche (behind whose steering wheel, Tonia thought, she looked like an elf from some Bavarian forest), to reappear on Sunday night. Once Tonia knocked at the door of the little cottage and Charity grudgingly let her in. The place was littered with newspapers, books, ashtrays full of butts, glasses half full of something stale, and coffee cups with tan circles of residue that sported bluish mold spots. All three of the plants that Tonia had put in the long windows had died and hung from their hooks as if from gibbets. Heaps of dirty clothes were strewn on chairs and the smell of the place—of unwashed clothes, cigarette smoke, lack of air—made her feel nauseous. As she stood there, a black kitten leaped up from nowhere onto the kitchen counter and began licking at a greasy bowl.

"What's that?" Tonia said, startled.

"That? It's a cat."

"I didn't know you liked cats."

"I don't. I thought it was your cat."

"I don't own a cat. Huh. I wonder where it came from?"

"I don't know. He hangs around and that's all right with me. He doesn't bother me much."

The cat was pretty, with one white paw and a dab of white on chest and chin. Well, thought Tonia, if she can tolerate a cat, maybe there's hope for her. Still, who could

live like this? Charity was pale and looked at Tonia with such
surly suspicion that she uneasily left. What is it? Tonia
wanted to ask her. Why are you looking at me like that? They
avoided each other. One night, coming in the kitchen door
with two bags full of groceries, Tonia saw a note on the table
in Charity's small handwriting. "Tom Ferrier coming out
Saturday night. Will you cook? 7 P.M. C."

She read it and smiled and something delicately
twanged inside her, like a bass fiddle string tentatively
plucked by a mere passerby. She began putting groceries
away—four boxes of cereal, peanut butter, canned soup, tuna
fish—and thought with sudden pleasure of the dinner she
would cook: it had been months since she'd cooked a good
dinner. Let's see, chicken Vallée d'Auge, whipped potatoes,
a spinach salad with mushrooms, or perhaps romaine with
slices of orange and a bit of rosemary, and for dessert, something light after all that cream and calvados—a lemon fromage. And to start, why not a soup instead of hors d'oeuvres,
a homemade Russian mushroom soup with a bit of dill and
a shake of paprika and a tiny dot of sour cream—Tanya's
recipe; I haven't thought of her in years.

And what to wear? She hardly thought of clothes for
herself anymore. Her velvet pants? No, too—uh—flashy.
Something ladylike; her old bottle-green velveteen skirt, a
shirt of palest coral silk to match the coral earrings that, Lord,
Ben had given her so long ago. And I wonder who Ben's
living with now. Must be someone, since apparently he's
alive, and knowing Ben, two nights without it and he's off
his feed. Ow, dammit. Where did that come from? Got to
clean this pantry out sometime. Well, two can play at that
game. Just because . . . just because . . . And wine: Taylor's,
Gallo, or Almadén? Haven't had French wine in years.
Doubt he's a wine snob, anyway. Good old upstate New

York. Simple food! Steak, roast beef, fresh corn rushed in from the garden, asparagus. Maybe, instead, I should have steak? No, men always cook steak for themselves; besides, it's expensive. What am I doing, planning a seduction?

She put the last jar away and thought: Yes! Exactly what I am doing. Wonder what he's like now. His smile and the way, all those evenings, in that cluttered Eighteenth Street apartment, a current of understanding had run between the sofa where she sat and his chair; and his shoes and those slumpy black socks and the way, when Charity left the room, he would suddenly stand and walk around, looking at everything. She smiled and Elizabeth, coming into the kitchen, said, "What's so funny?"

"Nothing," said Tonia, and Elizabeth glared. Elizabeth was in love with a boy who didn't love her and no one who lived with Elizabeth was allowed to laugh, smile, or even glance in her direction.

I wonder, Tonia thought, if he has changed. His wife, Charity said, had died in an accident. Drank. She remembered now, dwelt on his gravity, his sweetness, his smile, and most of all, that for nearly a week she thought she had loved him. And had always liked him and wondered now why Charity was going to all this trouble. Perhaps a good sign. These past few years Charity had lost interest in all her friends and acquaintances. Her illness, no doubt. She thought of Charity's pale sullen little face and the way, those few times Tonia had seen her getting in and out of the Porsche, Charity had looked at her so coldly, menacingly. And didn't know why. Illness changed one. It occurred to her that for several years now she hadn't really liked Charity, but because she kept on appearing in her life had continued to accept her because, oh, for old time's sake and—she glanced swiftly out the window—the money. Yes. That was it. Charity's glamorous money. Not that she wanted any of it. She had only thought that perhaps Charity's money, like gold leaf clinging electrostatically to a brush, might somehow brush off on her, enlarge her little world, which was so constrained with pedestrian concerns—food, mortgage, heat, schoolwork, getting along from day to day. She had thought that when Charity got her money she would bring into her little world (a little world all nailed up, it seemed to Tonia, with bars taken down from dollar signs) a scent of delicious freedom, travel, luxury—and here was Charity, the same but worse, saying: "It doesn't make any difference." If I had an eighth, a sixteenth of that money. I could take the kids skiing, I could travel a little, I could . . .

No use in that. Senseless. She had learned that long ago, after Jamie. We are all right. We will be all right. I have the kids, my mother, my sanity, my friends. Every night, although I don't pray, I plead with whatever it is: Don't harm my kids. My dark bargain—you can have my inner life, whoever you are out there, have everything I once cared deeply about. I have given it all up and ask only this: Don't touch my kids.

For a long time after Jamie died, and even after Ben was gone, Tonia was subject to sudden blanks of time—a strange whiteness accompanied by a deafening silence—when she thought of her elder son. It could happen anywhere; in the middle of a morning, at dinner, between dessert and coffee, shopping in some sterile supermarket with the Muzak playing, she would be seized by terror and have to stop and hold on to something—a table edge, a counter, a shelf. In time, these attacks lessened in duration, although not in severity. One day the year before, while at work, she had gotten a call from the school nurse. Joey was sick. She left her desk and went in to talk to Mr. Schletter, the supervisor, and then drove to the school in her ten-year-old station wagon. The car was rusty and dented and the chrome trim strips had long since departed and her kids were ashamed of it. In the school office they told her that Joey had gone home—he'd felt better and decided to walk.

She drove along the street, a surge of kids running on both sides, then turned down the narrow dirt lane in back of the school playground—she thought she saw Joey's orange sweater. She parked and got out of the car. The school grounds were filled with kids running, footballs flying; a soccer ball bounced along the packed rutted dirt field and she saw the orange sweater at the edge of the playground and then it disappeared into the trees. She walked through the yard, shading her eyes against the sun—it was late fall—and looked into the little woods near the school. Far down at the end of the ocher woods she saw a blond boy in a striped T-shirt and Joey. The blond boy had his arm around Joey's shoulders and as she watched, the boys looked at each other and smiled. She saw that the blond boy was Jamie and the boys laughed and ran off through the trees, over the stripes of tree-trunk shadows that lay on the ground, through the russet and gold and tan woods. She ran after them and called Joey's name, stumbling over tree roots and into sudden depressions that held rusted cans and broken bottles. She saw them, ahead of her, go through the gate of the yard nearest the school, where a large chained dog snarled and a clothesline held stiff gray clothes. When she got to the yard the boys were gone and only half a block later breathlessly caught up with them, two boys not Joey and Jamie at all but utterly, astonishingly different. They looked up at her with alarmed eyes, this crazy wild-haired lady.

She drove home, and through the glass of the kitchen

storm door saw Joey sitting at the table, his head in his hands. He said dully, his face red, his eyes fever-bright, "Hi, Mom. Don't be mad. I didn't want to make the nurse stay late." And he never knew why she seized his head and pressed it to her and stroked his hair for such a long time, or why, after she had put him to bed, she sat next to him in the darkened room not saying a word.

5

"Tom!"

He arrived with a bunch of yellow daisies wrapped in green tissue and, tucked under his other arm, a bottle of red wine. He had on a baggy raincoat and she noticed as he stood there, ceremoniously wiping his feet, that he still wore rubber-soled shoes. He was shorter than she'd remembered. She could, without any difficulty at all, look him right in the eye. "It's so nice to see you! Come right in! Isn't this awful weather! Charity's not here! She decided to go away for the weekend!" Babble, babble. The house, small as it was, seemed suddenly much too empty and she was as conscious of their aloneness as she once was at seventeen on a Saturday afternoon when Danny Reilly came by and her mother was out. "My kids are both gone for the evening—Elizabeth's at a basketball game and Joey's staying at a friend's house." Oh, Lord. Was that the wrong thing to say? He'll think I set it up to se-se-se— Christ, Tonia, will you calm down? The poor man will think you're crazy. Just relax. Pretend it's every Saturday night you se-se-se— Why is he looking at me so strangely?

He pointed. "You have a bit of soot on your cheek."

She peered into the mirror over the mantel. Sure enough, having made the fire herself—it hummed and crackled seductively in the grate—she had to mess up her carefully prepared face with a bit of soot from the damper. What to do? If she washed off the soot, half her face would be drab au naturel, the other half Elizabeth Arden pink. She put her hand to her cheek and gaily smiled. I'll seductively just smear it around a little so it blends in—a bit of wild gypsy along with sedate English pink—until I can get upstairs to my dressing table, in the bedroom, in the bed— Oh, why don't you just get your mind off the sack and pay attention to him? Look. He is a widower. He has teen-age children. He has, in that hospital of his, lots of young nurses he can— "Would you like a drink?"

He stood looking into the fire, rubbing his brown hands together as if it were twenty below outside when indeed it was warm for November and damp.

"No, thanks, Tonia. I don't drink anymore."

Doesn't drink! Doesn't drink! How am I to get through this without a drink? If he doesn't drink, can I? Oh, my God, you mean I have to take off my clothes stone sober? Maybe he's near-sighted.

"Glasses?" He looked at her curiously. "No, I've never worn them. I wonder why you'd remember that? In fact, my father is over seventy and can bring down a bagful of ducks without any trouble. Well. It's really been a long time, hasn't it?"

"Yes!"

"It doesn't seem that long ago."

"No!"

Silence. She was better at this when she was seventeen. When she was seventeen she didn't care and there was always, just around the corner, somebody else and carelessness had made her glib. Oh, yes—she remembered herself well —she had been a terrible tease; she'd been good at that. Where the hell is Charity and why, after setting this whole thing up, had she disappeared? Matchmaking again? She must be feeling better. Oh, but I'm a flop at this. I'm too old to kid around and what I'd really like to say is, Look, fella, after a point I can't be seductive and I passed that point when you walked in the door.

"Well. I am going to have a drink," she said, all smiles, and toddled off to the kitchen. Of course, she'd already had one—no, two—and as she poured Scotch into a clean glass her hand shook. It'll be all right. Think about *him.* Poor guy! Raised those two kids, Charity said, mostly alone. Wife in and out of rehabilitation centers. She fumbled in a drawer for cigarettes. Bet he doesn't smoke, either. Eats wheat germ. Practices yoga. I'll bet he jogs. No. I don't think he does any of those things; I think he's a nice man who works hard and is tired and he certainly didn't come out here to see Charity, Tonia, and just last week, Tonia, Steve, the mechanic down at Exxon Central—he's many years younger than you, babe —said, wiping his hands on a greasy rag, "All set, Mrs. Durham," and then, one brawny, black-haired arm resting on the edge of your open window, stooped and said without smiling, his dark hair falling forward, "I'll bet you wouldn't go out with just a grease monkey, would ya?" Silence. You were shocked. Sure you would, but not blackmailed into it by a sentence like that. You said, hoping to just sound surprised, "Aren't you married?" and he gave you a wiseacre look and shrugged and tossed the rag into a barrel and walked off and next day you switched to West Side Shell.

With this consoling thought, Tonia the Seductress moved confidently back into the living room, stumbling only once on the way and sloshing only a little Scotch on her bottle-green velveteen skirt. Ask him about his kids. Ask him about his work. You remember all those articles (don't you?) on how to talk to your date *(Seventeen, Glamour)*. You must have read a thousand or so when you were a girl. The fact is, though, Tonia, you are not a girl anymore and you are suddenly tired and when you come into the living room, he is lying aslant on the sofa with his head back and his eyes closed and his hands knitted together upon his chest and his mouth is agape and he seems to be, is, sleeping. There. He, too, is tired and maybe, just maybe, he will be too tired.

Silver, crystal, candlelight, yellow chrysanthemums in a low white bowl mixed with his yellow daisies. "This is fantastic," he murmured, but only poked at the sauce she had lavishly poured over the chicken: he had a gall bladder problem. Even the lemon fromage was left untouched. He didn't drink coffee after six o'clock. She had no Sanka. Plates cleared, they went back to the living room; she carrying brandy for one. (Say, aren't you drinking a lot? Three Scotch-and-waters, three glasses of wine, and now the brandy. What do you want to do, throw up?)

The living room was a pleasant brown-toned swirl, shot through somewhere in the center with what she thought might be the dying embers of the fire. They sat down and stared at the glow and suddenly he smiled—he hadn't yet smiled—and she remembered that moment at the top of the tenement stairs, which seemed so near in time, so far, and he asked about her kids, her work, and brimful of alcohol, she talked, and his deep brown eyes were so sympathetic, his long face lengthened (and suddenly, Tonia, you are blurting out all sorts of things, drowning in the morass of his understanding, and you want to say to him, terrified, Oh, don't!

Don't let me do this, give me a little distance, be ironic, say something funny, laugh—will you please just laugh? I don't want this to be deeply lugubrious, you have troubles of your own.).

But he had asked, and she had told him, horrified at herself, and then, alarmed, said: Smell that? Something must be burning, and weaving just a little, left the room.

She stood at the sink in the kitchen. Often, Ben would come up behind her when she was at the sink, her hands helplessly gloved in suds, and would rub up against her and sneakily put his hands on her breasts and say something filthy into her ear. This always made her indignantly scream and he would say, to tease her, "Ah-ah-ah. Watch your voice. You don't want to strain it."

"A lot you care about my voice."

"Your voice is all right, but your ass is fabulous."

Standing there, leaning against the sink, her cold hands held to her burning cheeks, feeling half or wholly drunk, looking out the window into the yard's autumn blackness, she began to cry. Salty tears slipped across the Elizabeth Arden and mingled with the rubbed-in gypsy soot. She remembered his ringing laugh and how, just when every-thing would get bogged down in feelings, he would come out with some awful crack, some piece of rueful nonsense that would restore the balance. Always, in the beginning and for many years after, he could make her laugh.

"Are you all right?" Tom Ferrier asked soothingly from the doorway.

"I'm fine," she said somewhat coldly, and put a bent wrist up to wipe her eyes, gritting her teeth because she knew this would get the mascara. Oh, well, she thought wearily, I don't care. And the truth of it was, she didn't care, which is what she realized standing there with her face turned away.

She did not care. She could not whip up so much as one ounce of lust for Tom Ferrier. Regrettably, she had no desire for him. No desire at all.

So that, having discovered this, she became gay and careless and talked pleasantly on many worthwhile and interesting topics and even got him to talk and the evening passed. Elizabeth came home and was her best public self instead of the broody teen, became before Tonia's very eyes a proper young lady (whew!) who shook hands, practically curtsied. At eleven, he did not suggest that they retire together but instead politely rose. Would she care to go out some evening, to dinner and a concert? The opera, perhaps. He had, believe it or not, become interested in the opera. She smiled. A music lover. Not that it made any difference. It made no difference at all. Life seemed to her suddenly, wearisomely mysterious—we never want the people we ought to want. *Misterioso! Misterioso!* There was no explaining love or desire. Once she knew she could not love him she was ready to like him and said at the door that that would be very nice and then asked, "Is there anything special you think I should do for Charity?"

"Do?" he said. He was struggling into the raincoat and she held one shoulder of it, this raincoat so baggy, so rumpled, so in need of a cleaner's attention, with one dejected button hanging its head—any other, less hardhearted woman would have loved him on the spot.

"I mean," she said, "because of the lupus. It is treatable now, isn't it? I know they use steroids, though the treatment I guess is exhausting."

"Lupus?" He sarcastically smiled. "She does not have lupus."

"She doesn't? But she told me so."

"She does not have lupus. Physically, she's fine."

"But . . ."

He sighed. "Tonia, you've known Charity all these years. You must know that sometimes, often, Charity doesn't tell the truth. She invents things. She *lies*. She does not have lupus."

"She seems so sick."

"She's had a difficult time and she is on a lot of medication. It makes her shaky."

"Funny. Now that I think of it—yes, thinking back, she'd often do these odd things. Like the business about the apartment when I first met her. Dragging me into that. I never understood it. And then you two getting married so suddenly."

"She was pregnant."

"Oh. She lost the baby?"

"She had an abortion." He said this matter-of-factly, but stared at the floor. "She had another abortion in West Virginia."

"But she told me—this was years ago, in New York— that she'd been sick and couldn't have children."

"No," he said. "That was a lie."

"Oh."

"Well. Thanks for the dinner. It was one of the nicest evenings I've had in a long time. I'll call you next week." He smiled at her, but how time had tempered that brilliant smile and what a sad smile it was. He brushed her cheek with a kiss and opened the door. The November wind rushed in, sweeping before it a crowd of gabbling leaves. She waved to him quickly and he waved back from the car. She shut the door against the wind. There. It was over. Well, she hadn't seduced him, but maybe after all it had been a pleasant evening.

6

"Tonia! How are you?"

To her surprise, Phil Merkle had instantly returned her call, and he sounded so fervent that she was wary.

"I'm just fine, Phil. And how are you?"

"Terrific, terrific. How are . . . the kids?"

"Fine, growing up. I'm calling to ask if you could help me with a small problem."

His turn to sound wary, but he said, "I'd be delighted to try."

"My mother's at your hospital. She's going to have an operation on Tuesday and I want Elizabeth to see her. The problem is, they don't allow anyone under sixteen on the ward. I thought that maybe since you were on the staff there, you could, frankly, use your influence somewhat on my behalf."

"I see."

"It seems such a stupid rule."

"I agree. It is a stupid rule. I'll tell you what—the surgery's scheduled for Tuesday?"

"Yes."

"What ward is she on?"

"She's on the fourth floor."

"And who's the surgeon?"

"Dr. Petrie."

"Have you talked to him?"

"I tried. I couldn't reach him."

"I see. Well, look. Suppose you and Elizabeth come in tomorrow, say at twelve. How's that?"

"Oh, that's fine."

"I'll call Petrie and all that business. What's he doing?"

"Pardon? Oh, you mean the operation? It's a resection of the right ventricle."

"I see. All right. Tomorrow at noon, then. I'll meet you at the information desk. And how are you, really? It's been . . . what? Seven years?"

"Yes."

"Incredible. Time flies."

"Yes. I'll see you tomorrow in the lobby. And thanks."

"Right-o."

"Many thanks."

"Anytime, love."

She wished he hadn't said that last.

His hair was smoothly combed but had turned completely white and if before he had often appeared colorless, now he seemed not so much bleached as drained. Life, the vampire, at work? He had divorced Laura, left Summerville for New York, and married the icy-voiced secretary. Laura had moved out of Summerville too and lived somewhere in Somerset County with several horses and many dogs. Tonia had seen her once or twice downtown. They had passed each other without speaking. Laura looked the same—still beautiful—but as if her features had been encased in some sort of ambergris, so that without definable change, they had become harder, set, as if her living face were a death mask. The eldest boy, Tonia had heard, was always in trouble—car theft, drugs—and had been in and out of boarding schools; the middle daughter was away at boarding school too, and little Kitty, who was Elizabeth's age, lived with her mother and went to a private day school. Elizabeth had met Kitty at several teen-age parties at Christmas time and when Tonia had asked about her had only shrugged. Tonia had seen Kitty downtown, sitting on the curbstone in front of the train station with a bunch of kids. She was a beautiful girl but already, at thirteen, jaded-looking, sitting there in jeans and a gauzy embroidered Mexican blouse, and a kind of smeared dopey look, smoking something or other.

"So here you are!" Phil said, and took her hand and smiled into her eyes. She let her face smile; her eyes wouldn't. "And this is Elizabeth!" He looked at her daughter keenly, and releasing her hand, took Elizabeth's. Elizabeth blushed and looked away and something smote Tonia's heart. Had Elizabeth guessed or was it only the tender way Phil looked at her? She had made Elizabeth put on a dress, stockings, high-heeled boots, so that she looked older, sixteen at least. When Phil finally let go of her hand, Elizabeth scowled and looked down at the rubber-tile floor.

He said smoothly, "I doubt there'll be any problem. I'll go up with you now and steer you past Mrs. Lanier. She seems stern but she's quite nice, really. Elizabeth, you're my Kitty's age, is that right?" He pressed the elevator button. Red-cheeked, Elizabeth muttered yes and to Tonia's irritation would not look up. Hadn't she always taught her children to look people in the eye when spoken to?

"Kitty is such a pretty girl," Tonia said, and the elevator arrived.

"So she is, so she is," Phil said gaily. They stepped in, he pressed four. On three, an elderly man in a wheelchair was brought on by a nurse's aide, and at four, when the elevator trembled to a stop, Phil took Elizabeth's elbow, saying, "Here we go!" and Tonia, amused now, saw that her daughter sensed what she had missed, that Phil had become that saddest, funniest of creatures, a dirty old man, and she saw suddenly his life at home with the icy-voiced secretary and thought: Well, so it goes.

At the nurse's station they stopped; Phil leaned over the

desk and spoke to a tall black-haired woman with the physique and posture of the Samothrace Nike. "Hi, Mrs. Lanier," he said soothingly. "How are you? Haven't been on this ward for quite a while. This is Mrs. Durham and her daughter. We're just going in to see her mother, who's a personal friend of mine. How's everyone on the floor? Did you finally get rid of Mr. MacGregor?"

Mrs. Lanier had a smile as cold as marble. "Oh, yes," she said in a deep voice with a British accent. "He had us all in chaos for a while, climbing in and out of windows." She glanced piercingly at Elizabeth and said, "Is the girl going in too?"

"She's seventeen," Phil said quickly. Elizabeth looked up. Tonia thought: Oh, hell. Why didn't I think of that? Just lie, that's all there is to it.

"Fine," said Mrs. Lanier curtly, and set her chiseled face to some charts she was checking. They all walked down the hall together.

"I'll leave you here," Phil said at the door to her mother's room.

Tonia held out her hand. "Thanks so much, Phil."

"No problem. My pleasure." He glanced at Elizabeth, who steadfastly refused to look in his direction.

"A lovely girl," he said, giving Tonia's hand a squeeze. "It really was lovely to see you again. Perhaps we'll have lunch together sometime." But he didn't mean it, for he didn't wait for an answer, and his arm, as he turned, lightly brushed Elizabeth's arm. Elizabeth looked up at her mother with cool furious eyes. Tonia pushed the half-open door of her mother's room and they went in.

"I hate him," Elizabeth said.

In the hospital bed nearest the door slept the room's other occupant, a very old woman who lay in the bed fetally sideways, who looked as brown and shrunken as the thousand-year-old corpse of an Indian found magically preserved in some Southwestern cave, whose long frizzled white braids needed combing and whose emaciated body gave no sign of life or breath. Tonia had the strange impression that the old woman's breathing had become disassociated from her body, for while this old lady peacefully dreamed, seemingly breathless, her mother's labored breathing filled the air with its gasping intake and wheezing release. She seemed asleep, although the hospital bed had been raised partway. On the adjustable table was a tray with a full hospital breakfast, oatmeal, fruit, juice, tea, cold and untouched.

"Mother?"

Her mother half opened her eyes. They looked small, sunken, and pale in color, more gray now than blue, and her skin, too, looked gray, with a hint of mortal lavender.

"How are you?"

Her mother shook her head and gasped. It was difficult for her to talk.

"Here's Elizabeth to see you," Tonia said, and her mother opened her eyes again, smiled briefly, and then relapsed into her halfdaze. Her lungs were filled with an accumulation of fluid; her circulation was failing; her heart was too tired to pump anymore.

Tonia sat down on the chair next to the bed and put her hand on her mother's arm, which had, these past few months, become thin as a stick. Elizabeth stared at her grandmother angrily. Why did I bring her? Tonia wondered. There was nothing to say, or too much, and Tonia felt now that Elizabeth's coming was a mistake, that it was pointless and wrong. The things she wanted to tell her mother she couldn't say with Elizabeth in the room, and was it possible, even, to say those things out loud? To say, Perhaps you are going to die, and if you die, we will miss you forever and ever? No, it certainly wasn't possible; you could only sit with a hand on an arm, meaning, in wordless communication, We are here, we love you, we wish you didn't have to suffer this way; and meanwhile Elizabeth stood at the end of the bed, would not touch her grandmother, and looked surly. She will be silent and angry all the way home, Tonia thought, and when we get home, she will slam all the doors. If Joey were here he would be silent and sad. If Jamie had been here, he would have cried and then, on the way home, been cheerful. If Ben were here, he too would look angry, and going home, he would drive too fast. There is too much I want to tell you. I will come back tomorrow, alone. I love you. I admire you. You have always seemed to me one of the bravest people I have ever known. She lightly squeezed her mother's arm, and in a doll-like response, her mother's eyes flew open. She looked at Tonia, gasped, and with an awful effort smiled, then her eyes closed again.

Driving through New York—it had begun to rain, a chill autumn rain—Elizabeth was silent and the windshield wipers ticked as regularly and soothingly as the beat of a healthy heart.

Just as they bore right off Thirty-ninth Street to go down the ramp into the Lincoln Tunnel, Elizabeth said, "Charity says he was your lover."

Oh, Lord, Tonia thought, and the car seemed to veer to the left all by itself so that she narrowly missed the staunch little line of yellow traffic cones closing off a lane of traffic. Easy now. She straightened the tail of the car and slid into the waiting poisonous jaws of the tunnel, whose dirty white-tiled walls always reminded her of something nastily reptilian. Easy now.

"Who is it," Tonia asked, stalling, "that we're talking about?"

"Dr. Merkle."

"Oh. When did Charity say that?"

"I don't know," Elizabeth said, staring ahead of her out of the windshield. "A while ago."

"I didn't know you ever talked to Charity."

"Sometimes she walks around outside. In the afternoon, when I get home from school."

"I see."

"Was he?"

"What difference could it possibly make?"

"A lot. Everyone in town thinks my father was a creep to leave you the way he did."

"I don't think everyone thinks that."

"Yes they do."

"I think most people are smart enough to know there are two sides to every—"

"Oh, bull, Mom. He left you alone with two little kids, just after Jamie died. That's what everyone thinks."

"That's what he did do. That is a fact. I think it's odd Charity told you that."

"She doesn't like you."

"Did she tell you that?"

"No. Okay, that's wrong. She *envies* you."

Tonia laughed. "Is that so? What is it she envies?"

"I don't know," Elizabeth said sulkily. "Your life. She said to me once she wished she could have your life."

"She's welcome to it," Tonia said dryly, and then, glancing at her daughter's set face, knew it wasn't true. Indeed, if she had any life, it consisted precisely in this exasperating child and her brother. "What else does she talk about?"

"Nothing much. She talks about Maine a lot. She said Dad used to be a good sailor."

"How would she know, for heaven's sake?"

"They went up to Maine together, once before he met

you. That's what she said. They went sailing together." The old station wagon had climbed out of the tunnel now and into a gray drizzle studded with traffic lights. "Is it true?"

"That they went to Maine together? I don't know. Maybe. So what?"

"Not that," Elizabeth said. "Is it true about Dr. Merkle?"

"I can't discuss it now, Elizabeth. I've got to get us safely onto the turnpike."

"Then it must be true."

"All right! No. It is *not* true."

Elizabeth glanced at her mother scornfully. "I don't believe you," she said, and turned her head and looked out of the car's side window.

In the morning Tonia got up while it was still dark and left the house to drive into the city. They had moved her mother from the fourth floor to the eighth, where the operating rooms were located. The sides of the bed had been put up, so that as Tonia looked down at her, her mother seemed to resemble a long thin elderly baby, very thin—so thin that the white plastic identification bracelet dangled loosely on her wrist. Her mother seemed asleep but her breathing this morning seemed lighter, easier, or was it, Tonia wondered, that she had already surrendered? Wake up, Tonia silently told her, please wake up. I need to speak to you before you go, and her mother opened her eyes.

"Tonia," she said weakly.

Tonia sat down, and put her hand through the side rails of the bed and felt her mother's hand. It was cold. She remembered, when she was little, coming in on a cold winter's day, how her mother had always taken her hands between her own and chafed them to warm them. Other chafings as well. As a girl and young woman, she had resented her mother's lapses into honesty, her chafings. She saw them now as warming. Who else would ever care enough about her to chafe her?

She said, "Later today you are going to feel so much better."

Her mother tried a brief smile, but only looked exhausted, then said, with much effort, "Thank you . . . for bringing Elizabeth. Tonia?"

"I'm here," she said.

"My . . . good girl." Oh, don't, Tonia thought. Please don't. I cannot break down now. I don't want to cry. I have to be cheerful and strong for both of us. I need now to give you strength.

"I want you . . ." her mother said, and it was like a command, "to be happy."

"Shush," Tonia said. "Maybe you shouldn't talk, Mother."

"Forgive . . ." her mother said, and then came a long terrible fit of coughing, followed by long rattling intakes of breath, the lungs straining to fill and release, and her mother closed her eyes, and her face constricted with effort.

"Don't talk, don't talk," Tonia said, feeling close to panic, afraid that she would die here, before the operation, before giving herself a second chance at life. Then the contorted face relaxed and she seemed to have fallen asleep. Tonia sat next to the bed with her hand on her mother's arm until the nurses came to prepare her for the operating room. Who? Tonia thought. Who is it I am to forgive?

She went downstairs to wait. The hospital lobby was full of people—black, white, yellow—every shade and disposition of the human race, alone or in groups, smoking, drinking coffee, reading, knitting, staring, sitting dumbly watching the floor. A Puerto Rican family had brought all five of their young children and the children were making a holiday of it, whining for snack bar food, playing in the corridor, crying, tugging at sleeves, pinching each other, running, throwing apple cores, and occasioning rapid outbursts of Spanish from their parents, who seemed to take turns at discipline. The old lady who sat next to Tonia, very white and pink and blue-eyed, smelling of face powder, tut-tutted loudly at them from time to time. "The very idea!" she said, glancing at Tonia, fishing for middle-class sympathy. Two plastic chairs away, a very old man, in hat and coat, sat hunched forward, one hand on top of the other on the head of his cane, looking into some other time, some other place, and quietly crying. The hospital walls were a depressing blue-gray, the floor tiles dark blood red. A young black man in jeans, black leather jacket, beret, mirrored sunglasses, chewed gum and held a transistor radio up to his ear, and across the room, a black man dressed like a pimp, in cape, high-heeled boots, safari hat, and shoulder bag, read a paperback book. The hospital PA system mercilessly chimed and droned. Hours passed. She heard her own name paged at last, and went to the telephone at the nurse's station and was told, on the telephone, to go upstairs. As she got out of the elevator, a young nurse, chart in crook of arm, dark hair in bun, said, out of a wide worried face, "Mrs. Durham? Your mother just died. Would you like to see her? They've just finished cleaning her up."

The door opposite the elevator opened and a nurse with a sweet oval face beckoned to her, and another nurse pushed aside the white folding screen. She walked and walked and walked the few feet toward the open door and entered the room, and turned past the starched pleated bosoms of the two young nurses and stood at the side of the narrow hospital bed and looked down at her mother. Even after she was grown, her mother was taller than she, and how was it that now in death she looked so small, so thin, so immensely old, her sticklike arms sticking out of the hospital gown and her face—her eyes were still open—ugly. Plainly now against the ashen skin you could see the dark hairs of an old lady's mustache over lips already turning blue. Dead. She closed her mother's eyes. Cold. And ugly.

The sweet-faced nurse said, anxiously, "Are you going to be all right, Mrs. Durham?" Tonia knew they were afraid that she was going to cry and that would make it difficult for them, their days were already so long and full of misery and pain, and it was awful when the patients' families cried, but she wanted to say something to them, for whom her mother was only another ugly dead old lady, and she said, while the two young nurses looked worriedly at her, "You see"—she wanted them to understand, so she went on stutteringly—"you—you don't know, you can't imagine, how beautiful she was when she was young." And then turned her head and looked a last time at her mother, who was not now her mother but a thing, and walked away.

They gave her a brown paper bag full of her mother's clothes. She went downstairs and sat in her parked car and cried. When she got home, she spilled the contents of the bag out upon the kitchen table and the little sealed envelope of valuables she'd been given looked suspiciously flat and when she tore it open, neither her mother's wedding ring nor her diamond engagement ring were inside, and outside snow had begun to fall in long oblique white strokes. She told the children. Joey sat with bowed head and silently cried and wiped his eyes with the heel of his hand. Elizabeth's face went bright red and she slammed the kitchen door and ran upstairs and slammed her bedroom door. Tonia sat for a long time with her arm over Joey's shoulder and found herself, childishly, longing for her mother. She wanted (and the thought amazed her) her mother to comfort her, now that her mother had died.

7

At her mother's funeral dinner, the Jews sat at one end of the long table, the Catholics sat at the other, and the sturdy upstate Protestants—all two of them, flown in from California—sat in the middle. Ken Weingarten, the son of David, the son of Alfred, sixteen and tall and thin and dark and intense, sat in a corner with his chair tilted back and talked to Elizabeth, whose pink color came and went and whose black-lashed blue eyes, so much like her grandmother's, sparkled with a vivaciousness that was entirely seemly, thought Tonia. Her mother would have smiled at this little adolescent dalliance and said—Tonia could hear her wry voice—"Life does go on."

Henry and Nancy Van Klock had, well, long wanted to come back East and see New York again, and Tonia, who had imagined they would look like the Grant Wood painting, a grim couple, backs straight as pitchforks, found instead two Californians, tanned, blond, lightly freckled, in tinted sunglasses and radiant smiles and pastel clothing. They loved the Coast. Why didn't Tonia move out with her kids? Tennis all year round! Swimming! Avocados! Tonia smiled and shook her head and couldn't tell them how much she loved the East and how much more beautiful (of course, no one would believe her) she thought green New Jersey than brown California. Besides, she'd never much cared for Spanish architecture.

And there were the Catholics from out of her Queens childhood. The Heideggers, now both gray-haired, although only a few years older than Tonia, both very fat and oddly loving with each other, and the Hallorans, from the house on the other side; they had prospered and together with Joe's sister Irene had bought a house in Douglaston and moved all five of their kids out there and everything was fine, Margaret Halloran said, except of course, she added, voice lowered, she wished to God *she* (Joe's sister Irene) would let the kids alone, not a minute's peace or privacy, always butting in where she wasn't wanted, thought the kids were her very own although she had never been married. You had to feel sorry for her, her whole life spent "in service," working as a cook for some rich lady in New York City who had only lately died and hadn't left her so much as a nickel in her will.

There was a large contingent of ladies from her mother's apartment house, who all sat together and had a bit much to drink, and how to tell these people, most of whom tactlessly asked, that she did not know where her children's father was presently located? Going home, Joey said, "Gee, that was fun, Mom—the dinner, I mean. I wish Dad had been there," and when she carefully drove into their driveway (everything was coated with snow; Elizabeth and Joey were both asleep in the back seat), she glanced toward the end of the drive and saw that the long windows of Charity's cottage were lit up. The small snow-covered house looked like a New England cottage, a seaside place in Maine, and suddenly as if she actually heard a click in her mind, she felt a piece of the puzzle move into place.

. . .

She knocked twice, lifting the heavy knocker and letting it fall. "Charity!" she called through the door. She stepped to the side and tried to peer in through the long windows, but the snow fell thickly against the panes, already lay heaped in the mullions' corners, and inside, the draperies were closed tight against the darkness. She took out her key and opened the door.

"Charity?" she called as the door swung open.

The door fell back, the lights were all on, there was no answer.

"Charity?" she called again. She pushed the door closed behind her and looked around. The room was extraordinarily neat, everything put away, no clothes, papers, books, ashtrays—not so much as a matchstick left out—but still the air had a foul, dead, rotten smell, perhaps, she thought, from being closed up.

She called out again, and walked across the carpeted room and pushed open the bathroom door. She flicked the light switch—nothing. The bathroom was empty, the mirror stared back at her, the porcelain tub and oval sink gleamed softly at her, wiped clean. She snapped the light off again and turned, went to the closet and pushed back the louvered sliding door. Nothing. No clothes. The empty hangers swung with a faint tinny music as she pushed shut the door again. Charity was gone. Of course. Stupid of her not to notice the Porsche wasn't parked in the drive. She had noticed only the lights behind the draperies, and now as she looked around the room she saw that things were not quite in order after all: the shade of the lamp on the desk was slightly askew, like a party hat on a drunk, and when she moved to adjust it she saw, held in place by the rubber feet of the telephone, a list of telephone numbers and she took the list—it was what she'd been looking for—folded it once, and put it into her coat pocket. Everything else looked—wait. In the kitchenette, things had been knocked over into the sink; a plastic bottle of detergent lay in a pool of its own green gel, and a plastic drinking cup lay on its side, and on the floor a Brillo pad.

She bent to pick it up, then saw, straightening, that one set of draperies hung crookedly, they were in fact off their hooks. As she walked toward them, she saw that the woven yellow draperies had been torn and were threaded in many places, and as she stood there, fingering the material and looking curiously up at the drapery rod, she noticed that the window mullions had been gouged and scratched. She pulled the drape aside for a closer look. The window, too, was scratched, and as she bent close to it, she moved her foot slightly and it struck something soft, and lifting the drapery up she saw just inside its hem, soft but very stiff, its paws already rigid in rigor mortis, the little kitten. Its white chin was streaked with blood, and its lips had pulled back so that its teeth were exposed; its amber eyes were open. Dead.

She turned and left the cottage, closing the door behind her. She walked through the snow and up the steps to her kitchen and inside went straight to the telephone. She dialed the first number on the list of numbers she had taken from the desk and her guess was quite correct. When he answered the telephone in faraway Maine, his voice was faint. She had to shout across the miles. "Ben, it's Tonia! We must see you! The children and I need to see you!" And he agreed to come.

He flew down as he said he would and stayed in a motel in town for two days. She had longed to see him, and standing there in the airport, watching him walk toward her, a big man swinging a small suitcase, felt almost foolishly happy. He was, on the other hand, reserved, and steadily refused to look directly at her. To Tonia's surprise, Elizabeth was cool to her father and when they were together, out to dinner, chose to sit next to her mother, and once or twice, Tonia felt her daughter's arm brush comfortingly against her. Strange, she thought. How strange kids are.

Just before he left—they were to drive him to the airport —Tonia asked him to come see their house. He had avoided it but he quietly consented. Joey, brown eyes alight, raced up and down the stairs, bringing his father school papers, airplane models, compositions, everything he had had an interest in the whole long fall. Elizabeth said coolly that she had to go out, to Karen's. After Elizabeth left, Ben stood in the little living room with his back to the fireplace, looking around. Tonia, too, looked around, pleased. She wanted him to see the house as she saw it, small, shabby, but a home— the clock ticking on the mantel, fall flowers on the table in front of the mirror, a bowl of polished apples. She wanted him to see . . . what? Not that she'd become independent (oh, God, she thought, we are all dependents; without her children she would have died or gone mad), but that, after all, she had survived. He stared at a print they had bought together in Germany, when they were first married (the river Main, a castle, a bridge), and then looked out of the windows, which were, it was true, much too close to their neighbor's house, and he said, "I'm sorry."

"About what?" she said.

"About this."

Abruptly, she sat down. "You mean the house?"

"Yes. The house, everything."

"But it's a lovely house."

He smiled ironically and shrugged. Funny. She had wanted him to see that she had made a life, maybe not much of one, but a life it was certainly.

"I'm sorry that things are so difficult for you." He sat down too, on the sofa where, a few weeks before, Tom Ferrier had fallen asleep.

"Everyone's life is difficult sometimes." He looked at her. He had on a brown-and-white-check wool shirt, open at the collar, and heavy, old-fashioned tweed pants, and high thick yellow boots. She had known from their first few minutes together that whatever feeling he once had for her was gone, and looking at him now, a tall, ruddy, healthy man, she saw, for her part, that the phantom she had slept with off and on all these years was exactly that: a phantom. Memory's cruelest trick. She had forgotten how crushed he could make her feel.

He said, "Did Charity tell you?"

"No. I found the telephone number in her cottage. I suppose . . ." She dropped her head. It was none of her business. "What is it you do in Maine?"

"I paint."

"You paint?"

"Yes. Watercolors." He smiled. "I've sold a couple."

She said, surprised, "But what do you live on?" Then blushed.

He said, "Oh, the money. I knew we'd get back to that. The money."

"I just wonder how you live."

"And if your next check will arrive."

"Don't, Ben."

"Don't what? Don't send the money?"

"Yes."

"My. You have changed."

She had decided even before he arrived not to argue—no matter what, to forbear—and she said calmly, "I have a thought about that. A proposal."

"Oh, good. Is it a modest proposal? I send you no money, you send me the children instead. To eat, I suppose."

"Yes."

"Yes, what?"

"I want you to take the children for the summer."

He looked away. "I see."

"They very much need that from you. And I—I need . . ."

"What?"

"Some time to myself." It wasn't true. What would she do all summer without her kids? But in the long run, what would the kids do with only a money-sending phantom father?

"There are some complications. I'm getting married."

She hadn't expected this and she hadn't expected to be quite so stung. "Well. That's a surprise. Congratulations. She's rich, anyway."

He frowned. "Rich?"

"If crazy."

"What?"

"It's not Charity?"

"Charity! Good God, no."

"But you're living at her place."

"I am renting her place. That's all." He stood up. "It's time to go. I can't miss this flight or I'll miss my connection to Rockland. I'll think it over and let you know."

"All right." Was he not even going to tell her? She said, "Who is it you're marrying?"

"Ramona." He shifted and put his hands in his pockets and jingled his change. "I suppose my idea was not to get married at all, but she's young and she has the right to . . . Well, I didn't want to lose her."

"Yes."

"I don't expect the kids to love her, but they seem to like her."

She wanted to say before he left how sorry she was, but it wasn't quite what she meant. She didn't feel apologetic; it was only regret for a past that in many ways had been good. She said, instead, "It's funny how life goes on. I always thought that when I got to be forty it would all be over and here I am still wanting to live, every minute."

"It was what I first liked about you, the way you wanted to live. The way you never wanted to give anything up."

"And you . . ." she smiled. "I liked your steadiness."

She thought it odd, later, thinking it over, long after he was gone, how the things they had liked about each other—those very same qualities—had, in the end, driven them apart. But surely they had learned from each other too. She had had to learn steadiness, and he had . . . why, hadn't he finally stopped marching?

Charity had gone for good, it appeared, and had forgotten to pay the contractor's final bill. Tonia's mother had left her a little money, but in January, when there was no check from Ben, and Bill Boland sent another bill, stamped in red "Second Notice," she at first regretted the foolish thing she had done. Of course she needed Ben's money; she always needed money. Instead of a check, there was in that mail a long letter from Ben to Joey and Elizabeth, asking them to come to Maine for the summer. He had always spent summers in Maine as a boy and he loved it. He would teach them how to sail. They would go on picnics to the islands. They would pick blueberries and dig for clams and early in the morning, before the fog had lifted, they would fish for mackerel. She sat there, at the kitchen table, reading the note and she felt wonderfully lightened, as if, after all these years, seven years, something had lifted.

She thought: Yes, he has stopped marching.

Elizabeth was on the telephone at the other end of the kitchen, saying, "Yeah, seven's fine. Wear jeans, okay? I've got this neat leather vest. Oh, and did I tell you? I'm going to Maine this summer. Go ahead, slobber with envy. . . . Uh-uh, my father. Uh-huh—isn't that super? I don't know. Wait. Mom?"

"Yes?"

"Where are you going this summer? You said you were going somewhere."

Tonia lifted her head. Suddenly, she felt taller, gayer, capable of girlish things. Her future seemed to her as full of promise as that of a young girl in a fairy tale who has endured seven years of bewitchment and finds her life at last magically restored to her. He had stopped marching. They had forgiven each other. They could forgive themselves. They were free of each other, at last. She felt, sitting there at the kitchen table, enormously happy, so happy that she might even sing, and certainly, certainly would fall in love, and she turned and said to her daughter, over her shoulder, "I'm going to New York. I'm going to sublet a place in the city, just for the summer."

8

These were the things then, Doctor, I had in my room when I was ten: twin beds covered with ruffled dotted-swiss spreads, a bureau, a desk. A bookcase with the usual girlhood books (Cherry Ames, Nancy Drew) on the top shelf, all pulled out with Prussian exactitude so that behind them there was room enough to hide my dirty pocket book collection, which I had bought, one by one, from Dorinda Snyder's older brother. The Grolier Children's Encyclopedia. *Cabbage Leaves,* a book on sex "for the older child," which contained many line drawings with plump pear-shaped organs coyly inserted here and there and that seemed to have no relation at all to my own simple stalk of a body. I kept at the back of said book the blurred photograph I had taken in Maine with my Kodak the summer I was nine, taken at great personal risk to myself, of a large black bull with nose ring and notched ear, mounting a sleek sedate clumsy black cow, whose tail switched furiously the while and whose eyeballs continuously whitely rolled. My impression was that her performance was a little stagy, the lady did protest too much, although esteemed professors at Harvard have since concluded that feigned female reluctance is not limited to the animal kingdom but remains an integral part of nature's scheme—goading on the poor male to ever bigger and better display, encouraging him to ruff up his plumage, roar, strut, parade, cackle his love song, whistle, hum, make more money, or inflate the air sacs upon his feathery breast.

As for the Maine coast, I hated it. It was chilly and boring and often too foggy, and one morning when the sun had at last appeared, my father took me out for a sail in our fifteen-footer. He had brought along (for warmth, he said) a flat vaguely convex silver flask that fitted the curve of his back hip pocket—I could see a glint out of the corner of my eye whenever it was lifted—and we sailed, so buoyant was the sea and his mood, farther and farther out of the blue bay on a brisk little northeast wind until the islands, which were really rather far apart, began to resemble broken-linked chains of stone that seemed to me to be saying, in a kind of visual Morse code: "Fare-thee-well! Good-bye-for-ever!"

I was lying prone under the jib, half asleep in the sun and spray, when a lurch made me roll, and opening my eyes, I saw slowly opening before me the foamy jade green jaws of a twenty-foot trough of sea water. It was like looking down the side of a sheer glassy green mountain. God, I was scared. We were well out of the bay now, in deep ocean, for all I knew, halfway to the Hebrides. I had read too much as a child and saw myself, of course, washed into the Port of New York (orange peels, bloated dead cats), frozen, with frozen eyelashes, lashed to a spar. Had not, at that very moment, a cheerful lobsterman appeared, with a sputtering two-way radio, a chugging motor, and a long tow rope (yes, we were ignominiously towed back; I loved my father, but God knows he was inept), we would certainly have drowned.

Sometimes, Dr. Walter, Harvard professors aside I understand enough about myself to know that I am marvelously attracted to small inept men, and I remember how my mother (it was blue and salmon twilight when we returned) stood at the end of the high dock (the tide was out), her white dress aflutter in the evening breeze, a martini glass in her hand, and flirted with the burly lobsterman while casting on my father a cold snigger of a look. Percival Jones, our caretaker, was at last allowed to take down the flags that we flew from the end of our dock: Old Glory, and underneath, the Bayards' own standard, a red star on a white circle on a navy ground. I went right past my mother, up the dock to the path to the house, and to the kitchen, where, with a cry, I sprang into Irene's arms.

I suppose it was sometime in the next year, the year after my parents died, that I noticed things were missing from my room. The Grolier Children's Encyclopedia left quietly, volume by volume. My camera. My watercolors, first the pinks and reds, finally the murky umbers. I asked Marie, the maid, but she simply stared at me and shook her head. The Monopoly game disappeared, and the Chinese checker set and the dart board and the indoor ring toss, and my dolls were reduced in number to five, then four, and I was afraid to tell Lucille about it because I knew she'd think I was crazy.

In that year after my parents died, I had gotten in the habit of coming home from school and, like any ordinary kid, heading for the kitchen. Irene would be there, sitting at the kitchen table, with the *Daily News* spread out before her, her elbows on the table, her face in the palm of one hand, exclaiming and clucking over the wantonness and infirmity of man and womankind. I would have graham crackers and milk and we would discuss the crimes of the day together, me pulling my chair closer and closer to hers all the while, finally letting my bare arm brush hers until she would say in a grumbly voice, "Ah, now don't be gettin' so close; it's hot enough in here to cook a goose."

I wanted to tell her everything that had happened to me at school, how I'd been cheated of an A by dumb Miss Baxley and how Peggy Rue had not asked me to her birthday party, but she only grunted and would go on tch-tching over the world at large or talk about her brother's family. They lived in Queens. There were five children. For fifty cents I would have ridden out there and dynamited their crummy abode. At every possible opportunity—birthdays, Christmas, Easter, Holy Communion—Irene would ride the subway out to Queens and take pictures of this freckle-faced group of hoydens, who, she claimed, were the best, the brightest, the wittiest children in the whole world, not one bit spoiled or whiny or demanding (like guess who), and the goal of her life, it seemed, was to live in the very same house with these hooligans and watch them grow into adulthood.

Sometime in that year Irene began to complain about

her feet. Cooking all day made her tired. Her back was all give out, her arches ached. One day I was in the white-tiled bathroom off the kitchen (it was the servants' bathroom; I was in there secretly trying out a Maybelline lipstick I'd bought at the five-and-ten) when I heard Irene's low grumble, followed by Lucille's crisp bark, then another grumble, louder, from Irene, and a volley from Lucille, and Irene said, "Well, it ain't enough, Miss Lucille, not enough by half."

"That's more than the going wage, Irene, as you know. In fact, I believe it is much more generous than you will find elsewhere. Besides, you're not exactly put upon."

"What would you mean by that, then?"

"I did hire you to cook and it seems to me that we have nothing but the most elementary sort of food. Frankfurters! Hamburgers! Campbell's soup!"

"Miss Charity likes those."

"I'm sure she does, but it seems to me that an occasional salad, a little veal, or perhaps even a pork roast . . . I may as well tell you that I've had my eye on someone else."

"Indeed," said Irene, her voice rising into a new dignity. "And who would take care of Miss Charity? The child spends the day in the kitchen, yammering, complaining, bothering me with her tales and her stories. It's a wonder I get anything done. And I've been kind to her."

"For a price."

"And wasn't it worth it to you? Some folks don't remember too well, do they, how expensive all them doctors was, and who it was brought Miss Charity straight out of her fit and depression."

"For a price."

"And what if I leave? Think of that! Think of that all over again."

There was a silence. I suppose Lucille was mentally

doing some fast arithmetic. She said, finally, "How much more do you want?"

And Irene's voice, now quite clear, triumphant, said: "Fringe benefits! Four weeks paid vacation! Ten days sick leave! A helper in the kitchen for dinner parties of eight and over! A pension fund! Medical insurance!"

Lucille sighed.

"I can put up with the child, I suppose, though she is a bit odd, not one bit like my brother's children."

"All right," said docile Lucille, "all *right.*"

You see, I thought Irene loved me.
And the next day, my dollhouse disappeared.

And you're right, of course.
I have always hidden behind my money.
I have always bought people with the promise of money.
I have always bought.
I have never given.
I have never been able to take.
Do you know what I dream sometimes? That I am poor. It is terrifying. I wake up sweating.

Epilogue

In June before the children left for Maine, Tonia heard a song that she hadn't heard before come from the piano in the living room. It was a melancholy little tune that wandered up and down, as if looking for something.

"What's that you're playing?" she asked Joey from the doorway.

He looked up. "It's my new song," he said. "I wrote it."

"You did?"

"Yes."

"Have you written other songs?"

"Yes. I like to write songs. I am going to be a composer. Mom? Remember when I was little and we lived in that big house and Dad was with us? You used to sing all the time. I loved it when you sang."

She sat down on the bench next to him. "Do you know," she said, "there has been a musician or two in every generation of our family for over a hundred years, maybe more. Your grandmother used to say that when they went to the Mercers for Sunday dinner . . ."

He wasn't listening. He was frowning at the piano keys, working something out, listening to something inside his head. She smiled and sat there on the piano bench thinking about her children and it seemed to her that her love for her children was infinitely strong, like the strings of a great unseen lyre that delicately, silently sing, these threads of generation, this unheard music handed down through time for ever and ever or at least until mankind's end.

She put out a hand and touched his hair. "Will you write me a song?"

"Yes. Will you sing it?"

"Of course," she said. (Tonia's summer sublet on the West Side of New York in the Eighties was only two blocks away from her new voice coach—a woman her age who had also taken lessons from Blakova. Rosa's beautiful contralto had been ruined for the stage by incapacitating stage fright. She was an excellent teacher, however, and had remembered Tonia at once. "You used to sit on the steps while I had my lesson. Blakova thought you were terrific. What happened?" Well. It was a long story.)

"Do you know," Tonia said to Joey (and was amused at herself; she felt like a twenty-year-old all over again), "it looks like I am going to be a singer."

"I know," Joey said, and went on playing. "Gee, Mom, I always knew that."

Isn't life surprising? The awful stubbornness of the human species, this desire, given even the poorest odds, to gamble on happiness. In the fall, after Ben's children had gone home to New Jersey, Ramona discovered that she was pregnant. The Durhams—Ramona and Ben—could no longer afford to live in Maine, so they moved back to New York City, where Ben got a job at a large medical center.

Now they have one small child and live on two floors of a brownstone in the East Eighties. Money, of course, is tight, but when isn't that true? Ben has a small city garden and would like to move to Connecticut, but Ramona refuses to leave New York. She was born in Indiana and wouldn't live in the boonies again for anything.

"No, lovey," Teddy said. "You are very wrong. It wasn't Dr. William E., it was Dr. Wilbur H. Haseltine, and his office wasn't on East Seventy-first Street; it was on East Seventy-third. I know very well who you mean because Mama occasionally went to him too. He was a vestryman at St. James, a small fellow with a little mustache." Teddy was lying, of course. He knew nothing at all about a licentious Dr. Haseltine and was convinced that this supposed affair of her mother's was simply another of Charity's strange obsessions.

Damn, thought Charity gloomily, I am just a manipulator manqué. She took the autobiography she had just finished writing, gathered the papers together, and stared at them sadly.

"Oh, now," said Teddy, "don't look like that. Come over here and sit next to me."

Charity looked up and smiled at him fondly. Since the night of his fall from the balcony of his parents' home right onto the polished wood floor of the living room, she had hardly left his side. They had been married in his hospital room while he was still in traction. When she'd married Teddy there were titters from everyone who knew them and scandalous speculations about their sex life. Charity startled the world by staying resolutely with him. He needed her (not her money) and no one had ever needed her before, and he trusted her, and she loved him. She loved him! The thought amazed her. Thus she spent those long dark winter afternoons while he was recuperating sitting in front of the fire in his bedroom, finishing her autobiography. Today, however, she was unhappy with what she'd just written and she morosely shuffled and reshuffled the papers.

"The truth is," Charity said, "I bore myself."

After all, late in the day as it was (she was forty), Charity had developed real feelings and a real inner life, but now that she was addicted to her work, tethered to her writing like a poor dog on a short chain, she never went anywhere, she hardly left the house: she had lost her outer life.

"Then why don't you write about someone else?" asked Teddy, looking up from his book.

Why, yes, she thought. That's just what I'll do. She would write a book, a novel, about someone she knew very well, someone—Tonia?—close enough to her to be almost another self.

"Charity!" Teddy cried from his bed. "What are you doing?"

She had stuffed her autobiography into the fire. "Oh, Teddy," she said. "I feel marvelous! I feel so free."

The papers curled blackly at the edges, buckled, then burst into a soaring yellow-red spire, and with a crackle and a roar flew up the chimney. If, on that cold winter night, you had been walking down East Sixty-eighth Street, and if, say, you had looked up at about seven-twenty, you might have seen, against the night sky, a flurry of tiny red sparks that hovered briefly on the chimney's coping before they flew off (these bits of imagined life, these little pieces of char) like released souls into the general blackness.

At the age of forty, when Tonia started singing again, she found that her voice had increased an octave in range.

It was Ben ("Don't tell Ramona") who agreed to pay for her singing lessons. The next year Tonia began singing with the Boston Opera Company and she and the children moved to a Boston suburb.

That year, the year she was forty-one, she fell in love again, she knew it at once, even before he had turned around. He was tall and homely and tone-deaf and he had a deep laugh. He went to all her performances and always fell asleep before the second act. Standing there on the stage, she would tenderly watch him doze off and then send him (as on a filament of airborne silk) a silent message: My love. Look up! He would shake his head, look sheepishly around and smile, and she would lift up her head and sing.

> *"We are the words,*
> *We are the music,*
> *We are the thing itself."*